SUMMER'S END

BAEN BOOKS
by JOHN VAN STRY

Summer's End

SUMMER'S END

JOHN VAN STRY

SUMMER'S END

This is a work of fiction. All the characters and events portrayed in this book are fictional, and any resemblance to real people or incidents is purely coincidental.

A Baen Books Original

Baen Publishing Enterprises
P.O. Box 1403
Riverdale, NY 10471
www.baen.com

ISBN: 978-1-9821-9229-7

Cover art by Sam R. Kennedy

First printing, December 2022

Distributed by Simon & Schuster
1230 Avenue of the Americas
New York, NY 10020

Library of Congress Cataloging-in-Publication Data

Names: Van Stry, John, author.
Title: Summer's end / John Van Stry.
Description: Riverdale, NY : Baen, 2022.
Identifiers: LCCN 2022039002 | ISBN 9781982192297 (trade paperback) | ISBN 9781625798855 (ebook)
Subjects: LCGFT: Science fiction. | Novels.
Classification: LCC PS3622.A585737 S86 2022 | DDC 813/.6—dc23/eng/20220824
LC record available at https://lccn.loc.gov/2022039002

Printed in the United States of America

10 9 8 7 6 5 4 3 2 1

SUMMER'S END

ONE

Earth—Holloman Spaceport

Dave,

I hope you won't be mad at me, but I hacked into your school files last night and accepted the job offer from Damascus Freight Lines for you. I know you were hoping something better would come in, and I'm sure it would have. However, Eileen's husband is involved in a very nasty political fight and apparently his opponent has found out about you.

You have become "inconvenient" as the holo-dramas like to say.

Best Wishes,
Ben

Shaking my head, I deleted the email from my tablet and turned it off. Two days ago I'd been woken up by an alarm that my brother had set when he'd hacked my tablet to send me that. I'd immediately packed my duffel bag, dropped the keys for my tiny micro-efficiency apartment in the rent slot at the manager's office with a note telling them I had left, and then spent the time since taking public transportation.

If he wasn't willing to send that to me via the usual email or chat programs we used, then I knew it had to be serious. Then, last night, just before I'd boarded this bus, I'd gotten several emails offering me interviews with some of the better companies out there. The kinds of offers that the *A* students got. The kinds of offers the connected got. Not the kind that a prole with straight *C*'s were ever offered.

Maybe I could have gotten a better deal. But waiting around was no longer an option. Elies like her husband really had no problems with making proles who caused them issues to "disappear." I wondered if she knew. I wondered if she'd care. Hell, I wondered if she even knew I still existed.

My dad used to tell me that the elies had the power to ignore anything that didn't fit into their worldview and would quickly forget anything embarrassing or inconvenient. And if anyone would know, it would be him.

Standing up and stretching as the autobus came to a stop, I got my bag and looked around the bus. The single bum sleeping in the back—buried under his coat, feet tucked up on the seat next to him as he laid there—looked quite uncaring. They'd gotten on in Albuquerque when all the rest of the passengers had gotten off. I was suddenly reminded of a similar scene from my youth, though back then there had been other people on the bus. All of whom had quite studiously ignored the man and pretended he didn't exist.

I was just glad I still had one of those jammers my brother liked to make, and that I'd activated it when I'd gotten on this bus in Amarillo, shutting down the cameras. I pulled it out of my pocket as I made for the exit and slipped it under the dash where no one would see it before I stepped off the bus. No one would know I'd been on it—well, no one who mattered at least—and no one would know when I got off. As for the guy buried under the coat in the back? People would think that this was probably the safest place to sleep if you were some homeless bum who couldn't afford a bed. So no one would bother him, I was sure.

Getting off the bus and going inside the cargo terminal, I looked at the sign hanging from the ceiling, trying to make out just where the ship I was going to board was located. Holloman was in the ass end of the New Mexico district and if what I was seeing was any judge of circumstances, probably the most run-down spaceport of all the spaceports in the North American United Districts.

I looked over at the little Information kiosk, which was not only completely abandoned but looked to be in even worse shape than the dust-covered sign that was suffering from a severe case of display burn-in.

Shaking my head, I slung my bag, dumped a few now useless items in the trash, made my best guess, and started walking down the long corridor to cargo wing Echo and hoped I'd made the right choice, looking for another sign along the way. The people mover belts didn't work, of course, and from the holes in them, I didn't even think it would be safe to walk on one.

Eventually I came to the end of the hall, where there was another display showing that, yes, I had guessed correctly. Again, there was no one here, but there was a large button with a sign that said CALL BUTTON.

So I pressed it.

And then I pressed it again.

After the third try the display flickered to show someone in a uniform.

"What?" they demanded.

"I'm here to report to the CCS *Iowa Hill*."

The door buzzed and I quickly grabbed the handle and pulled it open as the screen went dark. So much for security.

I stepped outside onto the tarmac and looked around. There was a line of ships several hundred yards away, gray steel box-like constructions of several sizes. The *Iowa Hill* was a convertible container/breakbulk hauler of the old Argon Six design by General Ship Designs. So it didn't take me long to pick it out of the lineup.

Looking around, I found a call box with a list of ships. Going down the list, I pressed the call button next to the *Iowa Hill*.

"*Iowa Hill*, what's your business?" a voice called back almost immediately.

"Fifth Engineer Walker reporting," I replied.

"Great, get your butt over here!"

I waited a moment to see if anything else was going to be said— like maybe how to get there without walking across the concrete in the middle of a summer day in hundred-plus degree heat?

Shaking my head, I started the very long trek across the hot concrete. At the school I'd gone to, when we'd done our training cruises, one of the guys had walked out onto the tarmac while looking around and thirty seconds later was facedown on the concrete getting jacked up by spaceport security.

Nothing like that happened here.

Then again, who'd want to be out in this heat if they didn't have to be?

It was a long, hot slog and the only reason I wasn't covered in sweat was the complete lack of humidity. When I got to the ship I saw that loading operations were going on, so I went over there.

"Hey! Drink this before you die!" someone from the loading crew said and tossed me a bottle of water. They had good aim as it hit me square in the chest and then fell to the ground as I completely missed the catch while trying to get my wits back. Bending over, it took me a minute to grab it, then standing up I moved into the shade of the ship. I opened the bottle and drank the entire contents before I took another step.

Next time, I'd see about wearing a hat.

When I finished, I looked at what was going on. Large cargo containers were being slung in through the side hatches, which had all been folded open and were touching the tarmac. I'd never seen a heavy cargo hauler up close on the ground. Most of the newer classes were just too big to land. The Argon class was the last design of GSD that had that ability.

"Yo! Walker! Get over here and report in!"

Looking over, I saw an older guy wearing a shipsuit and a headset waving at me. So re-slinging my bag I made my way over to him, making sure to avoid the moving loaders and not walk under anything that might crush me if it dropped. Something we'd been warned long and loud about back in school.

"Fifth Engineer Walker, reporting in, sir," I said and saluted.

"Great, and don't bother with that saluting stuff, you're in the real world now. I'm Chief Mate Ian Parks, or just 'Chief' to you onboard. Captain Roy is up on the bridge checking the gear. Go see him first."

I nodded.

"Welcome aboard, Walker," Chief Parks said and stuck out his hand.

"Thanks, Chief," I said shaking hands, then went up the crew stairs into the hold and started moving forward past the stacked containers. I stepped through the open hatch and looked at the faded direction arrows painted on the walls. The ship wasn't dirty, but it was definitely old. Older than me, maybe even older than my parents.

I dropped my bag outside the bridge and stepped inside. There was a team of people in there, but only one was wearing a shipsuit. The others all looked like techs from a ground support company.

"Fifth Engineer Walker reporting, Captain," I said, and saluted just to be safe.

"Oh great, you're here. Welcome aboard, son," he said, coming over to shake my hand. "Look, I've got these guys doing a systems check on all the running gear and a systems update on the nav consoles. Make sure they do what they say they're doing, sign off when they're done, and don't spend any money without checking with either me or Parks first, got it?"

"Umm, yes, sir," I said, eyes wide.

"Thanks! I need to go check with Briggs, our chief engineer. Oh, what's your first name, son?"

"Dave."

"Great! After they're done, I'll get someone to show you your billet and log you into the ship's systems."

I watched as the captain departed and then turned to look at all of the ground maintenance guys who had all turned to look at me.

"I used to work for Siemans and I've done this job at least a dozen times," I said. "So yeah, not an elie, I work for a living."

"What port?" the guy who looked like the lead asked.

"Boca Chica. Bill Evans was my boss."

"Why'd you leave a nice job like that for a place like this?" One of the other guys laughed, motioning to the outdated ship.

"Obviously for the medical plan," I said and several of them snickered as they all went back to work.

It took them two hours to finish up and I watched as they ran each of the tests and buttoned up the panels, not a single one of which had obviously been installed when the ship had first been commissioned. They all packed up their gear and then filed off the bridge as I went over the paperwork the lead handed me to sign.

"Seriously, why'd you leave a sweet gig like Boca Chica to fly on a scow like this?" he asked in a soft voice.

"I was only a temp worker while I went to college. Once

school ended, I got the boot," I told him as I signed the last of it off. "Pay sucked, too—temps don't get scale but still have to pay a fee to the union to work there. Only reason I even got that much was because my father's in the union and I grew up around most of the guys there, so they all knew me."

"Oh, yeah, that makes sense. Getting my daughter into the shop here cost me a month's wages in bribes. I can just imagine what it woulda cost your dad over there."

"More than it cost to go to a state college and get my engineer's cert, that's for sure," I said with a nod and handed him the tablet back.

"Well, good luck up there in space. Though why'd you want to go there, is beyond me."

"Thanks," I said and shook hands, and watched as he left.

"Yeah, why do you want to 'go up there'?" a woman asked from behind me.

"Ma'am?" I asked.

"Name's Dot, Dot Briggs, chief engineer. I'm your new boss."

She stuck out her hand and I shook it. "Nice to meet you, ma'am," I said, taking her in. If I had to guess, she was in her thirties, definitely a lot younger than I'd expect someone who was a chief engineer to be. She was shorter then me, with short black hair, what appeared to be a solid build inside the loose shipsuit she wore, and had rough hands that made it clear she worked and not just supervised.

"Dot, just Dot. We don't bother much with ma'ams and sirs onboard, this ain't the Navy after all. So, tell me, what does bring you here? If your father was a union man, surely you could've found a nice *safe* job down here somewhere."

"There aren't a lot of jobs for power plant and grav engineers down here," I said with a shrug.

"Still, I'd think there'd be better jobs with one of the big name shipping companies."

"Yeah, well, I wasn't exactly an *A* student," I admitted to her. "While everyone else got to spend their evenings studying, I had to work third shift so I could afford tuition."

"I thought the proles got free tuition?"

"That'd be the doles, and definitely not for engineering degrees."

"What about loans?"

"There's a limit to what you can borrow and my parents made

too much," I said and frowned at her, "Look, Damascus Freight Lines made me the best offer, so I took it. You know how it is."

Chief Briggs laughed. "Nope, can't say as I really do, I wasn't born here. I'm from Montana, the O'Neill colony, not the district."

"Oh? Then why are *you* here?" I asked.

She smiled. "That's personal."

I just nodded. Most proles didn't like to discuss private matters, unlike doles who never seemed to shut up about them.

"Well, go grab your bag, I'll show you to your own personal broom closet and then I'll introduce you to the boys."

"The boys?" I asked, retrieving my duffel.

"Yup, we've got two Siz-gees onboard for main drive and grav power and one Piper APU."

"We've got twelves?" I asked, surprised. "Where are they in their cycle?"

"The *Iowa*'s had two refuels, we're about ten years from a new core," she said, leading me aft out of the bridge via a different hatch than I'd come in.

"Think the company will replace the cores?" I asked as we walked down the corridor.

"Maybe, maybe not. Depends on the accountants. That's the captain's dayroom, there's his quarters." She started pointing to doors as we passed them. "These are the mates, kitchen, mess, cook. These last four are for dead heads. We bunk down by the engines, same for the bosun and the four ablebodied spacers we're supposed to have."

"Supposed to?" I asked as she came to a stair that was more of a ladder and started down.

"Damascus Freight likes to run light on the crew. We've got the captain, the chief mate, and a second mate. Add me and you to that, and that's all the officers that this ship's got. After that we've got the bosun, one ordinary spacer, and the cook."

"Wait, there's just the two of us in engineering?" I asked, surprised.

"Yup."

"Isn't that, like against the law or something?"

"The bosun's approved to stand watches; his name's Hank Smith. So now that you're here, we're covered," she said, turning and leading me down a second ladder. I thought about that as we came to the bottom.

"Okay," she said leading me forward. "I've got the chief engineer's quarters, right here. You get the second engineer's quarters, because guess what? You just got a promotion!" she said with a chuckle. "Bosun's quarters are two down from yours and the rest are for all that crew that we don't have."

"What about the ordinary spacers? Where do they sleep?"

"With the bosun. It's his current squeeze."

I shook my head. "This isn't anything like what they told us to expect."

"Sure isn't! But the smaller companies are all like this. We're a freight hauler, pure and simple. Point A to B to C and so on and so forth. Anything needs fixing; we get it fixed at the next stop if we can't fix it ourselves. You got any kind of space suit or pressure suit?"

I shook my head. "Couldn't afford one. The prices here are more than I have in the bank. This"—I hefted my duffel bag—"is all I own."

"I know a place at our next stop; we can get you fixed up with something that won't leave you broke. 'Cause trust me, you *need* a pressure suit. Accidents happen and the last thing I want is for you to be stuck in a cabin while I'm out making repairs."

I nodded at that.

"So when do we lift?" I asked.

"As soon as we're finished loading. Even at a dump like Holloman, parking spaces cost a premium, so the powers that be at headquarters want us out of here as soon as possible. Now, stow your bag and let me show you the good stuff!"

The engineering deck was huge. The ceiling was a good twenty-five feet above us, going up to the bottom of the first deck, and to either side of the central aisle were the two SS12G PWRs, or "Siz-gee" Pressurized Water Reactors. Each one was capable of generating three hundred megawatts, their design actually based off of the same power plants that had run the nuclear missile submarines of the old United States Navy. On the starboard side, aft of one of the Siz-gees, was the Piper Auxiliary Power Unit. They were fusion based and generated a megawatt worth of power, not enough to move something this large, but more than enough for the rest of the ship's systems, I was sure. The space aft of the port-side Siz-gee was empty.

"What used to go over there?" I asked, pointing at the spot as I took in the rest of the engine room. For the most part everything in here looked original. There really wasn't any need to change the controls or the instrumentation if you weren't changing the power plants. The display screens looked newish but were all obviously the same size as the originals had been. The turbines for generators looked new, or newer, but with design improvements they probably got replaced during the last refuel.

The Piper was new, of course. Or rather, newer than everything else.

"There used to be two fuel cell generators in here that did half a megawatt," Dot—Chief Briggs, that is—told me. "It was cheaper just to buy and install the one Piper when they did the last refuel."

"Why is it running? Aren't we on shore power?"

"Nope. Shore power here takes too long to hook up and remove, and you pay through the nose for it. Plus we'll need it for launch."

"What, those aren't big enough?" I asked, waving a hand at the two reactors.

"Max on each of my boys there is only two-seventy apiece, and we're going to use every last erg of it to climb out of the gravity well. So the Piper will be picking up all the other systems onboard."

"Wait, I thought they were rated for three hundred?"

"Yeah, well, apparently they 'saved'"—Dot made air quotes with her fingers when she said that—"a little money during the last refuel and only put in enough to make two-eighty and, well, after ten years we've lost a little. As long as they're above two-fifty-five they can supply enough to the drives to make top speed, but after that"—she shrugged—"we slow down."

I nodded; it made sense.

"So why did we land if taking back off is so hard?"

"Because it's cheaper to land and pay all the fees than to have it shuttled up to us, of course," she said with a smile. "Faster too. Even if it is gonna take us an hour to climb out of the gravity well."

I gave her another look. "Wait, we're making point one gravity in this, right?"

"Yes, but the ship was only rated for one point five when it was built fifty-plus years ago and just sitting still here we're at one, so the captain takes us up at a constant velocity, not acceleration, until we're well out of the atmosphere.

"So, it's slow."

I took another look around the room. It was neat and orderly, not overly clean like the training gear I'd learned on had been, but I didn't see any rust and not too much gunk.

"Where are the grav drives?"

"They're on the centerline down through the middle of the cargo bay, but it's best not to go back there while they're loading. We've got two Jansen two-twenties and one of the original four Muller fifteen hundreds."

I nodded and added the specs for those in my head and realized that there wasn't a lot of "headroom" between the engine ratings and the gross weight of this class.

"So, where do I start?"

She smiled. "I've got a list all nice and ready for you. Let's get your tablet slaved to the ship and I'll send it to you."

Earth—*Iowa Hill* Engineering

CHIEF BRIGGS "SUPERVISED" ME FOR THE FIRST TWO HOURS, which was mostly telling me where things were stored and her way of doing things. When the captain called and asked her to help him inspect the hatches and the load, she just told me to carry on and left.

In my last year of college I was never once left alone with a couple of nuclear reactors and told to "carry on." Things were definitely done differently out in the real world—or maybe it was just here on the *Iowa Hill*? This ship was flying with about half the crew it was required to have when it first left the shipyard. Obviously there were going to be a lot of crew functions that overlapped.

"Okay, let's get her ready to fly!" Dot said in a cheerful voice when she rejoined me several hours later. "Where are you on that list?"

"I just finished the leak check."

"Ah good, you're a lot faster than the previous guy was, I'll say that. Now as long as you do a better job, we'll both be happy."

"What happened to him, anyway?" I asked.

"He missed ship's movement. That's what happened," Dot said with a heavy sigh. "Now, I'll read the checklist and you can power everything up."

"Sure," I said sitting down at the control panel. "Any idea why he missed ship's movement?"

"Let's just say that borrowing money you don't have from a casino to cover a 'sure thing' is a good way to end up working your ass off to pay them back." She paused a moment and then with a rather nasty smiled added, "Literally."

"Sorry I asked. I'm ready."

It took about fifty minutes to bring the reactors up to full power; we could have done it faster, but the key to long life on the turbines, heat exchangers, and other gear is making sure that it all heats up gradually at an even rate. And Chief Briggs, or Dot as she kept telling me to call her, was very much interested in a long life.

"Remember," she said as all the temperature gauges leveled off, "money is *the* name of the game. We want to keep costs as low as possible wherever possible. The pencil pushers back in the accounting office, they'll just as happily cut your budget on things that will save your life as anything else. After all, *they're* not here, so as long as the ship isn't a write off, they don't care what happens to the crew.

"So it's your job to wring every last second of life out of the ship and her systems so they don't go looking for other places to save money. Now, let's power up the grav engines, run the self-tests, check the power feeds, and then bring up all the plates."

That took another twenty or so minutes. Again, we could have done it faster but Dot told me they'd been shut down long enough to have cooled off, so she wanted to be sure they warmed up gradually as well.

That done, she pressed the intercom button for the bridge.

"Okay, Captain. We're ready down here, both reactors are running, the grav engines and plates are active, and power's at ninety percent of design."

"Roger that, Chief Briggs. I'm bringing the engines up and transferring the load off of the landing gear. Now we're just waiting on departure clearance," the captain replied and then commed off.

"What *does* stop them from looking for other things to cut the budget on?" I asked, curious as we waited to depart.

"From looking for other places? Amortization charts. There are industry standards on what a ship and crew cost to operate over its lifetime, depending on its age and class, that the ship insurers all maintain and all the big companies follow. If we can squeak below that line just a little bit, while maintaining our schedules and still passing all the safety inspections, the folks doing the balance sheets will leave you alone, because nobody likes it when the insurance companies ask questions after an accident."

"What happens if you don't?"

"Then you better have one hell of a good excuse and be prepared for a very long argument. That or get your résumé together and move on to greener pastures. It's why we run older ships with half the crew—it costs less and lets the company charge less on shipping rates so they can compete against the larger companies while still maintaining enough of a profit margin to stay in business."

"Prepare to up ship!" the captain called out over the shipwide network. "All hands, prepare for lift!"

"Chief Briggs, I am taking us up and out," the captain called over the intercom to Engineering.

"Roger that, Captain. All green down here," she said after pressing the talk button.

"Acknowledged."

She released the talk button. "Now comes the long, boring part," she said with a sigh. "Landing on planets is always such a pain in the ass."

"I could go back to working down that punch list you gave me," I told her.

She shook her head. "Watch the acceleration gauge and the power settings to the three grav generators. Keep in mind that the two twenties get forty-six percent more power than the fifteen hundred, so don't let that throw you. Also three quarters of the grav panels are wired to the two-twenties. They're newer and more efficient, but they still draw more because they're larger. Captain Roy will take us up to a hundred kilometers an hour and hold us there as we climb out of the gravity well and the atmosphere.

"Normally if we have a problem underway, we can just coast until we fix it, but in a gravity well this deep, well, losing power can just ruin your whole day."

I thought about that and nodded.

"Also the internal gravity settings are going to be a bit wonky until we're under normal acceleration and that's the sort of thing that leads to accidents and accidents lead to expenses..."

"And expenses make the accountants unhappy," I finished.

She smiled. "Now you're learning!"

"This really wasn't one of the lessons they taught us about in school."

"That's 'cause most of the people teaching those classes either worked for one of the big outfits that don't worry as much about it, or they never crewed on a ship themselves."

I nodded.

"So just how do we manage with such a small crew? I mean, how do we even handle the watch?"

"Well, the bridge watch is split between the captain and the two mates—those being the chief and the second mate. If they need a break they'll call the bosun or one of us to come up and relieve them. They sit four-hour shifts and there's *always* someone on the bridge when we're underway. Unless it's an emergency."

"What about down here in Engineering? Isn't that the same?"

"Wellll," she said and grinned. "Yes and no. There's really only the two of us, and now that everything's running, the reactors and the grav drives only need spot checks and regular maintenance. As I've already entered you into the ship's systems, we'll just slave your tablet to the engineering console and set up a repeater on your display. There's also a larger one on the wall of your cabin. This way, no matter where you are onboard, you can check status, and if there's any kind of problem or alert, the ship's computer can notify you immediately."

"What about when we're sleeping?"

"There's a panel on the bridge, and one in each of the mates' cabins as well as the captain's. Now, we don't expect them to catch the minor things because they're not engineers like us. But they're smart enough to call us if they see something before the computer does.

"The reactors and the APU are the least of our problems, however. They're old and tired designs and the computers can handle them. Our real problem is the drives, or rather the five hundred and four grav panels that are run by the drives. They're also old, and while they don't have any moving parts, they wear out. We'll probably have to rebuild at least two of 'em on the trip."

I blinked at that. "I thought panels only got rebuilt in port, by certified machine shops?"

Dot laughed. "Yeah, well, we don't carry enough spares for

that! So when a panel fails, we swap it out with the spare we carry, and then bust our butts to rebuild it so when the next one dies, we've got something to replace it with."

"We only have one spare?" I asked, surprised. According to what I'd been taught, all ships were required to carry at least ten!

"Oh, no, we have two!" Dot said and then laughed at the expression on my face.

"Two? So then we have a backup if one fails while we're rebuilding, right?"

"Nope, the *Iowa Hill* uses two different types of panels because we have the two different drives and they're not interchangeable."

"Oh." I thought about that for a moment. "I've never rebuilt a panel before, Chief."

"It's Dot, please," she said with a smile. "Didn't I hear you say that you've got experience working as a yard tech on bridge systems?"

"Yeah, like I said, that's how I paid for school."

"You shouldn't have any problems learning, then. It's not like you need to know all the theory to rebuild the panel, they're a lot simpler than the drives. They're really only waveguides when you get down to it and they're a lot easier to rebuild than an actual gravity drive. The rebuild manuals are all in the ship's library and I'll teach you the rest."

"But what happens if we lose more than one? Won't that distort the ship?" I'd heard more than a few horror stories about that in class. "And shouldn't we be replacing them *before* they fail?"

Dot laughed again. "Live re-slots? Hardly! There's only the two of us and those are a lot more work than we're staffed for."

"But..."

"Look, the captain, or whoever has the helm, will just pull power back, all the way to zero if necessary, until we get it fixed. We're not on a tight deadline and this ship's only a point-one-gee vessel. Losing a panel, or even two, isn't going to stress the structure beyond limits. Sure, if the *Iowa* was a high-gee loader like some of those passenger clippers, then we'd have something to worry about, but for the most part we replace 'em after they fail and not before."

I nodded again.

"What about inspections? How do we get them certified?"

"We do that after each one is rebuilt."

"We can do that?"

"*I* can do that. I'm licensed to. Part of why I make the big bucks!" she said with another smile.

"I think my instructors would have had a fit at that idea," I admitted.

"Why's that?"

"Because what's to stop you from putting a subpar panel in, to save money?"

"Hmm, let's think about that," she said, arms crossed, her chin in her hand and one finger tapping the side of her face. "Why would someone want to put something that wasn't repaired properly into service on the ship that they lived on where they might die if it failed?"

"When you put it like that, it does sound stupid."

"Oh, I'm sure there are people dumb enough to do it, but those tend not to be the ones who spend money on the certifications in the first place and I don't think most captains would let them crew on a ship longer than the time it took to figure out just what kind of a knucklehead they were." She looked at the time on the engineering panel.

"Now, as long as we're going to be stuck here a while, let's go over the inspection routine for the rest of the ship."

"Wait, I thought you said you didn't inspect the panels?" I asked, confused.

"Oh no, we inspect them. There's always the chance one's going to go bad in a manner that's a lot worse than a simple failure. *Those* we fail and pull ourselves. The others, we just let 'em sit there until they die."

"Because it costs less?" I asked tentatively.

"Exactly! We'll make a cost-conscious engineer out of you yet!" Dot said with a cheerful laugh.

Apparently leaving Earth and the Earth/Moon system involved a lot more navigation than I realized because it was about two hours before we were told that the ship was done with maneuvering and now on course, and to set the regular watch.

"Engineer Walker, please come and see me in my dayroom," the captain called over the intercoms shortly afterward.

"Come back after you've seen the captain and I'll show you the grav drives," Dot said as I got out of my seat.

I nodded, went up the stairs, and made my way to the captain's dayroom, then knocked on the door.

"Come on in, Dave."

Opening the door, I stepped inside. "Engineer Dave Walker reporting as requested, sir."

"Close the door and have a seat, Dave. Welcome to the *Iowa Hill*. We're not all that formal here, just as long as everyone remembers who's in charge."

Closing the door, I sat down in the offered seat.

"Yes, sir."

"Now I've looked over your records and, honestly, I'm surprised you didn't wait for a better berth. I know what we're paying you, and you didn't even try to ask for more—which, considering that we couldn't take off until we hired another engineer..." He looked at me expectantly.

"I didn't know I could have asked for more, sir. I also didn't know that you were shorthanded," I replied. I'd have to let Ben know that if there ever was a "next time" to negotiate.

"You haven't broken any laws, have you, son?"

I shook my head. "No, sir. Well, not recently. Got in a few fights back in public school. But that's about it."

"So you just took the first offer you got?"

"I *was* going to wait, but my brother told me that I'd just be wasting my time. I think he looked at what was due to land and what the upcoming openings would be. He's usually right, and I barely had enough money to cover the bus fare, so I took his advice and took the berth, sir."

"Well, we all have our reasons, and to be honest, I'm happy we got you. You're a damn sight better than the last engineer we had onboard."

"Chief Briggs mentioned something about him. She said he got in trouble at a casino or something?"

"Yes, he wasn't the brightest diode on the display. I've already put in your records that you're the acting third engineer. If I'd put second, no one would believe it. Once you've got enough time in, I'll see about bumping you up a rating to get you a little better pay, seeing as you're already doing the job.

"We make a lot of long hauls on this ship, the company sends us wherever the money is, and that usually means long hauls, short turnarounds, and very little time for sightseeing. Any questions?"

"Um, yes, sir. Where are we going?"

"Jupiter. You didn't know?"

"I just wanted to get a job and get off Earth, sir."

The captain nodded. "Well, I'd say it's safe to say you've accomplished that. A little advice if I may?"

I nodded, "Yes, sir, I'd appreciate it."

"Stay here at least two years. People will want to see that you're able to stay in a job. For most people, working for a company like Damascus Freight is the end of the line, they can't find work anywhere else. Sure, the pay's not the best, but nobody here asks any questions. We don't sail to the nicer places; a lot of the places we sail to are anything *but* nice. So don't go wandering off on your own and don't go thinking you can beat the house when it comes to gambling. Do a good job and I'll write enough recommendations that when you do leave us, you'll be able to find something a lot better."

"Thank you, sir."

"Welcome aboard, Dave," the captain said standing up and offering his hand.

"Thank you, sir," I said shaking hands as I stood as well.

"And do come up with a better story for why you're here."

I blushed. "I'll get right on it, sir."

"Well, what do you think of our fair captain?" Dot asked as I came back down to Engineering.

"Perceptive," I said with a shrug.

"I suspect when you've been a captain long enough, you get to the point where you've seen it all before. Now, let me show you the grav drives before they call us for dinner."

She led me through a hatch on the aft side of engineering and this time there really was a ladder and we climbed up to the level above. We were out in the cargo hold and I could see the ladder went up another two levels.

"Ship's lifeboat is up there," Dot said pointing up the ladder. "Straight aft past the stairs that leads down to Engineering. There's supposed to be two, but with half the crew, they figured we only needed half the gear."

I just nodded and hoped we never had to use it.

She led me down the main aisle that split the hold in two, all the way to the back of the ship.

"Environmental is through there." She pointed to a hatch. "There's also a machine shop where we rebuild the bad panels and make anything else we need."

"Who's in charge of Environmental?"

"Bosun Smith handles it. He's pretty good at it too. Probably used to be an environmental tech or something before he ended up our bosun. Now, this is the panel to open the access for the grav drives."

I watched as she opened up a protective cover and pressed two buttons down together. A large red indicator light came on, and the deck we'd just walked down split open.

"There they are."

I looked down the trench that had opened in the floor and there they definitely were, bolted down to the keel with fastening nuts a good ten centimeters across, our three gravity drives. The first two, from the bow back, were the two-twenties. There was an open space next, then there was the old fifteen hundred. The cabling to them was all neatly laid out and secured on the starboard side of the keel, with a narrow passageway on the port side.

"The overhead contains a crane that we can use to lift anything heavy. It stows in the ceiling over there," she said, pointing to a spot just above hatch into Environmental. "We do a weekly inspection, and a monthly. Once a year we get a rebuild, that takes a week, and we also get a crew in to run some extensive tests two times a year."

She pressed the buttons and the deck laid back down into place.

"There's a hatch in the space between decks that leads to the space underneath the next compartment if you need to get in there without opening the floor, but other than making sure the hatch works and it's kept clear, we don't use it."

I nodded and looked around the hold for a moment. It was as wide as the ship and was three levels high. The containers on this level were stacked five high, or forty feet.

"How far past this bulkhead does the ship go?" I asked her.

"Fifty feet. Ship's plumbing, heating, and air-conditioning is on the level below; ship's computer, radio gear, gym, and miscellaneous gear is on the level above."

At that point the dinner chime sounded through the ship's intercom.

"Ah, perfect. Let's go see what Shelly's made us today!"

"I'm guessing Shelly's our cook?" I asked.

"Yup, and a decent one. She's the captain's wife too, so be polite."

"Got it."

The only person who wasn't at dinner was Chief Parks. Dot introduced me to Shelly. She looked a little younger than the captain, was thinner and shorter than Dot, though perhaps a little shapelier, but then her shipsuit was obviously tailored to show that she was an attractive woman. Not beautiful, but pleasant.

The second mate, Pam Wells, was there as well. Pam's shipsuit was a looser fitting one like Dot's, but couldn't contain the fact that Pam was built very impressively. I started to wonder if maybe she was Chief Park's wife, even if she looked a lot younger than him, because you wouldn't expect a woman with those kinds of looks to be on anything other than an elie passenger liner.

Bosun Hank Smith looked to be about my father's age, maybe a few years younger, and his "squeeze" was a handsome and well-built young man by the name of Chaz who was probably younger than me.

I smiled and shook hands with all of them as I was introduced and knew better than to comment on either the second mate's looks or the bosun's preference in lovers, even if the age difference was a little surprising. I just hoped that, if they had any fights, Chaz didn't end up coming to me about them because I was the closest one to his age onboard.

I had enough drama in my own life already that I wasn't at all capable when it came to helping sort out someone else's.

"So, Captain, what trick did customs try to use *this* time?" Hank asked when he sat down to eat.

Captain Roy laughed. "Oh! They were pretty creative this time! He told me that the new health regulations required that on hot days he needed to spend five minutes of every hour out of the heat. So I *had* to let him into the living areas where it was air-conditioned."

"What'd you do?"

"I took him over to the edge of the cargo bay and pointed to his car, which he'd left idling, and told him I'd wait up here while he took his break."

"How'd he take that?" Dot asked.

"Not well, he stomped around, told me I had to do it, but the union guys started giving him a hard time as *they* were being forced to wait in the sun for him to finish, and then threatened to file a grievance. *That* got him moving! He just signed off and left in a huff without inspecting the rest of the cargo."

"Why wouldn't you let him go inside?" I asked, a little confused.

"By treaty, unless the vessel is registered here on Earth, no Earth officials are allowed to go anywhere but the cargo deck, and only until after we've unsealed the bay doors," Dot said.

"If I'd have let him in," the captain continued, "that prohibition no longer exists."

I grimaced as the implications became apparent. "He'd search the whole ship then, wouldn't he?"

"Him and twenty of his best friends," Dot replied. "And anything that wasn't legal here on Earth, they'd confiscate and fine us for."

"Or worse yet, arrest somebody," Hank added with a nod.

"Is this a common problem?" I asked.

"Only here on Earth," the captain said. "Last time we were here the inspector claimed he had diarrhea, and I just pointed to the cargo bay door and told him he could hang his ass over the edge. Surely the loaders would understand."

I had to laugh at that.

The captain regaled us then with a few more stories about other, past times, where either customs, or some other port official, had tried to "violate the sanctity of the ship." I had to admit some of them were pretty ingenious, if not funny. But the lesson was clear and it was another one of those things that I wasn't taught in school, but should have been.

After dinner, Dot cut me loose to go get settled in. I found the storage cabinet for sheets, blankets, pillows, and towels, made my bed, set my alarm, and crashed. It had been a very long few days.

Iowa Hill—Ganymede Orbit

TRANSIT TIME TO JUPITER WAS ABOUT NINETEEN DAYS, WITH A
six-hour window of no acceleration, during which time they
flipped the ship and we'd spend the rest of the time decelerating,
or maybe it would be better to say we were accelerating *away*
from our destination. Not that we flew in anything even remotely
approaching a straight line. The course we flew was more of an *S*
shape, because everything was in motion, moving in orbit around
the sun or even another planet.

So we spent the acceleration portion of our trip matching
the ship's velocity to the orbital velocity of our target, as well as
accelerating toward it, until we were actually going faster than
our target. Then during the deceleration portion we also adjusted
that vector and velocity to rendezvous with our destination at
almost zero relative velocity.

I was told in school that military ships and the high-gee
passenger liners flew more of a single arc, instead of the *S* that
most cargo ships used, because it was faster. And because they
didn't care about the costs involved. But for ships like the *Iowa
Hill*, money and safety were the deciding factors on everything.
So we flew the cheapest, and hopefully safest, course we could.

Our destination was actually an artificial satellite of one of

Jupiter's moons, one of dozens that orbited it. There were hundreds or maybe even thousands of artificial habs that orbited Jupiter or one of the larger moons these days. There were probably more people out here than there were on Earth. Or at least, that's what some of the instructors back in college had claimed.

Dot had a pretty standard routine. We spent an hour cleaning Engineering every morning. The next four hours were spent inspecting gravity plates. After that it was lunch, then an hour or two inspecting one of the many systems onboard the ship, then off to the machine shop to repair or replace anything that needed repairing or replacing.

"What happens if we don't have anything that needs to be fixed?" I asked her that first day when we were repairing a valve that we'd just replaced from stores.

"Why, we take the rest of the day off!"

"Really?" I was surprised by that.

Dot laughed. "Honestly? I have no idea. On a ship this old there's always something that needs repairing or replacing, or cleaning, or inspecting. If we had a full engineering section I suspect we could catch up with it, but then what?"

I shook my head. "I don't follow."

"There's not a lot to do onboard ship during transit. If we didn't have all this to deal with"—she waved at the ship around her—"it'd get boring. The captain and each of the mates do a full ship inspection everyday during the non-bridge watch portions of their shifts. You'll see them doing inventories of gear or inspecting the cargo tie-downs. Just looking for anything out of place or things that might be a danger to the ship or the crew."

"Just to keep from being bored?"

"Well, that—and remember, if anything breaks out here, getting rescued isn't all that easy. Even if we stop accelerating, we're still carrying a lot of speed and inertia. Add to that the vastness of space, and, well, there are a lot of Flying Dutchmen out there and nobody really wants to join them. Objects in motion and all that stuff."

I nodded. I hadn't really given it all that much thought. Oh, there are the famous disasters everyone's all heard about, like the Harlow Lines *Firebird*, a fast passenger ship that experienced a complete engine room blowout just prior to flip and deceleration. Three hundred passengers who were now on a cometary orbit that wouldn't be back for a couple hundred years, circling the sun for the rest of eternity.

Nobody wanted *that*.

"What's the schedule for after dinner?" I asked.

"Sitting watch and if anything breaks, we fix it. If you've got any books to read, shows to watch, or studying to do, that's the time to do it."

"The captain said that once I get the time in, he'd bump me up a grade?"

"Yes, and...?"

"How much time does it take to go from fifth to fourth? They told us it takes a couple of years of sailing, but they never really told us what the requirements are."

Dot nodded, "It's pretty simple, you need a thousand hours on watch and to pass the test. So about three months."

"What?" I said shocked. "Three months? They told us it took a year or two!"

"Well, on a normal ship with a full crew, as the junior engineer you'd probably only get a four-hour watch a day, and maybe not even every day. On a larger ship with a larger crew, you might not even get that much. And that's only when you're underway. But here? Here you're legally on watch twelve hours a day."

"I am? Oh right! There's only two of us."

"And we spend as little time in port as possible. So you'll definitely have the time in four months. Moving up to third takes an additional two thousand hours, so say six to eight months."

"How hard is the test?"

"Not terribly. A couple of hours if I recall correctly. We've got study materials onboard, so if you're looking for something to do in your spare time, that's probably a good place to start."

"Is there anything else I need?"

"If your boss signs off on you, you don't have to take the physical examination, which is where they run you through an engine room and make you identify everything and explain how it all works."

"So I could make third engineer in a year?"

"Yup. Getting to second is a lot tougher, though, four thousand hours and five years as an engineer. It's also a much longer examination and for the physical part, they take you on whatever random ship they can get access to and you have to tell them how to run it and fix it."

I shook my head. "I don't even want to know what you have to do to make chief."

"Some folks never do. There's a lot who are happy as second. Hell, you can make a good living at third. The bigger ships and most habitats have engineers dedicated to specific areas like environmental, gravity, fission, fusion, waste processing, you name it. There's a lot of specialty ratings you can pick up at third and it's usually useful to pick up a couple."

"Such as?"

"Grav panel refurbisher and certifier," Dot said with a grin. "That alone right there lets me write my ticket on any ship with an opening and pretty much every habitat either wants to hire me, or has room for another shop offering repairs."

"Huh, they never taught us that."

"'Course not; most sailors think you gotta take it to a shop. Because most shops are run by engineers who decided to settle down and raise a brood."

"And how do I get one of *those* certs?"

Dot smiled again. "I'll teach you all about it. 'Course you can't file for it until you get your third engineer's rate, but once you do, it'll be worth it."

I spent the next two weeks mainly learning my duties and learning the ship. Inspecting the grav panels was interesting, because getting to them was often difficult. There were five hundred and four of them and half were in the top of the ship's hull while the other half were in the bottom. We averaged about ten a day and alternated each day between the upper ones and the lowers.

The grav drive theory was pretty complex, but simply put, the panels all had special superconducting coils wrapped around them, through which "gravitons" flowed in a circular pattern. The bottom panels flowed "right-hand" rule, while the tops did "left-hand." What this meant was a force was generated coming out of the front of the coil that pulled us along, and another force operated perpendicularly to the panel that provided gravity in the area between the two panels.

The ratio between acceleration and the artificial gravity that a panel provided was mainly based on the panel's construction. The *Iowa Hill* had "Ten-Ones," which meant that the gravity was ten times the acceleration—usually. There were things that could be done to change that ratio a little bit, like when they cut acceleration for the flip halfway through the flight we still had ten percent gravity, because being in pure freefall with only microgravity often led to problems.

There were also limits as to how much power you could push through a particular type of panel and the ones on the *Iowa Hill* were definitely at the lower end of the price point spectrum. There were of course specialty panels like the "Zero-One" panels that provided no acceleration while providing gravity. After two hundred years, the science behind them, as well as the engineering, was pretty well understood.

For the most part, the rest of the crew didn't really talk to me at all, just "hello" and not much else. Part of that was probably because of how much time I was spending with Dot learning my job, and part of that was probably because I was new.

Dot had told me that it wasn't uncommon for people to jump ship at the first port of call.

"Why's that?" I'd asked.

"Because we're a tramp spacer, we don't have a regular route, and we're socially and economically at the bottom of the barrel. Lots of folks sign on to outfits like ours because they don't know any better, or because they're just desperate to get someplace else. Once they realize you're staying, *then* they'll take the time to get to know you."

I had just nodded in agreement, because I figured she knew what she was talking about. As this was my first trip into real space, and on a *real* cargo ship, I had no idea at all what to expect. Other than that it was completely different from what I'd been led to believe.

I was allowed onto the bridge, which was nice, because the only windows in the ship where up there. The captain checked me out on the basic systems, then signed me off as a watch-stander, so if someone did need to take a break I could cover for them if no one else was available.

Four days into our trip, around 4:00 a.m., I was quite suddenly woken up from sleep by an alarm on the engineering panel in my room. It took me a couple minutes to figure out what was wrong as I got dressed. We'd lost a panel.

"Wake up," Dot's voice came over the intercom in my room. "We got a panel out."

"I saw. I'm almost dressed."

"Meet me at the spares," she replied and clicked off.

I got my deck shoes on, grabbed my tablet and my tool belt, and made my way back to the spares locker where we kept the extra panels, which was next to the machine shop. When I got there Dot had already gotten the "panel dolly" out and was undoing the dogs holding the eight-foot-by-twenty-four-foot spare that was what the two-twenties attached to. The fifteen hundred's panels were nine by twenty-six, needing to be larger because they were lower powered.

I helped undo the dogs holding it into place and then the two of us picked it up and set it on the cart. The panel wasn't all that heavy, maybe eighty pounds. Once we had it secured to the cart, Dot went and got the rigging bag for what we'd need to change it, then the two of us pushed the cart out into the hold.

This was where it got a little tricky. There was a hoist set in the ceiling, and we had to connect the dolly to that and hoist it all the way up. If the panel was one of the lower panels, we'd slide the hoist to either the port or starboard side and lower it all the way down, through a hatch, and into the interdeck space where the panels were located.

But for the upper panels we had to connect it to a second hoist that accessed the center interdeck hatch that led into the upper space.

That took about five minutes as Dot checked everything twice and had me check it all twice as well, while she engaged in some very colorful swearing about the pedigrees of engineers who couldn't make the second hoist reach down to the floor so that we wouldn't have to engage in such a senseless transfer.

We then hoisted it up into the interdeck space, moved it out of the way, climbed up there ourselves and moved the panel off to where the bad one was.

The thing that made swapping panels difficult was that the interdeck space that we had to work in was only a meter tall, so getting around inside was already difficult when you were just doing a panel inspection. Disconnecting the graviton feed lines, unbolting the panel, lowering it, moving it, putting the new one in and hooking it all up in such a tight space was both a time-consuming and difficult affair.

It took us an hour and I think I was the one doing most of

the swearing. When we were taught how to do this in class, we never had to do it in such a small workspace. While lying on our backs. Using flashlights.

"Okay, let's get started on rebuilding this," Dot said as we hauled the bad one into the machine shop.

"Can't we go back to bed for a few hours first?" I asked and yawned.

"Nope!" she said, sounding a lot more cheerful than I felt. "One of the opposing panels to this one will probably fail in the next twelve hours. They tend to go out in pairs. So we need to get this one done now, and it's a four-hour job if you know what you're doing."

I nodded.

"Now, let's get this opened up and get started."

I watched, interested, as she undid the top of the panel. The whole assembly was about ten centimeters thick and I'd never seen the inside of one. I watched carefully as she disassembled the entire thing, pointing out all of the fittings, the control box, everything. The "coil" in it was wrapped around a special board mounted inside and we lifted that out, once everything had been disconnected.

The fault in the coil was obvious, once she pointed it out to me. The coil was a brown ceramic material encased in a clear plastic tube, and was fairly solid.

"So, first we break up the old coil, flush it out of the tube, then we check the tube for leaks, seal any we find, and then refill it with new material."

I just nodded and helped her break it free of the board it was firmly wrapped around. Then we each grabbed a rubber mallet and worked over the contents of the tube until we could just shake them all out into a bucket.

"Now, if we were desperate, we could just add some solvent to that powder, and remix it, then reuse it. But that's a messy job. So instead we'll just bag it and trade it for new stuff."

"What happens if the tube has a leak?" I asked.

"We can patch it, if it's not too bad, or just replace it. I have a spool of tubing in the supply bin."

Refilling the tube with the new "paste" turned out to be a difficult job, and once that was done we had to rewrap the tube around the board, secure it, and then the whole thing went into a kiln that Dot had made to bake for several hours, "firing" the paste into ceramic.

While that was going on, we tested the control box and made sure it worked properly and replaced anything that seemed dodgy.

"How long does a panel last?"

Dot shrugged as she put the control box back into its mounts. "If you're easy on them, they can last a couple of decades, maybe longer. Usually what kills a panel is the ceramic coil cracks, like on this one. Physical shock can do that, so can heavy thermal cycles. That's why the captain brings us up to full acceleration slowly. It's also why on the high-gee ships losing a panel can cause the panels around it to fail and set up a distortion in the ship.

"When the lower panel fails next, due to this one's having failed, we'll probably see an overload in the control circuit and not a coil fault."

"Will we still replace the coil in that one?"

"Maybe, depends on how old it is. Now, let's get some breakfast—or is it lunchtime now? Then we can haul that out of the kiln, reassemble everything, and be ready for the other one to fail."

The other panel failed while we were eating dinner and the repair on it was a lot easier, as Dot had predicted. As the coil was only a couple of years old, we didn't replace it, just the controller. Which we then rebuilt, tested, and put into the spares bin for reuse.

Ganymede Orbital Two

FIVE DAYS LATER WE WERE DOCKED AT GANYMEDE TWO, ONE OF the several dozen artificial satellites that orbited Ganymede. Gany-Two was almost exclusively a transfer point for cargo being shipped down to the surface, or out to the other habitats or planets. Unlike Gany-One, which being the first one built had a lot of people living on it, as well as a lot of industry.

"Come on," Dot said after we'd secured everything and set the reactors to "banked"—low-power mode. "Put on your thermals and let's go see about getting you a pressure suit."

"Thermals?" I asked, surprised.

"Don't you have any thermal underwear?" she asked, giving me a surprised look.

"Umm, *no*?" I replied, looking as confused as I felt.

"Well, put on whatever you got that's warm under your shipsuit and I guess we'll buy you some of those too."

"Why?"

"You'll see."

Shrugging I went back to my cabin, shucked off my shipsuit, put on my one pair of sweats, then put the shipsuit back on and met her in the hallway.

"I checked with the captain, your shipboard account's been

credited with your pay, so you're not broke. Now, let's go do some shopping."

"How do you access your regular bank account?" I asked as I followed her toward the docking tube. Access to the cargo bay was now sealed as we were docked on the surface of Gany-Two and not in one of the larger bays inside it. So our cargo bay was now in total vacuum. The only way to get to the rear half of the ship currently was through the environmental duct that ran just inside the hull on the top of the ship, and having been in it a few times for inspections, it was pretty cramped.

"The day before we dock, when the captain checks to make sure they have a spot for us, he sends the crew manifest to the station. That gives the local branch of your bank enough time to update your account data. That's why they ask who you're banking with when you take the job."

"Oh!"

"You didn't fill that part out, did you?" she asked after a few moments of silence.

I could almost hear the smile in her voice as she checked the side access hatch for pressure, then opened it and we entered the docking tube.

"My bank wasn't on the list of choices," I said as I closed the hatch behind us.

"Well, I need to stop by my bank, so I guess you can open an account when we get there."

"Thanks," I said as we went through the hatch at the other end of the tube. "I really appreciate the help."

"Just doing my job, you're a part of the ship's crew now and you *do* work for me."

I looked around as we stepped out into the hallway. It wasn't exactly *dimly* lit, but it wasn't all that much brighter than that. There were pipes and cableways everywhere, the floor of the corridor being the only clear space, and it was covered in scuffs and scratches that showed just how many people and machines had gone through here over the years.

As for the paintjob, I had no idea what the original color must have been, but the current color was a kind of steely gray under about a century's worth of grime and dust.

"Damn! Don't they heat this place?" I said and shivered as I felt the cold radiating off the walls.

"Nope. Only the main concourse is heated, and even then it's not all that warm. Just be happy they keep it above freezing."

"How old is this place?" I asked as I followed her down the long hallway.

"I think it's about a hundred and fifty?" she said after thinking about it a minute. "They didn't start building it until traffic got to be too much for Gany-One and they couldn't expand it any further. Of course when they started on Gany-Three they had learned their lesson and they built it more like Gany-One. So of course most of the businesses that had come here left, making this even less desirable than it already was."

"And of course they couldn't fix it, right?" I asked.

"Wasn't in the budget and it would disrupt too much trade. It may look like shit and there may a lot of undesirables who call this place home, but more traffic comes through here than one and three combined."

When we got to the concourse, we had to go through another airlock, but this one I think was more for keeping the heat in than anything else. It was noticeably warmer, though definitely not as warm as we kept it onboard the *Iowa*.

The first thing I noticed were the people; there were quite a few here. The area also was a lot cleaner, brighter, and better cared for. The next thing I noticed was that there were a *lot* of women, and even a fair number of men, who were scantily clad and obviously looking for "dates."

"Okay, bank first, I need money and you need an account. Then we'll get you a pressure suit. After that, thermals and a few other things."

I nodded and followed her over to the bank and tried not to stare at any of the women "working the street." Some of them were pretty hot and I hadn't had a girlfriend in months.

"You can visit the hooks *after* we're done," Dot teased.

"I'm just window shopping," I said with an embarrassed smile. "I'm sure I can't afford any of that."

"Well, if you do decide you want some, don't mind me, but check with Parks first, he knows who's safe and who to avoid."

"Chief Parks? Really?"

"Yup, once the ship's unloaded he'll definitely be sampling their wares. Pam's a bit of a party girl too, once she's off ship."

"Really? Whenever I see her, she's always so serious."

Dot snorted. "Trust me; if you weren't on crew, a fine young man like you? She'd have jumped your bones, I'm sure."

I rolled my eyes at that. They'd warned us in school about shipboard romances and all of that. "I think two couples onboard the ship are probably enough. It's bad enough when Hank and Chaz have had an argument, I don't think I even want to be on the same ship when the captain and his wife have a fight."

"They don't," she said, leading me inside.

"Sure they don't."

"You'll see. Now, go over there and talk to the nice man about opening an account."

I rolled my eyes again. Sometimes Dot reminded me of my mom, even if she wasn't old enough.

Opening an account wasn't really all that hard, Dot confirmed my employment and they had my employer information on file. When I left I had more cash in my pocket than I think I'd ever had there before, and while my bank balance wasn't very big, at least I didn't have tuition to pay anymore. Just regular payments on my loan, which I took a few extra minutes to set up before we left.

Next we went and I got fitted for a pressure suit. That took most of what I had in the bank. Then while we were waiting for them to make it, Dot took me to a clothing store, where the first thing I bought was some thermal underwear.

"Okay, now, let's try on some of these parkas and winter pants," Dot told me after I'd got the thermals.

"Why? We live on a spaceship."

"Poor man's space suit," she said, smiling at me.

"Huh?"

"You put these on *over* your pressure suit. The fabric's tough enough that it won't rip or tear, and it conforms to your body to trap the heat. Plus it's got built-in heating and cooling in that little unit on the back. Add a good pair of boots and gloves and you can EVA for up to an hour without a problem."

I looked at her, and then at all the arctic gear. "You know, I'd been wondering why they had this here."

She nodded, grinning at me. "Most spacers rarely need a space suit, so they just buy this in case of emergencies. Also this packs up a lot smaller than a suit does."

It didn't take long to find a set to fit me, then after paying for it we went back to the place I'd bought the pressure suit. They'd finished making one for me, or rather their machine in the back had. So I stripped down and put it on and they tested everything to check it. Then I tried on the arctic gear I bought to make sure that fit, in case I had to return anything before we left.

At least I got to put my new thermals on under my shipsuit when I got out of the pressure suit so I wouldn't freeze on the walk back to the ship.

"Any idea how long we'll be here?" I asked on the return trip. I had my hands full, as the pressure suit had both a helmet and a small backpack that were all housed in a special hard-shell carrier that contained their battery chargers. Not to mention the bag with my arctic gear on top of all that.

"Seventy-two hours, more or less. Takes about eighteen hours to unload the ship here, then they have to put together the new cargo, make sure it's weighed and balanced, and then another twenty or so to load it."

"I'm trying to think of what to do tonight, seeing as I'm just about broke after this," I said, hefting the shopping goods a little.

"Is that a friend of yours up ahead?" Dot asked.

"All my friends are back on Earth," I replied and shifted my load so I could look down the corridor. I could see there was a man striding rather purposefully this way. "Maybe he's just walking from another ship?"

"No, he was waiting by the access way. He didn't start walking until he saw us."

"Maybe he's a friend of yours, then."

"I don't have any friends," Dot replied.

I didn't know what to say to that, so I kept my mouth shut and watched as we drew closer. I noticed he was looking straight at me, and as he came close I stopped and looked at him, turning to face him as Dot passed behind me.

"Dave?" he asked.

"No," I replied.

He smiled and pulled out a gun.

"Sorry about your friend," he said as he pointed it at me.

I immediately tried to duck behind the heavy case I was carrying and dodge to the side as I heard two quick shots, neither of which was very loud.

"Are you okay?" Dot asked from behind me as I heard something collapse onto the floor.

I dropped the stuff I was carrying and sure enough, the guy was on the floor with a red spot on his forehead that was quickly growing. I looked down at myself.

"He must have missed," I said, looking around. Dot came around me and she had a pistol with what looked like a long barrel in her hand. She kicked the pistol that the man had dropped away from his hand, then shot him again, point blank, in the eye.

"Well, if he wasn't dead, he is now," she said and quickly put her gun away.

I got a sinking feeling in my stomach and I went through his pockets while Dot grabbed my sweatshirt from the bag the parka was in and tied it around his head.

"What are you doing?" I asked her.

"Don't want to make a mess. We need to dispose of this before anybody comes along. What are *you* doing?"

"Looking for this." I sighed and showed her the picture of me I'd found, along with the name of *Iowa Hill* on it.

"Interesting. Well, first things first. Secure that pistol, and let's get rid of the body."

I stuck the stuff I'd found in my pockets, stuck the pistol in one of the leg pouches, then helped Dot carry the body down to the access way.

"Wait here, be right back," she said and went inside.

I ran back to where I'd dropped my stuff, carried it back, and set it near the body as she came out with a large plastic bag and a small bag. The body went into the large bag; my bloody sweatshirt went into the smaller one.

"You can wash that out later," she said handing it to me. "Now, let's get this bag into Engineering."

I grabbed one end, she got the other, and we hauled him inside and dumped him on the floor.

"I'll get your stuff, go grab some cleaning supplies and take care of that mess outside."

I nodded and did as I was told. There was a fair deal of blood on the floor, but the shirt had stopped it from getting worse. I ended up having to mop a much larger area, to keep the clean spots from standing out.

When I finally put everything away and went back into

Engineering, the body in the bag wasn't there anymore, and Dot was looking over my pressure suit.

"The shell stopped most of it; guy must have been an amateur or something. Anyway, I patched the hole and nothing else seems damaged other than a dent on the backpack."

"Why do you think he was an amateur?" I asked, dropping into one of the seats with a heavy sigh.

"He should have shot you in the head, that's why. Or better yet, he should have shot me first, as my hands weren't full. Let me see that pistol."

I reached into the leg pocket to grab it.

"Carefully!" Dot warned. "Don't shoot yourself! Or me for that matter!"

I resisted the urge to tell her that I knew what I was doing, because frankly, I didn't. I fished it out carefully and held it out to her.

"Ever use a gun before?" she asked.

"I've never even *touched* a gun before," I told her with a shake of my head. Guns were banned back home. Well, at least for people like me they were. Proles and doles tended to use other weapons when settling disputes or killing each other.

"Okay, watch closely and I'll explain. Here's how to unload it."

I watched as she removed the magazine, then worked the action, causing another bullet to fall out from the magazine well. After picking the round up she looked the pistol over carefully.

"Okay, this is a six-millimeter case-less. Pretty simple pistol, you can even make one in the machine shop in the back of the ship. It's got an integral silencer on it, to keep it from getting too loud. Ammo for these is common and again, not all that hard to make.

"This one was definitely made in a machine shop, same for that magazine. Most likely they cast it in a mold and then drilled out the barrel and just assembled the parts. Not a bad job overall. We'll see how well it shoots later."

"We?"

"What's the first rule of being shot at?" she asked with a grin.

"Don't get shot?"

"Nope!" She laughed. "That's the second rule. First rule is shoot back."

"Did you make your gun? The one you shot him with?"

"No, mine's a lot more expensive and shoots a more powerful round. What he was shooting you with might not penetrate the skull. Mine, as you saw, did. Quite handily I might add."

I nodded and looked at the gun, then around the room.

"Where's the body?"

"In the trash chute. We'll dump him when we're far enough from the station. Now. Any idea why somebody would be paying a common thug to kill you?"

I snorted. "'Cause they're self-centered idiots?"

"Ah, now we're making progress! And just who are 'they'?"

"Eileen's husband, maybe Eileen too," I said, frowning. "Eileen's husband is some big-shot elie politician, and from what my brother heard, I've become an inconvenience and, well, I guess they really do kill people for that."

"So that's why you took the job with us? To get away from Eileen?"

"I've been wanting to get away from Earth since I found out it was possible," I grumbled as I shook my head no. "The place is a hell-hole and life there just sucks unless you're one of the elies, and I'm obviously not. Yeah, I was hoping for a better gig, but like I said, my grades weren't the best. Besides, now that I'm here? I don't regret taking this one."

I shook my head again. "I just can't believe that they'd still try to get rid of me. I mean, I left Earth, I went to school for this!"

"So, let me guess, you were screwing this Eileen gal and her rich and powerful husband found out?"

I looked at her angrily. "Oh no, it's far far worse than that! Nobody cares who you sleep with when you're an elie. Or who you hurt, who you kill—nope, stuff like that doesn't matter.

"No, my crime is that I *exist*. That's it. The worst sin I could possibly have ever done, and it's not even my damn fault!"

"Whoa, you lost me there. What should that matter? So you exist? So what?"

"One of Eileen's husband's competitors for office has found out about me, apparently and, well, he wants to use me against him somehow. You see, to the elies, a prole is the worst thing in the world!" I paused a moment and thought about that. "Well, a dole might be worse, but they could use that at least to get votes."

"Do you always explain things like this? 'Cause really, Dave,

I'm lost here. How"—she looked me straight in the eyes—"are you two connected?"

"About twenty-two years ago, Eileen ran away from her incredibly wealthy and powerful elie parents to 'find herself' or some such shit according to my dad. They met; he had no idea who she was. They got married. Nine months later I happened. A few years after that Eileen decided that living life as a prole and working for a living was just too much of a hassle and she went home—without me."

"What about your brother?"

"My dad remarried, eventually. It's complicated. Ben's my stepbrother—but honestly, as far as I'm concerned he's my brother and Jenny, his mother, is my 'real' mother. Eileen abandoned me, got the marriage erased, and eventually married some other elie asshole. I think she even had kids by him.

"I don't think she even remembers that I exist."

"Well, if *she* doesn't know, how did her husband find out?"

"Because the *system* knows I exist. They track everything and everybody. The system knew who she was when she went into the hospital to have me, so even though *I'm* a prole and my father's a prole, as far as the system is concerned, my mom's an elie.

"And she's worth millions, maybe billions? Hell, I don't know." I sighed and shook my head again. "I figured as long as I didn't set foot on Earth again, at least until after the election, I'd be safe. But now? Now, I don't have a fucking clue."

I got up out of my seat. "I'll be in my cabin. Wake me when we leave. It's probably best I don't show my face off the ship. Maybe I'll get lucky and they'll think I'm dead."

Aboard the *Iowa Hill*

I SPENT THE REST OF THE DAY PLAYING WITH MY PRESSURE SUIT, until I understood every aspect of how it worked. I then did the same with the parka and the rest of the arctic gear. With the snorkel hood up it really was quite effective at keeping you warm. There were even D-rings on the integral belt, which made it clear that the manufacturer actually knew where most of their stock was going.

I could just imagine what the Earth government's responses would be if they knew. They'd probably ban arctic gear just to stop people from being able to do it, or perhaps require a pressure sensor be installed so the integral heaters and coolers wouldn't work when the gear was in a vacuum.

All for "your" safety, of course. The bribes they'd get from the actual space suit companies would have nothing to do with it at all.

After that I started studying for the "engineer fourth" test and, when that got boring, I studied the stuff on panel repair certifications that Dot had told me about.

I only left my cabin to get food, or use the bathroom.

Because yes, I was worried.

Not quite scared, but what the hell was I going to do about this? What could I do about this? If I was lucky, they'd figure I was dead and forget about me. "Out of sight, out of mind," right? If I wasn't lucky, they'd hire somebody at the next station. If I was *really* unlucky, they'd hire somebody who was a pro, and not some inexperienced idiot.

When we pulled out, the next trip was to Saturn, which was twenty-five days away. Because the Sun was in the way, we had to fly up out of the plane of the ecliptic, then back down into it again. According to Dot, that added a couple of days to the trip, but not really enough to matter.

"Why Saturn? Why not something closer?" I asked Dot as she showed me how to set up the target range in the lower hold. Obviously there were other members on the crew who practiced their marksmanship and, true to her word, she was going to teach me how to shoot.

"Local runs around the gas giants are usually handled by the locals, who get better deals, which makes them hard to compete with. So longer runs tend to be the rule, unless it's someplace nobody really wants to go. The other reason is that it was the best paying cargo that the owners could find."

"What'd the captain say about our little problem?"

Dot shrugged. "Didn't tell him."

"What? Why not?"

"Well, it didn't happen onboard, and I didn't want to lose my only engineer."

"You think he would have left me behind?" I asked, worried.

"I didn't want to take the chance. You really haven't been here long enough for anyone to care about you. Give it a month or two, and they'll all get behind you. It's not like any of us are saints on this crew."

"That still doesn't help with when we get to Saturn," I told her.

Dot smiled. "Don't worry, I've got an idea."

"Oh? What?"

"Worry about that later; for now, you need to learn how to shoot."

"And then what?"

"Learn how to shoot better," she said with a smile. "Now, be careful where you point this, because you can kill somebody with it," she said, handing me the pistol first, and then the magazine. She'd spent a good twenty minutes going over firearm safety with me back in Engineering before we even set foot onto the range.

"Now, load and fire at the target."

I put the magazine in, pointed, pulled the trigger, and nothing happened.

"You have to work the action to load a bullet."

"Oh."

The first shot surprised me but I hit the target. The second shot, nothing happened and I noticed I'd jerked a little.

"Huh, that's interesting," Dot said, carefully taking the pistol from me and removing the magazine, then working the action she picked up the bullet that fell onto the floor and looked at it. Then she looked up into the magazine well of the pistol.

"What's so interesting?" I asked.

"It jammed."

"So?"

"This pistol doesn't have an open slide. When you fire it, the action works to cock it and load another bullet. But as there's nothing to eject, there's no ejection port. That's why I had to remove the magazine to fully unload the pistol."

"And that means?"

"That if it jams or misfires, you're dead. I'm wondering now if this pistol has a defect, that it jams after the first shot. As you can't clear it, well, all you are after your first shot is a bullet sponge."

I watched as she reloaded it, worked the action, took a shot, and then nothing happened when she pulled the trigger a second time.

"Wow, he must have been surprised!" she said with a grin and unloaded the pistol again. "But *that's* why you always practice with a new firearm."

"So now what?"

"For now, you can use my pistol to learn."

"What about that one?" I said, motioning toward it.

"Well, we might be able to fix it, but I really don't like closed action pistols, because if they jam, you're in serious trouble as you've already witnessed. Probably just be better to salvage what we can from this one and build a new one. For now, just leave this one unloaded, and tonight before you go to bed, balance a coin on the front sight and practice pulling the trigger."

"If you say so."

"I do." She smiled. "Now, let me get my pistol and we'll get back to learning."

I went through about fifty rounds of ammunition shooting her pistol. After I got schooled a couple of times when she put "dud" ammunition in it and I realized I was jerking as I pulled the trigger, I got a lot better at shooting. I really liked her pistol, right up until she told me how much it cost.

Then we cleaned up the mess and it was back to business as usual for the rest of the shift.

"Hey, I noticed you didn't join us for dinner on the station last night," Chaz said, smiling at me as I sat down at the small mess table that I'd followed Dot to. There were four tables in the mess on the *Iowa Hill*, but normally we only used two, considering the size of the crew. Hank our bosun, Chaz, and Pam, our second mate, were already seated at it. Captain Roy and his wife, our cook, were seated at the other table. Chief Parks had the watch and whoever finished dinner first usually relieved him so he could eat.

I shrugged. "I needed to buy a lot of gear that I couldn't afford back on Earth, so Chief Briggs took me shopping. Didn't have anything left to go out with, after we got back."

"Captain says you worked your way through college as a tech?" Hank asked.

I nodded. "Yeah, I didn't qualify for any financial aid, and I didn't want to take out too many loans, so I had to work."

Hank smiled, the first time I'd actually seen him do it when looking at me. "Ah! Someone used to working for a living! No wonder Dot likes you!"

"I take it my predecessor wasn't?" I asked, looking around the table.

I noticed that Dot just smiled slightly, but Hank nodded and both Chaz and Pam, who were sitting across from me, smiled.

"He was always telling us about how special he was, because he came from an Earth school."

"Actually he came from one of the campuses the school had on Earth's Moon," Chaz put in with a sigh. "Acted like he had an elie stick up his butt."

I shook my head. "I've seen the type; they think that because they got a good job they're better than the rest of us. He was probably a doler who got lucky."

"I thought they didn't have dolers on the moon?"

"Probably a former doler who got lucky and had to leave town before his former dole friends got jealous and killed him for being successful."

"They do that?"

"Dole's never get over themselves," I said with a sigh. "They get everything handed to them, never have to work, and think their shit smells like roses. Most of 'em aren't very bright, but they all got tons of attitude and think that the world revolves around them. And heaven help you if you get ahead of any of the rest of them."

"And what about the proles?" Pam asked in a soft voice with a hint of a smile.

I smiled back a little self-consciously. "We believe that if we don't do it, it won't get done, so if we want to eat we need to get off our asses and go to work. Yeah, I'm sure I've got an attitude as well, but at least I try to actually *do* something."

"Why not sit on your ass and become a doler, then?"

"We're not allowed," I said with a sigh. "Not that I'd want to be one, to be honest."

"What do you mean you're 'not allowed'?" Chaz asked.

"Proles who won't work get sent to prison, and trust me, the stories you hear about that makes it pretty clear that you don't want to go there."

"Then why aren't the doles in prison?" he asked rather indignantly.

"Because they were born into it," I said with a shake of my head.

"No wonder they all feel special!" Chaz said with a laugh. "But still, jail? That's not very fair!"

Hank put a hand on Chaz's arm, causing him to look at him.

"If they didn't force the proles to work, everybody would starve to death and nothing would ever get done."

"Then why do they even have the doles?"

"Voting blocks. They live in a 'democracy,'" Dot said, making those air quotes with her fingers again. "The doles all vote as they're told, the elites—or 'elies'—get to rule, and the middle class—the 'proles' as they're called back on Earth—take it in the shorts."

"What happens if the proles don't work?"

"Riots," Hank said with a frown. "Last time was when my father was a young man; he told me about it. The doles all rose up and rioted and punished 'those nasty proles for being so selfish.' A lot of people died."

"Hence why you go to prison now if you don't work," I said with a nod. "And it's also true that while the doles all like to think they're elies, they get treated worse than we do if they even look like they're getting out of line. Killing a prole gets you sent to jail. Killing a dole just gets you a stern talking to."

"*Really?*" Pam asked, giving me a strange look.

"Well, unless you're an elie," I said with a snort. "Then nothing happens at all and everybody says that they had it coming."

"What happens if you kill an elie?" Chaz asked.

"They kill your family if you're a prole."

"What if you're a dole?"

"They kill everyone on your block," Hank said with a snort of his own.

Chaz shook his head. "How can anyone live like *that*?"

I shrugged. "Beats me. I hated every minute of it, and now that I'm gone, the only time I'll ever go back is when we land to pick up cargo. Where are the rest of you all from, anyway?" I asked, not only wanting to talk about something else, but wanting to be able to eat my dinner before it got cold as well. "They really don't teach us much about the rest of the solar system on Earth, being as it's the 'center of the universe' and all that kinda crud."

Everyone at the table snickered at that. I guess the Earther attitude was fairly well known.

"I'm from the colony on Ceres," Chaz said. "Not a lot to say about it really. It's a nice place, but everything there is either about mining, or about building habitats and space stations. My family's been doing it for generations, but me? I wanted to travel, I wanted to see things and go places. I always wanted to become a spacer and just travel and...well..." He smiled and looked at Hank, who smiled back at him.

"I grew up on Mars," Hank said next, looking over at me. "When I turned seventeen I decided to join the Martian Space Navy and see a bit more of the solar system than I'd ever see working in the steel mills down there like my old man.

"Honestly, I enjoyed it, but after a while hunting pirates and rescuing people or chasing down smugglers gets old. So when the time came I took all those skills they taught me and struck out on my own."

I glanced up at Pam, seeing as I already knew where Dot was from.

"I'm from Adonis," Pam said with a slight smile.

"Adonis?" I asked. "Where's that?"

"It's a small cluster of artificial habitats linked to the Adonis asteroid that used to be in the Apollo group. I trained with one of the groups there, but advancement was hard in my last job, so when I saw that Damascus had openings and had a faster track for promotion, I came here."

I nodded; I wasn't surprised that I'd never heard of where she was from. There were tens of thousands of asteriods that people lived in, on, or around, and most of them had been moved into better and more stable orbits over the last two hundred years. Many of which weren't even on any map, and some of which changed their orbits from time to time.

"I have to admit, I'm really curious as to what it's like growing up in a habitat or on an asteroid as big as Ceres," I said, pausing a minute between bites. "When I was a kid, my father would tell me stories he'd heard from some of the captains when he'd been working on their ships. The places you all get to go, the things you've seen. I grew up in a run-down apartment complex, never went anywhere until I went to college to become an engineer."

"It's not all fun and games, you know," Pam said, surprising me. I would have thought with looks like hers, every door would always have been open and life always *would* be fun and games. Then again, she was here, and Dot had warned me more than once about everyone onboard. A warning that even extended to me, I realized.

"Well...truth is my younger brother was a child prodigy and I had to watch out for him in the public school system for years, until he graduated—before me, I might add. Trust me, I haven't had any 'fun and games' since I was like twelve," I said with a short laugh. "But I take your point. The housing always looks sweeter on the other side of the quad, as they used to say where I grew up."

I looked down at my plate; I was done and I really wasn't interested in dessert. I still ate rather quickly, a holdover from school and work, where there was never enough time to enjoy yourself.

"I guess I'll go relieve Chief Parks," I said, getting up and carrying my stuff over to the counter. I actually enjoyed sitting the occasional watch on the bridge when somebody needed a break. It was the only part of the ship with windows, and while most of the times you only saw stars, it was still fascinating to look out at them.

"I got the watch, Chief, you can go eat," I said, coming onto the bridge.

"Ah, thanks, Dave! I saw earlier that Dot's teaching you how to shoot?"

I nodded. "I think she was a little offended to find out I'd never touched a gun before."

Parks laughed at that. "Yeah, I can see where she would be. Your predecessor not only wouldn't learn, I think he ran screaming from the room the first time he saw one!"

"And yet you still hired me?" I said, shaking my head. "Kinda surprised you'd be willing to take on another kid from Earth."

"Eh, I think the powers that be were pissed at us for letting that idiot get in trouble. That and finding entry-level engineers isn't easy. Most of the ones out in the system with actual certs and licenses are all threes and up, and they don't work cheap."

"So once I get my level three I'll be able to write my own ticket, then?" I asked, a bit curious.

Parks gave a snort as he headed for the exit. "Not at first you won't. You're gonna find that most Earthers aren't popular with the regular system types. Earth companies usually only hire Earthers and most Earthers don't want to work for anybody that isn't."

"Isn't Damascus Freight an Earth company?"

"Yup. But other than you and the captain, there isn't anybody else from Earth on the ship. Damascus isn't exactly *picky* about who works for them," Parks said with a grin as he left the bridge.

Shrugging, I got into the command chair and, sitting down, fastened the lap belt, but left the rest of the harness off. Regulations required the watch to be wearing at least one restraint when on duty, but I'd noticed that I was the only one who did it.

A few minutes later, Chaz surprised me by joining me on the bridge.

"We didn't say anything wrong down there, did we?" he asked, looking a little concerned.

"Huh? Why would you think that?"

"Well, you did leave kinda quick."

"Haven't you noticed I'm a fast eater?" I said. "It's a bad habit I picked up from school and work, where we only had, like, fifteen minutes to eat. Plus," I added with a grin, "I wanted to beat you up here for a change. I don't often get a chance to look out the windows."

"You don't have to be on duty to come up and look out the windows, Dave," Chaz said with a smile. "I think Dot's the only one who doesn't come up here at least once a day to take a look."

"Really?"

He nodded. "A lot of people who grow up out here aren't that fond of open spaces."

"What? But you live out here, in this!" I said, waving at the infinity on the other side of the windows.

Chaz laughed. "I know, right? But most of us don't go outside of our habitats, and most of them are *inside* an asteroid and not on the outside. So you can go months, or longer, without ever seeing a large open space. Because of all the mining and construction work, people back on Ceres go out into space all the time. They even have domes on the surface that they take you up in when you're a child, so you don't become afraid of it."

"Huh, I didn't know that."

"Well, for you planet-raised types, everyone worries if you'll flip from the lack of open spaces."

"Yeah, I can see that. But Engineering is pretty big and so's the cargo hold," I replied with a shrug. "Actually, I grew up spending a lot of my time inside. The complex we lived in was really just one big megalopolis. You didn't have to go outside if you didn't want to, and when the weather sucked, you really didn't want to."

"Yeah, that whole 'weather' thing was surprising when we were on Earth."

"Was that your first trip there?"

Chaz nodded.

"How long have you been onboard here?"

"On the *Iowa*?"

I nodded.

"About a year. I need another few months before I can file for my 'Able Spacer' certificate."

"And then?"

Chaz shrugged. "Won't know until then, I guess."

"What about Hank? I thought you two were a couple?"

"If we're still together a few years from now, then I guess

we'll be a couple," Chaz said with a chuckle. "Hank might be all grown up, but I'm anything but."

I laughed, "Yeah, I know *that* feeling."

"So, is your brother really a prodigy?"

I nodded. "Yup. He had it rough at first too. Until my dad sat me down and gave me this long talk about family and him being my brother now and how I had an obligation to take care of him."

"What, was he adopted?" Chaz asked confused.

I shook my head. "My father remarried when I was like ten. Up until then he'd been raising me by himself. Ben's mom—my mom now really—would babysit for my father while he was work-ing. As a single mother, she had it a lot worse than my dad did, and eventually they just decided to get married."

"What about your real mom?" Chaz asked.

"She *is* my real mom," I all but growled out.

"Oh, sorry...didn't mean to..."

I sighed. "It's a sore spot; my bio-mom ran off when I was, like, three; I can't remember anything about her. It was pure hell on my dad, though, having to raise a son *and* work a full-time job to pay the bills."

"Oh, I can imagine. Again, I didn't mean to pry."

"Eh, you didn't know," I said with a shrug. I still remembered when Dad had brought Jenny and Ben home; I was six going on seven. They'd been tossed out on the street after Jenny's husband had died; she was a doler who had been trying to move up into the proles, wanting a better life. When Dad had found her on the street, she was willing to do anything to protect her child, so I got a baby brother and dad got a live-in girlfriend and babysitter.

That he eventually married her and they had a daughter together had made me and Ben happy. Looking back on it, I could see now that she'd made my dad very happy. Because I didn't have a single memory of him ever being happy about anything until after she'd moved in. He'd always been either angry or sad.

"So, what's it like having a genius for a younger brother?" Chaz asked, snapping me out of my revery.

"At first it was a pain in the ass!" I said with a shake of my head. "A young smart kid who didn't know when to shut his mouth, always telling all the other kids in my school why they were wrong? Oh yeah, I got into a lot of fights teaching the other kids to keep their hands off my brother, *or else*."

"That must have sucked."

"Yeah, I got beat up or detention way too many times. But eventually he learned to keep his mouth shut and figured out how to help all the jocks. Once he got them on his side, I never had to beat anyone up again."

"How'd he win 'em over?"

"He'd watch their opponents' games before they played us, figure out their weak points, and then teach the team how to beat 'em. But it gets even better than that."

"Oh?"

I grinned. "He figured out how to make routines for the girls' cheerleading squads that would take them to the big national competitions. So at the age of thirteen he had one of the hottest eighteen-year-old girls in school as his girlfriend!"

Chaz laughed, "Damn! Now that's funny! He didn't leave you hanging, I hope?"

I shook my head. "No, from that point on, Ben always watched out for me, just as I watched out for him. There were a lot of girls who wanted to get to know me *better*, so they'd get a co-starring role on the team." I shook my head. "Honestly, I'm gonna miss him more than my parents.

"What about your family?" I asked.

Chaz spent the next twenty minutes, until Chief Parks came back, regaling me with stories about his own childhood and family. He had two brothers and a sister, and apparently one of his brothers had a reputation for practical jokes that was second to none, to hear him tell it. He'd actually been going to a trade school to be a deckhand on an ore hauler when he'd met Hank and decided to sign on with the *Iowa Hill*.

As I went back to my cabin, it felt nice to have finally connected with *somebody* on the crew on a friendly basis.

SIX

Saturn

BY THE TIME THE CAPTAIN HAD CALLED IN TO OUR DESTINATION, which was another transshipment point in orbit around Titan, I'd become friendly with Chaz, Hank, and Chief Parks, who preferred to just be called "Chief." Pam was always quiet around me, but considering the body I suspected that loose shipsuit was hiding, I really couldn't blame her. She probably didn't want me hitting on her.

Shelly, the cook, was even starting to warm up to me a bit, but I was still too afraid to try and make friends with the captain as I'd barely been here a month. Maybe once I'd been here a while longer and made a few more trips I'd be a bit more comfortable with talking to them.

Docking went off without a hitch and once cargo started unloading, Dot and I were both given leave of the ship.

"Here, put this on," Dot told me when I met her at the docking exit, as she handed me one of those athletic caps, the type with a bill on it.

Looking at her, I took the cap and put it on my head.

"What this for?"

"It's a disguise," she said, smiling.

"A hat? That's it?"

"There's a button on the underside of the bill, by the hatband. Press it."

I felt under the hat with my hand until I found a small bubble button. I pressed it and suddenly I noticed there was a slight glow along the underside of the bill.

"Look at me a moment."

I turned to face her and she smiled. "Perfect."

"What's it do?"

"Simple physics, it shines filtered light down over your face to change the color of your skin. Add a few simple variations and it alters the lines of your face faintly as well. Here, look."

She held up her tablet with it set for "mirror" mode and sure enough, my skin looked darker, somewhat swarthy, and I looked older.

"That's pretty cool!" I said as she put her tablet away.

"It's got enough battery power for about eight hours, then it has to be recharged. Now, let's go hit the station and get some supplies. Got your pistol?"

"Right here." I patted the vest I was wearing for extra warmth.

"Good. We'll see if we can find you a better holster while we're out."

I nodded and, checking the hat and making sure I had my own tablet, I followed her out onto the station. Coeus Station was one of the older stations and had started out as one of the original six colony habs around Titan, but over the last century the population had shrunk as a lot of people emigrated to either one of the many ultra-modern arcologies now down on the surface, or one of the much more numerous—and again, more luxurious—orbital habs that had been built on one of the many "captured" asteroids from the belt, or even some of the lesser moons of Saturn and Jupiter.

Given enough power, people had learned that if you weren't in a rush, you could use a gravity drive to move anything. Oh, a couple had crashed into Jupiter due to some magnificent engineering cock-ups, but after the disaster at Uranus where they'd accidentally dropped Miranda into the planet and killed a half million people, all the major governments got together and decreed that if you tried to move anything larger than ten kilometers in size and hadn't been licensed to do so by at least three of them, they'd kill everyone involved and seize whatever assets were left after that'd been done.

As Earth, Mars, Titan, Ganymede, Ceres, and Venus—all of whom maintained some large ships with some serious firepower— were a part of this agreement, nobody ever tried to move anything *that* big again. Though there was still talk about moving Oberon one of these days, not that I could understand why anyone would want to.

Leaving the ship, I noticed that the hallway we were berthed off of was a lot busier than the last one. There was a ship berthed to the other side of the arm we'd attached to, and there were people coming and going from that one, as well as several more spots we passed along the way as we headed for the commerce section of the station.

"See anybody following us?" Dot asked.

I shook my head. "No, but I don't know if I'd be able to tell. There's a lot more people here than I expected."

"Coeus is a major transfer station, unlike Gany-Two. There's still a large population of people living here as well."

"What's large?"

"More than twenty thousand, less than fifty, if I had to guess."

"Doesn't anybody know?" I asked, surprised.

"Oh, the people down in Environmental probably have a good idea, but that's not the kind of information that a lot of people want known. People out here tend to be a little paranoid when it comes to others wanting to know anything about them."

I thought about that a moment. On Earth, there was little to no privacy. The government knew everything about you that there was to know, and as was probably the case in governments everywhere going back to the beginning, what the government knew, way too many people who wanted something from you seemed to know as well.

"So what are we here to buy today?" I asked, changing the subject.

"Well, we need more materials to make more bullets; I also need to replace our stocks on materials for rebuilding panels. Then I need to order some general items for the ship's engineering stores. I also thought a few nice snacks from someplace other than the ship's freezers would be nice."

"How long are we going to be docked?"

"It'll take about forty-eight hours to unload the ship. They don't work around the clock here and as there's other ships on the same arm, they can only move so much out at a time. Captain says they already have a load assigned for us. So maybe another forty-eight to load. Count on three days, but it'll probably be more like four."

"Okay. Can we hit a bank? I really am just about broke."

"And you'll probably still be. The money you spent on Gany-Two was an advance on your salary I'd asked the captain to give you. As we only get paid monthly, I don't think you're going to find much in your account. Plus"—she turned and smiled at me—"you have to pay for the bullets you shot and the materials we used to build your new pistol, as well as all the new ammo we're going to buy."

"Didn't you say it was cheaper to make it yourself?"

"Yup. But until I teach you, or you learn how to do it yourself, you're going to be really short of ammunition, if you don't buy your own."

"Fine," I sighed. "Let's go find a bank so I can see just how impoverished I am after I pay you back and buy those things."

"That's the spirit!"

She checked her tablet, and then led us to a nearby branch for our bank. Coeus was actually a very large station, having a large asteroid as its original core. From what I'd read about it, there were a large number of processing facilities here, as well as cargo storage and other warehousing. A lot of people may have moved out of the station here, but there were so many habs in orbit around Saturn that many still came here to shop and trade for any major items. So while people were moving out, companies were moving in.

So I soon discovered that there were a lot of shops here, as well as a lot of people shopping and trading, some of whom were at small stands set up in the side corridors. I also noticed that barter, something I'd never really seen, was alive and well here.

When we got to the bank, I found that my balance was barely over three hundred credits. I took most of it out and added it to the forty-three credits I had left over from my last shopping spree.

"We're not buying anything expensive, are we?" I asked.

"Nope, and you owe me forty creds for everything."

I blinked and quickly forked it over. "That's it?"

"Bullets are cheap and the only expensive piece of your pistol was the stock we milled the receiver out of. Oh, and the hat was ten."

"You're charging me for the hat?" I said with a surprised look.

"TANSTAAFL."

"Huh?"

"There ain't no such thing as a free lunch."

"Oh! Right, PFWYG," I replied.

"Haven't heard that one before."

"Pay for what you get. The doles and the elies may get everything for free, but the proles have to work for every cred," I said with a grin. "The only freebies are at year's end and birthdays."

"Ah. Well, let's get our shopping done and head back to the ship. I think the captain wants to take everyone out to dinner tonight."

"What about the hat? Won't anybody say anything?"

"Stick it inside your jacket. As long as you're with a large group of people, I doubt anybody will try anything. Most folks go armed in the stations, so as long as you're with a crowd or around lots of people, you should be safe."

"That sounds like the voice of experience."

"It is. Now, shake a leg. I want to get back before they leave."

It didn't take us long to find what we were after, though the stuff for rebuilding the panels made for a fairly large package that, as the junior engineer, I got the job of carrying. But considering how fast Dot had been on the draw last time, I'd rather she kept her hands free and said as much.

"Just be sure to drop that the moment anything happens," she said, keeping a lookout as we walked. "Because I can't afford to have any of that shot up."

I sighed and shook my head as she just smiled.

At least the trip wasn't a long one, and we got inside unmolested.

"Well, I didn't see anybody who seemed to be all that interested in us," I told her as I carried everything into Engineering.

"I didn't see anybody either," Dot agreed. "Maybe they haven't gotten word back yet that your assassin failed."

"Or better yet, they think he succeeded."

"I wouldn't count on that. I'm sure he was supposed to show them a picture of your dead body."

I nodded glumly to that, and then took the materials for repairing bad panels back to the machine shop. By the time I got back, the entire crew was waiting for me and we all left for dinner, the captain locking the ship access behind us.

We trooped down the same hallway as I'd gone down earlier with Dot, but once we got into the commerce section with the shops, we took an elevator down into one of the lower levels of the station, which was a lot nicer, and much more posh looking than what I'd seen so far. The restaurant the captain led us into was definitely a very nice one.

He'd even reserved a room for us, so when we sat down for dinner, it was just the crew.

The waitress came out and took drink orders; I ordered a sweet tea, which I was surprised they had, while everyone else had cocktails.

"Dave! Unwind a little, have some alcohol!" Hank teased.

"Maybe once you're all used to me making a fool out of myself *without* any extra help," I said with a grin.

"Wise policy," the captain said with a nod. Then as the waitress left to get our orders he looked around the table. "This has been a good year, mostly."

I heard a few muted groans at that.

"Losing our last apprentice engineer caused a small bit of upset with the folks back in the head office, as they had to reroute a few of our trips to get us back to Earth so we could pick up Dave here," he said with a gesture toward me.

"Word of warning, Dave, never try to draw to an inside straight or I'll strangle you myself."

I shook my head. "Definitely not, Captain. I grew up playing poker. I know better."

"Excellent. Anyway, to get us back up to the levels of profit that the company is used to seeing from the *Iowa Hill*, we're going to be doing a lot of shipping along the Gray Routes from here on out. We probably won't hit a major hub again for at least six months, possibly a year."

"Do you think we'll hit any of the Blue Highways?" Hank asked.

"Maybe a few, it all depends on what and where we're going. Half the routes will probably be picked by me and Ian here," the captain said with a nod toward Chief Parks, who was sitting on his right, "if we come across any specialty or rush cargoes that we can fit into our routes. But from here on out it's all going to be fractional loads. The cargo we're picking up has six different destinations, so our route's going to be changing constantly."

"What about the dark stations, will we be going to any of those?" Dot asked in a soft voice.

"Doubtful. There are a few I'm willing to put into, but only because we've been there before, and only if it's a very special case."

"Like a lot of money," Hank muttered.

"Or an emergency, like last time," Chief Parks replied.

"More of the latter than the former," the captain said with a smile. "The folks back in the head office weren't too thrilled with me the last time. But the point I specifically want to make is that any entertainment you might wish to indulge in, or materials you might wish to bring onboard that you can't get easily elsewhere, well, we'll be pulling out three days from now."

He looked around the table. "Any questions?"

I raised my hand.

"You don't have to raise your hand, Dave, you're not in school anymore," he said with a laugh.

"Oh, sorry!" I lowered my hand. "But I've got two."

"Shoot."

"How many ships does Damascus Freight Lines have, anyways?"

"Eighteen, plus ours. Sixteen of them are the same class, two are smaller and do specialty runs. One's here in the Saturn system, the other's in the Jovan system. What's the other question?"

"Umm, what sort of things should I be looking to buy for entertainment?"

"Nothing breathing," the captain said and winked at Hank as everyone chuckled.

"Hey, I earn my keep!" Chaz protested with a frown.

"Yes, and we're pretty happy that you do too. That's why I put you on the ship's roster and payroll. But . . . there was this cat he brought on a few years back and I don't want to see a repeat of *that* debacle."

There were a number of snorts at that.

"Now, let's get our orders in and get some food," the captain said as the waitress returned with our drinks. I quickly looked over the menu, and thankfully I recognized most of the dishes and was able to order something I'd like.

"What are the Gray Routes?" I asked Pam, who I'd ended up sitting next to. I figured she was one of the deck crew and could both fly and navigate the ship, so if anyone would know, she would.

"Those are the trade routes to the smaller and sometimes less reputable places that no one wants to go to. A lot of them don't have enough trade to justify a large ship, even one as small as ours. That's why the captain said we'd be doing partials, dropping off a few containers here, picking up a few there, and just moving on."

"What do you mean by 'less reputable'?"

Pam took a deep breath and sighed, causing me to notice that she was obviously stacked under that loose suit.

"Every hab, every orbital outside of the gravity well of a major planet, makes their own laws."

"I thought they all did that?"

"To a lesser extent, yes. But the farther away you get, the more things change. Anything you can imagine, it exists out there, somewhere, maybe even in more than one place. And the worse something is, the more likely you are to run into it.

"That includes pirates."

I gave a small nod at that. "What about 'Blue Highways'?"

"Those are the secondary trade routes. Places that see more traffic because they either specialize in something, or they get a lot of tourists. Though some of them can be a little different as well."

"And dark stations?"

"They're people who are hiding, either from governments, police, military, or each other. Some of them are okay, but most of them are not. They're all run by gangs and if you get in trouble there, you can end up dead, or worse."

"Any advice on what I should get before we leave?"

Pam gave me a sly smile. "Sex toys."

"What?" I said, blushing. This wasn't the kind of thing I expected to hear from a pretty girl.

She laughed at me. "A lot of the places we stop at, we're not going to be at for more than twenty-four hours. Probably nothing for more than two days, and the kinds of girls, or boys if that's what you like, that you'll meet there probably aren't going to be ones you want to spend time with."

"Well, I don't see how I could really meet someone in two days."

"I was talking hookers," Pam said.

"Oh! Right! Yeah..."

Chaz asked me a question then about shopping the next day and I talked with him and the others until dinner arrived. Dinner was quite good, and I did my best not to wolf my meal down. Dessert was also quite good and the captain settled up the bill and left right after with his wife. Parks and Pam excused themselves not much later, though each headed off separately.

"Well, I'm gonna hit the facilities, then I guess it's back to the ship," I said, getting up.

"Facilities?" Chaz asked.

"Bathroom."

"Oh, the head!"

I nodded. "I'll try to be quick, as I don't want to have to try and find my way back on my own."

"If you get lost, just ping one of our tablets," Hank said. "The same codes we use on the ship'll work here."

"I'll do that," I said and left to take care of my business.

It ended up taking a bit longer than I'd expected, and when I came out of the bathroom, everybody was gone.

I thought about going out the back of the restaurant, but then I remembered that I had no idea what was there, just that it wouldn't be a street or an alley. So taking out my tablet, I called up the map of the station I'd downloaded and told it where I wanted to go as it zeroed in on my current location.

Leaving the restaurant, I stuck the tablet in my vest pocket and listened as it softly told me which way to go. I realized then that I'd forgotten my hat; I'd left it on one of the consoles in Engineering.

A minute after that I realized I was lost.

We'd come here on an elevator, but the navigation program wasn't leading me to it. I briefly considered backtracking to the restaurant and trying again, but I wasn't sure I could find it, after having made several turns.

So my only choice was to stick it out and hope that the path I was being led down would take me where I wanted to go.

Three turns and two doors later and I was at the base of a staircase that zigzagged up and down, out of sight. The program was telling me to go up, so that's what I did. Every fourth landing, there was a door, on which there was a level number painted. I wanted concourse one.

The first one I came to was Recreation Eight.

Four levels later, and I was at Recreation Seven.

I had no idea at all how many concourse levels there were,

and if that was even what came after I cleared the recreation levels. So I started pacing myself, though I kept moving quickly. I was used to walking and I was in good shape, a couple of flights of stairs shouldn't be too much of a problem. Still, going up twenty-eight or so flights of stairs was a daunting prospect.

I had just passed Recreation Four when I realized there was someone on the stairs a couple of levels below me, and they were slowly catching up. So I picked up speed and after a minute, I was pretty sure that they had too.

So I started to run. I watched the floors go by as I ran up the stairs; I could hear that the person behind me was now running too. I could only hope that they weren't gaining on me!

When I passed Recreation One, I gave a sigh of relief, or it may have been more of a pant, which turned into a swear as two flights later I came to Machine Level Two.

I didn't even hesitate; I grabbed the door, pulled it open, and ran through it.

I was instantly in a long hallway that had pipes and cableways lining the ceiling. The floor was smooth and wide, with what looked like tire scuff marks on it. I grabbed the handle on the first door I came to. Locked.

There was a side corridor and I ducked down that, just as I heard the door from the stairwell bang open.

I dodged down three more side corridors, left, right, right again, then I found a small side corridor and, ducking just around the corner, I drew my pistol and made sure the safety was off, then put it back in the holster and waited.

I heard him before I saw him, and the sound was coming from behind me!

Diving into the hallway I heard the muted sound of a shot and felt a burning sensation in my left leg as I fell to the floor.

"Stop running, Walker. You'll only die tired!" The guy actually laughed.

I scrabbled around a corner and waited. He wasn't trying to sneak up on me. I guess he didn't think I was armed. Drawing my pistol, I waited. The moment he stepped out of the side corridor, I shot him twice in the gut on purpose and once in the groin by accident. He cried out crumpled to the floor.

Getting shakily to my feet, I limped over to him and kicked his pistol away, then kicked him in the head as hard as I could, stunning him. Putting my pistol away, I straddled his body and dropped to my knees, pinning his arms to the floor. A tactic I'd used more than once in the past while dealing with people who'd picked on my little brother or caused me *other* problems.

Going through his clothes I found his tablet and, opening it up, I was surprised to find he had a password on it.

"I can pay you!" he gasped, coming to.

"Yup, you sure will," I said. "What's your password?"

"I'm not—" I punched him in the nose, breaking it and bouncing his head off the floor.

"Next time, I shoot you in the head, understand?"

He nodded. "*R* three, *F* four, *V* five."

I tapped it in and called up his mail program. Sure enough, there was an email there, a recent one too. He was getting ten thousand to kill me.

I opened up his bank app next. "What's the password for your bank?"

"Umm..."

I raised my fist in warning, and he gave me that next. There wasn't really all that much in it. But he had a contract for ten thousand, and all I needed was a dead body.

I looked down at him and thought back to a few things I'd done in the past that I wasn't too proud of. I put his tablet in my pocket.

"I need a doctor," he gasped.

I pulled my pistol out stuck it in his eye.

"Wait, no..."

And pulled the trigger, the sound of the suppressed pistol a little quieter than what I'd expected.

Wiping the barrel off on his shirt, I rolled off him and cursed loudly. Now that the adrenaline was starting to wear off, my left leg felt like it was burning. Looking down, there was a hole in the side of my pants leg, and a small bullet hole in my leg and it was bleeding. I'd been shot.

Looking at the dead body, I rolled it over, onto its side, shot it twice more in the back, then, putting my pistol away, I got his tablet out and set it down.

Next, I pulled off my belt and one of my shoes, then my sock. Pulling my pants down, I rolled up the sock and put it over the bullet hole and wrapped the belt around it to hold it in place and stop the bleeding, or at least slow it down. Then I pulled my pants back up, put on my shoe, and looked at the body. There was enough blood coming out of the back wounds, so I moved farther away and took a couple of pictures.

Then I got one of the face. That done, I relieved him of anything even remotely valuable or that might be used to identify him. Next I got his pistol, staggered back to my feet, and left the area.

Using the map on the phone, I found an elevator and made my way to that. Fortunately, the hole in my leg hadn't bled on the outside of my pants, so overall I was fairly clean. The problem was, where did I go next? I needed a doctor, but how did I find one? I didn't think I'd make it to the ship, but maybe I could rent a room?

I also had things I needed to do, and I needed to do them soon. While I'd never been shot before, I had been stabbed, more than once, and I was sure that this was going to be worse.

I took the elevator to Concourse Two and the maps claimed there was a cheap hotel where you just paid for the room at the door with creds or a card. Thankfully they were close to the elevator, and after I'd fed the slot by the door forty creds, it popped open. Once inside I closed the door and slumped down to the floor.

Getting out my tablet I pinged Dot.

I need a little help.

Where'd you disappear to? I came out of the bathroom and you were gone.

I sighed. It figured.

I'm on Concourse Two, in room 8 at the autohotel.

What are you doing there? You didn't hook up, did you?

I need a doctor. Got shot in the leg. Stopped the bleeding.

STAY!

Woof woof, I sent back.

Setting my tablet down, I undid my pants, and pushed them off. My left leg was a bloody mess. Picking up the dead guy's tablet, I took a bunch of blood and rubbed it all over my face, then closing my eyes I took a picture.

The picture didn't look too bad, but when I cut and pasted the blown-out eye socket from the picture of his face that I'd taken onto the one of mine, it looked better.

I then sent that picture, along with the one of the body with the bullets in the back, to the person who'd sent the contract and demanded payment. Then I put both tablets away, and started going through his things.

It wasn't long before there was a sharp rap on the door.

"Dot?"

"Yes."

Reaching up, I opened the door and was surprised when both Dot *and* Chaz came into the room.

"Holy shit!" Chaz said.

"The blood on my face is from my leg," I told him as he stared at me. "Could you get me a wet towel to clean up?"

"Yeah, right away!" he said and went over to the small bath-let, which combined a toilet, sink, and shower. Grabbing a small towel, he turned on the water and wet it. Then he came over and started cleaning off my face.

"What happened?" Dot said, looking at my leg.

"Guy followed me out of the place and we had it out a couple of floors down from here. He got me in the leg and, well . . . let's just say it didn't end well for him."

"Why is there blood on your face?"

"Staged my own death using his body," I said with a smile. "Got it all here on his tablet and have already sent off confirmation and demanded payment."

"Where's the body?"

"Far away from here. Like I said. Can we find a doctor to get the bullet out and patch up my leg?" I asked.

"Something like that isn't cheap, if you don't want any questions asked."

"Yeah, well, I've got ten thousand credits coming into this guy's account," I said, tapping the tablet again. "So let's just say I'm a little flush right now."

Dot smiled. "In that case, I know just the gal for you. Wait here. Chaz?"

"Yeah?"

"Stay here and take care of him. I'll be back as soon as I can. And keep an eye on that wound; make sure it's not bleeding."

"Got it!"

I watched as Dot left, then Chaz undid the belt and added a folded-up towel that he grabbed from the sink to the sock and used the belt to reapply direct pressure.

"So someone had a contract out on you?"

"Yup."

"Who?"

"My bio-mom's new husband." I sighed.

"Huh? I thought the proles didn't do that kinda stuff."

"She's an elie. She got tired of slumming when I was three and left me and my dad to go back to her elie parents."

"Damn, now I know why you hate them so much. So why's he want you dead?"

I shook my head and told him what little I knew, then he got a couple of wet towels and helped me clean up a bit more, then went and washed as much blood as he could out of my pants.

He was still working on that when Dot came back with an older-looking woman.

"Why are you on the floor?" she asked, looking at me.

"I didn't want to get blood on the bed?"

"Done this before?"

"Last time I got stabbed."

"Hurt much?"

"Oh yeah."

"How big was the bullet?"

I carefully pulled the gun out of my pocket and handed it to Dot. "Careful, it's still loaded."

Dot took it and immediately unloaded it, showing one of the bullets to the doctor, who nodded.

"Okay, I'm going to give you a shot to numb your leg. Then I'm going to remove the bullet. After that I'll clean the wound, then seal it up. Stay off it for a couple of days, then take it easy. Week to ten days, it should be healed."

"Thanks. I'm Dave. Where do I send the money?"

"Doc Hills. I'll leave you my bill when I'm done here."

I nodded and watched as she first gave me a shot that made the pain go away rather quickly. Then she carefully stuck something into the wound and after a minute she pulled it out and dropped a bullet on the floor. Then she started cleaning the wound, I guess.

About this time, I passed out.

When I woke up I was still in the room, only now I was on the bed, under the covers, and there was somebody snuggled up against me, with an arm around me.

I took a moment to process that. I was pretty sure it wasn't Dot; she didn't strike me as the type. Which meant it was probably Chaz. I could tell I still had my underwear on, so obviously nothing "untoward" had happened. Not that I thought he was the kind of guy to take advantage of the situation.

Stretching slowly, I winced. My leg hurt, but not as bad as I'd feared.

Chaz woke up then and rolled onto his back and stretched.

"I'm not getting you in trouble with Hank, am I?" I asked.

"Nah. I told him you got mugged and stabbed in the process and we had to get you a doc. He was the one who told me to stay the night and keep an eye on you."

"Really?" I asked surprised.

"Yeah, Hank's a Marsie. Those guys are the complete definition of loyal. I know he looks gruff and all that—hell, I bet you're thinking he'll cut me loose for a younger guy in a few years."

"That thought had crossed my mind," I admitted. Mainly 'cause I'd seen it happen to some of the kids I went to public school with, both gals *and* guys.

"Yeah, the only way we'll split up is if I leave him. Hope I didn't scare you there, but you were completely out of it, and, well, this isn't a big bed."

"I'm not scrambling out of bed screaming, am I?"

"I thought that was due to the leg!" he said with a chuckle.

"I'm not really into guys, but I don't mind sharing the bed. Honestly I'm surprised I didn't wake up sooner. Normally I can't sleep if there's someone else in the bed with me."

"Doc said she gave you a shot to help you sleep."

"That reminds me, I gotta pay her. Help me up, will you?"

Chaz climbed out of bed, having to crawl over me to do it, then helped me sit up, handed me both of the tablets, then found the doc's bill and handed me that too.

He didn't say anything as I opened up the guy's tablet, checked his bank account, and saw that, yes, the money had been paid. Looking at the time, I saw that I'd sent the "proof" of my death out about ten hours ago. The money had been deposited about five hours later.

Someone had obviously been waiting for a response, as Earth was about two hours transmission time from where Saturn was right now.

Picking up the bill, I looked at the amount and just transferred her the full ten thousand. What the hell, I couldn't touch it or they'd trace it to me. Assuming that mattered out here. If she didn't want the tip, she could always return it.

Chaz got dressed while I dealt with that, then helped me get dressed next.

"I need a new pair of pants." I sighed, looking down at mine and the small hole in them. At least the blood hadn't set too much before Chaz washed them out, but enough had that they were stained now. Thankfully they were dark enough that it wasn't obvious.

"Just be glad you weren't wearing your shipsuit, those ain't cheap."

I nodded. "True, but I could have patched that and no one would really care. That is, if we got the bloodstains out. Think we can buy me a new pair of pants on the way back to the ship?"

Chaz nodded. "It's not really that far out of the way. Probably should get you a cane or something too."

"That would help, I'm sure."

"Just let me call Dot and Hank and let 'em know what's up."

"Sure. Let's get some food, I'm starving."

I walked a few laps around the small room while Chaz let Dot and Hank know what was up. I could walk, or hobble at least. A cane would definitely help.

Once he was done, we cleaned up, took the bloody towels so we could dispose of them elsewhere, and left.

Chaz actually knew of a decent place for breakfast and Hank showed up while we were eating, gave Chaz a hug, then joined us.

"I'm surprised you're taking this so well," Hank said to me as we left the place in search of new pants and a cane. Chaz wanted to pick up a few things as well.

"Yeah, well," I sighed. "My life before I went to college was pretty messed up. Whenever I got in trouble, and I got in trouble a lot, the records showed who my bio-mom was, and, well, nobody wants to piss off an elie. Nobody in power that is. Kids at school? There's no crueler, harsher place in the world than a children's playground, and being a kid whose mom abandoned him meant I caught a lot of shit from the other kids until some doler bully thought he'd teach that bitch elie's child a lesson."

"Oh? What happened?"

I looked down at the ground. "I learned that bit about only getting a stern talking to."

"What? But how?"

"Like I said, the police, the prosecutor, the judge, they all knew who my 'real mom,'" I said making air quotes with my fingers like Dot did, "was. So they didn't know what to do. If I'd been a prole, I might have gotten jail time, even at my age. But because of her, I got told never to do it again, and sent home."

"What happened next?" Chaz asked.

"I joined a gang and started a reign of terror, what else?"

"Uh-huh. Right."

I smiled a little. "I did join a gang, and I did cause problems. It was actually Ben's idea. He told me that with a bunch of tough friends nobody would mess with either of us anymore, and he was right.

"Because I could get away with shit the others couldn't, and because they knew what I'd do if I had to, I suddenly got a lot of respect. And as Ben had a knack for building gadgets that were useful, the gang valued him too."

"I'm surprised you ended up here and didn't stay with the gang," Hank said.

I shook my head. "I did it to help Ben, and, well, maybe because I was angry at all the crap I'd gotten dumped on me because of what I was. When Ben left for MIT, I left the gang."

I didn't mention that my "grandfather" had one of his people tell me that the next time I dragged the "family name" through the mud it would be the *last* time. That "*we*" didn't do things like that, "*we*" were not "common thugs." Apparently they'd found out about me, my penchant for using ice picks—the weapon of choice among quad-gangs—and my stint as the gang's "picker." So while they wanted nothing to do with me and I had a different last name, appearances were still important. *Very* important.

The thorough beating I'd gotten then had also made that very clear.

Until that guy on the bus had tried to use a pick on me, I honestly hadn't touched one since back in high school. I was starting to wonder if maybe I should have kept it instead of dumping it in the trash back at Holloman.

"You can do that?" Chaz asked, bringing me back to the conversation.

"Yeah, we were all kids really. Not like we were in any kind of organized criminal gang. Kids' gangs are like the farm teams for the mobs. If you disappear, no one cares."

"It's different in most of the system, especially the Belt. Most gangs are family or clan affairs and nobody leaves, not even the kids."

"Huh, I'd heard stories that some of the Asian gangs were like that."

"What'd your parents think about it?"

I laughed. "My dad thought it was a 'rite of passage' kind of thing. I got the impression that he was quite the hell-raiser until I was born. My mom—my real mom, not my bio-mom—didn't care for it much, but when she found out that I wasn't just doing to for me, but for Ben too, I think she rationalized it."

"You did a lot for your stepbrother, didn't you?" Hank asked.

I nodded. "Yeah, my dad made it pretty damn clear that we were family now and as the eldest I had an obligation. That Ben was my *brother* not my 'step' brother." I smiled happily then. "And honestly? I'm glad I did. Ben may have started out as a clueless brain-case, but he looked up to me and listened when I started teaching him how to be popular.

"He also taught me everything I needed to know about engineering so I could get into a good school, then tutored me when I needed extra help."

"Family's important. It's nice to see that you've got your head in the right place."

I could see then that my words had made a pretty positive impression on Hank and I thought back to Chaz's comment on loyalty being a big deal to him. I don't know if he meant it was because he was from Mars, though, or because he'd been in the Mars Navy.

It was funny when I thought about it. I knew so little about the people who lived on the other planets, or the habs out in space. But from the sounds of it, they all seemed to know a fair deal about one another, and even Earth. I guess Earthers were just pretty self-centered.

I guess I shouldn't have been surprised. The doles and the elies never thought about anything other than themselves, and I'm not so sure that we proles were any better.

✧　　✧　　✧

The first thing we bought, or I bought, was a cane. Then I got two pairs of pants, and found a place to sit and relax while Chaz picked up a bunch of stuff for him and Hank. I also took a few minutes to write Ben and let him know what had happened and what I'd done. I didn't want him to think I was dead.

After that was done, we all went back to the ship and I thanked the both of them for their help, then climbed into bed and pretty much stayed there until we pulled out. Being in the low berths, I noticed once again that Chief Parks didn't come back to the ship until eight hours before we were due to depart, supervising the last of the loading while the captain worked up our routes. Pam didn't show up until quite a few hours after that.

Chaz had confirmed what Dot had told me, that Chief Parks tended to hit the brothels pretty hard whenever we were in a large port, but he had no idea what Pam was up to, whereas Dot had more or less said that Pam also partied pretty hard whenever we were in port.

The captain and his wife mostly stayed onboard and I gathered Dot was visiting with friends or something, though she came back each night. While Chaz and Hank hit the bars and came back pretty drunk each of the next two nights.

I did end up buying a lot of books and more than a few study guides from the station's online bookstore. I really wanted to get that engineer's three rating as soon as possible, as well as that repair cert. I bought a couple of movies too, now that I actually had the time to watch them, something I'd never had back when I was going to school and working.

Just before we pulled out I got a response from Ben, I smiled as I opened it.

Dave,

I got your message and thanks for telling me! I'm tapped into Eileen's husband's accounts now and I would have seen the message and worried about you. In fact, I did see the message, but I didn't go looking for it until after I'd gotten yours.

He bought it, if you hadn't already guessed. So for now that means you're safe.

College is still going well and I'm still having fun. I just finished my second doctorate, and thanks to my grades the school offered me a scholarship for a third masters in another one of those engineering sub-disciplines you like to make fun of. However, it is something I've been curious about for a while now, so I get to satisfy my curiosity on someone else's credit. Can't complain about that!

Still not sure what I want to do once I'm done with college—there's so many choices and there are definitely a lot of people who think they know and are all too willing to tell me what I should choose. As for me, well, as long as people are willing to pay me to go to school, I'm more than willing to let them. There are still a few things I'd like to learn.

Best Wishes,
Your Brother,
Ben

I stopped and reread that last paragraph a second time to be sure I'd read it right.

I got the message: they were starting to pressure him and he wasn't sure how much longer he had until he'd have to take a job. It wasn't urgent, but it was coming. I had faith in his ability to stall, but still, it was something I needed to keep in mind.

The Belt

OUR FIRST TRIP WAS TO AN ORBITAL HAB THAT WAS BETWEEN the orbit of Jupiter and Saturn. It was actually at Saturn's L5 LaGrange point. It only took us a week to get there, and once there we off-loaded at three different habs and picked up loads from two others.

As Engineering was active through the loading and off-loading procedures, I didn't set foot off the *Iowa Hill* during the five days we were there. Though to be honest, more than half of that time was spent flying from one hab to the next. We didn't stay docked at any of them any longer than it took to transfer cargo.

Next was another seven-day trip, which took us into the asteroid belt.

We spent the next six weeks going from place to place in the belt before the captain docked us at a commercial "rest and relaxation" hab named the Coyote Ranch. Its primary clientele were belt miners and other workers from the processing plants in this section of the asteroid belt. The only time one of the larger cargo haulers like the *Iowa Hill* put in was when they were delivering goods. Half of the cargo we'd picked up in the last month was actually destined for the Coyote Ranch, most of it being foodstuffs, but some of it was also replacement parts or things they sold.

We wouldn't be taking anything with us when we left, but instead of turning us around after the twelve hours it took us to unload and rebalance, the captain gave us all three days of shore leave.

Personally I couldn't wait.

"Okay, I got your test scheduled, you can show up anytime in the next few hours," Dot said to me as we secured the engineering systems.

"Test?" I said, looking at her a little confused.

"Yeah, you know, the Engineer Fourth exam? The one you've been studying for?"

"Wait, here? Now?"

"Of course now, you passed a thousand hours last week. With us being on duty with no time off the last two months, you've been racking up the hours."

"I thought you had to go to, I don't know, some major orbital, or a planet or something, to take the test!"

Dot laughed. "Nope. All the larger habs and orbitals have a testing office, and not just for ship's tests, but for anything you can think of. Most of the folks working out here, they may not get to a major orbital for years, maybe decades."

"But I'm not prepared!"

Dot raspberried at me. "You've been doing the practice tests for over a week now and I've seen your scores. That's more than good enough. I sent the address to your tablet. I'd suggest showing up in your shipsuit, then the whores'll all leave you alone 'cause they'll figure you're working."

I nodded and then had a thought. "I better check my bank account to make sure I can pay for this."

"Just make sure you've got the current access code to get back onboard. I don't think anybody's going to be on the ship until we leave."

I nodded. "Yeah, I'm thinking of getting a room myself. Any advice?"

"Don't gamble, and stick to the girls in the brothels, they at least won't roll you or sell your kidneys," she said with a laugh.

"Right, stick to the brothels," I said while rolling my eyes. I thought I might see if Hank and Chaz wanted to do a meal sometime over the next few days. But other than that, the idea of just walking around someplace that *wasn't* the *Iowa Hill* was uppermost in my mind.

Heading back to my cabin, I got my pistol, a spare magazine, put on my holster and slung that inside my shipsuit. Then checked in with the local branch of my bank, which did have my current balance.

I had to stop and look at it a moment, I'd never had this much money before and no bills or tuition that needed to be paid. Yeah, there were definitely jobs that paid more, but living onboard the *Iowa Hill* was effectively free. After that thought had settled in, I locked my tablet and grabbed the credits I still had left over from our last stop at Coeus Station.

I noticed the tablet then that I had from the guy I'd killed back there. I really had no idea what to do with it. I'd taken the time to completely wipe it and reset it. Tablets weren't cheap and I was keeping it as a backup for mine, if anything happened to it. I probably should've just tossed it in the trash someplace, but the idea of throwing one away just seemed a bit *too* wasteful. But now, now I was thinking maybe I should sell it, so it couldn't be traced back to me. Maybe on the black market where no one would ask any questions.

But I didn't know if this was the place for that. I'd have to ask somebody.

Leaving my cabin, I signed out of the ship and went straight to the testing place Dot had signed me up at.

I was a little surprised at how long it took me to find the room where the tests were administered. Apparently Coyote Ranch was a lot bigger once you got inside than I'd thought it was. Adding to that difficulty was their putting the testing room in the least attractive space in the entire hab, which was a smelly and noisy place right by the hab's main engineering department.

It was actually more than one room, and there were other people there taking tests, though for what I had no idea.

Checking in, I told them what I was there for, paid the fee, then they gave me a key to a locker in which everything on me was secured—including my pistol, which they didn't even bat an eye at.

That done, they sat me down at a terminal in the back, logged me in, and left me to it. The test was three hours long, or at least that's how long you had to do it in. I did it in half that, then spent another half hour going over my answers on the harder questions, just to make sure I hadn't made any stupid mistakes.

When I was done, I pressed the FINISHED button and someone came and got me from my test station. Then while I emptied the locker and put my stuff away, the computer graded the results. Ten minutes later I was told I'd passed, I paid another small filing fee, and they sent the results to my company, the ship, and then the licensing bureau of my choice. Which of course led to a dilemma: which licensing bureau did I want to use? Right now I was registered with Earth, but did I really want to continue with that?

Especially as it could lead to people finding out that I wasn't quite dead.

I decided, after thinking about it for all of one minute, to go with Mars. Then I got a wild hair and paid an extra twenty to have it sent to Ceres as well. That done, it was time to celebrate, which first meant going back to the ship, putting on something other than my shipsuit, and doing...

Well, doing something. A beer or two would be in order and definitely something nice to eat, followed by a day or two of not seeing anybody that I worked with.

Two hours later and I was finishing up a nice chicken dinner and a glass of wine that the waiter had recommended. That done, I settled up the bill, left a nice tip, and just went for a walk. I hadn't gotten a room yet, there really wasn't any rush. The place was really one big hotel with rooms everywhere. Some were fancier than others; some even had windows that looked out into space.

Not that I could afford one of those.

There were two other things that there were apparently a lot of, all over the hab. The first was casinos, they were literally everywhere, and in all sorts of shapes and sizes. They even had ones that advertised just how cheap they were. Obviously catering to spacers on a budget, or ones who didn't want to get in trouble.

The second was brothels, though none of those looked to be exactly "cheap." As I walked by one of them and noticed the young and attractive women inside looking back at me with a smile, I started thinking that maybe Dot was right. I hadn't had any female companionship since... since, well, since far too long.

"So, what's a young man like you looking for tonight?" an older woman, who obviously worked here asked, coming up to me.

"A nice young woman to spend some time in bed with," I replied, smiling back at her.

"Well, you've come to the right place. Rooms are included,

but anything beyond that is between you and the young lady you're entertaining."

"Any discounts if I want to spend more than just an hour?"

"That would be between you and her."

"Ah," I said with a nod and looked at the dozen girls who were all looking back at me now. They were all incredibly attractive, and all dressed to show it all off.

"Never been to a brothel before, have you?" she asked in a soft voice.

"Nope. But I work on a cargo ship now, so..." I shrugged and hoped I didn't get too badly skinned. I walked over to a brunette who I found very attractive, mainly because of the slight Asian cast to her features.

"How much for the night?" I asked.

"Four hundred an hour," she replied, looking me up and down.

"Two hundred an hour for eight hours," I told her, which was several weeks' worth of wages for me.

"Why would I agree to that?" she asked with a predatory smile.

"Because I can see that there's not a lot of business going on tonight? I'm no genius, but I'm sure one of you will take it. Besides, maybe I want to make you work harder for the tip," I said and smiled right back at her.

"Oh, I think I'm going to be getting a lot more than the tip tonight!"

The other girls all giggled then, but she took my arm in hers and led me off. "So you're a sailor on a cargo ship?"

"Yup, got in earlier today."

"First time?"

"Working on a ship? Yup. But not..." I said and smiled down at her.

She laughed again, and I had to admit it sounded good. I'm sure she was just as experienced at her job as I was at mine.

Several hours later I realized she was a *lot* more experienced at her job than I was at mine. Come the morning when she turned me loose I gave her a very large tip and thanked her for a truly wonderful time.

Then I staggered back to the ship, got the entry code right on the third try. Went inside and collapsed into my bunk and slept for the next twelve hours.

✧　　✧　　✧

When we pulled out of the Coyote Ranch hab a couple of days later, I was still feeling pleasantly mellow. I showed the captain my certificate verifying my passing the test and he made it official and sent a message to the company, informing them of my promotion as well.

"Congratulations! Nice to see you're interested in improving yourself, Dave!" he said, shaking my hand.

"Thanks Captain."

"So, are you going to take the third-class exam as well?"

I nodded. "As soon as I can. I also want to get that gravity panel refurbishment certification like Chief Briggs does."

"Well, at the rate we're bouncing around the ring here, I suspect you'll have the hours soon enough. I have to warn you, we don't have a bunk onboard for a second engineer."

I gave him a wry grin as I shook my head. "I think it'll be a long time before I go for Second."

"That's good, because I'm hoping we can hold onto you for a good long while. The crew all likes you; you obviously don't spook easy, and know how to handle yourself in difficult situations."

"Heard about that?" I asked looking a little embarrassed.

"Oh, let's just say that I put the vectors together and came up with the correct course. You didn't involve the ship, and you were onboard when we left. Can't ask for more than that—well, other than to suggest that you might want to be a little more careful about where you go when you're by yourself."

"Oh, I think that's been made more than clear to me," I replied with a rueful grin.

"Great! Well, keep up the good work and I'll be sure to let everyone know at dinner tonight that you've been promoted."

"Thanks again, Captain!" I said and, shaking hands again, I left his dayroom and went back down to Engineering to get back to work.

Sure enough, the captain did announce my promotion to fourth engineer, but it turned out that I wasn't the only one taking a test back at the Coyote Ranch. Chaz had finally been promoted to able spacer, which was a pretty major test as I understood it, and I found out later it had taken him two days, as there was a practical as well as a written test.

We all shook hands and Chaz and I both got congratulated.

"Two days, that must have been one hell of a test," I said to Chaz when we all sat back down.

"If I'd stayed and finished my schooling, it would have only been a day," Chaz replied.

"But you would have been stuck with ore haulers," Hank put in. "Now, you got the full ticket."

"Full ticket?" I asked.

Chaz grinned at me. "Deck hands have a completely different way of dealing with things than Engineering does. It's easy to specialize and only be rated as an able spacer on, say, an ore hauler or a cargo ship, but not both. You go to something else and you'll find yourself busted right back down to 'ordinary spacer.'"

"But this is a cargo ship, not a hauler," I pointed out.

"Yes, but I did most of my schooling for ore haulers and have a fair bit of experience on them. Then I have all the stuff I've learned here, and a fair deal that Hank's been teaching me about military ships. So I got to take the big test that covers *all* of them. Though a lot of the ore hauler stuff got waived due to prior experience, or it might have run three days."

"Huh, I had no idea. What about the mates?" I asked, nodding toward Pam.

"They're like you: typically they go to college and learn navigation, leadership, shipping rules and regs, and ship handling."

"There's also a lot of overlapping and specialties in the spacer category with both the ships officers and the engineering staff," Hank said.

"How's that?" I was curious as this wasn't anything I recalled them mentioning in college.

"Well, I'm certified for Environmental. I'm also certified as a ship handler, though the *Iowa* is just a bit outside of my weight class."

"Huh, I had no idea. What's the reason for it?"

"Because some ships have a lot of able spacers on board, but not that many mates or engineers. So training up the spacers to handle a number of specialty jobs frees the others up. Legally I could fly this ship, if the captain or one of the mates were giving me commands, whereas legally you couldn't do it, because you don't have the experience or the training."

"It's mostly the navies," Pam said, surprising me by speaking up. "Most navy ships don't have that many officers, but they've got lots of enlisted. So the enlisted have to learn the jobs and get the ratings. Our bosun there has what, ten different specialty certs on top of your able spacer rating, isn't it, Hank?"

Hank nodded. "It's why I can stand watches in Engineering and was able to help Dot with her engineering tasks when we were shorthanded."

"Here in the belt, a lot of the smaller ships have no officers onboard at all if they're short haulers," Pam continued. "Or they may have one captain and one engineer, who make the decisions and supervise if they just can't call for help when something breaks."

I looked at Chaz and Hank, who both nodded.

"The belt's pretty populated," Chaz said. "Most of the mining outfits are large operations, and even the small ones are rarely working in an area by themselves. So if you need a rescue here in the belt, you're a lot more likely to get one than when you're flying between planets."

I nodded; it all made sense. People flying here in the belt would also be moving at lower velocities because they were making shorter trips, so they'd be easier to catch up with, unlike a ship hauling in open space, where the distances meant you got up to some high velocities by the time you flipped and started your deceleration. High enough that, in some cases, no one would bother trying to get to you, assuming anyone even could.

"So, where are we off to next?" I asked. The *Iowa Hill* was running light now—we had only about a third of our cargo hold filled.

"Now we do the parts run," Pam grumbled.

"Oh, it's not that bad," Chaz said with a grin.

"What's 'the parts run'?" I asked.

"There's a lot of small outfits out here that make specialty equipment for habs. Shipping it to Ceres so it can be used in their hab construction can be an expensive proposition for some of the smaller outfits. So Ceres hires a freighter to come through here every four months or so and pick up all those shipments."

"And we'll drop off most of the cargo we've currently got along with way," the captain said from the other table. I guess he'd been following our conversation. "That's why most of what's left are half-size TEUs." TEUs were Twenty-foot Equivalent Units. "It's all spares or specialty stuff that those places ordered from Coeus when they found out that the ship the Ceres Hab Company hired was coming out of there. It's actually one of our more regular runs. Damascus Freight has a ten-year contract with Ceres Habs and several of our ships make this run at least once a year."

"So how many stops between here and there?"

"About one a week for the next four months," Pam said.

"That many?" I looked back at the captain.

"We sail for about a week, then we dock at a hab and wait for the locals to deliver their stuff to us, then we go to the next pickup," he said, looking back at me. "Layovers can be anything from a few hours, while we load, to a couple days if we have to wait for someone to show."

"And we *always* have to wait for some people to show." Pam sighed. "It took at least five months the last time we came through."

"Yeah, that was a bad one," the captain said with a nod. "But the folks over at Killian's did have a blowout and going over there and helping them out was the right thing to do."

"Actually that *was* kinda fun," Pam said with a smile. She turned back to me then. "Remember how I told you that everything you can think of, you'll find out here in a hab somewhere?"

I nodded.

Pam grinned at me. "Well, get ready for an education. Belters are *weird*!"

"Oh? And like Adonises are not?" Chaz retorted with a grin of his own.

"Compared to some of these people, we're positively high culture," Pam retorted, still grinning.

"Be aware that some of these places won't allow you to bring a firearm aboard, if we dock at any of them long enough to grant leave," the captain warned me.

"They won't?"

"Nope. Some of them are worried about leaks and the destruction of expensive equipment, because they're fairly small, poor, and remote. While others just have issues with firearms."

"So wear a knife," Dot said.

"Only if you know how to use it," the captain said and then got up. "Think I'll go check on Ian and let him get his dinner."

"You do know how to use a knife, right?" Hank asked after the captain had left.

"Do you really think I should bring a weapon?" I asked, turning toward Dot.

"I have a strong dislike of going unarmed. On most stations, people figure you've got a pistol, even if you're not showing it. So they're wary. But on these places they know you don't. So you strap on a knife, a nice big one, or at least one that it looks like you know how to use, and it keeps the disagreeable types at arm's length.

"Now, if we have to go aboard one of those places for engineering supplies, I would feel a whole lot better if you had some sort of weapon, and better still if you actually knew how to use it," she said, looking me in the eye.

"That makes sense, I guess. Looks like I'm gonna be using the machine shop tomorrow," I said. "By the way, do we have any Newtonian grip tape?"

"I think we have a roll. What would you want that for? That stuff's expensive."

"I only need a three-inch strip."

"So does that mean you know how to fight?" Pam asked.

"Remember how I said I had a little brother to stick up for?"

"Oh, right."

"You know this is going to feel even weirder than carrying a gun."

"Really? Why?"

"Well, because you're not allowed to carry weapons on Earth and here I'm going to be wearing one out in the open."

"You didn't have any problems with the pistol," Dot pointed out.

"But that was kept hidden. Parading around with a weapon out in the open?" I chuckled. "It just seems...wrong."

"Please don't tell me you've got problems with weapons!" Pam said.

"I'm just not a fan of showing off the goods," I said, turning to face her. "Surely *you* can understand *that*!"

She blushed as everyone laughed and I had to admit that I enjoyed seeing her blush.

The next morning I hit the machine shop. I had an eleven-inch-long, one-inch-by-one-inch-square piece of steel alloy. Setting it in the CNC machine, I programmed it to cut it down to the shape I wanted on the lathe, then once that was done it would execute another series of commands to drill some very fine channels.

After that was set, I grabbed a set of testing gear and went out to test panels. I'd earned enough of Dot's trust by now that I tested the top bank each day, while she tested the bottom bank. We even did the subsystems inspections separately. At this point the only task we always did together was the panel replacements and rebuilds. The first because it really did take two people. The second because I wasn't certified for it and she was still teaching me how to do it.

When we sat down for dinner that evening I pulled out my new toy and set it down.

"What's that?" Chaz said looking it over.

"It's an ice pick," Hank said looking at it. "Can I?" he asked.

"Sure," I said with a nod and he picked it up.

"Why'd you make an ice pick?" Chaz asked.

"I've heard about these," Hank said, looking it over.

"May I?" the captain asked, and Hank passed it over.

"This is rather nice," the captain said, looking at it. "I saw my fair share growing up on Earth."

"You did?" Chaz asked.

"It's a common weapon. Easier to hide than a knife and a lot easier to hurt someone with, or even kill them."

The captain passed it back to Hank, who passed it to Chaz.

"What's with the tape on the handle?" Chaz asked.

"Well, at one inch in diameter and four inches long, you can't really get a good grip on it, but the Newtonian grip tape grabs harder the faster it tries to move. So it lets you bring the entire force of your arm into a thrust or a swing."

"How long is the pick?"

"Three inches."

"Isn't that a bit short?" Pam asked, looking at it as Chaz passed it to her.

"The human body isn't all that thick and you don't want it going out the other side."

"Still, how much damage could it do?"

"Look at the tip."

She examined it a moment. I'd already shown all of this to Dot, who had been impressed.

"There's a hole going through the shaft, just behind the tip."

"That's right. And the handle is hollow and has a heavy lead slug set in it on a spring. That cavity is linked to those holes in the tip by a thin channel. So when the thrust or the swing abruptly stops because the wide base of the handle hits the body, the slug is pushed forward and due to the Venturi effect, a high-pressure blast of air cuts a cavity in whatever organ you just stabbed."

She set it down carefully. "That sounds nasty."

I nodded. "Because it is. You stab somebody in the arm or leg with that, and you've taken them out of the fight for at least a few minutes. Long enough to run away."

I didn't mention that a kidney stab or a heart stab would almost instantly kill you; same for anywhere in the head.

"Where I grew up, they'd put those little carbon dioxide canisters in the hilt and trigger it when they stabbed you," the captain said. "Those were quite vicious."

"I've heard of those. This is meant to hurt or disable more than kill, or I would have made the handle wider and the pick a little longer."

"You know, I don't think your wearing that will scare anybody off," Hank said.

I nodded. "Dot already made that point," I said, nodding toward her. "So I'm gonna make a big sheath knife and strap it on my leg. But if I have to fight"—I picked up the ice pick and spun it in my hand—"this is what I'll be using."

EIGHT

Burnside

THE ENGINEERING ALARM WENT OFF AND I WAS OUT OF BED AND into my shipsuit before I fully woke up. I hit the alarm cancel as I stepped into my deck shoes; the problem was in the cooling recirculation pump on the heat exchanger for the portside Siz-gee.

Either Dot or the computer had scrammed the Siz-gee already. I stepped out into the hallway, already feeling that gravity was about half of normal, and headed to Engineering. Dot was just sitting down at the main control panel as I came in, so I went over to the portside unit and it didn't take long to spot the problem: the pump was leaking coolant. Getting out my tablet, I took a couple of close-ups and sent them over to the engineering station. Then I got out an old-fashioned magnifying lens and started to look over the body of the pump, while trying to trace the leak to its source.

"Find anything?" Dot called.

"I think we have a micro-fissure. But with the pressure coming down as everything cools off, I can't be sure."

"We'll have to replace it. I'll go get the spare out of supply. Get everything together that we need."

"How long until this cools off?"

"Too long. We'll lower the coolant level, close all the valves, bleed off the pressure, and put a bucket under it to catch what we can."

I nodded and went over to the tool locker to get out what we were going to need.

"Need any help?" Hank called out, sticking his head in through the hatch.

"Yeah, a couple of large buckets that won't melt when we drain the coolant," I yelled back.

"Oh! And you might want to give Dot a hand carrying the replacement part back from stores!"

"On it!"

The captain showed up about the same time as Dot came back. Chaz was helping her carry the pump. It might weight half as much now, but mass was mass and that wasn't something that was going to be easy to lug around, regardless.

"How long for repairs?" the captain asked.

"Three hours to replace, then about two more to test it," Dot said. "If all is good I think we can have power back a few hours after that."

"Okay, do what you gotta do. I'll be on the bridge."

"Will do!" She turned to me next. "Go get all the welding gear, bring it back here and put it on."

I looked at her confused.

"This thing is going to let go with a lot of steam and boiling water when you crack those bolts. The welding gear is the best protection we've got."

"Oh!" I said and bolted off to get the gear from the machine shop in the rear. Running in half grav was not as easy as it looked. At least I didn't slam into anything too hard.

Once I was back and dressed, I took one of the power wrenches, and after everyone had gotten way back, I started loosening the nuts off the studs. Sure enough, as soon as I got to the second one, a jet of low-pressure steam started blowing out and not long after that there was coolant spraying out everywhere. If I hadn't been wearing the gear, I would definitely have gotten some serious burns.

By the time I'd gotten to the fourth bolt I had to stand back and take off the apron and the gloves, as they had all soaked through in spots and I was starting to get burned. Chaz had brought a second set down while I was shucking the first one, and gearing back up I got all the nuts loosened and half of them off.

After that, we slung the hoist, got a chain on the valve, and started disconnecting the pipe on the down-flow side from its mount so we'd have enough room to extract the pump. Once we had it out, we set to work cleaning the flanges where the pipes met, so when we put them back together, they wouldn't leak. If this part got screwed up, we'd have to strip it down and do it over again.

So we were both very careful, and we inspected each other's work.

That done, we applied a gasket-forming sealant to all the fittings and put it all back together.

"Not bad, only two and a half hours," I said to Dot as we started refilling the heat exchanger.

"Now let's hope there aren't any flaws in the new one." She sighed and checked the fluid levels. We'd have to purge all the air pockets and bubbles when we started testing it.

"Do you know something I don't know?" I asked.

"I know *lots* of things you don't know!" Dot chuckled. "But both of these pumps came from the same place, back when the last refuel was done. They've got the same lot numbers on them as well. As that one's flawed"—she pointed to the one now sitting on the deck in a puddle—"this one's probably flawed as well."

"And we don't have another one, do we?"

"Nope."

"Well, at least it lasted ten years, so hopefully the replacement will as well."

"Still, I'm gonna tell the captain that we need to replace that spare immediately. After that, we'll see about doing a magniflux on it to locate the crack and weld it up. Probably won't be to spec, but it'd allow us to run at reduced power."

I had a very bad thought then.

"Let me guess, the recirculation pump on the other heat exchanger is also from the same batch?"

Dot nodded. "I checked the casting on it to be sure when you were getting that one out," she said, making a motion toward the one on the floor.

"How about I haul that up to the shop and perform the magniflux and start prepping for welding? I'm sure Chaz can help you with purging the lines."

Dot nodded, and then smiled. "Good idea. Though I'll need you in here when we put this back online."

✧　　✧　　✧

The captain came down to Engineering to talk to us while we were bringing the reactor back up to power.

"So, how's it looking?"

"Not bad, but we do have a problem," Dot said, and then told him about the other two pumps being from the same production batch. She then called up the pictures I'd taken of the leak, along with those of the magniflux test.

"Now, Dave and I are going to weld that one up. I don't think it'll be quite to spec, but it'll be better than nothing at all if the starboard side fails before we can get a new spare."

"I'll order one for Ceres, then I'll start beating the bushes for the stations between here and Ceres to see if anybody else has one. How common are those pumps?"

"Fairly common. The reason we've got new ones is because they couldn't source the old ones anymore and they upgraded them when they upgraded the turbines."

"Okay. Once we've got the portside back online, I want you to reduce the starboard reactor fifteen percent. When we get into Ceres, I'll get somebody in here to x-ray it and tell us if it's flawed or not."

"Sure thing, Cap."

Dot turned to me after the captain had left Engineering. "I think I'm going to go weld up that casing now. If you see anything strange, don't wait to holler."

"That worried?"

"I just don't want to tempt fate, it never seems to be able to refuse the opportunity!"

"Okay, got it, 'Chief'!"

Dot rolled her eyes and left me to monitor the startup of the reactor. At this point, I really wasn't too surprised to be left unsupervised for something as important as this; after all, I'd been on board over four months now and was no longer a lowly "fifth" engineer.

Plus there was a repeater back in the shop. I was sure Dot would be keeping an eye on things.

Twenty-four hours later, the starboard pump let go, only it cracked a lot more spectacularly, making a pretty big mess. Changing out that pump actually went a little faster because we'd just done the other one. But the cleanup took a lot more time.

Also we couldn't run the reactor at more than a seventy percent load. Dot had told the captain running it up to eighty percent should be fine, but the captain decided to play it safe and added a bit more of a safety margin.

Dot went to see the captain while I was cleaning up the mess from hot coolant spraying all over the place. It was definitely going to take a few days to get the place back to rights. When she finally came back she picked up a mop and joined me.

"The captain located a new part; we'll be picking it up at Burnside Hab."

"That's a relief. When will we be getting there?"

"Ten days. We're decelerating now to another one of our cargo pickups. Burnside is the one after that, so we won't be detouring at all. That should keep the accountants happy."

"Are we going to replace the portside pump when we get to Ceres?"

"Yes. Two of them failed, so it's not even worth inspecting the third one. We may even replace the one we're picking up at Burnside if it looks like it's been used or rebuilt."

"Guess we won't be seeing much of Ceres then, will we?" I said with a sigh.

"Well, it would cost less if we did the replacements rather than having the yard dogs do it. As I don't think that we're the only ship running these pumps, the accountants are probably looking at a lot of replacements and are very much going to want to keep the costs down as much as possible."

"So what's Burnside like? Any idea?"

Dot shook her head. "Never gone ashore there, so I have no idea. It's a large one, but it's mostly corporation miners, so probably not a lot of fun. Everyone there'll be working for the corporation and they'll all be on a contract. So don't expect to see a lot of happy faces."

"Why's that?" I asked cautiously. "Is there something wrong with working on a contract?"

"Ever heard of 'the Company Store'?"

I shook my head.

"You might want to look up a little Earth history from before we went into space. Let's just say that some things haven't changed all that much."

I nodded and when the end of the shift came I went back to

my cabin after dinner and did just that. The history, of course, was a pretty bleak one. When I looked into the more recent practices, it wasn't as horrendous—they had to provide you with a trip back to wherever it was you'd came from, but a lot of people came back with very little money.

Not all the outfits were bad, some were actually fair about their treatment. But those were in the minority and Burnside wasn't one of them. At least they weren't among the worst.

We spent the next ten days—well, Dot and I, at least—inspecting those pumps for any signs of leaks or cracking. In order to keep up with his current schedule the captain was forced to keep the gravity at a lower rate and pump more into the drive aspect of the panels. As this wasn't what the panels were optimized for, it increased our failure rate, and we'd had four failures by the time we got to Burnside.

So we were both fairly tired when we went through the docking tube to Burnside Hab. The rock it was built on was fairly large, the site of a very profitable mine. There were also several other nearby rocks that were being mined by the same concern.

Guns weren't allowed, so we had our knives strapped on rather prominently. Chaz had been sent along to help carry the pump back, considering how much it weighed.

When we stepped out of the airlock into the hab I had my first real culture shock: the place was filthy. It was also poorly lighted, and the air stank.

"People *live* like this?" I asked, looking around. We were docked in the sole cargo area, because we were taking on several containers of processed materials. Most of what we were getting, however, was coming from other ships that were meeting us here and they were docking on the far side of us to transfer their cargo through the starboard cargo hatches. So it wasn't like we were off in a remote part of the place.

"Yeah, some people can be real slobs." Chaz sighed.

"This isn't their home, they just work here, so unless they're paid to keep it clean, they don't," Dot said with a shrug. "Don't wander off, either of you. Wherever I go, you go, got that?"

"What about if you have to go to the bathroom?" Chaz teased.

"Like I'd want to do that in a place like this," Dot said, making a face as she pulled out her tablet and examined it. "Okay, this way," she said, pointing to the right, and we followed her off.

When we got to the end of the cargo corridor, we passed through a large airlock into the main hallway for the installation. There were a surprising amount of people who really didn't look like they were working. As they were all men, I could understand why Dot didn't want to be alone, ever, while we were here. I could hear some muttered comments and a few muted conversations that were obviously about the new woman and how nice and clean she was.

Most of them went fairly south after that, and I could see that Dot was studiously ignoring them. The corridor we were walking down was lined with shops that were mainly for repairs, but a few of them appeared to sell clothing or other supplies. Most of the men we saw here were actually working. The men lounging around and not doing anything appeared to be the most unkempt and scraggly looking.

"Don't they work?" I asked in a low voice.

"Maybe. Maybe not," Chaz replied. "Some folks get 'stranded' here. They're involved in some sort of illicit operation or other, and keep from being kicked off by bribing the right company manager. Others are just lazy assholes who do whatever they can to shirk their jobs, or they're off shift and just looking for whatever trouble they can get into."

"You got these types at Ceres?"

Chaz snorted. "Hell, no. You don't pull your own weight, we toss your ass out the front door."

"You live in a hab. How the hell can you toss them out the front door?"

"Hence why anybody with a lick of sense or half a brain doesn't do shit like this," Chaz said looking around.

"You kill them?" I said, amazed.

"No, we don't kill them."

"But you just said…"

"The vacuum of space kills them," he said with a smirk.

"Stations and habs don't have much in the way of resources to waste on layabouts," Dot said. "And the really nice ones don't have much truck with people whose only goal seems to be pulling everyone else down with them."

"Wait, you can't be telling me there's no crime. I've already run into two people who were being paid to off me."

"There's always crime, Dave. But even the criminals pull their

own weight and aren't trying to make things worse for everybody else. But in a place like this, as long as nothing cuts into
the profits, the bosses don't care. They don't live here, after all."

"Hell, I bet they don't even visit," Chaz said. "I can tell you,
when they finally do pull out, somebody will pop this place with
a missile and make sure it's completely vented to space, to deal
with any 'vermin issues' that got left behind."

I thought about that while we walked, making sure to keep
my eyes open. This was almost as bad as when we used to raid
Doler territory back when I was in the gang.

"Okay, we're here," Dot said, turning down a narrow corridor
and pressing the buzzer on the door at the end of it. The door
had a sign saying HYDROMATIC PARTS SIX and there were several
cameras set up to see us.

"What's your business?" a voice asked from a hidden speaker.

"We're here from the *Iowa Hill* to pick up a pump we ordered."

"You can come in, the two guys wait outside."

"Oh, fuck no!" Dot swore loudly. "I'm not going anywhere
without my assistants, and I'm sure as hell not gonna carry that
thing by myself. Now open up or you don't get paid!"

I heard some grumbling, but then the door buzzed and we
all stepped through, Chaz leading and me bringing up the rear.
We came into a small waiting area with a counter across the far
wall and a man standing behind it.

"Where is it?" Dot asked.

"Let me see your money first."

Dot growled. "Do you want me to tell my boys to kill you?
'Cause they *will* kill you. Show me the part first, and then, *if* it's
what we ordered, *then* you'll see some money. If not, my captain
and your boss are going to have a conversation about why we
left your dead corpse nailed to that wall over there."

I kept my face passive, but internally I was shocked! Dot was
always cheerful and always smiled. But she was ripping into this
guy with an attitude like some of the nastier heavies we used
to deal with every once in a while. I didn't know if it was just
posturing or what, but I had my hand on the handle of my pick,
figuring out the quickest way to get over that counter and ice
the guy behind it.

"Look I make the—" he started saying, but then his eyes met
mine and suddenly he shut up. Because I was looking *through*

him. I'd learned a long time ago that you never make eye contact with a target, it distracts you. I guess he'd seen that look before.

"Let me go get it."

"We'll go with you," I said.

"It's okay, wait right—"

I was over the counter without even thinking about it, and Chaz was right behind me.

"We'll go with you," I said.

"What, don't you trust me?" he said, with his hands held up and away from his body.

"Not anymore," Dot said, sliding over the counter as well. "Me and my boys don't like it when somebody tries to shake us down. You deal fair, no chop, and we'll pay you and take what's ours and go. Now, you know what we're here for, let's go."

I followed the guy, almost on his heels, while Dot and Chaz hung back. It wasn't all that far back in the supply racks; obviously it'd been brought up from some other supply room for us. Chaz stood by the guy, looking menacing, which considering that Chaz was pretty well built wasn't all that hard, while Dot and I quickly went over the pump. I checked the connections and the sensors on it, then the threads on the fittings. Dot was checking the flanges for trueness across their surface, then she ran a small camera up inside to do a quick inspection of the pump vanes. After that she took a small hammer and tapped all over it. That last one would tell you if there were any major cracks or flaws in the case from the sound.

"It's good. Got a dolly we can borrow?" she asked, looking up at the guy.

He pointed over to a corner. "What about the money?"

Dot unzipped a pocket and pulled out a rather thick wad of credits and started to count them off while Chaz went and got the dolly. There turned out to be quite a lot there, two thousand.

"What about for the dolly?" he asked.

"We'll leave it at the lock. You can pick it up later."

He nodded slowly. Chaz moved the dolly over and then the two of us picked up the pump and set it on the dolly, securing it with a strap.

"Now, be a nice man and show us to the exit," Dot said with a smile that wasn't as kind or friendly as they ones I was used to.

"Yeah, I like that idea. Follow me," he said.

When we got to the door, Chaz went out first, followed by Dot. I stopped in the doorway and looked back at the guy.

"If we run into any surprises, I know what you look like and I know where you are," I said to him, then held up my tablet and took his picture. "Have a nice day."

Letting the door close I took a couple of quick strides to catch up with Dot and Chaz.

"What'd you do that for?" Chaz asked.

"General principles," I said and smiled. "You saw how afraid of me he was."

"And fear is a great motivator," Dot agreed. "Now, let's see if we can get back to the ship without any problems."

The trip back down the main corridor was about the same as the trip in, though I thought the comments were a bit ruder and perhaps a bit louder. The expression on Dot's face was pretty stoic, though her lips seemed to be pressed together rather tightly.

"Turn left here," Dot said suddenly as we drew close to the airlock to the cargo corridor. Chaz didn't question, and turned down the large side corridor just before the doors. I saw several surprised expressions on a couple of the guys standing near the doorway.

"I hope you know where you're going," I whispered to Dot as I kept an eye on the two guys, one of whom was starting to follow us.

"I'm the only woman without a price tag on this rock. Yeah, I know where I'm going," she whispered back.

"Right, Chaz," she said in a voice loud enough for him to hear.

As soon as we went around the corner, I flattened myself against the wall.

"I'll catch up," I said and Dot just nodded as they continued on ahead.

I got my pick out and waited. The guy following us dashed around the corner and didn't even realize I was there. I got him in the kidney with my ice pick as my hand hit him in his Adam's apple, cutting off his voice. Looking around, I dragged him into a dark spot just inside one of the shops that looked deserted and dumped him on the floor.

A quick once-over and I found the comm he was using. I grabbed it and fled out the door. As I left, a couple of locals ran in and started stripping the body of whatever I'd left behind.

Ignoring them, I rushed to catch up with the others.

I passed the comm to Dot just as she directed Chaz to turn right again.

"Thanks. Any problems?"

"'Course not." I smiled.

She looked around; the corridor we were in was a short one and empty. It ended in an airlock.

"Okay, this is a side passage to the cargo dock. You're gonna have to carry the pump from here on out, though. I don't think that dolly is gonna fit."

"You think there was an ambush on the other side of the main lock?" Chaz asked.

"Yup. And they're still gonna be in the cargo hall waiting for us. Just now they're not between us and the ship."

"Let me message Hank," Chaz said.

Dot nodded and cut the strap holding the pump down with her knife. "Get that side, Dave," she said with a nod and then the two of us picked it up, while Chaz brought up the rear.

We all crammed in the lock; it was a tight fit with the pump.

"Chaz, you and I will take the pump, Dave will be rear guard."

"What? I know how to fight with a knife! Dave's only got that little ice pick."

"Don't argue with me, Chaz, okay?" Dot said in a voice that was so happy and sweet you just knew that if you did argue, you'd count it as one of life's great mistakes.

"Yes, ma'am!" Chaz said and he took hold of the pump and I let go, then cycled the lock open and stepped out first. I walked out slowly into the hallway and glanced back toward where our ship was. It was clear. Then I turned to look back at the lock we were supposed to have gone through, a good fifty yards away, as Chaz and Dot passed behind me, carrying the pump between them and going as fast as they could without dropping it or tripping over their own feet.

There were four of them, and it took them almost a minute to realize that we were behind them. I just stood there, arms out, with my pick in my right hand, and acted like I didn't have a care in the world.

"The bitch is getting away!" one of them suddenly yelled and took off running toward me. The other three followed behind him, but only one was at all close to him. I gave a small shake of my head. Here I was, a billion kilometers from home, and I might as well been back running with the Howlers.

The leader had his knife out and was pointing it at me as he charged. I dodged left at the last moment and his own momentum drove my pick right into his chest and between the ribs. This was the real reason I used the Newtonian grip tape. He died instantly and his legs and lower body pivoted around my arm as the life went out of him. The sheer force and shock of it would have ripped the pick out of my grasp, but now it was as good as welded to my hand.

I let the force of the collision spin me around like a top, ripping my pick out of his chest. I spun around so fast the second guy didn't even know I'd driven my pick into his skull.

He went right down on top of his buddy, his body twitching because his brain just had the equivalent of a small firecracker go off inside it.

Numbers three and four came to a stop so fast their soft-soled shoes made a screeching noise on the floor.

"Not the party you were expecting, is it?" I said with a big-ass smile, and lunged at the closer of the two.

He dropped his knife and started backing up as the other one just flat-out ran and left his buddy.

"Tell you what, if you can get to the airlock before I can, you get to live." Damned if he didn't turn and hightail it out of there.

"You okay?" Hank yelled, coming up behind me.

"Yeah, I'm okay," I said and bent over to wipe my pick off on the jumpsuit of the guy I'd gotten in the head.

Hank eyed the bodies. "Get the one on top; I'll get the one on the bottom."

"You might want to flip him over, I got him in the chest," I told him as I grabbed the leg of the other guy and started to drag him down the corridor toward the ship.

"Dot told me you left one back in the station?"

I nodded. "But the rats were already stripping him, so I don't think they'll pin it on us."

"Rats?"

"The other lowlifes."

"Ah." Hank was quiet a moment, then he laughed as he dragged the other guy's body behind me. "'Reign of terror,' indeed."

I shrugged. "I was a very angry kid and I fell in with a bad crowd."

"You mean they fell in with you," he said with a chuckle. "Thanks, by the way."

"For what?"

"Protecting Chaz and, yes, Dot too. Chaz is a good kid, but no way could he have taken these guys on. He hasn't got a mean bone in his body."

"Like my dad said, you gotta take care of family, and you're all the family I got these days."

"Think I'd like to meet him someday."

I just shook my head at that. Dot met us at the hatch with two plastic bags and we wrapped the guys up and then dumped them in the garbage chute.

When all was said and done, we locked the hatch and disconnected the docking tube, then immediately went to work on replacing the bad pump.

"How'd you know?" I asked Dot as I started undoing the bolts on the pump.

"You picked a weapon whose main purpose is killing, and you custom-made it to fit your hand." She shrugged. "You've seen my pistol, now you know why I have such an expensive custom job, when I could make something almost as good."

I nodded and then I looked at her. "Oh, there's one thing you're wrong about."

"And that is?"

"You have one friend."

She grinned, and then she smiled and laughed. "Hi, friend!"

Ceres

I WAS REALLY LOOKING FORWARD TO DOCKING AT CERES AGAIN.
When we'd been here last, four months ago, I don't think I'd spent
more than twelve hours off the ship, as Dot and I had to replace
both recirculation pumps, and then test everything involved until
she was satisfied. Then the captain had a local company come
in and test everything again, and both of us watched everything
they did, just to be safe—because it was our asses on the line if
they broke again.

In the last four months we'd been to Saturn's L4, then the
L5 again. After that we then swung through the asteroids once
more to again make deliveries as well as pick up shipments for
the Ceres Habitat Company.

At least we'd taken another three-day leave at the Coyote
Ranch, and while my bank account may have been lighter for
it, I know I enjoyed it.

The biggest reason I was looking forward to leave this time
around was that we'd be here almost a week—we were getting
a lot of special equipment loaded aboard for a new habitat that
was being built out past Uranus, none of which would fit in a
TEU container. Getting that loaded had to be done by hand, by
specialists, so it was going to take a while. After almost a year

of living onboard the ship, the idea of *not* coming back to it for a few days was truly something special.

The second biggest reason was that I now had enough time in to test for my third engineer's rating, and as soon as I got off the ship, that's what I was going to do. Then after that I was going to take the test for the gravity panel rebuilder certification.

The third-class rating would get me another raise in pay. The rebuilder certification would make both Dot's life and mine easier—we'd be able to take turns on the panel inspections and rebuilds, instead of her having to do it all the time.

And after all of *that* I was either going to get falling down drunk or blow a fortune in a bordello.

Unless, of course, Chaz caught up with me first and dragged me off to show me the sights and meet some of his family and friends. All of which sounded like fun; I really needed some time to unwind. But that last one would definitely cost a lot less money than the other two.

Ceres was kinda weird in that it was built like an onion. Not all of the surface was covered with habitats but just about every square kilometer of the surface *was* being used by somebody for something, which was nearly three million square kilometers. Several thousand of that was habs, which was a lot.

But when they'd started mining, they'd decided to do it in uniform levels for the most part, or at least it looked that way now. Each of the first three levels added over a million square kilometers in area to the colony. Chaz had told me once that by the time they were finished they'd have more usable area than the surface of all of Earth's landmasses combined. I hadn't bothered to do the math, but I wouldn't be surprised to find out he was right.

All I knew was each of the levels were huge, the ceilings a good ten meters high in most places and even higher in the town centers. The buildings weren't built into the walls; they all stood separately along the wide avenues. It really felt like you were on a planet and all that open space was a nice change after spending almost a year on the ship, where the only large spaces were in the cargo bay.

Given the size of the place they had to have a mass transit system, and it, like all things on Ceres apparently, was fairly efficient. So getting to the test wasn't terribly hard. The place I ended up at was similar to the last testing center I'd been to. This one was a lot busier, however, but then again, considering the population and the number of ships that came through here, I wasn't all that surprised.

The rules were the same as the last place and three hours later I had my engineer's third certificate. Five hours after that, I had the panel rebuilding certificate. The panel test really wasn't hard, but it was grueling. You rebuilt four panels, each with a different problem, which you first had to troubleshoot. Next you inspected four more, and then, after that, you had a general knowledge test.

However, it was an open book test. There were so many things you had to know, because there were so many variations in panels, that no one expected you to know all of it. But they did expect you to be able to look up the answers, find them, and apply them properly. I'd helped Dot rebuild over a hundred panels by now, so I had most of it memorized by this point. But I still looked everything up and double-checked it just to be safe. Just like Dot had taught me.

The next cert I wanted to go for had to deal with rebuilding, fitting, and tuning grav drives. Dot didn't have that one, and for the minor stuff you'd encounter on a ship that already had drives installed, it was something you were taught in the ship's engineering course work. But when it came to putting *new* drives into an existing ship, or drives into an entirely new design, well, that was something a lot more involved.

There were always ships out there getting their drives either replaced or upgraded as the old ones hit their end of life. It wasn't a popular field as that cert took a lot of work, but I figured I had a lot of spare time on my hands anyway and that one would definitely guarantee me work for the rest of my life.

I mean, running around on a ship was kinda fun, and I'm sure it'd be even more fun if I moved up to something bigger with longer layovers. But I didn't think this was going to be the kind of thing I'd want to do for the rest of my life. Sooner or later I'd find a place I liked, and I'd set up shop and settle down.

I pinged Chaz when I was done and he told me he'd come get me, rather than tell me how to get where he was. Apparently getting lost on Ceres was common for folks who didn't grow up here. They even had a legend about their very own "flying Dutchman," a visitor from one of the planets who got lost a hundred years ago, and his ghostly figure could still be seen navigating the mass transit system as he continually strived to try and find his way back to his ship.

So sitting down outside the building, I wrote out a brief email to my brother. Told him about my promotion and new certifications, about life on the ship, even the busted pump and a little about some of the other crew. Hopefully I'd get his reply before we shipped out. Mail didn't follow you when you left a port, it would just sit there and wait for your return. It was too costly to try and forward it, as most ships didn't publish their itinerary due to concerns about everything from pirates to competitors, and smaller cargo ships like ours often didn't know where they were going until they got to the next port.

Not that I suspected it was that hard to find out where most of the larger ships were going just from a look at their cargo manifest.

While I was finishing up the letter, I got that "hair standing up on the back of my neck" feeling and surreptitiously scanned the people standing around me. I was sitting with my back to the building. I didn't like people sneaking up on me without my being able to see them—an old habit from my public school days when I was still in the gang and getting in way too many fights and "other" trouble.

There was a dark-haired guy standing in the back of the group. He wasn't wearing a shipsuit, so I didn't think he was here for testing, but then I wasn't wearing mine today either as I wasn't planning on going back to the ship right away. Still, something about him didn't seem to fit in well with the rest of the folks who, like me, had just finished some test or other and were now taking a break.

I hit SEND and put my tablet away, then got out my earbud and put it in my ear. Standing up, I looked around, then waved down toward the end of the street like I was trying to get someone's attention and started walking that way. Chaz would call me when he was close, so we could meet up. But first I wanted to know if I had somebody paying a little *too* much attention to me.

Sure enough, the guy started following me as I walked down the street. There were a fair number of people coming in my direction; the area really was set up like a street and full of shops and buildings like they would be on a planet's surface. All the open space probably helped to keep people from getting too claustrophobic or becoming agoraphobic when they had to go outside.

Thankfully, this also meant that there were alleyways between the "buildings" that led into the service ways in the rock walls behind everything. So I kept glancing down them as I passed, looking for one that wasn't a dead end and had something I could hide behind.

The moment I came to the right one I bolted into it, immediately, but I ducked around behind a couple of containers that were stacked there. Squatting down, I pulled out my pistol and waited.

"Shit!" the dark-haired guy said, running into the alley, passing by where I'd hidden.

I stood up quietly and pointed my pistol at him and waited to see what he'd do.

He stopped, looked around a bit, then turned around and saw me.

"Surprise!" I said with a smile. "Don't move, or I'll kill you."

"You're bluffing," he said, but he didn't move.

"Nope, not bluffing. I already called some friends to help me dispose of the body if you don't cooperate," I said, and tapped my earbud. "Now, tell me what I want to know, and you save me having to pay for getting your dead carcass dragged out of here. Why are you following me?"

"Look, I just turned down the same..."

I put a bullet just past his ear, into the wall behind him.

"Okay, next time you lie is the last time. Put your hands on your head, interlock your fingers, and get down on your knees," I told him as I carefully circled around behind him, keeping my pistol aimed at his head.

He complied, though slowly.

"Eyes forward," I warned him as I got behind him.

He stopped trying to look at me.

Just then my phone beeped, so I tapped the bud with my free hand and answered.

"I'm in the alley between Hojo's and Smith's," I said.

"What are you doing there?" Chaz asked.

"I've got some guy who's been tailing me."

"Ah, shit. Please tell me you haven't killed him? I got my brother with me, and he's in uniform."

"As long as he stays nice and still, I promised not to shoot him in the head. I know how much our admins hate paperwork, so by all means, send in the enforcers."

The guy started as I said that, trying to get to his feet, his hands coming off his head. So I kicked him in the kidney, hard, and holstered my pistol as he collapsed in pain.

"Better hurry," I said and, putting a knee in the guy's back, I dropped my full weight down onto him and stripped him of his pistol, his wallet, and his tablet. I hit the power button on his tablet and slipped it into my pocket with mine, then I opened up his wallet and looked at his ID, memorizing the name, then stuck it back in his pocket.

He started to groan and struggle so I put my knuckle in the middle of his spine and pressed hard, making him think it was the barrel of my pistol.

"If you want to live life in a wheelchair, just keep struggling," I growled.

"Don't move!"

I looked up and saw a Ceres officer with what looked like a shocker out that was pointed at the both of us.

I smiled.

"Show your hands!"

I carefully lifted mine out to either side, showing my palms. While the guy under me slowly slid his out into the open as he laid on the ground under me.

"Cuff him," he said, making me blink.

"Umm, I don't have a set?" I said.

The officer rolled his eyes. "Chief's gonna yell at you again," he said and, reaching behind him, he pulled out a set of plasti-cuffs and tossed them to me.

Catching them, I quickly put them on the guy beneath me. This part I knew how to do, seeing as I'd had it done to me more than once back in my gang days. Getting off the guy then, I hauled him up to his feet as the officer put his shocker away. Then he came over and frisked the guy, coming up with a couple of knives, some drugs, an injector, and a garrote. He pulled out the guy's wallet after dealing with all of those and checked the ID.

"So, Richard Specter, perhaps you might want to tell us why you're following around one of our code enforcement officers?"

"He hit me! He tried to shoot me!" Richard groaned. I knew

from experience just how much kidney punches hurt, and I'd kicked him. He'd be pissing blood for a week.

I pointed to the pistol on the ground.

"Well, maybe you shouldn't have pulled a gun on him, then!"

"I did no such thing!"

"Then why is *your* gun lying on the ground over there?"

"He did that! After he hit me!"

The officer went over, picked up the pistol, looked at it, then fired a shot into the back wall.

"Will you look at that! It's even been fired! Well, I guess we're going to have a very long discussion with you down in the tombs tonight!"

I noticed the guy's face went ash white at that point.

"Car's here, Jeff!" I heard Chaz's voice call out.

Jeff took control of Richard then. "Wait here," he said to me sotto voce, then marched Richard out of the alley. Chaz came back then and smiled.

"Thanks for not killing anybody."

"So that's your brother?"

Chaz nodded. "Yeah, he joined the local enforcers years ago. So you think that guy was paid to kill you?"

I shrugged. "I just know he was taking an unhealthy interest in me."

"Well, he followed you into an alley, so I doubt he was thinking about being your friend," Chaz said with a shrug.

Jeff came back into the alley then, smiling at me. "So, you must be Dave."

I nodded and stuck out my hand. "Yup. Thanks for the save; I really did *not* want to kill him."

Jeff shook hands with me. "So what makes you think he wanted to kill you?"

"Because my bio-mom's husband seems to have found me to be inconvenient and has tried to have me murdered, like, three times now?" I said with a shrug. "I was hoping leaving Earth he'd leave me alone and forget about me."

Jeff looked at Chaz, who just nodded. "His bio is an Earth Elite. I guess Dave here is like a blot on the family tree now or something."

"Oh, this must have fallen out of his pocket," I said and pulled out Richard's tablet. "I suspect if you hack into it, you'll see an email contracting him to kill me."

Jeff shook his head. "Sorry, I must have missed it when I searched the alley."

"Huh?"

"Unless you're planning on staying around for the trial, all we're going to be able to get him on is the unlawful discharge of a firearm. He'll be quietly told to forget he ever saw you, that he obviously confused one of our undercover officers with whoever it was he was looking for."

"And he'll believe that?"

"Well, as you won't be testifying, there are only two logical explanations. The first is that he tried to kill a cop, which will encourage him to take a long vacation away from here 'cause he'll be on our 'special' list."

"And the second?"

"The second is that you are indeed the person he thought you were, but you're under the protection of Ceres's ruling council, because the police wouldn't be covering for you if that wasn't the case."

"And being on *their* list is probably worse than being on the enforcers'," Chaz said with a grin.

"Well, anybody know a good place to get this thing hacked? 'Cause I for one would like to know if he really was paid to kill me, or if there was something else he was going to do."

"Like just rob you?" Jeff said with a laugh. "Yeah, I know a guy. Let's head back to my place first so I can get changed. Then I'll take you by there."

"Jeff works in this district," Chaz told me as we headed out onto the street. "That's why I grabbed him on the way here to get you. After we drop that off"—Chaz motioned to the tablet as I put it away—"we'll hook up with a few more of my sibs, some local friends, and get drunk."

"Sounds like a plan!" I said, smiling. "'Cause right now I could definitely stand to be drunk!"

Jeff definitely knew a guy, and we left the tablet with him.

Chaz definitely had a lot of siblings, and even more friends.

He also had a very cute sister named Kacey and at some point, after latching onto me for most of the night, she dragged me off to bed and had her way with me. Or at least that's my story and I'm sticking to it.

Waking up in her bedroom in the Doyle family house was a bit of a shocker, especially as it was Mrs. Doyle sticking her head in the room and telling us to hit the shower if we didn't want to miss breakfast. Either social mores on Ceres were a lot different from what I'd grown up with, which was probably true, or Kacey and Chaz's parents really liked me. Because they didn't seem to have any problems with it and nobody was yelling at anybody about me being naked in their daughter's bed.

"So, does your mom and stepdad really want you dead?" Kacey asked as we sat down for breakfast, still damp from a nice hot shower together.

I shrugged. "I don't know if my bio-mom does, but according to my brother her husband seems to."

"Ever meet him?" Rob, their father, asked me.

I shook my head. "Honestly, I can't even remember what my bio-mom looks like; my dad got rid of all her pictures after she left. Hell, I doubt she even remembers I exist."

"Ever think of writing her?"

"Hell no," I said with a shake of my head. "If she'd wanted to talk to me, she would have. I mean, what would I say to her? 'Hi, remember me? The son you abandoned?'" I snorted. "I'm sure that'd go over real well. Besides, I think the fact that they're trying to get rid of me kinda makes it clear where they stand on having me in the family."

"So what's your plan for dealing with it?"

I shook my head. "I dunno, make myself scarce, I guess, until they eventually just forget about me and move on? I mean, if my own mother can forget about me, I'm sure they will too."

"Do you really think that guy Jeff arrested was going to kill you?" Kacey asked, rubbing her leg up against mine. I don't know why she liked me as much as she did, but I was happy that she did. She was pretty, and she'd definitely rocked my world last night. I was hoping to spend my entire shore leave with her, or at least until they got tired of me and threw me out.

"Honestly? I hope not. But I won't know until they crack his tablet and his email account. I thought I'd fooled them when I staged my own death back on Coeus station."

"Chaz told us about that," Kacey said with a smile, "as well as a few other things."

"Other things?" I asked, trying not to blush.

"Jeff said he could find you a job with the enforcers if you ever decided to give up being an engineer. With a job like that, no one 'round here would even think of going after you."

I looked at Kacey, who was giving me the same kind of look I'd seem Mom give Dad a million times. I didn't know if I should run or propose! Hell, I hadn't even known her a full day and I suddenly got the feeling that she was already lining me up for a lifetime obligation.

I turned and looked back at Rob, their father, who nodded.

"You might want to keep that in mind. Ceres is a good place to live. Lots of space and it's always growing. Lots of work here too, for enforcers *or* engineers."

Chaz came into the room then yawning; surprisingly—or maybe *unsurprisingly?*—Hank was with him. Where I grew up, being gay wasn't that big of an issue, but I don't think a lot of parents would have appreciated their son bringing home their boyfriend when he was almost as old as they were.

Chaz's father and mother, Maureen, didn't even bat an eye. In fact, I think they approved of Hank. Then again, I'd learned that Hank was a pretty stand-up kind of guy.

"Stop trying to marry our engineer off to Kacey, Dad," Chaz said, dropping into a seat with Hank taking the one besides him.

"Just lettin' him know that there's options," Rob said with a smile.

"So what do *you* want to do today?" Kacey asked, now shamelessly leaning into me.

"Your brother told me that you have parks here? Actual large outdoor spaces?"

"Well, they're not exactly 'outdoor,' but yeah, we do. Want to see one?" she asked, smiling at me.

I smiled back and nodded. "I could use some wide-open spaces after being cooped up on the ship for the last eight plus months. Then maybe just do a little sightseeing?"

"Oh, I've got some sights for you!" she teased.

"I'm sure you do," I agreed. "But we can put *those* off until bedtime, I'm sure!"

I was surprised that she didn't even blush as everyone else at the table snickered. Then again, maybe I shouldn't have been. Everyone had to have known what we were doing last night, but nobody seemed to be the slightest bit bothered by it.

Not what I'd grown up with at all.

We talked a little bit more, about what we'd been doing onboard the *Iowa Hill* since we'd been here last, then the four of us headed out, Hank, Chaz, Kacey, and me. We did a little shopping for a few odds and ends that Chaz and I needed. But other than that it was mostly just sightseeing. We spent several hours in the park, it was in a surface hab and the clear glass roof was high enough that I hardly even noticed it. The place was huge; I'd never been to a park that big growing up on Earth! The folks on Ceres really did know a thing or two about how to build a habitat.

When we finally got back to Chaz's family's place, Jeff was waiting for me with a folder.

"What's this?" I asked as he passed it over to me.

"It's everything they found on that guy's tablet that would interest you."

"Why not put it on a memory stick?"

"Less chance of anyone finding out this way. I'd suggest shredding it when you're done, just to be safe."

"That bad?" I asked, a little worried.

"That's hard to say. But he wasn't looking to kill you."

"He wasn't?"

"Nope. He was going to hit you with that injector we found on him and knock you unconscious. Apparently he was supposed to kidnap you."

"Kidnap me? For what?"

"No idea. But the information's all in there if you want to read it."

I looked up at the door leading to Kacey's room; I could see her inside, slowly stripping off her clothing and smiling at me.

"I'll read it later," I said as I folded it up and stuck it in my back pocket. I had three more days of leave and I had better ideas on how to spend it. I'd read the file once I was back onboard the *Iowa Hill*.

Kacey made love to me that night, and I realized then that she really was serious about me. Looking at her, I honestly had to admit that I really could see myself spending a lot more time with her.

"Deep thoughts?" she asked me as we lay there, entwined, beneath the sheets of her bed.

"Why me?" I asked her.

"Hmm?"

"Kacey, I may be young, but I'm not dumb. You want me; I can see it when you look at me."

"Oh? And how do I look at you?" she teased with a smile.

"Like my mom—my real mom, not my bio—looks at my dad." I pulled her close against me and just enjoyed the warm softness of her body. "So, why me? We've barely known each other a day."

"What, you don't like me?" she asked, teasing me again.

"Oh, no. I like you. Trust me on that!" I chuckled and gave her a kiss.

"Well, it's because you're strong and you're tough..."

"Oh? I am?"

"Chaz told me about those guys you stopped," she said, snuggling into me a little closer, "and then Hank told me what really happened, as well as the one you dealt with back at Saturn. Then, of course, there's the simple fact that you actually *work*. Two ratings and a cert in less than a year? You're going places, and you take care of what's yours and your friends. Plus, you're good-looking and fun in bed!" She said the last with a giggle.

I nodded and shifted in bed, tucking her under my chin, and thought about that. I was suddenly struck by an old memory, from about a year after Dad had taken in Jenny and Ben. Ben was sleeping in my room, and Jenny was sleeping in Dad's bed. I hadn't realized it then, but looking back on it now, Jenny was paying for staying with us—not just with her babysitting all day long, but with her body each night as well.

But all I could remember was how happy Dad had become, and how she'd smile at him, even when he wasn't looking. Then one night I got up to use the bathroom and Dad was just finishing up.

"Dad?"

"Yes, Dave?"

"How long are Jenny and Ben staying?"

"What? Don't you like sharing your room?" he had asked, frowning a little.

"No, it's not that," I said shaking my head. "It's just..." I'd sighed and then just blurted it out, "It's just that I want to call her 'Mom' like Ben does, but I don't want to do that if she's going to leave us!"

My father had blinked and just looked at me, I guess he was shocked.

"What? Don't you want her to stay?" I'd asked, just plowing on ahead in all innocence. "I like her, Dad, and I can tell you like her too. You're always smiling at her and she's always smiling back, even when you're not home."

"So you want her to stay?" he'd asked, softly.

"Well, yeah. She'd make a good mom! Don't you want her?"

The next morning, they were engaged and got married after he'd gotten home from work.

"More deep thoughts?" Kacey asked, rolling over and rubbing back against me as she reached up with a hand to stroke the side of my face.

"I need to put another year in with the *Iowa Hill* before I can realistically think about getting a job somewhere else."

"And after you've done that?" she asked.

"After I've done that, I think that maybe, just maybe, I might be convinced to take a job someplace, oh I don't know, closer to here, perhaps?" I replied, teasing her for a change.

"Oh? Only just maybe?" she asked and then started rubbing her butt into my crotch. "And just what, might I ask, could *possibly* convince you?" She giggled.

"How about we spend the rest of my leave finding out?"

"Ooo! A challenge! I *love* a challenge! Think you're up to it?"

"Try me," I said with a chuckle.

Iowa Hill, Far Space

"SO, THINKING OF SETTLING DOWN ON CERES?" DOT ASKED ME as we swapped out the panel I'd just rebuilt. We'd left Ceres four days ago and last night a panel had burned out and, as usual, its "twin" followed it the next day.

I nodded. "Yeah, maybe. I definitely like the place and, yes, before you say anything, I definitely like Chaz's sister."

Dot laughed. "You all but had to peel her off there at the docks when we left."

I shook my head, but I had to laugh as well. "The temptation to drag her aboard and tell the captain we had a new hand was strong, trust me on that one."

"Give it another year and try asking him, he might surprise you," Dot said, still laughing.

"Really? You think he'd go for it?"

"That's what Hank did, and you've seen how well that worked out. Besides, it's not like we're lacking on space or life support. All it would really be is another mouth to feed, and when you consider how hard it is to find a good engineer these days? Oh yeah, if it was the difference between losing you or keeping you, I suspect the captain would go for it. Worse comes to worst, he just takes her food budget out of your pay."

"Pass me that wrench?" I said and after she'd handed it to

me, I started tightening down the bolts on my end of the panel as I thought about what she'd just said.

"I wonder if she'd go for it, though? I mean, living here on the ship isn't much of a honeymoon."

"When you consider how much off time we're gonna start seeing with two engineers on this boat who actually work, I'd think it'd be quite the honeymoon!" Dot said with a laugh. "Honestly, though, it depends on what she wants to do for a living. Most folks on Ceres work at something in the trades that are related to ships or habs, and most of those can get you a working berth on a ship."

"Guess I should ask her the next time we put in at Ceres. It's just all kinda shocking, you know?"

"Oh please, don't tell me you've never had somebody latch onto you before!" Dot said with a snicker.

"Not anyone that I wanted to keep," I said with a sigh. Yeah, there'd been the girls who wanted an "in" with my brother so they'd get one of the starring roles on the cheerleading squad, and more than a few who had a thing for "bad boys in gangs," especially if that bad boy was the gang's head "picker."

But they were just tourists.

"They weren't there for me, I wasn't the main attraction. They just wanted me for what I could do for them. For what they could get for themselves from being with me. With Kacey it feels like I'm the main attraction. It's just . . . well, different."

"Well, it's going to be quite a few months before we put in there and you see her again."

"True, and there's always the chance someone else may come along while we're gone," I said with a wistful look. "Where *are* we headed anyway?"

"Somebody's building a bunch of habs out in the Neptune L5 Trojans."

"I'm surprised somebody hasn't already," I said, finishing up with the last bolt. Sitting up, I pulled my tool bag over to start packing up.

"Nobody's wanted to go out that far," Dot said with a shrug and unlocked the wheels on our little trolley after making sure the panel we were removing was secure.

"What about all the people on the moons around Neptune? They're out just as far."

"Yeah, but there's a lot of moons out there, so there's mining and research and all the usual. The Trojans are well off the beaten path. It's like Pluto or Eris, the only people out there are researchers working for one of the major governments. There aren't any real colonies or settlements, just a handful of research stations."

"Well, I can understand Eris, in another few decades it's gonna be out past Pluto again. That's going to be one very long trip for anybody living there."

"Oh, I'm sure there's people out there who'd be willing to do it, now that you can actually travel that far. I mean, it's not like we don't already spend months aboard this ship, right?"

"Yeah, but the idea of being so far away from everyone else?" I shook my head. "I'm too much of a people person to want to do that."

"Well, you could probably make an okay living running supplies and such out to them, but not as much as just doing a lot of shorter runs closer in. Otherwise I'm sure Damascus would have us going there as well."

"It might be interesting to go out that far, that's really out there into deep space. But I don't know if I'd want to make a habit of it," I said as we got our gear together. We started moving the trolley and its panel back toward the hoist so we could move it up to the shop and repair it.

"You want a hand rebuilding this one?" I asked.

"Nah. You got the hard one yesterday. I'll probably be able to knock this one out in an hour or two."

"Well, I guess I'll go finish the daily inspections while you handle that."

"See you at dinner, I guess."

Nodding, I made my way back to the ladder that led up to the top level in the back of the ship. The ship's computer was back there, as well as the ship's radio gear, our small gym, and the lockers for a lot of the ship's gear—things that got used outside of the ship in space during loading or unloading, if we had to do it without a loading dock. There was also a lot of stuff stowed there in case we had to go outside and do actual work on the ship. There was even a large airlock off the back of the ship, but it was rarely used and we only function checked it once a quarter.

But a lot of environmental equipment ran through the upper level of the ship, same for a lot of the control ways. Also the computer system's environmental unit was up here as well. My job for today would be to clean the computer's cooling system and do the usual tests. After that, I was going to inventory some of the gear in the lockers.

It took me a couple of hours to clean and check the cooling system, then after that I was in the storage lockers for at least another hour. When I came out, I glanced into the gym and saw Pam in there, working out. This was the first time I'd ever seen her in something other than that bulky shipsuit she always wore, and I had to stop and watch a moment. She was seriously hot.

"Enjoying the show?" she asked when she noticed me standing there in the doorway.

"Appreciating it would be a better description. I guess now I know why you wear that baggy suit and try to keep me at arm's length. Still, I'm surprised you're not on one of the top-end Earth space liners. Everyone always says that they hire for looks."

Pam nodded. "They do, and I was."

"Why'd you leave?"

"Because you need to sleep with people to get ahead, and while I didn't mind that with some of the crew, most of the passengers weren't anybody I wanted to even touch, much less screw."

I made a face. "Ugh. I'd say I'm surprised, but from everything I've ever seen of the elies, I'm not really. I'm guessing that didn't go over well with your bosses?"

"They fired me on the run in to a pleasure hab on one of the asteroids. Getting out of there wasn't a lot of fun, but I got rescued by one of Damascus Freight's other cargo ships and, well, they had an opening and I didn't have to screw anybody to get it, so here I am."

I nodded. "Well, I promise to behave."

"It's not you I'm worried—"

Just then there was a loud *BANG* and we lost gravity.

"Holy shit!" Pam yelled and pushed off the exercise machine she'd been using for the door leaving the gym as I stepped aside so she could get out. All of the airtight doors were swinging closed and engaging as the ship's general quarters alarm sounded.

I pulled myself down the hallway, but Pam shot past me like a rocket. Apparently she was an expert in zero-gee. I myself wasn't very good at it, it wasn't something I'd had much time or experience with.

Though I'd be lying if I said I didn't appreciate the view.

"The doorway to the cargo deck is sealed, it's losing atmosphere."

"Damn," I said, floating up beside her. "Can you see anything through the porthole?"

"Just the cargo bay!"

"Excuse me," I said and, grabbing her gently, I pushed her out of the way.

"Just what do you think you're doing?" she said, turning toward me angrily.

"My job. This is an engineering failure. Now, be quiet or I'm going to get really condescending," I said as I peered out the window. The upper walkway was in the center of the hold, same as the lower two. But it was grated, so I could see through it, and from what I could see, it didn't look good.

"Damn." I got out my tablet.

"What?"

"Looks like an explosion in the grav generator bay, but the last one in the back."

"Which means?"

"That a quarter of our grav plates are out."

"That means we've lost drive!"

"Some of it, yes," I mumbled and looked at the repeater function. The reactors were spooling down to a ten percent setting—ninety percent of the power to the two-twenties had been cut, so they were providing about two tenths of a gravity to the rest of the ship—but the display for the fifteen hundred was zero and had a lot of flashing icons on it.

"We're going to go Dutchman!" Pam said. "We're on a cometary orbit! I don't have my pressure suit! We're trapped back here! We need to get to the lifeboat! We need to get out of here!"

I started tapping out a message to Dot, asking if she'd made it back to Engineering.

"Dave! What are you doing? Aren't you listening to me! We're trapped back here! Trapped!"

She grabbed my arm and I turned to look at her. I was honestly surprised at how much she was panicking.

"Everything is fine, Pam."

She started shaking me.

"No! It's not! We're cut off! We can't get out of here! We're trap—"

I grabbed her by the collar and smacked her across the face. The look of complete and utter fear then surprised me. She started trying to push away.

"I'm not going to rape you! Calm your ass *down*. I got this! *Alright?*"

"Don't-kill-me-please-don't-kill-me-please-don't—"

"I'm *not* going to kill you." I sighed.

"But I heard Hank telling Ian that you killed those guys on Burnside who tried to get to Dot."

"Pam!" I said, waving my hand in front of her face. I was surprised at how badly she'd lost it; then again, maybe she'd been afraid of me after hearing what I'd done? That or something really bad had happened to her.

"Pam!" I said it again, and this time she stopped whimpering and looked at me.

"I will take care of you, I promise! I'm not going to rape you or kill you. Yes, I'm a big, bad, nasty man, but I'm *your* big, bad, nasty man, okay?"

She stared at me, but she wasn't whimpering anymore.

"Okay?" I said in a softer voice.

She nodded. "Okay," she said in a soft voice.

"Now, stay with me. We're not trapped. There's an engineering passage that connects the back to the front for use when the cargo deck is in vacuum. Understand?"

She nodded and I grabbed my panel from where it was floating.

I'm fine, Dot sent me. *Pam's missing.*

She's with me, I texted back. *Looks like the 1500 blew up. I can see the damage from here.*

That shouldn't be possible.

I know. We're coming forward. I guess we'll be suiting up and going inside to look.

"Come on, we need to get to the passage."

"Where is it?"

"In the computer room. It's on the starboard side, so it doesn't block the lifeboat hatch."

"So..." She stopped and took a deep breath and it was hard not to appreciate the effect it had on her rather impressive bust in zero-gee. "So we can get to the lifeboat?"

"Yes, but I doubt we'll use it. We can still fly with what we've got, just not as fast. So our trip's gonna take a bit longer. C'mon, follow me."

I pushed off the sealed hatch and drifted back toward the access to the computer room. The door was closed, but there was atmosphere on the other side, so I opened it and we went inside. I then pushed off and went over to the access way as Pam closed the door and then followed me.

I'd just opened the hatch when my tablet pinged with an urgent alert.

"Go through, I'll follow you," I told Pam and got my tablet out.

Pirates! We've been ordered to abandon ship or they'll fire on us! Hurry!

"Shit," I swore.

"What's wrong, Dave?"

"We need to get to the lifeboat as quickly as possible. Now, *go!*"

"What is it?"

"Pirates."

Pam lost it then, and I mean *completely.* She started crying and shaking and I ended up having to grab her and hold her against me with one arm, while I pulled myself through the convoluted passageway with the other. I heard a loud *clang* from the back of the ship. I recognized it from some of our in-space transfers. A ship had just magnetically locked on to the stern of the *Iowa Hill.*

It took me a moment to figure out what that meant, as Pam started thrashing wildly for about a minute.

The rear lock could be opened from the outside. In fact, you couldn't lock it! That was against the law, in case someone got trapped outside.

We were being boarded.

My tablet pinged again, but I was too busy trying to get down the damn passageway with a panicking woman flailing and crying, which was made even worse now that we were in gravity again.

My tablet pinged yet again, but I couldn't get to it and keep moving forward.

Just as I got to the access hatch to get into the front of the ship I felt the entire ship shudder.

"Oh fuck, they didn't!"

I pulled out the tablet there were several messages from Dot.

Hurry!

They're boarding! Hurry!

Parks is losing it! He's convinced you're dead and they're raping Pam!

The last one was short and sweet.

Parks hit the emergency release, I'm sorry!

I'll deal. I hit SEND and hoped they were close enough to get it.

Pam started to scream and I grabbed her by the throat, cutting her off, then I undogged the hatch with my free hand and pushed us both through it, falling onto the floor in the lower gravity.

Straddling Pam, I got right into her face and growled. Her eyes went wide and she froze.

"Okay, now get this straight. You belong to me now, got that? I *own* you. Because I own you I am *not* going to let any man, pirate or otherwise, rape you. You're mine. I don't share. Not now, not ever.

"Do. You. Understand?"

She nodded.

"Now, I need you to run to your cabin and put your pressure suit on and meet me on the bridge. *Do not* grab a gun or any weapon. I have to get mine. I will meet you there shortly.

"Do you understand?"

"Yes." She nodded, then asked in a soft voice, "You won't let them hurt me?"

"They'll have to kill me, and I don't intend on dying. Now, go!" I said and, rolling off her, I flew down to my quarters as fast as I could, grabbed my pressure suit, and ran back up to the bridge.

Pam was climbing into hers, which of course meant she was naked and I honestly wished I could have taken the time to appreciate the view, but I was too busy stripping down and getting into mine.

I checked my pockets and moved my tablet, wallet, and pick to the pockets of my pressure suit. I didn't know what, if any, of my stuff I'd be able to grab, but right now my first concern was not dying.

After that, it was taking care of Pam.

Walking over to the radio, I grabbed the mike and keyed it.

"You scared them off too quickly, two crew members got stranded."

"Who is this?" came back immediately.

"Dave Walker, third engineer. The second mate's here too. We were trapped in the back when the cargo hold lost pressure and, well, they thought we were dead, I guess. We're on the bridge, and no, we're not armed."

There was a long silence then.

"Do you want me to unlock and open the cargo bay doors?" I asked next.

"Yes, unlock them and then shut down all gravity in the cargo bay."

"Will do." I looked over at Pam. "You heard the man."

"You're going to help them?" she asked, looking at me, still in shock.

"Pam, what did I tell you?" I warned.

She blushed and did as I told her.

"Anything else you need us to do from up here?"

"Bring up all the loading lights."

"You got it," I said and nodded toward Pam, who this time did what I asked without questioning me.

"Why are you being so helpful?" another voice asked.

"Because I'm hoping you'll take us with you," I radioed back. "I've got no desire to be a *Flying Dutchman* for the rest of my life."

"Oh, I'm sure you'll be rescued."

"I'm not. The rest of the crew thinks we're dead and this ship has got a hell of a lot of delta-V. Also..." I took a deep breath and played my first card. "I don't think I want to be talking to the police all close and personal-like when it's obvious that we've been sabotaged."

"You think they'll pin you for it, don't you?"

Actually I was afraid that if word got back to my bio-mom's husband, he'd float a big fat bribe to the police and have me killed. Or maybe he'd just tell them I was a wanted killer and it would be better if I didn't make it into port.

I just didn't want to take that chance. Ben's last email to me had said that they hadn't yet discovered my ruse. However, the information that Jeff's "friend" had gleaned from that tablet had made it very clear that the guy had been trying to grab me for Eileen's husband's political rival. I guess he thought he could use me as some sort of leverage or something.

But in either case I now had *two* groups interested in me, and their interests didn't coincide with any of my personal plans for long-term survival.

"Let's just say that I'm not a fan of the police," I said over the radio, "and they're not a fan of me. Sure, they *might* come out and get us. But right now they're not the kind of people I want to meet, okay?"

"What, you kill a cop or something?"

"Let's just say that there are moneyed interests out there that hate me just about as much as they're gonna hate you when this gear doesn't arrive."

"Someone's coming through the mid-deck lock," Pam whispered.

"Come here and stand behind me," I told her.

She scurried over and hid behind me. She couldn't press in too close, as I had my helmet hanging open on my back, same as her.

I waited and heard them as they approached. We still had gravity in the front quarter of the ship—not a lot but more than enough, if things turned ugly.

Four men entered the bridge; they had their helmets off and folded back. All four of them had sidearms that they were currently holding in their hands.

"Move out from behind him and show us your hands!" one of them, the biggest, said.

"Do it, Pam," I told her.

The big one frowned at me. I pegged him pretty quickly, he was the muscle, but he wasn't the one in charge. That was the older-looking guy in the front of them who was already putting his gun away.

"Damn, she's a pretty one, Marcus! I say we take her!"

Pam whimpered a little and I frowned and looked at him.

"That's my woman and you will *not* be putting your hands on her."

"Or?" he laughed.

"I'll kill you."

"I don't know if you've noticed, sonny, but I've got a pistol and you've got squat! All I have to do is shoot you."

"You mean you'll try, and you'll fail. And then Marcus will have to hire me to replace you."

I looked at the one I'd pegged as Marcus, and I broke the cardinal rule—I made eye contact.

"Put your gun away, Greg," Marcus said as his eyes met mine. We looked at each other for a moment and I knew I could kill him before any of them could stop me. I'd probably get to kill Greg for good measure. I had my pick in my hand and they weren't even fifteen feet away.

Marcus's eyes widened a hair, and then narrowed as that thought went through my mind.

"I'm not in the habit of taking on freeloaders," Marcus said.

"Pay for what you get, right? Nothing's free. You get me and my woman here out of this mess and I'll give you six months."

"I don't need another killer," Marcus said and I noticed Greg flinch.

"What, him?" Greg said, sounding surprised.

"Greg, he'd kill you before you got your pistol back out. That thing in his left hand is an old assassin's weapon."

"*What?* No, he—"

"Quiet! I don't want to have to tell my sister that you got yourself killed being an idiot."

He turned back to me then.

"This really is quite a mess. Normally we run the crew off before we take the ship. What did you say your name was? David Walker?"

"Yes, and I'm a rated third engineer. Surely you could use another engineer?"

"I have more than enough engineers, David, for what we're doing."

"Oh? How many do you have that are certified to repair grav panels?"

I smiled then as I saw his eyebrows go up a hair.

"Are you now?" he asked.

"How do you think we keep an old ship like this running? Go check the spares, we've got two, and they're not even the same size. We repair them in our machine shop in the back."

I watched as Marcus pondered that a bit.

"What's the story with your girl Pam there?"

"She's just a regular second mate. She had a bit of a run-in with some unpleasant types. Elies."

"Ah, and you dealt with it." He paused a moment and looked Pam over. Pressure suits were skintight and even looking scared with red eyes from crying, Pam was still the kind of woman that a lot of men killed for.

"I have issues with rapists," I told him. "So if there are any on your crew, let 'em know not to mess with Pam or to let me know what they are."

Marcus smiled then, surprising me. "Yes, I'm not much of a fan of them myself. I'll warn my men. So, you want to work for me?"

I nodded. "I figure six months of my repairing all of your panels will cover Pam's and my room, board, and the price of a ride back to the main trade routes."

"And just what will you tell everyone after you've been released?"

"That I made a deal to save our lives and I honored it. It's not like I would go to the authorities. Even if I could, I doubt they'd believe me. Look, you tried to run the whole crew off, that tells me you're not just some cold, hardened killer..."

"Unlike you," Marcus said with a frown.

"Cold, hardened killers don't go rescuing damsels in distress, now do they?" I said, rolling my eyes.

Marcus laughed. "Ah, a romantic! Fine, six months, then you can leave. That includes your woman, Pam."

He stuck out his hand and we shook.

"Welcome aboard."

"What? You hired him? Marcus! You can't trust him!"

"We have a lot of panels that need fixing, Gregory, and none of our people are certified or actually trained to do it. Besides, what's he going to do? Sell us out? He works in a trust business. Or did, at least?" Marcus asked, turning back to me.

I nodded. "I don't do it for money anymore. Just to protect me and mine. I made a promise to my grandfather and, well, family's everything."

Marcus smiled widely when he heard that. "Get your things together. We'll take you with us when we transfer back to my ship."

"My tools for repairing panels are in the rear of the ship. You won't have a problem with me going back there and getting them, will you?"

"Take Miguel here with you. And don't hurt him, please."

"You're the boss," I said and, taking Pam's hand, I led her off the bridge.

"That's right, I am, aren't I? So don't kill anybody!" Marcus called after me as we left.

When we got to Pam's room, the first thing she did was collapse against me, wrapping her arms around me and holding me tight.

"I'll wait outside," Miguel said and I nodded.

Pam put her head on my shoulder and cried softly for a little while as I put my arms around her and just held her.

"Thank you," she said when she finally settled down.

"I promised you, didn't I?" I said with a smile.

Looking up at me, she smiled back, a little shyly, then putting her hand behind my head, she pulled herself up to me and kissed me.

I was impressed, she tasted good and she really knew how to kiss. I held her against me and savored it. It felt good to be alive and, for all my bluster back there, I might have been able to kill one, maybe even two, of them. But there were four of them and *lots* more on the other ships that I was sure were out there. I would have been a dead man.

"I seem to recall you promising me something else?" Pam whispered, still looking up at me shyly. "Something about my being your *property*?"

I grinned down at her and kissed her on the nose. "Yup. And I ain't going back on that one either, *but* I'm not going to rape you or even ask you to have sex with me, Pam. I know what you've been through and I don't want to add to that."

"Oh?" She looked surprised at that.

I sighed, smiling down at her. "I won't kick you out of bed, but I won't force myself on you. Now, pack your stuff, we got a bunch of things to do before we leave."

"We do?"

"Yup. I want you to program a new course in the ship's computer for after we leave. Have it flip and decelerate at fifteen percent thrust for a couple of weeks. Just make sure you give me a copy along with all the current course data."

"Why?"

"So when we go back to Damascus Freight Lines we can tell them where to find their ship so they can salvage it and we get to keep our jobs, why else?"

"Are you going to tell Marcus?"

I nodded. "Yup. I suspect he won't mind. Worst he can do is tell us not to do it. Now, pack, and keep it light. Leave the sex toys behind."

She grinned at me and quickly packed her things. When she was done she had a single large duffel and her pressure suit carrier. She was wearing her parka, not that I blamed her. It would definitely keep the men's eyes off her.

I didn't have all that much to pack, so it didn't take me very long either. I'd told Pam to pack her pistol in the bottom of her duffel and I did the same. Miguel's only response when I told him was "As long as you're not pointing them at me."

Crossing the cargo deck, we had to be careful as there was a very large group of people transshipping the habitat equipment out of the *Iowa Hill* into another, larger cargo ship that had locked onto ours and warped in so close as to be touching.

When we got to the shop, I grabbed an airtight crate, put all the tools and other supplies I'd need into it, sealed it up, and wrote my name on the side as well as Marcus's. When we went back out to the cargo deck, Miguel directed one of the men to take it over to the cargo ship and see to it that it was delivered to Marcus "once they got back." Wherever "back" was.

I did manage to get a brief look through the catwalk at the fifteen hundred. Something had punched a ten-inch-wide hole straight through it and out the bottom of the ship. Which explained the loss of pressure as well as the loss of the generator.

"So, I guess we're pirates now?" Pam said in a soft voice when we'd finally returned to the bridge.

"We're not pirates, we're buccaneers," Marcus said as we turned to look at him.

"What's the difference?" I asked.

"Pirates pretty much just rape, murder, plunder, and not much else. We only take what we need, and, well, we *need* that habitation gear. We're not going to sell it; we're going to *use* it. For us, this is a matter of survival. We have ethics and morals and we're not interested in slaughter, even on a small scale. Otherwise we would have just killed the crew and you two as well."

"That reminds me. Would you mind if we put in a program to put the ship on a better orbit after we leave?"

"Why would you want to do that?"

"So when we go back to our employers we can tell them where to find it so they can salvage it—and hopefully they'll give us our old jobs back."

"Sure, knock yourselves out. If nothing else it'll keep you out of trouble until they've finished off-loading."

"Thanks," I told him and then I set about writing my own little program for the reactors. I'd run them up to fifty percent when we left, so Pam's nav program wouldn't have any power issues. But after three weeks they'd run a gradual cooldown program until one was completely shut down and the other one maintained temperatures a few degrees above freezing.

It took them eighteen hours to off-load the gear. After we'd finished our programs, Pam and I went into the mess and made food for ourselves as well as anybody else who wanted some while they were working. Why let it go to waste, right? Besides which, I was starving.

When they finally pulled their cargo ship away, I closed the cargo doors and engaged the locks, then Pam and I downloaded our programs, and I shut down most of the ship's systems, as they wouldn't be needed anymore. Then we followed Marcus out of the front section, across the cargo bay, into the back, and then out through the rear lock into his ship, which was grappled on there.

It looked like a frigate to me, though I'll be the first to admit that I don't know a lot about military ships. We were shown to a cabin that wasn't much bigger than the six-by-four-foot bed in it.

"Okay," Miguel said, "this is your cabin and where you'll be staying. No one will enter without knocking. Marcus has told everyone you're onboard and working for him. So no one should mess with you—*either* of you," he added, giving Pam a glance.

"Stay in here, don't come out except to use the head." He pointed over to the sign on the wall flagging its location.

"What about food?"

"Someone will come and get you."

"How long are we going to be in here, anyway?" I asked.

"Just a few days. When you hear the acceleration alarm, lay down on the bed. This thing can pull a lot of G when it has to."

"Got it, and again, thanks. Dying out there would have really sucked."

"You know, I gotta ask. Would you really have killed us?"

I frowned. "Marcus and Greg wouldn't have stood a chance; they were way too close to me. You and the other guy..."

"Walt."

"Yeah, you and Walt might have survived, if you'd gotten to your guns fast enough."

"So, why didn't you?"

"Because I promised Pam I'd take care of her and protect her. Can't really do that if I'm dead, can I?"

Miguel smiled then, surprising me. "You should join us, man, you'd fit right in."

"Huh?" was about all I could think of to say.

"Like the big man said, we're not doing this for money; we're doing it for survival. It's all about protecting others. Probably why he was okay with hiring you on—you *get* it. You already think like one of us. Who knows? A year from now you might even *be* one of us."

I smiled and just shook my head. "Stranger things have happened!"

He closed the door then and I stripped out of my pressure suit while Pam got out of hers. I'd been up so long at this point I have to admit that I didn't even look at her. I just got the small towels out of the case, cleaned my suit, stowed it, put those back in the case with it, then plugged it into a wall receptacle to recharge.

I didn't even remember lying down.

I was woken up by Pam, whose hands were fondling certain portions of my anatomy, which, as always, had woken up just before I did.

"Morning, sailor," Pam said, smiling at me as I yawned and stretched.

"Does somebody want something?" I asked, smiling back at her. She really was incredibly hot, and she was naked, and she was in bed with me and there was no way I wasn't going to take advantage of the situation.

Though it may have been debatable as to who was taking advantage of whom.

"Well, as 'your woman,' it's only right that I take care of my man's needs," she said and then winked at me as she slid down and put her mouth to better uses.

One thing of course led to another and I discovered that Pam was a far more accomplished and talented lover than I was, not that she wasn't afraid to show me what she liked. She was also rather demanding, of both my attention and my affections.

If somebody hadn't knocked and told us food would be ready soon, I don't think we would have stopped.

Thankfully the head had a shower and we both made quick use of it. Even more thankfully it only fit one at a time.

We were dressed in shipsuits and ready when they came and took us down to eat with the rest of the crew. Pam was cuddled up against me and I had an arm around her as we came into the mess, got our food, then sat down to eat. The crew talked amongst themselves but mostly ignored us. Or rather, ignored me. Even though Pam was wearing a bulky shipsuit, with the way she was leaning into me, it wasn't hard to figure out what was under it. As there wasn't a single woman other than her in the mess, she was definitely getting a lot of looks.

Miguel, Walt, Greg, and Marcus were all there, and had nodded to us when we sat, but beyond that, there really wasn't any conversation. I was fine with that because I was still trying to process Pam going from a woman who was afraid of me and wanted me at arm's length to one who was very obviously now wanting to be my girlfriend and lover.

As soon as we got back to our small cabin she pulled the zipper down on her shipsuit, shucked it, and pulled the zipper down on mine.

"Okay, just what's going on with you?" I asked, looking down at her.

"What, don't you want me?" she asked, giving me an innocent smile that I knew was anything but after this morning.

"Oh, I want you, Pam, and from where your hand is I'm sure I'm going to be having you—a lot. But yesterday you were terrified of me, of sex, of damn near everything. Before that, you were always quiet and reserved on ship, especially around me."

"Well, you 'own' me now, you said so yourself," she said, giving me a shy, sexy smile. "I just want to please my master."

"And your master wants very much to be pleased and to return the favor. But, Pam, love"—I noticed she brightened when I said that—"I think I'm missing something, and your master would greatly appreciate it if you clued him in."

"I'm from Adonis, the Adonis group."

I nodded. I remembered her telling me that. "And that means what? You're all sex slaves by nature?"

She gave a soft and very feminine giggle and shook her head slightly.

"No. It means I'm genetically enhanced. For looks, for sexual pleasure, for a great many things."

"They built you for sex?" I looked at her confused.

"Not exactly. Everyone on Adonis has been 'adjusted' a certain amount. Modified if you like. Genetic modifications are the norm there, it's part of who we are. Everyone is modified to be beautiful—men, women, all of us. We're immune to a lot of common diseases; we're given above average IQs and reflexes. We're very resilient and healthy. And, well, while they were in there tinkering they improved our sexual responses and increased our appreciation for the act."

"So you're saying they made everybody horny."

Pam bit her lip and smiled rather sexily. "More or less. Whenever we hit port, I go party and get laid, not unlike Ian. Though in my case I'm not paying for it."

"I'll bet," I said with a chuckle.

"I don't get involved onboard, because...well, because I just don't want those kinds of problems anymore."

I nodded. "Got it. Which brings us to here and now."

"You're very handsome, Dave. You're also very well built." She smiled and ran her hand down my body inside the now unzipped shipsuit. "You're big, tough, ruthless when you have to be, and you made it clear to everybody that I'm yours and you'll protect me." She shivered a little, and I started to realize that Pam was definitely a little kinky.

"You protected me; you put your life on the line for me. Without you I'd be getting raped, or worse, right now."

"So you're rewarding me?" I asked with a smile.

"You also made it clear that no one else is allowed to touch me, and I like sex, I *want* sex, and I'm gonna give you all you can stand, and then some."

She put her other hand inside my shipsuit and slid them both around me, pulling her naked body up against me. I shrugged off the suit, letting it fall down my legs, and put my arms around her as well, enjoying the warmth and the nice firm curves of her body. I guess I was about to live every young man's dream.

"You're mine, Pam," I whispered softly. "Until we leave here, I *own* you. You're all mine and I promise to protect you and love you."

She grabbed me a lot tighter then and ground into me, shivering.

I started to realize that *maybe* I'd bitten off more than I could chew, but sometimes you just have to go all in.

"And I'm going to screw your brains out," I teased.

She damn near raped me after that, not that I wasn't willing. I've had some rather attractive women as lovers in my life, mostly due to Ben or being in the Howlers. That girl back at the Coyote Ranch I'd seen twice now was also pretty hot, and Kacey was most definitely a looker.

But Pam was by far the hottest and sexiest of them all, and without a doubt the most talented and the most shameless; and she was turning it all on me.

It felt like winning the lottery.

There was no way this wasn't going straight to my head.

Location Unknown

FOUR DAYS LATER WE DOCKED AT OUR DESTINATION, AND IF there was an ounce of fat left anywhere on my body, it deserved an award. Pam really put me through my paces the entire time we were shut up in that small cabin and I was just vain enough to keep encouraging her. It made me wonder just how many "tourists" to her home screwed themselves to death. I think the only thing that had saved me was my youth and overall good condition.

Still, I must have done something right, because she was still puppy-dogging me and was being affectionate as hell.

"Come on, I'll take you to your new shop," Marcus said as he came and got us.

"Are my tools here yet?" I asked as we picked up our belongings.

"No, they'll be another couple of days. But you'll need to set up your shop first. Until we get the new parts of the hab online, we're pretty limited on space," he said, as he led us off of the ship.

"Okay, I'm gonna need to build a kiln, so I can get to work on that first."

Marcus gave me a puzzled look. "What do you need *that* for?"

"The graviton coils are made from superconductors. *Ceramic* superconductors. So I need to bake 'em before I install 'em. I grabbed all of the slurry we have for making them from the *Iowa* before we left. Hopefully your people can get more."

"What if they can't?" he asked, frowning.

"I can reuse the old stuff, but it's a little more work. I have to turn it into a powder, then add solvents to liquefy it. Then press those out and put it in something that will allow me to squeeze it into the tubes that hold it in place while I fire it in the kiln."

I shrugged. "It's a bit messier, and you always lose a little, but if you've got any chemical engineers, I'm sure they can whip me up a new batch eventually."

"I'll put my staff on it. I'm sure that's not the kind of thing we'd want to go and buy."

"Why not?" Pam asked, surprising me. Mainly because she hadn't said a word to anyone other than me since this had all started.

"Because someone might figure out that somebody's got a dark hab out here," I told her. "Companies always try to figure out where their product is going, and, well, sometimes they share what they learn with the governments, and I don't think the people here want to be found. Right, Marcus?"

"Perceptive. Where are you from, David? I've been trying to place the accent."

"Earth, Texas District."

"Really? You don't sound like you're from Earth! And how'd you end up as a ... well ..."

"Killer?" I prompted.

"Umm, actually I was going to ask about your being an engineer, out here far from your home."

"I had a rough childhood; I guess you could say I'm the black sheep of the family, the blackest. And some of that family wants me dead."

"Oh? What'd you do? Betray them or something?"

I laughed. "Oh no, it's far worse than that. I exist."

Marcus glanced over at me as we headed out of the docking area, into the main part of the hab, which was decidedly busy. There were a lot of people here when I stopped to compare it to all the places I'd been to so far, none of which had ever seemed so crowded.

"Sounds ... *complicated*," he said after a moment. "But then you don't sound like any of the elies I've ever met."

"Like you said, it's complicated. Once I get to know you better, I'll fill you in on the details—that is, if you really want to hear the boring truth," I said with a chuckle.

"After the way you stood up to us, I don't think it's going to be boring, David."

"So why are you folks out here, anyway? Who are you all hiding from? If you don't mind my asking, that is."

"The tyranny that comes with infallibility," Marcus replied with a heavy sigh. "But that's not your battle, so I wouldn't let it concern you."

I just nodded and figured I'd find out eventually. Not like I was going to be anywhere else for the next six months.

"Do you use regular credits here?"

"Only if you've got them on you. It's not like we can have a bank here or tie into the regular credit networks."

I nodded. "So you have your own currency, then?"

"Yes, but it's all digital and not worth anything anywhere other than here."

"How's your black market?" Pam asked.

Marcus shrugged. "No idea, really. We don't tell people what they can and can't do with themselves. So they're free to trade or barter whatever they want."

"Libertarians?"

"More or less, I guess. We believe in the right of self-determination, but with all that's happened to us"—Marcus sighed and shook his head—"simple survival has forced us to, at the very least, put some of our higher beliefs on hold. We all hope that over time we can return to how we were, but"—Marcus shrugged and motioned to the walls around us as we walked down the corridor—"there is so much we have to do, and we honestly don't know how long it's going to take us. We were, to put it bluntly, unprepared for what happened and what came next."

"Aren't we all?" I said softly as I thought about my own life.

"I don't know, you seem to be coping well enough," Marcus said with a slight smile.

"You don't learn to land on your feet without face-planting a whole hell of a lot first," I said, looking around. "But I suspect you've already learned *that* lesson."

We came to an elevator then and Marcus looked thoughtful for a moment.

"You're right, of course. I must say that I'm surprised that someone as young as you has learned what is apparently one of life's more important lessons."

Now it was my turn to shrug as suddenly I felt uncomfortably guilty. The lessons I'd learned had all come with a price, even if I wasn't always the one paying it, and I started to wonder just how big that price must have been when it involved what had to be tens of thousands of people. This place was big, I could tell that just from what I'd learned from the habs and orbitals I'd already been to. Add to that the number of people I was seeing in the corridor...

Yeah, this wasn't a pirate camp or some random bunch of outlaws. This was a society that had been torn out by the roots, forcibly no doubt, and then had to run for its collective life.

I just hoped I hadn't ended up with the equivalent of the "white glove society" or something like that.

The elevator arrived and getting in we rode down in silence. I watched the numbers count off as we descended. The elevator had a keypad display, so I had no idea how many levels there were, just that we'd gone down twenty-three when we stopped.

"I'm going to want to meet with your station engineer at some point," I said to him as we stepped out onto a level that was so new that there were people still working on it.

"Why's that?"

"Hab panels are different from orbital panels, which are different from ship panels. I need to know how he's setting this all up," I said with a nod to the stuff going on around us as we walked. "Trust me—as soon as he hears about me, I'm sure he'll want to tell me what he wants me to do."

We stopped in front of a door that was already open and Marcus motioned inside. Looking in there was a fairly large, and empty, room. There was also an older-looking—as in gray-haired and most likely in her sixties—woman in the room.

"Yes, that would be me and when Marcus there told me about you, I made sure to be here to meet you," she said, sticking out a hand, which I immediately shook. "You must be Dave." She then did the same with Pam. "And you're Pam, right? I'm Mabel, habitat designer and head engineer. Marcus, thanks for bringing him here, I can definitely use him. Now, I suspect you've got more important things to deal with?"

Marcus smiled and nodded at his obvious dismissal, "Yes, I do."

Marcus turned to me before he left. "I will be around, David; there are things I'd like to discuss with you." He smiled at Pam next. "If you need help, don't hesitate to ask."

Giving another nod he smiled, turned, and went back to the elevator.

"You might want to go explore a bit, Pam. This is going to be a long and very dull conversation, I'm sure," Mabel said with a warm smile.

"Umm, no. I'll stay with Dave if you don't mind," she said, taking a firmer grip on my arm and leaning into me a bit more.

"There weren't any problems with any of our boys, were there?" Mabel asked with a frown.

"No, and I don't want there to be any."

"It's from before we came here," I said. "Now, before we get started, where are we going to be living?"

She pointed to a doorway in the back of the room. "Your room is back there. I already checked, it's got power, water, and everything works."

"Well, let us get this stowed." I hefted the pressure suit's case I was still holding.

"Of course!"

Mabel led us to the back of the room, showed us how the lock worked, then opened it and we went inside. There wasn't much, it was about as big as the apartment I'd grown up in, with one less room. The bed in the bedroom was part of the structure, and there wasn't a mattress or any blankets, but it was a start. Dropping Pam's and my duffels and setting down my pressure suit carrier next to Pam's, I put my arm around her and steered her back out to the "common room," which was really a combination kitchen/living area. The table there had bench seating, all of which was built into the walls as well. I had Pam sit down and slide in, then I sat down as Mabel sat across from me. I pulled out my tablet as she pulled out hers.

"Okay, first off, I'm going to need a good power tap down here," I said.

"For?"

"I need to build a kiln, at least one, though probably more like half a dozen."

"Oh! Right." Mabel started making notes on her tablet. "I

forgot about that! Good thing they're not finished running cable. I'll get them on it immediately.

"Do you think you could build panels from scratch?" she asked, looking back up at me.

"Why would you want to do that? Don't you have enough?"

She shook her head. "Not for what we've got planned."

"Well, the ceramic is the main limiting factor. Then there's the plastic tubing to hold it in place and protect it. After that... well, building all of those controllers isn't hard—it's a pretty standardized design—but that's going to take time."

"I got lots of kids we can train up to do that stuff; I just need someone to teach 'em."

I nodded. "I can do that, *but* I gotta warn you, I'm gonna need someone to test all of their work. And it better be someone responsible, or they're going to find my foot up their ass if they start passing on shoddy work."

Mabel laughed. "I hear you on that! I'm just glad we got you. All the panel techs we've now got are pretty much self-trained, and, well, our repairs haven't been the best."

I sighed. "I guess I'll be training them up as well, then."

"Sure you want to?"

I nodded. "Yeah, I am. Right now I *live* here. And while I may not plan on staying, I sure don't want to be killed or injured by someone's mistakes. Onboard a ship, if something breaks and you can't fix it, well, good luck waiting for help to arrive before you die. So I've been trained to be a bit pedantic about all of this," I said with a grin.

"Our chief engineer is a stickler for doing things right," Pam piped up. "If she found out Dave was doing substandard work, she'd come out here and kick his ass."

After we'd gotten that all out of the way, Mabel spent the next couple of hours showing me what her plans were for the future, as well as what I was going to have to deal with for now. Half my day would be repairing panels, while teaching one of her current techs and getting them up to speed. The other half of my day would be going over her planned production facility. First making sure it was put together right, then after that was done, making sure people knew what they were doing and overseeing its operation while training someone else to take it over for after I'd left.

Evenings would be teaching the basics to the people who were going to be working there.

In short I was going to be pretty busy. I had to make sure I penned in plenty of time to spend with Pam, because I owed her that much. Also, because I didn't want to risk losing her. For all that I'd told her that I "owned" her, I couldn't see myself enforcing it if she decided to leave. Right now, a lot of people believed I was a lot worse, and a lot more dangerous, than I really was. As that was working in my favor, I really had no plans on correcting them.

When we finally finished I looked at Pam, who had fallen asleep cuddled up against me. I couldn't help but smile.

"She's from Adonis, isn't she?" Mabel said in a soft voice.

"Yeah, please don't spread it around. She had some really bad moments when we were told pirates were boarding."

Mabel sighed and gave a small shake of her head. "Marcus mentioned something about a problem with some Earther Elites?"

"Yeah, among other things."

"Well, she's definitely clinging to you."

"That's 'cause I told her I'd kill anyone that messed with her, and she knows I'll do it."

Mabel gave me a look then.

I shrugged. "What else was I supposed to do? She was freaking out and crying. I had to get her under control and it's not like I *was* going to let anyone hurt her."

"And she believed you?"

"That I'd protect her? Well, obviously."

Mabel smirked. "No, I mean the part about you killing for her."

"A bunch of men tried to ambush me and another, younger deckhand so they could rape our engineer when we had to put in at one of those corporate mining facilities for emergency repairs a few months back."

"What happened?"

"I killed three of them. Single-handedly. The rest ran away." I shrugged. "I used to be a very bad person—well, at least that's what everybody else likes to say." I looked at Pam. "Yeah, I'd kill for her. I promised and I keep my promises." I turned back to Mabel. "I guess Marcus put it best when I warned them what would happen if they laid a hand on her back when we first met.

I used to work in a 'high trust' business. You keep your word—no matter what. This place"—I waved my free hand at the room around us—"I'll never tell anyone who was here or where here even is—assuming I figure it out."

"That's a pretty evolved code of ethics for a young man like you."

"I was the top picker for a very large street gang for most of my teenaged life. The street gangs on Earth have been around for centuries. Their rules are pretty strict; so are their ethics. After a while, if you survive, it becomes a part of you."

"Picker? What's that?"

I reached into my pocket, carefully. I didn't want to wake Pam up yet. Pulling out my pick, I set it on the table. "When I found out we wouldn't be allowed to take our pistols, I made that before we went ashore on that station."

She picked it up, and noticed the weight inside it.

"I've heard of these."

I frowned at that. "Yeah, apparently Marcus has as well. I thought they were solely an Earth thing because we're not allowed firearms. So where'd you hear about them?"

Mabel set my pick down and gave me a wry grin. "Earther police dramas are all the rage in the Venusian cloud cities. One of them had this killer, they were after him for, like, three years on the show, and he used one of those," she said with a nod at my pick as I reclaimed it and put it back in my pocket.

"According to that show, only the pros use them."

I shook my head. "Lots of people use them. Just some of us know how to use them right. I can pick someone without doing any serious damage, or I can really mess them up for a while."

"Or kill them."

"Yeah. But you all carry guns, so it's not like I've got a monopoly on deadly weapons, Mabel."

"While that may be true, I doubt there are many people on this hab who have even killed three people, and I'm guessing you've killed more than that."

"Marcus has killed more than three."

I noticed her eyes widen slightly. "Why do you say that?"

"He knew I wasn't blowing smoke up his ass when I laid down my terms."

"Very astute. Yes, Marcus has had to do a great many unpleasant tasks since this journey of ours started. I just hope he can find peace when we finally are safe again."

"Yeah, I keep hoping for a little of that myself." I sighed and Pam took that moment to yawn and stretch, sitting up.

"Sorry! I kinda dozed off there. You all done?"

Mabel smiled at her and nodded. "Yeah, we're all done."

"Great!" Pam bounced a little. "Now, do you think you could tell us where we can buy some blankets and towels and sheets and stuff?"

"And a mattress," I added.

"Oh! Right! A mattress," she said, leering at me.

"I know a place," Mabel said, "but I don't think it's going to be cheap."

"Oh, that's okay. I have some creds on me and I heard Marcus say people will take them."

"Well, let's get a move on. I'll show you where those shops are, but then I need to get back to work."

Among Strangers

IT TOOK A WEEK TO BUILD AND TEST ALL THE KILNS I'D NEED. When I'd taken my test, I'd seen pictures of some existing shop layouts and I was copying one of them as I could best remember it. I wanted this place set up as best as I could make it—not so much for whoever would be running the place after I left, but more so when the time came for me to set up my own place, I'd know what I was doing.

So I took a lot of pictures and made a lot of notes.

Mabel had someone come in and build the workbenches I'd need and when my tools showed up, she sent a couple of machinists down to take pictures and measurements of them. They were going to make several sets of copies, two of which would end up in here.

When I got all of *that* done, I then ended up spending two whole weeks helping them build their new production facility. Any plans for just working half days on it went right out the window the first day, when I made them tear out everything they'd done that morning and start over.

So evenings became my "panel repair" time and I got introduced to the four current repair techs, who were all very polite and very grateful. I suppose there was a chance that they really

141

did feel that way, but my Earth upbringing had me suspecting that it was more likely they'd been told all about me, and been reassured that if I didn't punish them, someone else would.

Still, they were all nice enough, and they were all definitely willing to work, so I was looking forward to training them.

Pam was starting to settle down a little, in that when I was out of the shop working down the hall, she was content to sit in our little apartment. With the door locked. And her gun out.

Then again she was no longer dressing down, and when we went to the general mess to eat—food was one of those things still being carefully managed—she got a lot of looks. Then they'd notice me and quickly look away.

That last bit felt both good and bad. It's nice to know that people don't want to mess with you, and are perhaps a little bit afraid of you to boot. But I wanted these folks to like me. Six months is a long time and I didn't want to spend it with only Pam to talk to in my few off hours.

'Cause private time with Pam usually involved lots and lots of sex and very little talk.

"Don't you ever run down?" I teased her after the end of that first month.

"What? Don't you want to?" she asked with a smirk.

"'Course I want to," I said and gave her a hug. "Sex with you is definitely something I enjoy. But I also just enjoy *you*, Pam. I don't want you thinking all I see when I look at you is a sex toy. There are times I'd like to know just what's going on behind those green eyes of yours."

"Are you saying that you—*gasp*!—want a relationship?" She was grinning when she said it.

"It's going to be a lot of months yet, Pam, before we leave here. So yeah, I am. What's so strange about that?"

"Because most regular guys just want the sex toy and not much more beyond that."

"And the guys from back home?"

"Back home sex is pretty casual, as well as common. It's not really what most relationships are based on."

I thought about that a moment before I responded.

"So, you're saying if we were just hooking up for sex several times a day, that would be all that there was?"

She nodded. "Pretty much. I mean, we might not even know each other's full names. Could be we just enjoyed sex together and left it at that."

I could see where that would take a little time to get my head around.

"Okay, but we do live together, and we sleep together, we do damn near everything together. Plus we *do* have a relationship."

"That's right, you *own* me," she said in a husky voice. I was starting to learn that just as certain things panicked her, there were other things that also set her off, but in much more enjoyable ways.

"Yeah, so I want to get to know you. Who knows, maybe I'll decide to stay here so I can keep you and never let you go!" I teased and noticed her eyes widen.

"You..." She stiffened and then shivered, closing her eyes.

"Can't make up your mind if you like that idea or not, can you?" I said with a snicker.

"You really are a bad man, Dave, you know that?" she grumbled, panting just a little.

"This from the woman who loves playing my devoted love slave," I said, and hugged her again. "Look, if you don't want to talk, fine. I get it. You're with me because you know I'll protect you and take care of you. Honestly, it's a bit of an ego boost to know that a woman like you has faith in a guy like me."

"A woman like me?" Pam said with an amused snort.

"Hey, you believe I'm a cruel, cold killer and all that kind of thing, so why can't I believe that you're just some little helpless, gorgeous, and hot sex goddess who just needs a strong man to care for her?" I said, giving her my best wide-eyed and innocent look.

From the resulting laughter, I guess she got the point.

"Okay, okay, I think maybe I see your point, Dave. But sex goddess? *Really?*"

"Cold killer?" I said back.

"Well, you did kill those three, then that guy back at Saturn..."

"And you've been trying to do the same to me in bed now for how many weeks?"

She blushed and actually hid her face in my shoulder.

"I...Umm...I *do* like you, Dave, and honestly, after what happened on the bridge that kinda got me all excited and stuff... And let's be honest here, you've been doing a fair bit of encouraging yourself."

I sighed. "This whole thing hasn't exactly been easy on me; it bothers me to have to done those things." I didn't want to tell her the *real* truth: that killing those people didn't bother me at all—what *really* bothered me was just how easily I'd backslid. "I don't even want to think of how it's been for you."

"Actually, for me it's been pretty easy," she said, surprising me.

"*Really?*" I'm sure I sounded as shocked as I felt by her reply.

She nodded. "Once Marcus took us aboard his ship I realized that you really were going to take care of me and I didn't have to worry anymore. It also helps that Marcus seems to be a man of his word.

"I mean, I'm not ready to go walking around the rest of this place without you around, but right now I got a sexy man to please me, who's more than happy to take care of me. So"—she looked up at me and smiled—"I'm good. But I can tell *you* need some taking care of, and honestly? That's been a lot of fun as well. Even if you are a dangerous bad man," she added with a giggle.

"I'm glad," I said and then kissed her.

"Really?"

I nodded. "I really do worry about you, Pam. I spent half my life watching out for my little brother, so you just kinda fit into that spot in my head. Just with a lot more 'rewards' for doing it!" I said, winking at her.

"Why did you leave Earth? What was the real reason? Was it just to get away from family?"

I blinked at the change of subject, and shook my head. "It wasn't really that. I just wanted to get away from the way of life there. It's so rigid, controlled. Monitored. Everybody has their little place and they'd damn well better stay in it! Out here, it's different. It's actually better than I'd thought it would be. You can pretty much do what you want and nobody really cares. What about you?"

"The ship I was working on was taken by pirates," Pam said and shivered. Not the good kind of shiver either. "It wasn't pretty what happened next. All of us women were sold off to be sex slaves, because we were Adonis."

She didn't say anything then for a minute.

"How'd you get free?" I asked softly.

"A Mars cruiser came and busted up the operation. Freed all of us that survived and killed everyone else there. They even nuked the orbital as they pulled out."

I gave her a tight hug. "Well, I guess that explains what happened back on the ship."

She nodded and shivered again. "Anyway, I really had nothing to go home to, so when I got out of the sick bay, I took a job with one of the Earth passenger liners. That was okay at first. But eventually my boss told me if I didn't start sleeping with the customers, 'like a good little Adonis,' I'd be fired."

"Ouch."

"I stabbed him with a stylus, got my shit, and got off that ship." Pam sighed. "The stories I've been telling you and everyone else about what I do on leave are just that, stories. I really only started sleeping with men again recently."

"Oh? How recently?"

Pam blushed and looked up at me. "Five weeks?"

I opened and closed my mouth a few times. Eventually I was able to talk again.

"Why me?"

"Because you didn't die. Because you won. Because suddenly I wasn't afraid of you anymore. Because the last person to do that before you came along died. Horribly. In front of me. But *you* didn't. You didn't..." She shivered again and started to cry quietly.

I kissed her softly and just held her. Here I'd thought my life was pretty screwed up and now I'd found someone whose life was worse. Way worse. It didn't take a genius to figure out it was her boyfriend who'd been killed; maybe he was even her husband? Or to figure out what'd been done to her afterward.

I was suddenly a lot happier with myself for having taken that risk for her, and not because I was getting laid. But because for the first time in my life since Ben, I'd actually saved somebody who'd needed to be saved. That might not sound like a lot to most people, but when you'd done as many bad things as I had, it meant a lot.

She kissed me then, a lot more tentatively than she had before. I guess having unburdened herself to me she was worried about how I might feel about her. I kissed her back unreservedly, and then for the first time we made love. It wasn't just sex, it was actual caring and sharing tender love.

I think I had the best night's sleep after that since I'd left Earth.

✧   ✧   ✧

The next morning Pam was a lot more relaxed and easy with me, as well as affectionate in those little ways that just give you a warm feeling inside. It actually reminded me, rather suddenly, of Kacey. That gave me an uncomfortable moment. I wondered if Kacey knew I was alive or not. The next thought was about Pam. I realized that up until now, I really had been thinking of her more as someone I was screwing, not someone I had any real feelings for. Last night she'd become "real" to me, in that I now had real feelings for her.

Like I had for Kacey. Which brought me back to: what was I going to do when we left here? Would Pam want to stay with me? Would I want Pam to stay with me?

Suddenly this was all starting to get a lot more complicated in ways I hadn't considered, and I realized that I really did want to see Kacey again. I wanted to get to know her better and I wanted to find out if she was "the one."

But I still wanted Pam.

That gave me a lot to think about while we ate breakfast that had nothing to do with building or repairing panels, or even our current situation on a dark hab out in the middle of space. Namely: What the hell was I going to do? Assuming Marcus *did* live up to his word and let us go, then what? Would Pam want to stay with me? Would *I* want her to stay with me?

What if they didn't let us go? What if they all decided they needed me here? I could think of any number of excuses they could make, as well as any number of threats to keep me in line, because Marcus had to know that if he put Pam's safety on the line, I'd fold. Then again, they could just decide that it wasn't safe to let me go, and it wasn't safe to keep me around. The very thing that was protecting me, my reputation, could end up being the death of me.

I thought about Kacey again. Would *she* even wait for me? Especially if she believed I was dead? That did make it easier to justify what I was doing with Pam, but that wasn't really true. I got involved with Pam because I was just happy to be alive at the time and I wasn't very optimistic about my long-term prospects.

Maybe I shouldn't have gotten involved, but damn, who could have said no? And not just because she was hot and she was good in bed.

Sometimes even cold-blooded heartless killers needed someone to hold in the middle of the night.

Screw it. I'd just have to see what happened, and if—no, *when*—we got away from here, I'd worry about it then.

After we returned from breakfast I started on what I'd hoped would be my "usual" schedule and work. Which was actually repairing panels. I had all four techs working in my shop for now, and we each did our own panel that morning. The only thing different was each of us took a turn troubleshooting each panel, and then when it was done, we tested all of the panels.

Several of their panels failed, so I had to take a minute to let them know that was okay. Everyone makes mistakes, just do it again, and if it failed again, don't worry about it, just figure out what you did wrong, and keep trying until you got it right.

The reason for my concern was that I still was getting a feel for the people here and the way they did things and lived. I knew that there were places back on Earth where if you failed at your job more than once, they kicked you to the curb, or worse. Out here, where these people were struggling to survive, I was worried that it *might be* "or worse," and it wasn't just that I didn't want to have to train someone up from scratch. It was also because I'd had my own brushes with failure growing up, but I'd had Ben to help me work past them. I doubted they had anyone like that at home, so I felt it was only fair to do what I could.

Come noon, I had lunch with Pam, then after I'd spent a little time making sure she was happy, I went down to the "factory," which was really only a hundred feet from my shop. Most of what they were doing really didn't need my supervision now that we'd gotten it set up and running. Building the casings, the holders, all of the mechanical stuff, they had shop guys for that who knew what they were doing and could train the new people without my help.

Building the controllers and wiring them up was, again, something their regular engineers could oversee and teach them how to do. Though I still planned to make a point of testing each of the units as they turned them out, at least until I had faith in their testing procedures.

The hard part was the fittings to connect the coils and, of course, the actual coils. That stuff had to be done right and the fittings to connect it to the grid had to be exact, or the problems that could happen were severe. When rebuilding a panel you didn't have to worry about the fittings, because they so rarely broke. So it was very much a matter of "getting it right the first time."

Things were going well, as usual, until I came to the one of the newer guys who just didn't seem to be taking me seriously.

"Look," I told him. "These measurements aren't suggestions, they have to be *exact*. Close isn't 'good enough.' I need you to take this seriously. You mess this up and this panel, as well as the one it ends up pairing with, could have problems!"

"Oh, come on, it's just a few millimeters! What's the worst that could happen?"

"This," I said and, grabbing a wrench off of the workbench next to me, I whacked him in the head with it, laying him out, cold, on the floor.

Suddenly everyone got really quiet. I guess they'd been following our little argument.

"Okay, listen up!" I said looking around the room. "If this isn't done right, someone could get hurt, or worse yet, *die*. And that someone could be me, so I'm not going to stand for any of it.

"And I want all of you to remember what I just said. It could be *me* that gets hurt, or dies, which of course means *you*. Or it could be your wife, your girlfriend, your *mother*. How do you think you're gonna feel if you fuck up and somebody you love pays the price for it? Gravity panels are *not* something you want to make a mistake on, especially not the big ones we're going to be making here. You're living in a hab! With *artificial* gravity! Not with natural gravity! This stuff can *kill* you! *Pay attention to detail!*"

I pointed to the guy now groggily sitting up on the floor and holding his face, which was bleeding heavily. "Someone take him down to Medical and get him patched up."

"What should we do with him after that?" one of the supervisors asked, coming over to check on him.

"Bring him back here and put his ass back to work. What, did you think I was going to fire him?" I asked, looking around the room.

I saw more than a few people nod.

I just shook my head. "He made a mistake, he was corrected. Just remember what I said and how it applies to you. This is serious business, people! After you go home tonight, see if you can't find some holos on grav panel failures. Just don't do it after you've eaten."

Someone helped my "victim" to his feet and took him off to get stitched up, and I went back to going over people's work and checking that it was done right. Thankfully nobody gave me any more trouble.

I had an insight then as I finished up. That little speech I gave was pretty close to the one that one of my instructors had given in one of my classes on grav panels and grav drives. Because we were all Earthers, none of us had ever seen or dealt with artificial gravity before, so we really were all pretty ignorant of the dangers.

Just like these guys.

There weren't a lot of places out there where you weren't exposed to grav panels as a daily part of life, and I already knew these people weren't from the one I'd grown up in. I recalled Mabel's comment about Venusian holo-dramas and suddenly I knew where they were from. Now if only I knew the why.

Later that evening, when I was just finishing up with the training class I was doing for the four repair techs who really didn't know as much about the engines that powered the panels as I would have liked, Marcus surprised me by showing up.

"Okay, guys," I said, looking at them as they all looked at Marcus with that kind of expression that tells you he's more than just a "boss" to them. "I think that's enough for today, see you all in the morning."

They all nodded, and quickly filed out, each stopping to say hello to Marcus before leaving.

"I'm impressed," Marcus said, coming over to me and shaking hands after the others had left. "You got this place up and running pretty quickly; same for our little production facility that Mabel's been bothering me to build."

"This place wasn't all that hard, I've been doing repairs for almost a year now, so I know most of what I need. But don't go giving me any praise on that factory yet," I said, shaking my head. "It's going to be months before I'm satisfied with that place."

"Oh? Why so long?"

"Building's a lot harder than repairing. My teachers used to be really quick to point that out back in college and damned if I'm not learning that to be true. I just hope I can have them up and running at least a month before I leave, so they can get used to me not looking over their shoulders constantly."

"What about the techs you're training here?"

"None of them are engineers. They'll do fine with the repair work; they're already good at it. But it's more of a case of finding the problems before they can become problems, if that makes any sense to you."

Marcus nodded and smiled. "Actually, it does. As the leader of our small community, heading problems off *before* they become problems takes up a great deal of my time."

"So what brings you down here? From the amount of stuff I see going on, I know you're a busy man."

"Mostly, I just wanted to see how you and Pam were getting on. Where is she, anyway?"

I nodded toward the back of the shop. "She tends to stay in our apartment when I'm in lecture mode. She's not all that interested in engineering."

"No problems?" he asked, and I could see he was genuinely concerned.

"Nope," I said with a shake of my head. "She's actually starting to feel safer and a bit more at home. This obviously isn't a pirate base and no one here is looking to turn her into a sex slave or any of that. Plus"—I smiled—"apparently the rumor mill has let it be known just what I'll do to anyone who hurts her."

Marcus nodded. "That one's my fault. Our society is still undergoing a fair bit of chaos and, well, some of the younger men tend to go astray and do stupid things when they start to believe that there aren't any rules. That none of what they do matters anymore. So I dropped a few hints about your past and, well, Greg and Miguel backed those up with some of their own comments pretty quickly."

I nodded. "Well, come on in and sit down. I'm sure Pam wouldn't mind some company."

"You sure?" he asked, giving me a look. "I mean, I did rob your ship."

"She trusts you."

"She does?"

"Yeah, because you kept your word rather than just trying to shoot me and rape her."

"That's a pretty low bar for trust, you know," Marcus said as I led him back to our small apartment.

"Not for that situation, apparently that's about as high as the bar can go. Let me warn her first." I stuck my head in the door. "Company, Pam. Marcus is here."

"I'll be right out!" she called from the bedroom, closing the door.

"Come on in," I said and led him over to the table. "Water is about all I can offer to drink."

"Water's fine."

I got a couple of glasses, filled them from the tap, and set one down in front of him as Pam came out of the bedroom, wearing shorts and a loose shirt. I let her slide in the bench seat and gave her the other glass of water and sat down.

"Hello, Pam. I hope you're well?"

"Marcus," she said with a smile. "About as good as can be expected for the circumstances. It's a little boring, though."

"Well, if you want me to find you a job or something, let me know and I'll see what I can do."

She nodded and Marcus smiled at her again, then turned back to me.

"Getting back to business, I still want to thank you, David, for your work. You're taking this all a lot more seriously than I'd hoped and folks are starting to notice."

I shrugged, trying not to feel too embarrassed. "Well, I did give my word, and to be honest, I'm learning a lot from doing this, so I don't see it as a waste of my time or effort."

"You gave your word to open up a repair shop and fix panels for six months. Not to train our techs or help us set up a factory."

"Yeah, well, who knows? Someday I may need a place to hide out myself, and it wouldn't hurt if I was welcome to come back here."

"That's assuming that you even know where here is," Marcus said with a laugh.

"I'm sure I'll figure it out if I ever need to come back."

"Or you could, of course, decide to stay," Marcus said, giving me a serious look. "Hard working go-getters are just the kind of people we need here, David. For a lot of us, this isn't the kind of environment we grew up in. We're learning, but that takes time, and a number of us have noticed that you're not afraid to step up and do what needs to be done."

I smiled. "Thanks, but I have a few commitments yet that I need to take care of. First is that I need to get my brother off of Earth. Second is that I've promised Pam that I would see her safely out of here and back to her old job. Then, of course, I really do want to learn how to tune gravity engines for habs and spacecraft."

"Still, I'd like you to think about it. A young man like you could make something of himself in a place like this. We're not even close to finishing what we've got planned on building."

"What about your ship raiding?" Pam asked. "When does that end?"

Marcus sighed and for a moment I could see he looked troubled.

"I don't know, Pam. I honestly don't know. We've got a lot of minerals that we're mining and processing. We do hope to start trading soon, but it's hard to trade and get fair value when it's all 'no questions asked.' Or when some of the equipment you need is heavily tracked."

"Why not set up trade runs? You've got at least that one cargo ship that we saw."

"Unfortunately, the people we're hiding from know about that ship as well as most all of the rest of them. So we can't take it into any port, or they'd soon find out about us. We'd like to set up with some independents, but again, who can we trust? We're nowhere near being able to defend ourselves."

"Still, there has to be a better way."

"I'll tell you what, if you can help me find it, then I'll do it," Marcus said, looking her in the eye. "Because I really don't like what it's made me become."

I could see that had an impact on her; she looked away and nodded slowly. "I'll think about it, Marcus."

Marcus gave a small nod and turned back to me.

"So, David, just why are they after you back on Earth? I think you promised an explanation?"

I smiled at him. "Well, I don't know if I exactly promised, but the long and short of it is my mother is an elie, from a very rich and powerful family. My father is a prole. Mom ran away to 'find herself' and married my dad, had me, and then decided that she'd rather find herself back in the lap of luxury.

"Apparently her new husband has issues with my existence and wants to put an end to it and his political rivals want to get their hands on me for other reasons. I thought leaving Earth would put an end to all of that. Apparently I was wrong."

Marcus snorted. "There was once a time when I wouldn't have believed a word of that."

"Yeah, I know. I guess I'm just numb to it now. I've seen the worst that people can do to each other. I don't expect to change the universe or really anybody else anymore. I'd much rather build than tear down. Probably why I became an engineer."

"Well, you're definitely helping to build something here."

"Thanks."

We talked a little more after that, mainly Pam asking where we could find certain things, like beer, more clothes, or other luxuries that we hadn't been able to find at the one place that Mabel had taken us to.

When that was done, Marcus excused himself and took his leave.

"So, are you going to stay?" Pam asked a couple of minutes after he'd left.

"Well, there is one tempting aspect to his offer," I said, looking thoughtful.

"Oh? And what would that be?" Pam said, looking a little concerned.

"Simple," I said leering at her. "You belong to me until we leave. If I don't leave..."

"Have I told you that you're an evil bad man?" she said, playfully swatting at me with her hand.

"As a matter of fact"—I grinned—"I think you did this morning."

"Can we at least go check out some of those places he mentioned before you drag me off to the bedroom and ravish me?" Pam asked with a giggle.

"I'll think about it," I said and, grabbing her arm, I pulled her toward me. "Nah, who am I kidding? Off to the bedroom!" I laughed and, picking her up, took her to bed.

"I'll take you there during lunch tomorrow," I told her before tossing her onto the bed. "It's late, and it's time for some fun and then sleep."

THIRTEEN

A Quiet Place

COME LUNCHTIME I GOT PAM AND WE WENT TO FIND THE PLACE that Marcus had told us about. It would be nice to have some beers, I thought, though any kind of drink other than water to put in the fridge would be nice! Same for some snacks or such.

It wasn't very hard to find the area we were looking for, though it was a much farther trip than any we'd taken before, including the one from the docks to my shop. But you could easily see that the shops here definitely specialized a lot more in "recreational" items than the other place we'd been to. It was obviously an older part of the hab, suspiciously looking a *lot* older than I would have expected. That made me start to wonder just how long they'd been here.

We started to go shop to shop—there were maybe a dozen here—to see what they each had. I was all but tapped out on credits at this point, but Pam had kept a fair amount of ready cash in her things. A lesson she'd learned after she'd had to quit that Earth liner she'd been working on and found herself penniless on a strange hab.

We found a place that sold beer in gallon-sized reusable jugs, which you could bring back and get refilled, so we bought one of those. We also purchased an assortment of powdered drink mixes, as well as a pitcher to put them in to chill in the small refrigerator in our apartment.

There was, of course, another problem that this part of the hab had, which considering its age and what they sold around here, I had more or less expected.

"Hey, aren't you that tough guy from Earth?" some guy with a black crew cut and a heavy build asked, stepping out in front of me as we started to head back to the shop.

"I work for Marcus, you may have heard of him?" I said, looking through the guy, so I could pick out his friends with my peripheral vision. There was only one who looked like he was seriously paying attention, though I suspected that would change here real quickly.

"That's not what I asked you, dirtworm."

"I think the word you're looking for is 'Earthworm,'" I said and smiled. "Now, how about you step aside and let us by before there's trouble."

"Oh! There's going to be trouble, alright!" he said in a loud voice, and *that* caused a lot more people to suddenly take notice. "I've been hearing from people that you're this tough, nasty killer who can kill a dozen people with his bare hands and not even break a sweat!"

"Is there a point to this?" I asked, looking at him as Pam moved behind me.

"Yeah! I don't think you're so tough! I think you're full of it! I don't think you've killed anybody!"

"Oh? And you have, I take it?" I asked.

"Yeah! I have and I'll tell you—"

He stopped talking at that point as I'd let go of the packages I was carrying. I had my pick in my left hand and I came around with it, hard, taking him in the side of his hip, just above the hip joint and driving the pick in to the hilt, while drawing my pistol with my right hand and taking aim at his friend, who was in the process of pulling his own weapon. I shot him in the left knee.

The guy in front of me was already screaming in pain and falling as I yanked my pick out, then got him in the right bicep for good measure. The "air shot" from the weight in my pick had been injected right into the joint and I'd dislocated his hip. The wound to his bicep had completely disrupted his arm, so he wasn't able to draw his pistol as he crashed to the floor in front of me.

A quick check on his friend showed that he was holding his knee with both hands as he rolled around on the floor, pistol forgotten. A few other people looked like they might be thinking of getting involved, but as my eyes swept the crowd, the pistol pointing at the head of the guy on the ground who was gibbering and crying, they all raised their hands and backed off.

"That wasn't fair!" the guy all but whined between sobs.

"Next time, I'll kill you, got that? I'm not a kid, and this ain't a game. Just be glad you didn't put a hand on my woman or I'd be sending you *and* your friend to the morgue."

I holstered my pistol, picked up our things, and took another look around. Pam had her pistol out and was watching the crowd.

"Put that away, love. I don't think anyone else here wants any trouble," I told her.

Pam nodded, but she kept her hand on the butt of her pistol as she holstered it, coming over beside me as we headed out of the area and back toward the elevator two hallways down that'd left us here.

"Are you okay?" I asked as soon as the doors closed.

"I'm fine," Pam said, panting a little. "I can't believe how fast you moved! I've never seen a natural move like that before!"

"Natural?" I asked.

She blushed a little. "That's what we call the unadjusted. People who didn't have their genes tinkered with before they were born."

I took a deep breath and sighed.

"Pam, my bio-mom was an elie. Elites believe that they are the reason the sun rises in the morning and that God exists only because they allow the doles to believe in him. Do you really think that people like that haven't been tinkering with their own genes for the last hundred years?"

"Oh! I...I didn't know!"

"It's part of why I'm so good with a pick. I'm faster than everyone else."

"What do you think is going to happen next?"

"I'll probably get yelled at for totaling that moron and shooting his friend in the knee. But he told me flat out he was a killer and was calling me out, so I'm figuring my chances are good."

By the time we got to our room, Miguel was there waiting for us, the four techs looking at me a little nervously.

"Damn, word travels fast around here, doesn't it?" I asked Miguel as we walked in.

"Marcus wants to see you," he said, shaking his head.

"Fine, let me put the beer in the fridge, then we'll go."

"He said to bring Pam along as well."

I looked at Pam, who nodded.

"Sure."

I put the beer away, set the other stuff on the table, and then we both followed Miguel out the door.

"You know, I really have no idea where we're going," I said to him. "I've never been to—well, I assume we're going to his office?"

"It's our town hall," Miguel replied. "We have a council of elders there that Marcus leads."

"How much trouble are we in, Miguel?" Pam asked.

"You? None at all. You didn't do anything. Dave here?" He shrugged. "I guess we'll just have to see."

I found that to be just a little bit cryptic, but I had all but wasted that kid. A dislocated hip isn't a small thing. Even with modern meds he'd be off his feet for a week.

Miguel led us back toward the part of the hab we'd just come from, which I found interesting, but to a lower level. While this part was easily as old as where we'd been just a little while ago, this was much brighter, nicer, and not exactly expensive looking, but it was obviously a step above most of the hab I'd see so far.

This area also had something that I hadn't seen anywhere else: a high ceiling with wide halls. Oh, it wasn't as high as the ceilings on Ceres, but the corridor was almost as wide. I wondered if they held gatherings here. Maybe when the population was smaller? Which would mean that maybe Marcus and his friends weren't the original tenants of this place.

Miguel led us over to a very imposing set of double doors set into a rather nice archway and we went inside. Once inside, the place really did look like a city hall. There was a lot of open space with a balcony surrounding it, office doors, a receptionist, all of that. We went up a stairway that led to the balcony, down a short hallway, and then through a door that had MARCUS Diebold—Chief OF STATE written on it.

Inside was a rather imposing desk in a very large office, but Marcus wasn't sitting behind it; rather, he was sitting on its edge, one foot on the floor, listening to a man who was obviously very agitated, while Mabel, some other woman, and three more men stood around watching Marcus and this other man.

I noticed as I glanced around the room that there were a *lot* of monitors on the wall across from the desk, all of which were showing status reports for both the hab and the space in the surrounding area. I could see that we were obviously on something a lot bigger than an asteroid.

"Marcus," Miguel said, and both Marcus and the man arguing with him turned and saw me there.

The guy who had arguing with him immediately started walking toward me, looking rather angry. He was a fairly well built, but older man. Probably about as old as my dad—early forties, maybe? He had short-cut black hair and I pegged him immediately.

"How dare you attack my son!" he thundered, pointing at me as he strode closer.

I shrugged. "He threatened to kill me."

"He did no such thing!"

"Funny, I don't recall seeing you there," I said and got ready to dodge. I was sure he was going to take a swing at me, and I didn't think defending myself would go over well with this crowd.

Especially as defending myself would probably end up with him rolling and screaming on the floor like his son.

So I stood my ground and just waited, and sure enough, he took a swing and I ducked and slipped past him, turning to make sure he didn't go after Pam, or then he really would be regretting his decisions.

"Kiesler! Stop!" Marcus yelled as the man, obviously Kiesler, spun around and started to come at me again.

"Or what? He attacked my son!"

"Or I'll let him hurt you, that's what!" Marcus said. "Your son's a bully, Kiesler, and everyone knows it, and that he's been hiding behind your position for years now. Well, he picked on the wrong guy and he got hurt."

I noticed Kiesler had stopped moving closer, but I wasn't going to stop keeping an eye on him.

"He attacked my son without warning!"

"I'm not in the habit of warning people who mean me harm," I said in a soft voice. "Your son threatened me, he got his card slotted. So I tuned him up a little. Maybe he'll learn not to act like a dole."

"See! He even admits to ambushing my son!"

"No, I just didn't warn him that I was going to take him down when he threatened me," I said, backing away slowly.

"He didn't threaten you!" Kiesler said, moving forward to keep the same distance.

"How would you know?" I asked, holding my hands out to the sides, taking another step. "You weren't there."

"Because he told me!"

"Well, that'd make him a liar then, wouldn't it?"

Sure enough, Kiesler came at me again, only this time he tripped over my leg as I dodged, just a little too slowly, out of the way, and he face-planted right into that nice big desk of Marcus's. I didn't even have to help him along—well, not all that much. It's really all in the way you sweep the leg.

"Ooh! That had to hurt," I said, moving back away from him as quickly as I could.

Marcus gave me a look, but I just shrugged. I noticed that Mabel and the other woman were smirking. Of the three men, one looked disgusted and the other two were obviously trying not to laugh. Kiesler was obviously not a well-liked man.

"What happened, David?" Marcus asked as Kiesler gathered his wits, and discovered that his nose was now bleeding rather freely.

I shrugged. "His son confronted me, told me I didn't look that tough, refused to get out of my way so Pam and I could leave. Then he told me he had actually killed. So I took him and his backup down, and left. Not like I killed anybody."

"Backup?" Mabel asked.

"Yeah, he had a guy back hiding in a doorway ready to shoot me if he lost. Well, he lost and I kneecapped the other guy before he could start shooting into the crowd."

"You know, that's twice he attacked a man who offered him no threat," the other woman said, nodding at Kiesler, who had pulled out a cloth of some sort and was getting his bleeding nose under control.

"And I'm sick and tired of him covering up for his bully of a son," said the man who had looked disgusted a moment before. "I say we put his son on punishment detail for a couple of years and maybe let his father there join him for a few months."

"Then who's going to run the incinerator for you? The break-down tanks?" Kiesler said, looking up from the floor, an almost feral snarl on his face. "You put me in punishment and just who are you going to leave in charge? I'm the only guy who knows how that stuff works! Without me, it'll all back up, or *worse*."

"Yes," Marcus said, "you are, aren't you? Ten years now, Kiesler, *ten years*, and yet, no one on your crew really seems to know what to do. Why is that?"

I noticed the look on Marcus's face as he said that. I'd seen that look before, back in the Howlers, when Big Jim, our local quad top man got into it with Kauf, the guy who ran all the quads in our city. It hadn't ended well for Jim. He'd pushed too hard, too long. Kauf had laid a trap, and Big Jim had just strolled right into it.

Marcus had that same look on his face that Kauf had had, just before he moved in for the kill.

"You're not putting my son in punishment either! Understand? He gets out too, or I swear to you, I'll shut it down! I'll shut it *all* down! Then what'll you do? We've got almost a hundred thousand people here now, Marcus! You gonna let them all suffer, get sick, die? Over what? Some Earther scum?"

"We need David here to train us how to deal with our gravity panels; he's actually doing exactly what he promised to do. Unlike, say, *you*." Marcus said, looking down at Kiesler, who was smiling rather nastily up at him, still thinking he had the upper hand.

"You've promised *time* and *time* again to train up your techs, so they can run our hazardous waste processing facilities—without your oversight I might add—for years now. Yet, each year, no one seems to understand how it all works, and oddly enough, whenever someone does, they always seem to have an 'accident.' A *fatal* accident. *Why* is that, Kiesler?"

"Maybe some people are just too smart for their own good!" Kiesler said with an ugly laugh. "All I know is, you need me, and without me, this place will go to pieces."

"Yes, well, as much as I'd rather not have to do it, I guess we'll just have to hire a replacement. I'm sure we could have someone here in a few weeks, maybe a month."

Kiesler snorted. "I got a couple thousand gallons of volatile toxic waste down in the plant. Just what do you think is going to happen if I'm not there to deal with it come tomorrow? Just how big of an explosion do you think that will be? What'll you do then, 'Chief of State'? How many people will you be able to save this time?"

"Miguel, if you would, please?"

Miguel quickly walked over to Kiesler, smacked him across the face with a sap that I only just then noticed, then quickly rolled him facedown, cuffed him, and emptied out his pockets.

Two uniformed men came in, grabbed a groaning Kiesler by his arms, and hoisted him to his feet.

"For your continued crimes against the well-being of the community, and no doubt for the deaths of several workers under your care, I'm putting you off the station, Kiesler," Marcus said. "You and your son both."

Kiesler spit out a mouthful of blood, hitting the front of Marcus's shirt. "You can't do that! You'll die without me!"

"Actually, no," Marcus said with a smile so cheerful that I started to look for the knife. "It seems we have a highly trained hazardous waste engineer in residence here on the hab. As a matter of fact, she even told me just the other day that she was bored and was looking for a job. Isn't that right, Pam?"

I turned and looked at Pam, and I noticed that Mabel and the other woman were smiling as well. Pam herself was looking a little embarrassed.

"But I'm only going to be here until Dave's done and we leave!" she protested.

"HER?" Kiesler screamed. "HER? That ADONIS *bitch*?"

I almost stepped forward and punched him in the face, but Miguel beat me to it, then he pulled out a piece of duct tape and slapped it over his mouth.

"Yes, Kiesler, her. Apparently the people of Adonis happen to like making their children work in all sorts of dirty jobs while they're growing up. And Miss Wells there actually comes highly recommended. But then her mother is the chief reclamation engineer for one of their habs, so"—Marcus smiled again—"I guess there won't be any explosions tonight. So, when the pressure starts to drop, you can feel secure in the knowledge that we're all going to be safe and sound, inside here.

"Take him away," Marcus said to the two guards, who dragged a now violently thrashing Kiesler out of the room. He then turned back to Pam.

"Pam, I'm sorry, I wish I didn't have to do this, but unfortunately, events have forced my hand. I know you're not planning on staying here, but we really need your help and you can name your own price. The only thing I'll ask of you is that you help us find your replacement, and start teaching some of the better workers here just how to do your job."

I looked at Pam and she looked back at me.

"You're rated for waste processing?" I asked her with a silly grin.

"Umm, can we talk about this later, Dave?" she said, looking a little uncomfortable.

"Sure," I nodded.

She gave me a shy smile and looked back at Marcus. "I'll help. You don't have to pay me or anything. But I want someone like Miguel here with me, when Dave's working."

"Of course! Mabel, Joan, would you be so kind as to show Pam where she'll be working?"

"I'll be happy to!" Mabel said.

"And you can pay her what that Kiesler bastard was getting," Joan, the other woman, said.

I went over and gave Pam a hug. "Will you be okay without me? I need to talk to Marcus a minute, and then I need to go deal with the factory."

Pam nodded. "I'll be fine."

"Miguel?" I said, turning to him. "If you would be so kind?"

Miguel looked at Marcus, who nodded and then smiled back at me. "I'll keep her safe, Dave—because I know my life depends on it!" he added with a laugh.

I gave Pam a kiss and a pat on the ass and watched as everyone filed out of the room, with the last one out closing the door behind them, leaving just me and Marcus.

"That was one hell of a setup, Marcus," I said, turning to look at him. "Hell, I'm not even mad."

Marcus sighed and gave me an innocent smile. "I have no idea what you're talking about, David."

I shook my head and laughed. "Please, don't go pretending you're innocent. You got someone to drop rumors to his kid, so he'd come after me, knowing full well what I'd do to him. Hell, I'm sure you even knew he was going to attack me, given that you had two officers waiting just outside your door."

I almost laughed again, as Marcus looked a little embarrassed. "That bit with the desk, how'd you get him to do that, anyway?"

"It's all in the leg," I said, grinning. "When I tripped him over it, I actually kicked him in the back of the other foot, just enough to make him stumble. How'd you find out about Pam?"

"I ran both of your backgrounds after you came here. I needed to be sure that you weren't some special deep-cover agent being sent by our enemies. I suspect your stepfather has figured out you're alive now, by the way. As for Pam?" He shook his head. "When I found out about it, I started thinking. We actually have been working on a replacement for Kiesler for a while now. But we're pretty sure he killed the last guy we brought in; his son just *happened* to get in a fight with him and killed him *accidentally*."

"Why not wait until your new replacement showed up, then?"

"Because he won't be here for months, and we need somebody who *really* knows how these systems work. Pam's an expert. Hell, I don't even know why she's flying ships and not home working with her mom. She had a pretty important job there."

I blinked as it clicked.

"I know," I said with a sigh.

"Oh? What happened?"

"Not my place to say and I would strongly suggest you don't ask about it either."

"Or?" Marcus asked, frowning.

"Or you'll feel like a complete heel," I said with a sigh. I shook my head and thought about what'd just transpired. "So why'd you leave Venus?"

"Are you sure you want to know?"

"You just hijacked my woman to fix your problem—not that I blame you—but, yeah, I think now I need to know."

"About twenty years ago, we had a new leader rise to power, very charismatic, had a way about him. He also had a lot of people with a lot of money and power backing him. His bio claimed that he was of humble beginnings and all the usual, when actually he was about as 'elie' as your mom.

"Anyway, he ended up in control of one of the larger groups of city-states that the cloud cities on Venus are arranged in. It didn't take him long to start taking his message to the other city-states and the people believed in him so strongly. It became like a religion."

"And you dissented," I said.

"Oh, quite a few people dissented. And they usually died. And in one case an entire city lost its flotation and twenty-million people ended up in a sea of boiling acid. So we moved our city away from theirs, but they pursued us. They were the pure and the chosen. They knew the truth and if you didn't agree with them, well, then you were evil. Bad. You had to be punished and shown the error of your ways."

"And they're still following you?" I said, surprised.

"Of course! We have to be shown the error of our ways! We have to be silenced! We must be stopped! There were millions of us, David, *millions*! Hundreds of thousands have died. They followed us from place to place, until we found this one, this home.

"Now, we're building it up as fast as we can, to bring our scattered survivors back together, to give us all a safe place to stay. Why do you think I want you here with us? You know what it's like. Your own family won't let you go; they'd rather see you dead. Yet you still fight on, you're still determined to live your life on your terms, not theirs."

"Wow," I said and I had to admit, I felt it. They were living large what I was living in a microcosm. "I . . . I don't know if I can stay, Marcus. I told you before, I have things I need to do. But maybe I'll be back. You've definitely given me a lot to think about, and now I know why Mabel's got such grand plans for this rock."

"How'd you figure out where we were from?"

"Oh, that was easy. None of you really understand grav panels, and the only places that really have Earth-like gravity are Earth and Venus. Well, that plus a few off-hand comments."

Marcus nodded. "My apologies for using you like that, David. But, well, it had to be done."

I nodded. "Yeah, it did. That guy was a piece of work. You really gonna kill him and his kid?"

Marcus sighed and gave a nod. "If I don't, their particular brand of cancer will spread. Plus they know where we are, and I can't afford to have them telling our enemies just where to find us."

I nodded. "Better you than me, I guess. You might want to talk to the one I kneecapped and make sure you get all of his friends back on the path."

"Way ahead of you there," Marcus replied.

"Well, I need to get to back to work. Next time you come over, you can bring the beer."

Marcus smiled at that and, giving him a wave, I headed off to deal with the folks at our little factory for the rest of the day.

✦ ✦ ✦

Pam didn't come home until several hours after dinner. Someone had let me know she was going to be late, so I wouldn't worry.

"So, how bad was it?" I asked her as she came in to our apartment and literally collapsed into my arms.

"Bad. He was intentionally running everything on the edge of capacity, so if he was gone for more than a day, the system would start breaking down and sounding alarms. He also kept the maintenance on the edge, so all of his people were always too busy fixing things to figure out how it all actually worked."

She shook her head. "I told Marcus that if he didn't kill that bastard, I would!"

That took me back a little. "Who are you and what happened to my little sex slave?"

She blushed then and put her arms around me. "I'm sorry, but what he was doing wasn't just criminal, it was dangerous. He was blackmailing the people in charge by holding everyone here hostage. The systems they use here aren't like the ones they used on their home planet. And, well, after they got it up and running the other three engineers who helped build it all died in accidents, and suddenly he was the only one who knew how to deal with it."

"Somehow I'm not surprised," I said and, pulling her up, I gave her a kiss. "If you don't want to tell me why you're working as a mate instead of..." I gave her another kiss. "That's okay."

She closed her eyes and sighed. "I was deadheading on the ship; the first mate was my fiancé. I was taking a vacation with him, when we were attacked. After they killed him..." She stopped and took a couple of deep breaths. "I couldn't go back home. I couldn't go back and face everyone. That life, the life I'd...*we'd* planned, I couldn't live it anymore. I had the basic mate's certification, that was how we'd first met. So I just got a berth and decided I wasn't going back."

She started to cry then, and I held her close until she settled down. Then I undressed her, carried her to bed, and just comforted her until she fell asleep.

Captain Roy had been telling the truth when he'd said that for the crew of the *Iowa Hill*, that job was pretty much the end of the line for most of them. Hank and Chaz were possibly the only two there who were normal, and I wasn't all that sure about Hank.

FOURTEEN

Acceptance

THINGS CHANGED AFTER THAT. BECAUSE SUDDENLY WE WEREN'T just some part-time interlopers who nobody was sure they could trust. No, we were members of the community, *important* members. Word about what Kiesler was, and what he'd been doing, made the rounds pretty quickly. That or there'd always been a fair amount of suspicion about him. Pam's job was an important job, a key one, one that gave her a voice in the community. Not that she seemed to want to use it.

Because I was "her man" and was rather protective of her, everyone quickly found out about what I was doing for Mabel with her factory and the training I was giving to the repair techs. Which everyone appreciated, especially as I wasn't getting paid for any of it, yet I'd still gone above and beyond what I'd promised to do.

It was nice, to be honest. Though for the first month, as Pam got the recycling systems under control, she had to work a lot of very long hours. I often ended up straddling her butt and giving her a back and neck massage because she'd come home so completely stressed. While my job still had a lot of rough edges and even a few rough people, I was used to living in a stressful environment. So I figured she needed the attention and the pampering a lot more than I did.

But the more she got that place under control and straightened out, the happier she was.

"It feels good to be doing something important again," she confided in me one night.

"Does this mean you're going to go back home when we get out of here?"

She gave a small shake of her head. "I don't know. I'm sure they've replaced me by now. It's been a couple of years since I left. Plus they'd never let anything get as bad as it was here. We've been invited to dinner tomorrow."

"We? Or just you?" I teased.

Pam grinned and kissed me. "We. They all know I'm your woman and you 'don't share,'" she said with a giggle. "It's nice. Nobody hits on me, because they figure if you don't set them straight, Marcus will."

"Marcus?"

"You did tell him, more than once if I recall, that no one was allowed to touch me or there'd be hell to pay. The last thing he wants is to have anything happen that interrupts your work."

"I'd think what you were doing was a lot more important, Pam."

She shrugged. "Not so much anymore. Now that everything isn't being stressed to the limits and is working like it *should*, the job's a lot easier to do. In another month, unless there's some sort of major system failure, I think they'll all be able to deal with running the place without my constantly having to look over their shoulder. I got Marcus to send someone out to buy up all the training aids that that bastard deleted to keep everyone else in the dark.

"I'll have that department running like a Martian Navy ship in no time!"

"They run that good, do they?"

Pam chuckled. "They're the only real reliable military force out there. Earth barely has enough ships to protect everything in lunar orbit. Saturn and Jupiter have so many small factions that they barely agree on anything, so neither of them have any sort of a unified government, much less a military or even a police force. That's why there's so many pirates out beyond the asteroids."

"But Mars takes care of everything closer in?"

She gave a slight nod. "Yeah, they do, and a *lot* of habs and orbitals are not only very welcoming of any Mars Navy ship that might come by to visit, but they're willing to help shoulder the cost of having them come by and patrol. Earth may *think* they're the power in the solar system, but Mars *is* the real power."

"I wonder if the people running Earth know that?" I asked with a chuckle.

"Who knows? I mean you grew up there, do they really seem to care about what's going on in the rest of the system?"

I thought about that a moment and had to shake my head. "You know, probably not. People tend to think that the folks out here are pretty unsophisticated and not all that bright. Which is pretty funny when you consider most of the doles are as dumb as bricks. The only time you even hear the talking heads on the holo go on about anything not on Earth is when either a lot of people died, or some Earther elie 'discovers' something or 'saves those poor off-worlders' from some terrible fate.

"But the truth is, I'm pretty sure nobody cares about what happens out here. It's not Earth, so it's not important. I only know about some of the disasters that happened because they were engineering mistakes and we were taught about them in college. But take what happened to these people—I don't think it even made the news."

"So you figured it out?"

"Some of it, but Marcus confessed the worst of it to me, and gave me an idea of just how many they lost."

Pam nodded. "People avoid Venus now. Maybe when their leader dies, they'll start to be more rational."

"Well, whatever their problem is, I hope they just keep it to themselves."

"They killed off something like a quarter of their population. I don't think they're going to be bothering anybody for a long time."

"Well, Marcus sure does."

"That's because he's a 'heretic' and I wouldn't put it past the idiots running things to build a couple of ships solely to come out here and 'punish' them. There have been other incidents where they've gone after refugees on some of the habs and orbitals out there, which of course has made it hard for those refugees to find a place to stay."

"Huh, I didn't know that."

"Those who know don't like to talk about it much."

"Whistling while walking past the crazy man, huh?"

"That's as good a description as any."

I nodded.

"Well, dinner tomorrow night would be nice. I'll make sure I've got everything wrapped up early."

"Thanks, Dave."

When our six months were finally up, there were a lot of people who most definitely did not want us to go.

"You sure you don't want to stay?" Mabel asked me the night before we were due to leave.

"Sorry, but I have things I need to do yet," I told her with a smile. "Maybe after you get those big parks set up in those chambers you're mining out I'll come back."

"Seeing as you have no idea where we are, that'd be a trick."

"Well then, drop me a line a few years from now, you've got my email, and maybe we'll talk."

"I just may do that!" She gave me a hug then. "You're a good kid, Dave, and just between you and me"—she lowered her voice—"I think your whole 'deadly hit man act' was just that, an act. Not saying you're an innocent, not by far, but you're no devil either."

I smiled at her. "Thanks, Mabel. And keep an eye on the folks building those panels. Drag Josh and the others down there in a couple of days and do a 'surprise' inspection. Wouldn't want them slacking off."

"Sure thing!"

They threw a going away party for us later that evening, and when we got back to our apartment Pam and I were both a little frantic.

"After this, you won't own me anymore," Pam teased, smiling.

"We'll be on ship a few days, so you're not off the leash yet," I teased her back.

"Are you going to go back to work for Damascus Freight? Or are you going to go look up that girlfriend of yours on Ceres?"

I sighed and rolled onto my back, pulling her against me as I did.

"Honestly? I haven't a clue. Probably both. I just never thought ahead to this moment."

"Really? Why not?"

"I wasn't all that sure that they'd let us go."

"Marcus keeps his word; I thought you'd realized that."

"Oh, I have. But we're dealing with a lot more than Marcus here. Though I can think of worse places to be stranded."

"Thinking of staying, are we?"

I laughed. "Thinking of coming back, if I can't resolve my family problems and get them to stop trying to kill me. You?"

"Oh, I've thought about it, more than once. But I did promise to stay with my man until he got me out of here," she said and gave me a hug.

"Thanks, Pam. I'm just glad I was able to do right by you."

The trip back was in two stages. The first was in the frigate we'd come out in, and we were pretty much confined to quarters same as before. We also ended up doing the same as before. Somewhere along the way I started to realize that Pam was saying goodbye. I guess she figured I'd made up my mind and was going to go back to Kacey, and maybe I was.

But leaving Pam was not going to be easy for me to do.

After five days under drive, we met up with another ship, a very small cargo ship, one a lot smaller than the *Iowa Hill*. As we transferred off the frigate and onto it, I noticed a large number of people leaving the cargo ship for the frigate, along with a fair amount of gear of some sort or another.

It was another day's worth of flight before we made port, then; we were at a small hab.

"Where are we?" I asked the captain as I gathered my things and made for the exit with Pam in tow.

"The Jupiter Trojans, one of the smaller habs. You shouldn't have any problems getting a flight from here to the main transfer station."

"Actually, I'm broke," I said with a sigh.

He handed me an envelope. "There's a thousand credits inside. Marcus said he didn't want you left high and dry. Said you earned it."

"Thanks," I said and stuck it in one of the pockets of my shipsuit.

We transited the tube and once off the ship, I set my things down and turned to help Pam.

Who wasn't carrying her things anymore and was giving me a sad smile.

"Dave?"

"Yes?"

"I want to thank you for everything. You kept your word to me, and I kept my word to you. We're here, we're safe, you protected me. But I'm also not your woman anymore, okay?"

I closed my eyes and took a deep breath. How did I not see this coming? Or maybe more to the point, I knew this was coming, had done everything I could to pretend it wasn't, but still, why was it bothering me? If anyone had ever mastered the "cat's goodbye," it was me.

I opened my eyes and nodded. "Yes, it's okay." I smiled a little ruefully then. "You get to make your own choices now, not that I don't think you haven't been already."

She grinned at me then and it hit me.

"You're going back, aren't you?"

"Yes. I am. But I wanted to stand here, free, next to you, so you'd realize that it was my choice. That no one was forcing me."

"Who is he?" I frowned.

She laughed and wagged a finger at me. "I never cheated on you, Dave. Not once."

"But there is somebody, right?"

She nodded. "Yes, there's somebody. We became good friends, while I was working on the recycling plant. We were always respectful of our situation; after all, neither you nor I were really free. But now I am, and now I'm going back to him, because I think I have finally found my place and someone who can replace Wyatt in my heart."

"You never told me his name before," I said, a little surprised.

"You never asked," she said with a sigh and a sad smile. "I do care about you, Dave, and I think I even love you a little. You were there for me, and you helped me in ways that I don't think you really understand. But we're not for each other. It was fun, and even a little kinky"—she winked at me and grinned—"but we're still strangers to each other, when you get right down to it."

It hit me like a bolt between the eyes. She was right. I knew more about Kacey, who I'd barely spent a week with, than I did Pam, whom I'd been sleeping with and living with for six months. We'd never talked about our pasts, and rarely talked about our futures. We'd just talked about our current problems, when we talked at all. We'd been there for each other when we needed it, but neither one of us had really opened up about our pasts or who we really were.

Mostly, we'd just had sex.

I sighed. "I feel like a heel."

Pam grinned. "Don't. You *know* I enjoyed everything we did; you're good people, Dave. Don't be so hard on yourself. But we're not just meant to be."

"So who is it? Anyone I know?"

"Marcus."

"*Marcus?*" I said, surprised. "He's old enough to—"

She put her finger on my lips, stopping me. "He lost his wife, just like I lost my Wyatt. He's had a hard time of it, and he's had to do it alone. He helped me face my fears almost as much as you did, David, and somewhere in there, we *did* connect. So I'm going back to him and we're going to make a go of it."

I nodded. "Good luck, Pam. I'll miss you, but you're right. I wish you two the best." I stepped over and hugged her and she kissed me goodbye.

Then she turned and got back on the ship. I picked up my things and started heading for the station center. I was numb. I felt like a complete idiot. All that time, Marcus had been putting the moves on Pam and I hadn't even noticed it!

Maybe if I *had* spent more time asking about her past, asking about her, getting to know the real her, things might have turned out differently.

I shook my head and tried to console my totally deflated ego. At least I was now saved the pain of having to choose between her or Kacey.

And *that* made me feel like a heel all over again. Kacey. Yeah, if she'd decided I was dead and moved on with her life, it wouldn't be anything less than I deserved after everything I'd done with Pam.

I shook my head. If I was going to be serious about Kacey, then I needed to start being serious about Kacey. Whether she was there or not.

Between Planets

I WAS ABLE TO GET A LIFT FROM THE HAB TO THE MAIN TRANS-
fer station in the area after only a half day of waiting around. The
transfer station here wasn't terribly large for all that there were
a lot of asteroids with habs in the Jupiter Trojans. There were a
surprising number of ships coming and going from it, though
most of them were small cargo ships that really didn't haul a lot.

Finding out where they were going next was pretty much
impossible. The only two destinations I could reliably make from
here was either Gany-Two, which I'd been to before, or I could
wait a week and possibly get a ride to Ceres.

I opted for the ride to Ceres, because Kacey was there, and
Damascus Freight Lines had contracts with Ceres, so it was most
likely the best place to hook back up with them. Assuming, of
course, I still had a job.

I was able to connect with my bank account, because my
bank did have a small branch there. Though getting my account
activated there so I could *use* it took two days. I sent Kacey an
email, letting her know that I was still alive, I was going to try
and get space on the next ship to Ceres that put in here, and I
would love to see her again, if that was possible.

I know I was worried she might have found someone else. I

was sure everyone thought I was dead, or worse. I also sent my brother a short message letting him know I was still alive and would hopefully be on Ceres in a few weeks.

I thought about contacting Damascus Freight Lines, but these messages weren't cheap. I also noticed I hadn't been paid in five months. But after my second day of sitting around by myself and being bored to tears, I decided to spend the money and I sent them an email letting them know that I'd been let go, I wasn't dead, I'd like to come back to work, I was trying to make my way to Ceres, and oh, I have the *Iowa Hill*'s orbital information so they can salvage it.

Five very boring days later, I was contacted at the small auto-bed hotel, which was about all I could afford, that there was a ship in port from Ceres and they had a berth. So I gathered up my duffel and my pressure suit and quickly made my way down to the docking bay.

When I got there, I pressed the button by the docking hatch. "Yes?"

"Engineer third, Dave Walker. You said you've got space for a deadhead to Ceres?"

"Two hundred creds to cover food and air."

"That's fair. I've got the creds on me."

"Come aboard. I'll meet you just inside the airlock."

I opened the door, grabbed my stuff, went down the docking tube, and then went onboard.

"Welcome aboard the *Star Treader*," an older man in a shipsuit with the ship's name on it said and stuck out his hand. "I'm Bill Ryan, the exec. Captain's supervising the loading."

I shook hand with him and then got out my much smaller stack of credits, counted off two hundred, and gave them to him.

"Dave Walker, as I said. Do you need to see my engineer's cert?"

"Nah, that's okay. The station sent it over with your request for a ride back to Ceres. How'd you end up stranded out here?"

"Me and the girlfriend decided it was time to call it quits and well..." I shrugged. "The captain liked her more."

"Ah...I see," he said, shaking his head. "Well. We'll be pulling out in twenty hours. Let me show you to your bunk. Hope you don't mind the general crew quarters?"

"That's fine by me. What's the transit time to Ceres from here, anyway?"

"Five days. Ceres is actually fairly close to the Trojans right now."

"Great, it'll be nice to be back," I said and followed him into the engineering berths. He showed me the bunk room, which had six racks in it, but only one looked like it was being used.

"We have a pretty small crew onboard: two engineers, one deckhand, the captain, and myself. If you know how to cook, you can run the galley for us and I'll give you half your money back when we arrive."

"Beats sitting down here doing nothing all day," I said, and stowed my duffel on one of the open racks along with my pressure suit.

"Great, I'll show you to the galley."

By the time we'd gotten underway I'd figured out where everything was and wrote out a simple menu for the meals for the next five days, which I sent to the captain and the exec for their feedback. It's not like I was going to be doing any fancy cooking—most of the meals were prepackaged. They just needed someone to prepare them and serve them. But I'd learned from Shelly, the cook on the *Iowa Hill*, that a few small changes could make a world of difference, and they did have a bunch of spices in one of the cabinets.

"So, you're the guy deadheading back to Ceres?" the one deckhand asked me the next day when I was cleaning up after dinner. So far, nobody had complained, but with a crew this small, nobody spent much time in the small mess either, taking their food back to their watch station or cabin.

"I'm Dave," I told him and nodded as I scrubbed down one of the pans I'd used.

"Chet," he said and nodded back. "Bill tells me you got dumped when the captain took a liking to your girl?"

I shook my head and chuckled. "More like she decided it was time for us to go our separate ways. Captain would probably have kept me, but well…" I shrugged. "Time to move on."

"So what were you doing out here?"

I shrugged. "Beats me. I was just one of the engineers. Mainly I mind what goes on in Engineering and don't involve myself in cargoes and the rest of that. Why?"

"Eh, just wondering. A lot of black and gray market stuff runs through the Jupiter Trojans. Rumors are that some of the pirates even trade there."

I laughed. "You all don't really strike me as the pirating type."

Chet laughed as well. "No, we're not. But we do haul a fair bit of gray market stuff around from time to time. Captain has some good contacts with a number of companies on Ceres and we get all sorts of rebuilds on the cheap and then come out here to sell it at a pretty nice mark up."

I thought about that a moment.

"So all the dark habs can go there and get their parts without being traced?"

"Exactamundo," Chet said with a grin.

"Damn, that's smart. Coming from Ceres, the stuff you're getting is probably better than anyone else's too. Still, you'd think the Marsies or one of the other militaries would be hanging around a place like that."

"Way I hear it, they come shopping there too, to support their own little secret projects that they don't want anyone to know about."

"Huh, all I know is that it's expensive to stay there, and pretty boring," I said with a shrug. "I didn't see any bars, no hookers, nothing. Just dullsville."

"Where you from, anyway?"

"Earth."

"Earth? Then why are you going back to Ceres? Hell, why're you all the way out here?"

"Eh, long story. But I'm a lot more likely to find another berth on Ceres than where we just left. What's your story?" I asked and hoped this guy would take a hint.

"Oh, I used to work deckhand on an ore boat. But this job's a lot better. Good pay, we only run out once every other month, and they're all fast trips. So I get a lot of downtime."

"What's it like working the ore boats?" I asked, then listened as he talked about it. I found his account to be a fair bit different from what Chaz had told me. Then again, Chaz really hadn't wanted much to do with working on the local ore haulers.

"So, what was your girl like?" he asked, coming back to me after a couple of minutes.

"She was nice," I said and left it at that.

"What'd she look like?"

"Eh, rather not dwell on it." I said and, finishing up, I put the last tray away and cleaned my hands off. "Well, I'm gonna go crash for a while. I need to get up early to put together breakfast for you guys. Nice talking to ya, Chet!" I said and shook hands with him, then left him staring at my back as I went down to my bunk. Back home I would have pegged him as an informant or something. But on a ship with a crew of five, that idea was just ridiculous.

When we pulled into the dock I had my tablet out and sent Kacey a note letting her know that I was here, now that the ship's systems were linked to the local network on Ceres.

What ship? came an almost immediate response.

The Star Treader. Does this mean you still want to see me?

Yes, ya goof. I'll come down and meet you at the dock. Wait for me.

Thanks, hon. It's been one hell of a ride. I'll be waiting.

"Chatting with someone?" Bill, the first mate and executive officer, asked, coming up to me as I sat on the end of my rack.

"Yeah, close friend. What's up?"

"Well, here's your hundred credits back. Thanks for helping out with the galley."

I smiled, took the credits, and stuffed them into one of my pockets.

"You're welcome. I just hope I can find a job or another berth before the money runs out."

"Well, the ship's docked, we've settled up our business, and I've got other things to attend to."

"Right!" I smiled and got up and shook hands. "I'll get off your ship so you can get back to work. Thanks for the ride."

Grabbing my duffel and my suit, I made my way off the ship, and out through the docking tunnel.

Where I was met by a half dozen of Ceres's finest. Several of whom were pointing shockers at me.

"Please put your hands up!"

I dropped my stuff and did as they asked. I recognized Jeff, Kacey and Chaz's older brother.

"Hi, Jeff. Does this mean Kacey's not coming?"

"This is serious, Dave," Jeff warned.

"Yeah, I got that. Trust me. My pistol's in a holster just inside my shipsuit and my pick is in my left hip pocket. Do you want me to set them on the floor? Or would you rather get them off me?"

"Turn around, put your hands on your head."

"Got it," I said and did as I was told. Jeff came up and grabbed each of my hands one at a time and cuffed them behind my back. Then he carefully divested me of the pistol and then my pick.

"What else you got?"

"My tablet, some credits, pocketknife, penlight, ID, and I think that's about it."

He relieved me of the pocketknife and then led me away from the hatch.

"Could you have someone pick up my stuff, please? That's all I got left."

"Jeff! What the hell is going on here!" I heard Kacey say as she came striding down the docking arm hall.

"He's under arrest."

"Duh, I can see that. Now why?"

"Suspicion of piracy."

I frowned and turned my head to look at him. "Huh?"

"How in the hell did you come up with that?" Kacey yelled at him.

"I didn't, the folks up in headquarters did. They asked me to come down here because I know him."

"Of all the stupid, vacuum-brained, dust-snorting..." I listened as she ran through a list of insults, curses, and other put downs as the other enforcers all tried not to smile and Jeff just sighed.

"You done, sis?"

"I'm just getting started!"

"Kacey? Hon?" I asked.

"Yes?" she asked, looking at me.

"Could you get me a lawyer please? Assuming I'm entitled to one?" I asked, looking at Jeff again, who nodded.

"What do you need a lawyer for?"

"Because I have absolutely no idea what's going on, that's why. Plus, after spending six months as a prisoner, I'd *really* rather not end up in any kind of jail again."

"Okay, I'll have one waiting at..." She looked at Jeff. "Where are you taking him?"

"Level one processing. I'll tell Judge Pimm that you'll be sending a lawyer over."

"Fine." She looked at me. "I'd hug you, but that'd probably get me in trouble with Jeff."

"Thanks, Kacey."

"Let's go," Jeff said and started marching me down the hall-way as Kacey got out her tablet and started to call somebody.

"Don't forget my stuff!" I said.

"We won't. So just where've you been?"

"No idea, they didn't tell me. Any idea what's going on?"

"Not really. I know your ship got hit; Chaz and the rest of the crew came back here. The first mate—Parks, is it? He was positive you were dead and that they were raping the second mate to death."

I sighed. "If that asshole had waited a few more minutes, or came and helped me, we would have all gotten off together."

"So what happened?"

"What happened is we got lucky and the pirates who took the ship were more interested in making money than in living up to a bad reputation. So I made a deal."

"Oh, what kind?"

"The kind that had me slaving away for six months."

"Huh, I'm surprised they lived up to it."

"Me too."

Ten minutes later, they got me to the local courthouse and I got the usual treatment as far as fingerprints, retina photos, mug shots, and the rest. When they were finished I was shown to a room with a gray-haired woman in it.

"Ma'am?" I asked as they undid the cuffs.

"I'm your lawyer, Cheryl Pimm."

"Ah!" I said and smiled and shook hands. "And relation to the judge?"

She smiled. "He's my husband. Now, have a seat."

I did as she instructed.

"Tell me what happened."

I nodded and did just that. Though I didn't give her any descriptions of my "assailants," I just left them all in their hel-mets. I also didn't tell her anything beyond my threats and offer, their acceptance, and how I'd spent the last six months repairing panels and training their four techs.

"What happened to the other woman, Pam Wells?"

"She left with me. But when we got off the ship she decided she'd had enough sailing and was going home."

"Why'd she do that?"

"Because she'd been caught by pirates before. That's why she freaked out. She's an Adonis. She found a ship going her way and left. I wanted to come back here, so I had to wait."

"People are going to find it hard to believe that they just let you go."

"Cheryl, I spent a good many years of my teenaged life in a street gang on Earth. A violent street gang. I gave them my word that I would fix their stuff, train their people, and not hurt any of them if they took me and Pam with them, and let us go after six months."

"And they bought that? Why?"

"Because I was standing close enough to them that I could have killed their leader and maybe all of his bodyguards, and he suddenly realized that I had a dangerous weapon in my hand, that I knew how to use it, and that I'd keep my word."

"And you trusted him, why?"

"Because when a gang leader gives his word in front of his men, he has to keep it. Or he'll lose trust. Being a criminal in a gang involves a lot of face and a lot of trust. I spoke to him on a level he understood, because I know the lingo.

"Besides"—I shrugged—"I'm a certified grav panel repair tech and we don't grow on trees. He got his money's worth out of me."

"Why didn't you just stay with the ship? You told me they were going to let you."

"Because if the rest of my crew thought we were dead, would anyone even bother coming out?"

"Good call. I looked up your ship. They didn't send anyone out, it was too far away and you're right, they figured you were both dead."

"Great, so now what?"

"Now you tell the judge what you told me. The fact that they didn't send anyone out to your ship means you made the right choice. Though I suspect there's going to be some suspicion as to why they let you go."

"Umm, well, to be honest, I think they were afraid of me, just a little bit."

Cheryl looked at me with a frown. "And just why would that be?"

"Have you ever seen that Earther crime drama? The one with the assassin who used a pick to kill people?"

"*The Iceman Chronicles*? What does that have to do with anything?"

"Well, I've been trained to use a pick, had one in my hand, in fact, and they'd all seen the series. They thought I was a deadly Earther assassin and I wasn't about to disabuse them of the notion."

She started laughing so loud then that the guard actually came and checked on us.

"Really?" she said, looking at me and still giggling.

I nodded. "They even asked me about the show. I guess they were all big fans."

"Well, it *was* popular. Now, let's go see the judge."

She left, then a bailiff came in and they handcuffed me again, and ten minutes later I was standing before the judge as the charges were read.

There was some discussion back and forth, between Cheryl and the prosecutor, mainly over the lack of evidence. I don't know what the rules for evidence were out here, but I was gathering that just being associated with pirates was a pretty serious crime. The prosecutor also let drop that they had testimony from a government agent that I had shown up at a known location where pirates traded and offered a rather flimsy story, which was completely at odds with the truth.

That made me wonder as Cheryl then told the judge my story, with a few minor details left out. Surprisingly, she left Pam completely out. When the prosecutor asked why the pirates had been willing to deal with me, she took my pick off the evidence table and then told them the part about the holo show. A number of people in the courtroom snickered when she finished. Even the judge—her husband—smiled.

"Okay, but assuming that's true," the prosecutor said, "then why did he tell the crew of the ship that brought him here that he'd lost his berth because his girlfriend had dumped him for the captain? Our agent is positive that he came off a ship known to do business with pirates!"

I noticed Judge Pimm rolling his eyes as he turned to the prosecutor. "William, of course he came off a ship that dealt with pirates. They let him go. Being captured by pirates isn't a crime. That he made a deal with them to protect himself and eventually gain his freedom isn't a criminal act. I'll give you ten days to present evidence of actual criminal wrongdoing and make a case. So far, all you've offered is hearsay." Then he turned to me.

"Mr. Walker!"

"Yes, Your Honor," I said standing up.

"You're released without bail. Don't leave Ceres, understand?"

"Yes, Your Honor."

He hit his gavel on the block. "Next case."

The bailiff came over and undid the cuffs, and Cheryl escorted me out of the courtroom. I saw Kacey was sitting in the back, along with her brother Jeff, and they followed us out.

"Thanks, Cheryl," I said, shaking her hand. "I am curious as to why you didn't mention Pam."

"Because this isn't about what happened to her, it's about what happened to you. You were faced with the same situation, regardless. That you didn't abandon her, and that you took on her defense, says a lot about you. So what are your plans now?"

"Well, first to see if I can get my old job back, I guess. I know the location of the wreck, so I'll give it to them so they can salvage it. I saw the damage; it's not really all that bad."

"Get your old job back? What, did they fire you?" she asked me as Kacey and Jeff joined us.

"They stopped paying me, so I guess they thought I was dead. I sent them an email from the hab in the Trojans before I left. I told them I would be coming here. I guess I need to follow up."

She nodded. "Let me know how that goes. They're not allowed to stop paying you; they have insurance to cover that."

"Thanks, I will."

A bailiff came out with my possessions then, and I quickly put them away as he set my duffel and pressure suit case on the floor.

"I'll have Kacey forward you my contact info, as well as my bill."

I smiled and shook hands with her again. "Thank you again."

"You're welcome. Kacey, Jeff," she said and nodded to them, then left.

I turned to Kacey and, wrapping my arms around her, I kissed her, and she kissed me back just as passionately. Eventually we had to acknowledge Jeff, who was coughing up a storm.

"I missed you," I told her.

"I missed you as well. Now, how about coming home and you can tell me all about it."

"Sounds like a plan." I picked up my duffel, Jeff had grabbed the case, and Kacey and I walked out of the courthouse, arm in arm.

"So, just how much of that was true?" Jeff asked.

"Aren't you an officer of the court?" I asked, looking over at him.

"Umm." Jeff blushed a little. "Maybe you should marry her, then you're family and I can't testify against you."

"Oh! I like the sound of that," Kacey said, and I gave her a squeeze.

"To be absolutely honest, it was all truthful. I told her damn near everything, though she did leave some things out."

"Oh? Such as?"

"Pam, the second mate. Part of why I stood up to them and threatened them was because she'd been raped by pirates before and was terrified it would happen again." I shook my head. "If they'd been real pirates, the nasty kind, I'd be dead and she'd probably be as well. But"—I shrugged—"I would have taken a couple of them with me."

"And the holo show bit?"

I laughed. "Oh, when I found out about that, I encouraged it. Trust me on that!"

"So what happened to Pam?" Kacey asked.

"She went back home. I think her days of sailing are over. She was grateful for all I did..."

"How grateful?" Kacey growled.

"Very," I said, looking down at her. "But I'd like to point out that I'm with *you* and not with *her*."

"And why's that?"

"I didn't love her." I realized it was true as soon as I said it. She really had been more of a friend. One with great benefits, true, but Pam was right, we hadn't connected. When it counted, I knew I could count on Kacey. She wasn't the type to go to pieces.

"She's a friend, and that's all she'll ever be." I looked down at Kacey and smiled happily. "You, on the other hand..." I stopped us a moment so I could give her a kiss.

Kacey leaned into me, looking quite pleased with herself.

"So, where's Chaz?"

"Damascus Freight bought a ship to replace the *Iowa Hill*. Most of the crew are on it now."

"Most?"

"Apparently the first mate had some sort of accident."

"Oh? What kind?"

"The kind," Jeff spoke up, "that happens when the rest of the crew gets pissed off about your behavior."

"But we can talk about that later," Kacey said. "I think right now, I'd like to spend a little time reconnecting with my boyfriend."

I smiled. "Yeah, I'd like that."

SIXTEEN

Ceres

WE WERE LYING IN BED TOGETHER AT HER PARENTS' HOUSE. I
had no real idea what time it was, and no desire to find out.
After the initial rush of jumping into bed and making love to
each other, we'd had a long talk.

I'd told her everything. And I do mean *everything* that had
happened. How Pam had lost it, how we'd been stranded, my
fears of just what might happen to me if we got "rescued," my
decision to take my chances with what I'd thought were pirates,
and my decision as well to protect Pam, even if that meant lowering my own chances of survival.

I even told her of Pam's decision to reward me, as well as
what Pam told me later about her last run-in with pirates. I told
Kacey flat out that I wanted her to know who I was and, yes,
what I was. That I wasn't ever going to hold anything back.

And I wanted to know all about her as well.

"Why? Why are you telling me all this?" she asked sometime
late in the middle of the night.

"Pam told me that the reason we couldn't make a go of it
was because we really didn't know each other."

"So you're trying not to make the same mistake again?" Kacey
asked, frowning.

"No," I said with a shake of my head. "When I saw you, I

realized that I'd never asked about Pam's past, who she was, what she wanted, because I really didn't *care*. My ending up with Pam was a complete fluke. The only thing we had in common was that we were both crew on the *Iowa Hill*. I didn't ask, because I didn't want to know. Same for her.

"But you? I *want* to know about you. I *want* you to know about me. Pam was afraid of me, because I've killed people. You're not, because you like the idea of what I'll do if I have to. You're used to men like that and instead of scaring you, it makes you feel secure."

Kacey snorted. "Yeah, I can't understand her going to pieces like that, when the smart thing to do was run. She just fell down and was waiting to die."

I nodded. "Deep down, I knew I couldn't count on her. Not like I could count on my brother, my old gang mates, or"—I smiled—"you."

Kacey blushed a little and leaned into me. Then she started to tell me about herself, what she was doing, where she wanted to go in life. After that we traded stories about our past. I actually felt better lying in bed, tired because we'd been up all night talking, than the mornings I'd woken up with Pam tired from having sex all night.

Sort of like the difference between filling up on dessert, or filling up on a good meal.

"So, what do you want to do today?" Kacey asked, yawning and stretching while I watched appreciatively.

"Eat, go to the park and enjoy some open spaces, then maybe come back here and do what everyone probably thinks we were doing all last night?"

Kacey smiled and kissed me. "You know, usually this is where the guy starts looking for a ring."

"A ring?"

"Yeah, silly. An engagement ring!"

I paused and thought about that a moment. "I thought only the elies and stuff did that sort of thing?"

"Maybe on Earth, but not out here."

"Guess we can do that tomorrow, then? I still need to let my bank know I'm here and then see how broke I am. I also need to find out if I still have a job and, if not, figure out what I'm going to do for money."

"Maybe you should check your email? You told them you were coming here, didn't you?"

"Maybe after breakfast."

"What, don't you want to know?"

"Just not yet. Right now I can pretend that it's going to be good news."

"It's an email, it's not Schrödinger's cat, Dave!"

"Fine." Reaching over her, I grabbed my tablet off the nightstand and unlocked it. Then I logged into my email. I blinked and gave it another look.

"Wow, I got a *lot* of emails!"

"Some of those dates go back quite a ways," Kacey said, looking at the tablet. "There's one from Damascus."

I nodded and opened it, quickly reading it; the rest could wait a while longer.

"Well, I'm getting my back pay and it'll be deposited within the week. They're *not* interested in salvaging the ship, seeing as insurance has already paid out on it and they've replaced it."

"Does that mean it's open salvage?"

I shrugged. "No idea. Would have to ask a lawyer."

"Ask Cheryl, she'd know."

"I don't think I have the money to go salvage a derelict."

"How bad is the damage?"

"One of the grav drives got destroyed. Though..." I thought about it. Three quarters of the drive panels *were* still operational, and the dead ones were in the rear. "I'd have to talk to a structural engineer. It might be able to make it back here, though it'd be a long trip."

"Something to think about. Now, the all-important question: do you still have a job?"

I scanned over the last part of the letter.

"Maybe..." I said.

"Maybe? How can they not know?"

"They need to talk to all the captains out there, and see if anybody needs an engineer, then figure out just how much it'll cost to link us up. But, on the bright side, until they figure that out, I'm still getting paid, only I'm just getting half salary as I'm on 'extended shore leave.'"

I saw that Kacey had forwarded me Cheryl's email address, so I sent her an email so she could bill me directly.

I saw that there were also emails from Dot, Chaz, two from my brother Ben, a slew of bank statements, and an invitation to the spacers guild, now that I'd been in space over a year. Another invitation to an engineers society, because I'd made engineer third; a letter from my father and my mother; plus another one from my little sister, Dianne.

"Guess I'll sort through these later," I said, locking my tablet and setting it down. "Right now, how about a shower and then some food?"

"Sounds good to me!"

When we finally made it down to the kitchen, Kacey sat me down and started making me breakfast.

"You sure you don't want any help?" I asked, watching her.

"Don't fret, I'll let you do it tomorrow," she said with a chuckle, then glanced back at me. "Were you serious upstairs?"

"About what?"

"About buying me an engagement ring," she asked.

"You suggested it," I teased.

"True, but from what I've seen, that's usually the cue to the guy to start hemming and hawing and looking for the door."

"But you want a ring, right?" I asked.

"You understand that if you give me that ring, you're proposing marriage?"

I nodded, slowly. "Yeah. I do."

"And we've only known each other for, like, a week?"

"No, we've known each other for months, Kace, it's just that we've only spent a little time together."

"Aren't you worried we might be rushing into it?"

"Well…" I thought about it a moment. "A proposal is just that, right? We set a date and from that point on, we're pretty much got an exclusive claim on each other. That's how it works, right?"

"This isn't just dating, Dave. There's a wedding at the end of that corridor."

"Look, Kace, I *really* want to get to know you better and I sure as hell don't want anybody else out there competing with me, okay? I want…I guess you'd call it 'exclusive rights.'"

"Is *that* all you want? *Exclusive rights?* To me?" she said a little angrily.

"Well, isn't that what you want of me? I mean, isn't that the whole purpose here? To see if we can live with each other? I mean honestly, I'm pretty sure about you. But, well, I'm the one with all the baggage here."

She stopped and turned around and looked at me.

"Let me see if I'm hearing you right. You're worried that I might change my mind?"

"Which is why I want to get rid of the competition, to improve my chances," I said with a goofy grin. It suddenly occurred to me just what I was getting myself into. She was serious.

"*We*"—she pointed the spatula in her hand at me—"are going shopping right after we eat and *you* are buying me a ring and proposing."

"Yes, ma'am!" I said with a grin.

"Don't you start on that now!" she said, grinning back at me.

"I'll behave."

"Yeah, right!"

"Poorly," I teased.

"Uh-huh." And she went back to whatever it was she was cooking. I watched her and thought about what it would be like to live with her for the rest of my life. My dad had gotten married to my bio-mom at twenty, before he'd finished tech school, and they'd had me just after he'd graduated, a year later. A lot of the kids I'd gone to school with had hooked up and moved in together while I was in college. Proles tended to get married early, or at least start living together. I think the elies were the only ones who put it off until they were, like, in their thirties or something.

Still, the idea of marriage had never really occurred to me before. I guess living with Pam had primed the pathways in my head to start thinking about it. It had been nice being with her, I couldn't lie about that. But it seemed to me that being with Kacey would be better.

She made up two plates of food, set one down in front of me, and took the other one for herself and we just ate, smiling at each other. I couldn't recall a single time when Pam had cooked for me, or taken it on herself to do anything unasked. Well, other than sex.

"What are you thinking?" Kacey asked, smiling back at me.

"That you beat out an Adonis, that's what."

"Wait, what?" she asked, giving me a sideways look with a slight frown.

"Pam was an Adonis, born and bred to be hot, and I guess they train 'em for sex or something. And you just beat her out," I said with a smile.

"Are you for real?" she asked, but I could see she was starting to smile.

"Yeah, I am," I said with a nod. My relationship with Pam had been more of a master/slave kind of thing, I realized as I looked back at it. Not exactly healthy and while perhaps I'd inadvertently set the terms, she'd sure enjoyed living up to them. Obviously what she'd gone through had changed her in some fundamental way—either that or Adonises were just raised pretty damn kinky.

She smiled, a little shyly. "Are you saying that you'd rather have me than her?"

"Hands down."

"Finish your breakfast and grab your ID. You are going to be spending a *lot* of money today."

The ring we picked out really wasn't as expensive as she'd warned me. Kacey was rather practical when you got right down to it. After I paid for it, I took it from the salesman, smiled at her, then got down on one knee like I'd seen in the holos and asked her.

"Kacey, will you marry me?"

"Yes!" she said and I gave her the ring, we kissed, and then I damn near jumped out of my skin as everyone in the shop applauded. I felt my face get hot as I blushed, but she just preened and I put my arm around her as we left the shop. We spent the rest of the day walking through the "city" until we came to one of the park entrances and went up onto the surface. After six months of living deep in that hab, and then the small spaces of the habs in the Jupiter Trojans, I was starting to feel a little claustrophobic.

When we finally got back to her parents' house, I sat down in a chair in the living room and started to read my mail, starting with my brother's first one from around five months ago, while she went to talk to her mom.

Dave,

   Still enjoying my time here at school. I put in my thesis for my third doctorate. Turns out the master's degree I was working on was a lot easier than I'd expected, so when I finished it, I just kept going and did the doctorate work. I can almost hear your muttered "of course you did" from here!

   While I'm waiting on that I've started on masters four and five. They're mostly side disciplines that I figured I needed *to learn a little bit more about. Still, as I've said before, as long as they keep offering me new things to study, who am I to turn them down?*

Besides which, I like the weather up here in Boston. No more hot and humid Texas summers, or springs, or falls.

I continued reading as he went on a bit about family things, how Mom, Dad, and our sister were doing. It wasn't until down at the end I came to this:

On the minus side of the equation, I'm not sure how much longer I'll be able to use the crutches I've been on since I got here. The doctors are all positive now that it's ALS, and they're fairly positive that they can arrest the progress here before it gets any worse. Still, I suspect I'll be in a wheelchair in six months, a year at the latest. If only they'd caught this back when I was in high school, right?

Still, all things considered, I'm grateful. Part-time in a wheelchair still beats becoming a total vegetable.

> *—Ben*

As soon as that one was finished, I immediately started in on the next.

Dave,

I'm happy to hear that you got away from those pirates! I was a little worried when I received the notification that your ship had been taken, but to be honest, I was a little more concerned with what you'd be doing to them, than the reverse. I hope you didn't hurt them too bad! :-)

Unfortunately, those events led to Eileen being notified of your capture and I suspect once you've straightened out your affairs with your company, she'll get another notification that you're alive, which means her husband will probably become a problem once more.

On the positive side, my thesis was accepted and I now have my third doctorate! The school approached me last week about taking a professorship and I have to admit that I'm sorely tempted. Who knew learning could be so much fun, right?

Plus I've been doing the routines for the cheer squad on the side and the payoffs from that have been even better than they were in high school. ;-> So there's a lot of reasons to stay. But I've apparently come to the attention of the corps now—I've been getting some serious offers to join two of the more prestigious research groups, and the amount of creds they waved under my nose were enough to make me take their offers seriously.

I'll give it all some serious consideration when I finish the current masters degrees I'm pursuing. I know whichever way I jump, that I won't be able to continue my studies at my current rate.

On the ALS. The doctors are positive that they've managed to rein it in, however I'm more in a wheelchair now than not. There's been talk about using some new techniques to get me back up on my feet again, but I've told them I'm too busy right now to be a guinea pig. Besides which, it doesn't seem to be getting any worse. So why tempt fate?

Let me know how you make out, and if you're ever this way again, we should do dinner.

—Ben

I leaned back in my chair and took a few deep breaths as I thought about what he'd written.

"Dave?" Robert, Kacey's father, came into the room, interrupting my thoughts.

"Yes?" I asked, looking up at him.

"You okay there?"

"Oh, just a note from my brother. What's up?"

"Did you just propose to my daughter?" he asked, looking a little concerned.

I smiled and nodded. "Yup! She started dropping hints this morning."

"Don't you think it's a little too soon? This is only been the second time you've been with her."

I gave a small shake of my head. "No, no, I don't. We sat up all night talking and getting to know each other. I mean, I liked Kacey a lot when I left here, and after last night"—I smiled—"I'm not taking any chances. Besides, we've got a few months before the wedding, not that I expect anything to change our minds."

"Does that mean you're going to find a job here on Ceres?"

I thought about Ben's letter, and shook my head slightly. "Not right away. Maybe in a year? I'd like to get a little more time in, working as a ship's engineer."

"I thought you had your panel rebuilder's certification?"

"Yeah, I do. But what I *really* want is the engine tuner's certification. There are only a few people doing that here, and with all the ships that put into Ceres for rebuilds? And all the talk about building more shipyards here? *That's* where the real money is going to be.

"Besides which, maybe I can swing a job for Kacey onboard and find a ship that's making the run to Earth so I can introduce her to my parents, and my brother," I added with a thoughtful look.

"Just don't mess with her schooling; she's still got a year of college left to get her degree."

I nodded. "I know, I like that she's getting a business and accounting degree. That'll come in handy for us when we open up our shop."

"Nice to see you're thinking ahead."

"Did I mention just how *late* we stayed up talking last night?" I said with a chuckle.

"And here I figured you'd both be doing something else," he said with a laugh.

"Eh, there's always going to be time for that. But I didn't want her to think I was taking her for granted. Also"—I smiled—"I really wanted to get to know her."

"Well, if you're going to get married, it's usually better to do that before, instead of after—fewer problems that way."

I nodded.

"So what's up with your brother? I saw that concerned look on your face and I thought you might have already been having second thoughts about Kacey."

"Never that. My brother's in a wheelchair now."

"Wheelchair? What happened?"

"He's got ALS."

"I thought there was a cure for that?"

"Sorta. If they'd caught it sooner, they could have stopped it, but they really didn't discover it until he was in college. Proles like us, we don't get all that great health care, 'cause we're supposed to be earning, not living off the government teat."

"Is he going to be okay?"

I nodded. "Yeah, but he's probably going to spend the rest of his life in a wheelchair. They stopped it, just not soon enough."

"Maybe he should come out here? They could turn the panels down for him, so he'd be light enough to walk—well, at least in his own home and wherever he ends up working."

I shook my head. "It's not that easy. My brother's a genius. He's up to three doctorate degrees and, like, five masters. The government passed a 'brain drain' law years ago, because all of the best and the brightest were leaving Earth and coming out here, into space. So he's not allowed off planet."

"I had no idea. That's a shame."

"Yeah, it is."

"Anyway, don't make any plans for dinner tonight. I've invited everyone over so we can celebrate."

"Who's 'everyone'?" I asked a little warily.

"Jeff, Carl and his wife, Wade and his wife, Sheila and her husband, my sister Cheryl and her husband..."

"Cheryl, as in my lawyer?"

Rob smiled. "Yup, and her husband is Judge Pimm. I'll see if my brother Dennis and his wife can come as well. But don't worry; I won't invite all the nieces and nephews."

"That's a relief," I said with a mock sigh.

"Big families are pretty common out here. If Kacey hasn't warned you about that, well, now maybe you won't be surprised."

"I'll keep that in mind," I said as he got out his own tablet.

"Well, I got some calls to make, so excuse me for a bit."

I just nodded and went back to my emails. My parents were doing well, just the usual there and a bunch of questions about how things were going. I felt guilty that I hadn't sent them a message letting them know I was okay. My father was probably alerted the same time that my bio-mom was. So I immediately sent them a message, same for my little sister. I then read her letter, she was quickly advancing through the grades. While she might not be as big a genius as Ben, she was still well above normal.

The letter from Chaz had made it clear just what they'd done to Parks for freaking out and leaving without me and Pam, and they all hoped we made it home safely. He told me that Dot had gotten my last message. He also filled me in on the new cargo ship they'd all been assigned to, though the company was in the process of finding a new first mate and second mate, as well as an engineer to replace me.

While I was reading over that, I got a new mail from him;

I guess either the company or Kacey had emailed him letting him know I was back. He congratulated me on my safe return, was relieved to hear that Pam had also gotten away. Told me Hank and Dot both sent their regards, as well as Captain Roy and his wife, Shelly. They'd be in port here in about a month. He added their expected itinerary so I could get a reply to him. They were doing a circle route that included the Titan orbital, then the Saturn Trojans, and a tour through the belt before they ended up here again.

Dot's email contained a couple of pictures of what they'd done to Parks, and I immediately replied to her, using Chaz's itinerary with my hopes to see her again soon, and *please don't kill him!* I reiterated that a few times to let her know I was serious and things had turned out for the best.

Because I had no doubts in my mind at all that she was thinking of doing just that, once she was sure she could get away with it.

I also asked her to say hello to everyone and let Chaz know I was going to marry his sister. You know, the one I had to peel off last time we were here? And I added a little smiley face to that.

None of the rest of the emails were important, not really. So I went back to thinking about what Ben's last email had said, not directly, this was something we'd talked about years ago, before he'd gone to college and I'd decided I was going to leave Earth.

Ben had as little desire to stay there as I had. He saw what it had done to his mother, and what it had done to both me and him. No, the message was clear, Ben was ready to leave.

Now I just had to figure out how to make it happen.

The dinner party was nice. Everyone was happy for us, even if for a few of them it seemed to be a bit sudden. When the party finally broke up and we went to bed, Kacey and I celebrated in our own way, which this time really didn't involve much talking. When we finally snuggled up to go to sleep, I found I was having trouble sleeping. My mind kept coming back to getting Ben off of Earth.

I also wondered about our parents and our younger sister. Should we take them? Should we even mention it to them? Dianne would probably have a better life out here, where she could be whatever she wanted to be. My father wouldn't have any trouble finding work; he was an experienced repair technician, specialized in spaceships. As for Mom, well, she was a housewife, so I didn't think she would really mind at all.

I wished I could talk to Ben about it; I was sure he'd already given it a lot of thought.

"Something bothering you?" Kacey asked.

"Yeah, my brother's email."

"My dad said he's got ALS? That's pretty bad, isn't it?"

"It used to be. But that's not what's got me worried."

"What, then?"

"He wants to leave Earth."

"He said that?"

"Yes, but he said it in code."

"Why would he do that?"

"Because really smart people aren't allowed to leave Earth. Years ago, before I left, we arranged a code between us, because while he wanted to get a good education, once he got it, he wanted to leave. So the plan was, I'd look for a good place, where I thought he'd be happy, and then when the time was right, I'd smuggle him off planet the next time my ship went to Earth.

"But..."

"But you're not on a ship and there's a good chance you won't have a job on one for a while yet."

"Yeah, exactly that. I figured the folks on the *Iowa* would be okay with it, by the time we got to it. Just pay the freight and bribe them to keep quiet about it. They all knew me, after all."

"You can always start over, with another ship."

"I don't have the time," I said with a sigh. "He needs to be off soon, I figure I got six months to a year."

"Did he say why?"

"No, we didn't come up with that involved of a code, just a flag that he was ready to go and a general sense of how urgently."

"Well, worrying about it isn't going to make it any easier. Go to sleep and in the morning we can talk to a few people, maybe figure something out. Your old crew will be here in about a month, so who knows? Maybe they'll give somebody the boot and put you onboard instead."

"Then I just gotta get them to fly to Earth."

"One thing at a time, Dave. One thing at a time."

She yawned and then I yawned and I closed my eyes and was able to fall asleep this time. It felt good to have help for a change.

SEVENTEEN

Doyle House

AFTER BREAKFAST, KACEY DRAGGED ME OUT THE DOOR. IT WAS a workday and her parents were already gone.

"What's the rush?"

"I've got classes today, so I need to get you over to Cheryl's."

"Why Cheryl's?"

"You didn't ask her about salvage rights. Also, immigrating to Ceres isn't all that easy. You've got a skill and you're marrying a local, so for you it'll be easy. But you probably should talk to her about your brother. Make sure there isn't any way that they can extradite him."

"You think it's safe to talk to her?"

She rolled her eyes. "She's your lawyer. She won't talk to anybody about your plans. Though she will tell you how to do it legally, if there's any possible issue."

"Ah, okay. But how are we going to get out to where the ship is? It's not all that close."

"First things first."

It didn't take us long to get to Cheryl's office, and after saying "Hi!" to Cheryl, Kacey kissed me and left.

"Where's she off to in such a rush?" Cheryl asked with a chuckle.

"School. She's in her last year."

"Ah, right. I think she's going for business?"

I nodded. "Which will be great when I open my shop up."

"So what brings you here? You could have just paid me via email."

"I want to salvage the ship I was on, the one the pirates raided."

"You company has first rights, Dave. So I'm not so sure that you can."

"They told me they're not interested. I have all the orbit information for it, saved it when we left. I'd figured they'd want to get it back, it's not that damaged. But they told me they already settled with their insurer and replaced it. So..." I shrugged. "I know where it is and I know how to fix it—well, mostly. So why not?"

"Do you have the email they sent you?" she asked.

I nodded, got out my tablet, and called it up, then handed it to her.

"Hmm, ah, here it is. They took the insurance payout on it. I'll have to check the records, but if the insurance company hasn't commissioned a salvage operation and filed a claim, then it's open to anyone salvaging it." She looked up at me. "Did you send them the orbital data?"

I shook my head. "No, I didn't have the money for that much traffic."

"Then odds are they haven't, and by now they can't, so it's probably fair game."

"Great. Also, I want to smuggle my brother off of Earth and bring him here."

"You what?" she said, looking at me like I was crazy.

"My brother is a genius. Geniuses aren't allowed to leave Earth."

She nodded. "I've heard about that."

"Well, he wants off, and we've got a basic plan, something we came up long before I left home. *But* can I bring him here? Would that be legal? Would we get in trouble? Would he be sent *back*?"

"You said he's a genius?"

"Yeah, he's got, like, three doctorates from MIT now and I think, like, five masters? Think he's got a couple of bachelors and stuff as well."

"Well, being as he's your brother, that shouldn't be a problem."

"Actually, he's my stepbrother. My dad remarried and Jenny

already had a son, Ben. He's four years younger than me, and, well, being a total brain-case, there were issues and I had to stand up for him, a lot. We became really close."

"Hmm, well, he probably doesn't qualify as family, because he's not blood. But, if he's a genius, I'm sure they'll want him to immigrate here. They're always looking for smart people."

"What about my parents? And my little sister?"

"Is your sister a stepsib?"

"No, Mom and Dad had a kid together after they'd gotten married." I smiled, remembering. "Ben and I both thought it was cool, because now we were related, through her. Also, she kinda takes after Ben. She's not as smart as him, but she's a damn sight smarter than the rest of us in the family."

"Thinking of bringing the rest of them, are you?"

"Maybe?" I shrugged. "We never mentioned it to them, but after seeing how things are out here, I've starting thinking about it. My dad's a top-rated tech, though he struggles to get by because of all the taxes he's gotta pay. Dianne, my sister, well, I doubt she'll get the opportunities back there that she could get here. And Mom will go where Dad goes, especially if Ben and Dianne are there."

"Okay, I'll see about getting the paperwork set up, so if and when they show, I've got it all ready. The big thing is that you have to be valuable to society here. We don't accept dead wood."

"Got it."

"So, what's your next step?"

I shook my head. "I don't know. I don't know if I still have a job or not. Or if and when I'll have to leave."

"What about your old ship? The *Iowa Hill*? That's a lot of money floating out there, or a lot of opportunity, depending on how you look at it."

"I know, I know." I sighed. "But it needs one of the grav drives replaced, though it should be able to fly back under its own power without it, as long as we don't go too fast. But that's a lot of money up front. Also, how am I going to get out there? And I'll need a crew. I don't know how to handle a ship, and then there's food, tools, gear. A whole bunch of stuff."

"Form a company, with the goal of salvaging the ship. Take investors; there are a lot of people who would jump at the chance, because the return, a functioning cargo ship, is worth a lot of money."

"But what if I want to keep her?" I said as a wild idea floated through my head.

"Either buy them out, or offer them a spot in the new company. You can even make that part of the first company, tell them that if you can swing the repairs, you're going to start running it."

"Still, that's a lot of risk. Do you think people would go for it?"

Cheryl smiled. "We live on a rock out in the middle of space. Most of the people here are either miners, make stuff for miners, or build habs for other people who want to live in space. This place is full of risk takers. The trick is just to make it look like your risk is low and the payoff is high."

I nodded. This was something I needed to discuss with Kacey. She'd probably know who to talk with about it.

"Just remember, when you decide to do it, bring your contracts here for me to go over. Same for your incorporation and company documents. You want to be sure everything's in order."

"Thanks, Cheryl. I appreciate it."

She smiled at me. "Well, I want to make sure that everything is set up right, Kacey's my favorite niece. Also, I think I just might want to invest."

"Honest?" I said, looking at her and feeling a little shocked.

"Family businesses are the best businesses. The hard part, as always, is finding a good market out here. Small shippers can't always compete with the larger ones, but if you can find steady work, you can do really well."

I remembered then something that Marcus had said about wanting to start trading, but needing somebody he could trust.

"I know that look, Dave. I've seen it a hundred times on people I've defended in court."

"You know those people I worked for?"

"Yes, what about them?"

"They're refugees. They're hiding out because the people they ran away from want them dead. Well, they've got a lot of mining going on, so they've got stuff to trade and stuff they need. Wouldn't it be better if they could buy it, instead of stealing it?"

"I thought you said you didn't know where they are?"

"I don't. But..." I smiled at her. "I'm pretty sure I can figure it out."

"What else haven't you told me?"

"Lots of stuff. Those people got a raw deal. That's why they didn't just kill us out of hand. Their whole plan was to scare the crew off the ship so they wouldn't have to deal with anybody. Once they realized I would keep my word, they agreed to take us on. They're actually nice people. If it wasn't for my brother and Kacey, I might even have stayed."

"I checked the reports from the rest of your crew. They said those pirates had a frigate."

"Yeah, they did. They like to think of themselves as 'buccaneers' actually, because they've got some ethics."

"Really?" she said, giving me a sarcastic look.

I laughed. "Mostly, yeah. Oh, it's not all wine and roses, and there were some folks who definitely needed to be cut down to size. That's part of why their leader wants to get out of the whole piracy thing. It's hurting them, their society. They only took our cargo because they needed it to live." I looked at her, hands spread. "You can't fault people for stealing when it's life or death."

"They're from Venus, aren't they?"

"How'd you guess?"

"Because that's the only place so messed up right now, that their government would follow you across the system to get revenge. They're like a cult. Government as religion almost. There's no disagreeing with them. If you do, well, you're evil and you have to die. I think that's part of what holds them together. If you don't believe what they do, you just keep your mouth shut and your head down."

"So, think it'd put any noses out of joint or break any laws if I started to bring their stuff in here and sell it for them?"

"Just don't connect them to the piracy; come up with some other story. Nobody really cares where ore's coming from, as long as it's not stolen. The trick is going to be to keep anyone from following you to try and steal your business."

"Just don't tell anyone about them, okay?"

"Oh, I won't. Last thing anybody wants out here is the Venusian Moral Collective. Besides, you're right, if they can trade they won't pirate, and we can make the system a better place while getting paid to do it!" She grinned at me. "Oh, did I mention we can be just a little bit mercenary out here on Ceres as well?"

"Why do you think I want to live here?" I replied, smiling back at her.

"Well, I have work to do. Don't forget to pay your bill!" she added with a smile.

I nodded and waved, then left her office. I needed to replace the tools I'd taken from the *Iowa Hill* when I'd left, as well as a fair deal of the supplies for fixing panels. I'd also need to get an idea of what a Muller 1500, in working condition, would cost, so we could replace the one that got destroyed.

Looking for those things and getting a price on them was as good as any place to start.

"Hi, hon!" Kacey said, coming over and giving me a kiss. "What's up?"

"I'm trying to get an idea of just what we'll need to salvage the *Iowa Hill*."

"So you talked to Cheryl about it?"

I nodded and then told her what we'd discussed.

"Makes sense," she said when I was done. "Only we'll just start a trading company with the initial goal of salvaging the ship. That'll be our contribution to the company."

"Our?" I asked with a smile.

"Yes, 'our,'" she said and hip-checked me, then went to get something to drink. "Though I guess I could also be our accountant and general manager, well, at least at first."

"Did you find the engine that you needed?"

"Yeah, there's still a fair number of them in storage at a lot of the different yards here. Lots of ships have been upgrading and the old drives just go into a warehouse for those that haven't and may need a replacement."

"How much are we talking?"

"A quarter million, which, from what I've seen, is not that bad."

"What about the rest?"

"I'm not sure. I really need to go over this with someone a lot more experienced than me, but right now, I think we only need about a million, not including crew and transportation."

"How much do you have in the bank?"

"Six months' wages plus what little savings I have comes to sixty grand. I'm guessing you have even less than that?"

Kacey nodded. "However, I have something you don't."

"Oh, you have a lot of things I don't, that's why I'm marrying you!" I teased.

She came over with her drink and sat in my lap.

"I know people. Lots of people. I can probably get us some

better deals on the stuff you need. Might even be able to get us a better deal on the engine. Then, of course, there's investors. Between me and my family, I think we should be able to round up enough money. Especially as Cheryl told you she wanted in."

"Why does she make a big difference?"

"Because she's your lawyer and undoubtedly knows all those things you'd rather not make public. Keep in mind that she has to answer to an ethics board for everything she does. So if she thinks it's a good idea, then it probably is, and it's going to be legal as well."

"So who do we ask first?"

"My parents, of course. Then we'll ask my brothers and my sister. Most of the family is pretty well tied into the hab construction business; Chaz is the only one who decided he wanted to do something different. Well, I guess Jeff counts too, though at least he still lives here on Ceres."

"Think any of them might be crew? Or have a ship we can rent cheap to get out there?"

"How far out there is it, anyway?"

"Out past Neptune."

"That far?"

"Yeah. When we lost the engine we were still in the boost phase, and we just lost a fair bit of thrust. So I had Pam write a program to reverse thrust with a slight vector change thrown in to get the ship into a stable orbit. We only had about fifteen percent of the normal thrust to work with, and from what I'd been told, two weeks was probably about as long as you wanted to trust the helm on that ship to fly by itself."

"So it's still on an outbound track, but just not as far as it would have been."

"Exactly. It's on a fairly parabolic orbit, but it still won't be inside Neptune's orbit for, like, fifty years, I'd guess. Once we find us a good helmsman to fly the ship for us, I'll go over the data with them, to get a better idea."

"Show it to Mom. She's pretty good with that stuff."

"Really?"

"She plots a lot of the routes for the hab gear deliveries, so they can make their schedules."

"Well, that's one less thing to worry about. That's our biggest secret and I don't want that getting out. Also, I've been thinking that maybe we should show up at Marcus's people's hab and offer to sell their ore for them, as well as bring back the stuff they want to buy."

"That sounds like a good idea, assuming they don't shoot us on sight. But how are you going to do that, if you don't know where they are?"

"Remember I told you that I helped set up their grav panel factory and taught them how to run it?"

She nodded.

"Well, while doing that, I had to find out exactly what their local gravity was." I smiled. "Also, their head hab engineer, Mabel, showed me her plans for what they were trying to build."

"And the name of the place was written on it?" Kacey asked hopefully.

"No, but I got a pretty good scale for the size. That, along with the gravity, I'm pretty sure they're on one of the dwarf planets."

"But those are all pretty well settled, aren't they?"

"Not the ones that are about to go way out into deep space. I think those have pretty minimal science teams, and these people aren't stupid. They may have just gotten their people onto the teams and moved in. Then just stay out of sight when anybody visits."

"Let's go upstairs and do a search on my computer, see what comes up."

I nodded and we went into her room, and I gave her the gravity for the planet.

"Wow, looks like they're on Eris!"

I looked over the data and it fit. "I guess that frigate of theirs has a pretty strong drive," I said, looking at the distances involved. "And that also explains the tidal forces I was seeing during some of my tests."

"Yeah, but look at that orbit! Five hundred and sixty years? They're going to be way out there, and I mean really way out there."

"And by the time they come back, everything and anything that was going on with Venus will be over and they'll probably be forgotten."

"Assuming they survive."

"It's a long trip, but it's not impossible. They've got one really large cargo ship that I know of. So they'll be able to get whatever they need, just the turnaround will be, like, eight months."

"Well, that's not for another two hundred years, so I don't think we need to worry about it."

"How long until your parents get home?"

"Oh, a few hours," Kacey said, and then winked at me and went over to sit on the bed. "Whatever will we do to pass the time?"

Apparently, Kacey's parents really did have a lot of resources. Between them and the rest of the family, they put up all of the money we needed and got us a much better deal on the drive, as well as the supplies that we'd so far determined that we needed.

Maureen had run the data I'd gotten from Pam and it looked like a three-week run just to get to the area we thought the ship was in, then probably another week searching for it with radar. I was just happy I'd forgotten to turn off the navigation lights; hopefully that'd make it easier to find.

We didn't have a ship, yet, but several options had been discussed, including using an ore hauler to get there, then putting the *Iowa Hill* in the cargo hold and hauling it back with us. It would mean we could use the same crew, but I wasn't sure I liked that option much. I was starting to think of hauling the Muller 1500 out there with us, installing it, and going straight to Eris. That would bring us back with a money-paying cargo. We could then go back with a load of what they wanted, and run off to Earth next.

I wasn't sure if we could just take a load of ore to Earth. I knew they took ingots of a lot of different metals that had already been smelted, but I wasn't sure if they did any of that on the planet, and I definitely needed a cargo that would allow us to land.

I'd tell whoever ended up scheduling our cargo to get us one going to Earth once we had the ship up and running.

But right now, before we started worrying about our crew, and about just how we were going to get there, we had something that took priority over all of that: setting up the business.

There were a lot of contracts, forms to file, fees to pay, people to see, all of that. We needed an office. We needed officers for the company. We needed a clear contract between the company and all the investors. We also needed to understand just who owned what and how it all ran.

Then we needed to arrange for warehouse space, because there was a good chance that we'd need to store cargo, until a load was put together to go onto the ship, or a load had come off and hadn't been sold or delivered yet. And that cargo space came in three flavors, which depended on security. The more you had, the more it cost.

Then there was insurance, payroll, health care, and other benefits.

Thank God that Kacey understood it and that Cheryl was there to help, because I was completely lost through all of that. My biggest problem, however, was crew. I needed at least one more engineer, for the long term at least. For the retrieval I could do what was necessary myself. As the engine was the same as the now destroyed one, replacing it shouldn't present any serious problems.

I also needed at least one person who could fly the ship and who had their captain's certificate for a ship that big, and then either another mate, or a couple of able-bodied spacers. Mostly people to help with the watch-standing. And, of course, a cook.

For a big company able to pay good wages, hiring was easy. There was the spacers guild and the different societies for each of the professional classes. There were also employment agencies that would screen people for you. There was even open recruitment.

But a small mom-and-pop like us? With no track record? We were almost the epitome of "Two Guys with a Spaceship."

During this time I was offered a space on a ship working the other side of the ring, which all things considered I don't know that I would have taken even if I wasn't trying to start a business. So I declined and filed my resignation from Damascus Freight Lines, and thanked them for the opportunities that they had given me. I also told them I was getting married to a woman on Ceres, which was why I was turning them down, and would be pursuing more local opportunities.

It was at this time that the *Eatons Neck*, the Damascus Freight Lines' replacement for the *Iowa Hill*, made port. So, of course, we had a party.

"Dave! I can't tell you how happy I am to see you're alive and well! Dot tells me that Pam's fine too? Just that she decided to go back home?" Captain Roy said, shaking my hand as he came into the bar we were all meeting at.

"Hi, Captain! And yeah, she's fine, but I think she's decided to go back to her first love, which was managing and running hazardous waste processing facilities. Mrs. Roy, it's nice to see you again," I said, shaking hands with her next. Dot was next and she surprised me by giving me a hug.

"I got your last message before we got out of range of the ship's comms," she told me. "I was worried, but I guess you weren't lying, you really did 'deal' with it!"

I grinned at her, "Remember, I ran in a gang for a *long* time. It's all about the negotiations. Hi, Hank! Chaz!" I said, shaking hands with them.

"How'd you keep them away from Pam?" Dot asked.

"Simple, I told them she was my woman, and I didn't share. Also I'd kill anyone who laid a hand on her."

"How'd she take that?" Hank asked.

"I told her I'd protect her when we were first boarded. So she was more than happy to play the part."

"So you really did make them an offer of six months' work repairing their panels in exchange for getting you out of there and taking you someplace safe?" Shelly asked.

I nodded. "I figured they're pirates, where the hell can they go to get their panels replaced? Wherever it is, they had to be paying a premium. Then they took me to the folks on the dark hab they were selling the gear to, and we both ended up there. Those folks were maybe a bit rough around the edges, but they trusted me to do the work and kept their word."

"They were probably too afraid of what would happen if they crossed you!" Chaz said and laughed.

"Turned out they were all fans of some old Earth crime drama and when they found out I knew how to use a pick, I think it was a combination of fear and hero worship," I said with a laugh of my own. "Now, how about introducing me to the new guys?" I asked, motioning to the three men hanging back a ways.

Dot spoke up first. "The young man on the end there is your replacement, Charles, or 'Chuck.' He's actually out of Ceres here."

Chuck came over and I shook hands with him.

"Sorry about taking your old job," he said with a shrug.

"That's okay; I'm starting a new business with Chaz's sister."

"That's right, Chaz mentioned that. You're going to salvage the *Iowa Hill* and start a small cargo line," Dot said.

I nodded. "I asked the folks at Damascus Freight if they wanted the orbital data, but they said they weren't interested. They just let it go for whoever wants to claim it."

"Probably because it's ten years from needing new reactors." She looked over at Captain Roy. "That sound about right to you, Steve?"

Captain Roy nodded. "Yup, had that discussion with them when we got back here. I'll send you all the master passwords for the systems before we head back out. Should make your life easier. Now this is Ken, our new exec and first mate." I shook hands with him. "And this is Jamaal, Pam's replacement." I shook hands with him next.

"Now, as I'm sure you've all heard from Chaz..." I said, looking at them all as Kacey came over to join me. All of Chaz's family had come to welcome him and Hank back. "I'm engaged to his sister, Kacey, and yes, we've actually already started a business and we're going to go get the *Iowa Hill* back and put her back into service. Before any of you ask, yes, we'll give you your stuff back when we clean out the cabins."

They all cheered when they heard that, but I wasn't sure if they were cheering my engagement or getting their stuff back. I figured I was better off not asking.

After that we mostly broke into groups and talked. Captain Roy told me to stop calling him "Captain," seeing as I wasn't on his crew anymore, and he had a lot of advice about running the *Iowa Hill*. As he'd been the captain on it for almost ten years, it was worth listening to.

Eventually, Dot got me alone and gave me a look.

"Are you really sure you don't want me to take care of Parks?" she asked. "I mean, that was pretty bad what he did to you and Pam."

"Honestly?" I said with a sigh. "Yeah, just leave it. Pam lost it really bad when we heard them docking with us. She'd been taken by pirates once before and until the Mars Navy had saved her she'd had it pretty rough. I honestly had no idea someone who seemed as together as she was could lose it that badly. Parks probably has something like that in his past as well. Besides, I doubt he'll ever get another job as a mate, or even a deckhand."

"Oh that's most definitely the truth. Captain was pissed and put the word out on him when we got back to port."

"Oh? Did he help with that beating?"

"No, he wanted to, though; I think that's why he was mad when he found out about it," Dot said with a big grin. "So, found a crew yet?"

I shook my head. "We've only just figured out what we'll need. I got the chance to inspect the damage before I left, so I know how bad it is."

"I hope you weren't planning on me leaving Damascus. I don't think you could match the pay and I'd rather not leave Steve high and dry having to replace me on such short notice."

"I understand. As it is, I suspect Chaz might want to leave and join us, seeing as it's the family business."

"It is?"

I nodded, "Yeah, we've even named it Doyle Shipping."

Dot laughed, "Well that does sound better than Walker Shipping—people would think you weren't in a rush!"

I had to laugh at that too, as that connotation hadn't even occurred to me.

"Actually, the Doyles here have a *lot* of connections. We didn't even have to go outside the family for the startup funds, and one of the big-name lawyers and her husband, who's a judge, are investors."

"That can't hurt. I better warn Steve that he might be looking for another deckhand before we leave."

"You think Hank'll follow Chaz if he goes?"

"Let's just say that I don't think Chaz will go if Hank says no. In fact, if you're considering Chaz, you might want to consider Hank as well. He was a Marsie Navy guy—if you ever have to repel boarders, he's definitely your man. Hell, he wanted to fight off that last bunch, but the captain told him no."

I thought about that, then I remembered just *who* I wanted to do business with! Yeah, I definitely needed to have a conversation with Hank.

"So, how was Pam?" Dot asked.

"Huh?"

She gave me a sly grin. "You were locked up for six months with an Adonis who you'd just told everyone was your girl, and you'd kill anybody who touched her! I know you ain't a saint there, Dave."

I tried not to blush too much. "It was every young man's fantasy," I admitted to her in a soft voice. "She really put me through my paces."

"I'm surprised you didn't keep her. I mean, after something like that, she was probably still all sorts of grateful."

I smiled and shook my head. "We had a discussion about it, albeit a short one. She knew I didn't love her, and after she said it, I knew it too. Also, to be totally honest? The next time something bad happened, I don't think I could have trusted her not to go to pieces on me again. Not like Kacey," I said, and nodded in her direction. She was chatting with Chaz and Hank.

"Must be a bit rough for her, having to follow after Pam."

"Actually, Pam was a hell of a lot of fun and all that, but there's something to be said for actually loving the person you're in bed with. Pam never made me forget about Kacey, but now? Unless someone brings her up, I've already forgotten about Pam. Hell, I've already shuffled her off to 'old friend' status in my head, not even 'old lover.'"

Dot got a thoughtful look on her face and nodded, "Good for you, and good for Kacey too."

"Well, I better go corral Hank and see if I'm going to end up looking for deckhands or not," I said.

"Too bad you didn't offer Pam a job, then you wouldn't need to find someone to fly the ship for you," Dot said as I grabbed my beer.

"Nah, even if she wasn't planning on going home, I'd already decided on Kacey, and that probably would have been all sorts of uncomfortable."

I went over and gave Kacey a hug and joined her, Chaz, and Hank. They were talking about our plans for the company, of course. I set my beer down and caught Hank's eye.

"I'll be back in a couple, need to hit the head."

I ran into Hank just as I was leaving the bathroom.

"What's up?" he asked.

"Let's take a short walk," I told him.

Hank nodded and followed me out the back of the bar.

"So, what's the problem?" he asked when we got "outside."

"I want to know if I should tell Chaz no if he decides he wants to sign on and you decide you don't," I told him. "I'm guessing you two are still pretty much in love, seeing the way you both are with each other."

Hank smiled. "Yeah, I think we've gotten pretty close. If I tell him we can't take the job, I don't think he'll like it, but I don't think there'll be too big of a fight over it.

"Now, why do you think I don't want the job?"

"Those 'pirates' I worked for, for the last six months?"

"Yeah, what about them?"

"I'm thinking of going back there, after we get the ship fixed, offering to take the stuff they've been mining that they can't sell, and sell it for them. See if I can't set up a clandestine trade route with them."

"Why?" Hank asked, looking at me a little concerned.

"'Cause they got screwed?" I said with a shrug. "They're nice people, just in a bad situation. So why not help them out and make some money in the process?"

"They're Venusians, aren't they?"

"What makes you say that?"

"I got a look at that frigate that landed on us when the lifeboat was jettisoned. It's a Venusian one, and the only people, other then the folks living on Venus, who have them are the ones who fled their new 'government' and got slaughtered by the hundreds of thousands for having the gall to not want to prostate themselves before the Venusian Moral Collective and their 'New Way of Life.'"

"Yeah, that's them. They said they had to steal the load because they desperately needed the hab gear to finish setting everything up. They don't like being pirates. But it's that or die. So why not help them make the money they need so they can buy it instead of stealing it?"

"I'm not all that convinced that they 'stole' that shipment we were carrying."

"Huh? What makes you say that?"

"Go ask Chaz's mom how often they send that equipment out on a small cargo ship without an escort."

"Huh?"

Hank gave me one of those "patient" looks that I guess he learned to use on new recruits in the navy. "That gear is worth tens of millions of credits. That whole shipment was probably worth over a hundred million. Do you really think they're going to send stuff like that out in a small cargo ship run by the lowest bidder? And without an escort?

"Hell, even the 'Let-Be's' showed up with at least one frigate. Odds are they had another one there as well, to run off anybody who might have gotten ideas."

I scowled back at him as I thought about that. "So you're saying it was a setup?"

"Sure looks like one to me. Tell me, you saw the damage that took out the grav drive, did that come from a ship's weapon?"

"Huh? No, it was from a shaped charge. It was sabotage."

"Which explains why no one came out to try and rescue the ship. Look, if anybody asks, that motor was taken out by some sort of weapon. Weld a big patch over the hole, replace the section of grating above it, maybe even the one above that, and put another patch on the ceiling."

"Do you think Captain Roy knew?"

Hank shook his head. "I doubt it. Though I wouldn't be surprised if the folks at Damascus Freight Lines were encouraged not to try and salvage the wreck."

"Think I'll have any trouble?"

"Nah, just as long as you play along, I don't think anyone will care. It's been half a year, the press has moved on, the insurance payments have all been made, the case has been closed."

"So who *do* you think was behind it?"

Hank shrugged. "Might have just been the manufacturer, though I doubt it. I'm sure a couple of governments, Ceres's at the very least, were backing it and helping to set it up."

"Why?" I asked.

"Because the folks on Venus have made it clear they don't want anyone helping 'the renegades,' and they'll do something if anyone does. They've gone after a few of the smaller habs, I think they even blew a couple up. All the Let-Be's ever wanted was to be left alone and so they left, leaving the rest of the world to the new order. So it's either folks got tired of seeing them getting screwed, or they figured they'd help them solve their problem and find a place that the righteous back on Venus won't find.

"Who knows? Maybe they owed somebody a favor. I do know a lot of governments are looking at the Venusian Moral Collective and making sure they stay on their own damn planet. They sunk two of their own cloud cities and killed God only knows how many tens of millions, just because they wouldn't say the right things. Right now I think they're all hoping that their 'enlightened and most glorious leader' dies before he can start exporting his little revolutionary enlightenment. Otherwise you're going to see *all* of those cloud cities sunk and the place turned into a pure company planet."

"I'm surprised that they haven't done that already."

"Because nobody wants that. Well, least not on our side."

I nodded and started heading back inside the bar. "So does that mean you don't have any issues with my working with them?"

"Nah, I'm good."

"Thanks, because I suspect Chaz is going to want to sail with us."

"And you need somebody to keep all of you out of trouble."

"That too," I said as I went back to the party with a few more things to think about. If someone in the Ceres government was helping out Marcus's people—the Let-Be's as Hank was calling them—that meant we might have some help when it came time to sell and trade for them.

I just needed to make sure that, if there were, I didn't give *their* involvement away.

Ships Docks and Space

IT TURNED OUT THAT THE HARDEST PART OF ALL OF THIS WAS finding us a captain and pilot. We needed somebody I felt I could trust to keep their mouth shut if I should decide to go on to Eris. They also had to be licensed to fly a ship as big as the *Iowa Hill*.

Because it was a salvage, we probably could have gotten away with making the first trip with just anyone who knew basic ship handling, then just park it a couple hundred kilometers away and have a local pilot come out and take us into the dock.

I actually gave that a lot of thought, because I might just be able to pick up a pilot at Eris from Marcus. From a security point of view, it would definitely guarantee that their secret would stay secret. But I didn't want any divided loyalties up on the bridge. As one of the ship owners—Kacey and I would own fifty-one percent, our shipping company the other forty-nine—I wanted someone who would listen to me or Kacey, first and foremost. The company next, and any customers, secret or otherwise, last.

Kacey did have a few cousins who were qualified, the problem was just figuring out which one we thought would be the best fit *and* convincing them to quit their job and come work for us.

In the end we resorted to bribery. One of Kacey's close friends, Emiliana, was apparently interested in Kacey's cousin Chris—who, I got the impression, was equally interested in her. However, nothing is ever as it seems when it comes to serious dating, I guess. Either Chris felt she was out of his league, or maybe he was just interested in playing the field. Guys who could captain the larger ships made a good living, and I guess Kacey's friend was maybe a bit too proud to go throwing herself at him. Whatever their problem was, Kacey understood what was going on, because I sure didn't.

As Emiliana, or Emil, was a good cook, as well as rated as a cargo master for reasons that I decided weren't my business, Kacey signed her onto our crew, then dropped the bug in Chris's ear that maybe he'd like a month or two all alone on a ship with Emil and no one else chasing her.

What made this work was Emil was definitely worth chasing.

And, of course, Kacey was quite sure that Chris was interested in Emil in the same ways that Emil was interested in Chris.

"You know, if this doesn't work out, I'm holding you responsible for the inevitable murder/suicide," I told Kacey with a grin.

"Emil's hot for him, no idea why, but she's been so ever since she met him. Trust me, we get them alone together and she'll reel him in like a floundering spacer. Just like I did you!" she said with a wink.

"Oh, I wasn't floundering; I knew *exactly* what I was getting myself into. Speaking of which, how do we make sure no one else interferes in this little plan of yours?"

"Simple, Chaz and Hank are pretty much not interested in anyone else and I don't think Chris is into guys at all. I seem to recall you saying that you wanted to have the wedding before we left?"

I nodded. I figured if we did go to Eris, it would be for the best to be already married when I ran into Marcus and Pam. There would definitely be a lot fewer issues. Plus I wanted Kacey to come. If it delayed her getting her degree by a few months, it wasn't really that big of a deal, seeing as she was part owner of the ship and the company, along with me.

"What about the crew of the ship taking us out there?"

"Well, until we pick a ship, that's up in the air. And speaking of ships, I've been going over what's available out on the docks right now and I've got, like, five possibles. I thought we could go down to the docks and talk to the captains, see what they can do and find out what it's going to cost us."

I looked up at the clock on the kitchen wall. We hadn't signed any leases yet, as until we came back with the *Iowa Hill*, there really wasn't any point. So our "office" was her parents' kitchen. "Why don't we go run down to the charter docks and start talking to them now? I definitely want to inspect their ships, if we're going to be onboard for almost a month."

"Yeah, probably a good idea," she said, standing up. "Let's go."

I followed her out of the house and down to the station, where we got a tram to the charter docks, which was where all of the local operations worked out of. I was finally starting to figure out just how the transit system here worked. There wasn't really a set route. Every car could go anywhere, but its destinations depended on the passengers onboard. Now while there was a certain preference for cars in certain areas to stop at certain places, the computer that ran the system looked at where you were going when you got on board and then figured out your route. Depending on where everyone who'd already gotten on was going, you might simply stay on the car and it'd take you there. Or it might tell you that you had to transfer at a particular station, onto another car to get where you needed to go.

To me it sounded like pure chaos theory. But the computer managing the system did quite well. Apparently it was some sort of "expert learning system" and had gotten quite good at its job, though Kacey told me that about once every few months a car would stop and kick everyone off, because it needed to reset the logic stream for each car every so often, and could only do so when a car was empty.

That didn't happen to us today and we got to the docks without having to change at all, but then again, they were a popular destination with all of the warehouses and repair shops. There were actually a number of different docks on Ceres, but this one was closest and wasn't private, like the military's docks or some of the private corporations' docks.

"Who's first?" I asked Kacey as we entered the charter docks complex, which had its own moving sidewalks and in some cases even tramways to sections too far for most people to walk. This was different from the normal dock complex as there were offices across from each access way for the company that owned the ship. Some of the larger concerns took up entire segments.

"Anatoly's. They specialize in moving crews and equipment out to operations farther around the ring."

I nodded and we went down to their offices and stepped inside. Looking around, it was neat and orderly inside; there were several desks, but only one was occupied by a middle-aged woman.

"Can I help you?"

I smiled. "Yes, we need to take a crew of six and about four tons of equipment out to a ship we're going to salvage."

"And where is the location of the ship?" she asked, picking up a phone.

"Exact details won't be provided until we're underway, but it's about a month's travel at point one grav."

"Two months? Sorry," she said putting the phone back down without even calling anyone. "We're limited to six weeks total round trip."

I didn't even ask why, we just said thanks and walked back out.

"Next?"

"Brennin's," Kacey said with a pensive look. "I wonder if that's going to be a problem?"

I shrugged. "Guess we'll find out."

"Can I help you?" an older man asked as we set foot into the next office, which wasn't half as nice looking as the last one.

"Yes, we need to rent a ship to take a crew of six and about four tons of gear out to a ship we're going to salvage. It's about a month out from here at point one."

"That's a pretty long trip," he said, looking us over.

"I'm aware of that."

"Well, we can do it, but it's not going to be cheap. What kind of equipment are you talking about?"

"A grav drive, several pieces of sheet-steel for hull patching, the rest is tools and food for our trip back."

"So two months out and back," he thought about that. "Three hundred thousand."

"Before we agree to anything, can we see your ship?" Kacey asked.

He nodded and got up. "Sure, it's right across the way."

We followed him out the door over to the access hatch on the other side of the corridor and then into his ship.

The first thing I noticed was the smell. It was faint, but it didn't bode well for what the rest of the ship would be like in my mind.

The tour didn't take very long. The ship was basically a

converted ore carrier with a large bunkroom added on, which took up about a quarter of the hold. It wasn't exactly filthy, but it wasn't all that clean either. The state of the engine room really didn't want me risking my life on it either.

"So, what do you think?" he asked when we stepped back out into the main corridor.

"We have several more outfits we're going to talk with," I said to him with a smile that concealed the fact that I had no desires to sail anywhere in that heap.

"Well, don't take too long, or I'll be under contract to someone else."

I nodded and shook hands with him, so did Kacey.

"Can we find a bathroom?" I asked her after he'd gone back into his office. "I feel unclean..."

Kacey made a face. "Yeah, I need to wash my hands too. There should be one down the corridor before we get to the next place."

The next place was Weeks Transfer service. Their offices looked a lot more professional and there were several people working in the office. I told a young woman who didn't look all that much older than me what we were doing and what we needed, and she sat down at a terminal and started putting in information.

"Okay, soonest we could fit you in would be in three weeks from today. That ship is a bit tight, with six people on it, but it's got more than enough cargo space. We usually use it for hauling equipment out to mining sites. That'd run you about three hundred and fifty K. If you want to wait another two weeks, we'll have one of our larger ships in port that we can send out on something that long, but it'll cost you four hundred and ten. Salvage, you say?"

"Yes," Kacey said with a nod.

"How accurate is your orbit data?"

"Fairly," I said.

"Well, for every week extra you have to look for it, that's going to be another thirty-five K to help you find it."

"You have experience with this?" Kacey asked.

"Oh yeah," the young woman said with a nod. "Every few years someone loses an ore carrier or prospector boat, and they send a crew out to retrieve it. Hope you're used to dealing with dead bodies," she said with a face.

"I was the last crew member off of it," I told her. "It's empty."

"Well, that's good. Give me your contact info and I'll send you a quote for each ship, along with their specs and a contract if you decide to sign with us. If you wait more than a week, the first ship will probably be under contract to someone else by then, but we've got five ships in our fleet, so I'm sure we'll be able to help you out regardless."

"Thanks," both Kacey and I said, and she provided her with an email address to reach us.

"That's really going to push our budget," Kacey said after we left.

"Especially if it takes us several weeks to find the ship. Still, sounds like they've got an experienced crew."

"Well, we've got two more I want to check out, let's see what they say."

"Lead on."

One of the remaining places wanted about the same as Weeks did, the other wanted a lot more. Their ships were nice, but again, we'd have to make a decision soon, because they didn't expect to be without a contract for long. Most of these places were in the same business of supporting all the different mining operations going on.

"Hey!" a voice called out shortly after we exited our last prospect. "I hear you're looking to hire a ship to go out past Neptune and salvage a ship?"

I looked up. There was a guy who I'd put in his sixties, *late* sixties, smiling at us. He was wearing an old, but clean, shipsuit and had on a wool cap.

"Excuse me?" I asked a little warily, checking our surroundings. We were still out on the dock proper; there were more than enough people around.

"Word travels fast down here and someone wanting to salvage a ship out in deep space always gets the rumor mill goin'. So calm yerself down. This ain't a scam. I've heard you say this thing's a month out at point one?"

"Yeah, what about it?" I asked, still feeling a little cautious.

"We can get you there in two weeks, probably less."

"Oh?"

He smiled. "We can run at up to half a gee if we have to. We're a small charter yacht for rich people on vacation, or companies that can't afford their own when their execs need to go someplace. So, we get a fair bit of downtime. I figure we can get you there, hang out a few days, maybe a week, to make sure things are okay, and still be back here in the barn within a month of leaving.

"Plus," he added with a wink, "we got better radar and scanning gear because we're a fast mover. So if it's out there, we'll find it."

"And you are...?" Kacey asked.

"Captain Edgar Hanson. Ship's the *Norse Star*. We're docked way down the far end. Come on, I'll give you the tour."

"What would this cost us?" I asked.

"Four hundred fifty K, fixed price."

"That's a lot," Kacey said a sounding a little worried.

"Yeah, but if we can't find your ship, we'll call it a hundred and fifty to cover fuel, food, and expenses and chalk it up as a nice vacation," Captain Hanson said with a laugh.

"You sound pretty confident," I said.

"'Course I am, I was a destroyer captain in the Mars Navy. The *Norse Star* is a converted frigate. Long legs, lots of speed, touch of armor..."

"Weapons?"

"Yeah, a few of those too, but nothing like she was built with," he said while we followed him over to one of the slideways. "We run a pretty small crew, just the four of us, really. Though we do take on a couple of cooks and stewards if we're running a cruise or a bunch of VIPs."

I noticed that Kacey was working her tablet. She looked up at him.

"Well, Mom's heard of you, at least."

"You're one of the Doyle clan, aren't ya?"

"Guilty as charged."

"And she's my fiancée," I added.

"Ah! Sailin's a lot easier when you can bring the wife along. Wife and I have been plying the system for longer than I can recall," he said with a chuckle.

"She's on your crew?" Kacey asked.

"She's my engineer. My brother's our exec and his wife's our other engineer. Between the four of us, we pretty much got it all covered. Ah, we're here."

We followed him off the slidewalk and across the corridor to a ship's access hatch. I noticed there was a small office across the way with a sign over the door that just said NORSE STAR CRUISES.

I was surprised at just how clean and tidy everything was.

"How do you keep this place so clean?" Kacey asked.

"Oh, we have a service come through every time we put back into port. Plus we're all ex-navy sailors, so we're all used to cleanin' up after ourselves."

I'd never been in a warship before—well, not one I got the free run of, at least. The helm station and bridge were right next to the engineering deck, in the middle of the ship. Which made sense, I guess. The crew quarters were right near that as well.

The front of the ship was for the passengers and that part had been modified to enlarge several of the ports to give a rather commanding view. I noticed there was a small second deck to the back of the area up higher.

"What's up there?" I asked.

"Small conning deck. For docking and any other maneuvers where you'd need to look out the ports. We don't use it much. The hologear we've got on the bridge now is more than capable."

"How old is this ship?" Kacey asked.

Captain Hanson smiled. "They laid her keel down over ninety years ago. The Mars Navy sold her off to the breakers about thirty years back and me and the wife got her cheap, and over the years converted her. She'll actually do two gravs if you need it, but that's hell on the plates, so we limit her to a half, tops."

"Do you have enough cargo space to fit a Muller fifteen hundred?" I asked.

"Shouldn't be a problem at all. We used to charter for high-risk, limited-time cargoes before we decided to take the easy life."

"How soon can you be ready to leave?" Kacey asked.

"Tomorrow, though I think it'll probably take a day to get that Muller delivered."

"Let's plan on five days from now," I said. "That'll give us time to get the Muller loaded and make sure everyone's ready."

"Everyone's ready now," Kacey said.

"No, everyone's not ready," I said and smiled at her. "We have a wedding, remember?"

Kacey blushed. "You know, with everything going on, I sorta forgot we'd agreed to take care of that before we left."

✧   ✧   ✧

A week later and we were underway in the *Norse Star*. Emil took over the cooking duties almost immediately, and when Kacey finally emerged from our stateroom after she and I engaged in a very lengthy celebration, she went and helped her for the rest of the trip, while I spent a fair bit of my time down on the engineering deck.

They had fusion reactors down there, four older ones, which I really wanted to learn about. The *Iowa Hill*'s SS12G PWRs were nearing the end of their life cycle. They had ten years left, twelve at best. When that time came, they'd have to be decommissioned, which meant pulling them out and replacing them if we wanted to keep working the ship.

Fusion reactors didn't suffer from that problem, as they weren't subjected to the same kinds of radiation that the fission cores in the PWRs generated. So where the PWRs' cores eventually turned the rest of the reactor vessel too dangerously radioactive to use, on fusion reactors you could just change out the parts. True, they did lose efficiency over the years and required more maintenance as they aged, and true, some of those parts were difficult and expensive to replace, but they were still cheaper, and safer, to run than a fission reactor. This is why everyone had switched to them, once the price came down enough so that people other than the military or the government could afford them.

I was hoping to find a good set of older, used ones for the *Iowa Hill* by the time their replacement came. So I needed to start learning about them and keep an eye out for any deals out there. Both of the engineers, Beatrice Hanson and her sister-in-law, Wilma, were pretty knowledgeable when it came to fusion generators. Then again, they'd both been chief engineers since long before I was born, and done full careers in the navy, working on this very type of fusion reactor.

So it was educational.

When we were about two days out from our destination, I gathered our "crew" in the lounge so we could go start going over just what our plans were.

Chris Doyle, the *Iowa Hill*'s new captain, was sitting with Emiliana. I didn't know when they hooked up, because Kacey and I had been in that stateroom for a lot of days. Sure, we'd been sleeping together for over a month by then, closer to two, but we still really wanted to celebrate and we wanted to do it in private, and very much alone.

Chris was a fairly good-looking young man, tall, dark haired, with a fair complexion. He was only a few years older than me, so we hadn't had any problems connecting. Emil was a redhead with a lot of freckles and a nice slender figure.

Hank and Chaz were there, of course, and I suspect were enjoying the staterooms as much as the rest of us.

"Okay, so we're about two days out, and if what Captain Hanson has told me is true, they'll probably pick up the *Iowa Hill*'s signature fairly soon. I did leave one of the reactors running when I left, the ship's gravity was on, though it was set low, and I'd left the navigation lights on as well."

"How long ago was that?" Chris asked.

"At this point, about nine months," I told him. "It's possible that something happened and tripped the auto-scram on the reactor, but at a low power setting I doubt it. But even if that did happen, both reactors generate enough heat just sitting there to keep the temperature in the front half of the ship from getting too far below freezing."

"You said that only the cargo hold lost atmosphere?"

I nodded. "The living spaces, front and back, were all fine. I brought some sheets of hull metal to patch the spot were we were hulled. There should be enough atmosphere in the ship's tanks to re-pressurize the hold, but we brought a few extra tanks with us just in case. Once that's done, we'll swap out the fifteen hundred and hook it up. Then we'll be good to go."

"Can we fly it without the replacement?" Hank asked.

I nodded. "The grav engine that we lost handles the rear quarter of the ship, from about the rear cargo wall back. I checked the ship's specifications, and talked to a few of the shipbuilders on Ceres. They agreed with me that without a load we could run the ship at normal speeds, and with a load fifty percent of normal would still be safe. We'd just have to run the internal gravity at half a gee in either case."

"So we're good to go, even if we can't fix it or something goes wrong with the new one?" Emil asked.

"Yup."

"Are we going to ask Captain Hanson to hang around for a few days, just in case?"

"At least one. Maybe two. I think we'll know within a day whether or not we can sail."

"Maybe we should put it up to a vote?" she asked, looking around.

Chris immediately shook his head. "Once we're aboard the *Iowa*, *I'm* the captain, and when it comes to the crew's safety, that's going to be my call. If Dave over there"—he pointed to me—"can't convince me that the ship can fly, and can support us all safely, then we'll be leaving it there and returning on this ship."

"Why does he have to convince *you*?" she asked, looking genuinely curious.

"Because I'm the captain?" he said with a smile. "It's my license, my certifications that are on the line if anyone gets hurt or anything gets damaged. So I'm not going to endanger anyone's life, especially not my own. Nor will I endanger the ship."

He looked over at Kacey and me. "You two don't have a problem with that, do you?"

We both shook our heads.

"We hired you because you're an expert," Kacey said. "So it would be kind of stupid for us to waste all that money we spent and ignore your advice, now wouldn't it?"

"My thoughts exactly," I said, agreeing with her.

"So, are you going to be the chief engineer from here on out?" Hank asked. "Or just for this trip?"

I smiled. "Probably from here on out. As much as I would love to hire someone and just work for them until I got my hours up enough to get my second engineer's tag, I don't know that we can afford it."

"Is that legal?" Chaz asked.

"What, my being the chief engineer?"

"Yeah, 'cause you're only a third right now. I know for this trip we're just running a skeleton crew, but what about when we start hauling cargo?"

"The owners were willing to sign off on it because of my extensive experience with this particular ship," I said with a grin.

"Really?" Emil asked with a skeptical look.

"Yeah, what she said," Chaz agreed.

I gave a small sigh. "It's legal. If we were carrying passengers it wouldn't be, but for just cargo? I've got a lot of time in that ship and as a third engineer I am allowed to run a ship's engineering division. Once I become a second, I can even run a passenger liner, just not a big one. There's tonnage restrictions involved, just like on a captain's tag."

"What's the plan for the rest of the crew?" Hank asked.

"We're not sure," I said, looking over at Chris. "It's something that Chris, Kacey, and I are still discussing. We'd like two more mates to cover the flying duties, but we could do it with just one. The problem is, someone rated as a first officer costs a lot more than a second or a third."

"Well, you have to have one, don't you?" Chaz asked.

Chris shook his head. "As the chief engineer and also as one of the ship's owners, Dave could take that role."

"But I'm not so sure I want it," I said with a frown. "Because a lot of extra duties come with that role and I've already got a lot on my plate with being the chief engineer."

"Yes, but we're only going to add two or three more people," Chris said. "So I don't think you'll be that overwhelmed."

"A lot of that is going to depend on how good the engineer I hire to be my assistant turns out to be," I replied.

"How long until we get back home?" Emil asked.

Kacey shook her head. "That's going to depend on what we find when we get onboard the *Iowa Hill*. We've got a possible contract already lined up, so if the ship's up to it, we're going to pick up a cargo on the way home to help cover the cost of this trip."

"So?"

"Anywhere from a month to a couple of months," I said. "That's not a problem, is it?"

She smiled and leaned into Chris. "Oh, not a problem at all..."

There were a couple of snickers at that response, one of which came from me.

"So, Hank, enjoying flying on a Mars Navy ship again?" Kacey asked.

Hank grinned. "I've actually been on this class of ship before—not this particular one, though. I've spent quite a few hours with Captain Hanson and his brother, Stew, reminiscing about our days in the service."

"Turns out they crossed paths, more than once," Chaz said. "When the ships they were on formed up for a mission."

"I'm just happy we found these guys—or rather, that they found us," Kacey said. "It might be expensive, but the time we're saving almost makes up for it."

I noticed a slight smirk on Hank's face; I guess he didn't think it was a coincidence that we'd run into Captain Hanson.

On the off chance that he was right, I decided that I'd weld up all those patches we'd discussed *before* I let any of the *Norse Star*'s crew aboard to inspect. Last thing I wanted was to lose that ship after all the work it'd taken us to get this far.

"How long do you think it'll take them to find the *Iowa*?" Chris asked.

"Not very," Hank said. "They still have the original detection suite in the ship. When the navy sold it, none of it was classified anymore, so it was just cheaper to leave it in than to rip it out. In fact, Captain Hanson asked if I wouldn't mind joining them on the bridge tomorrow to help run it."

About halfway through the ship's day on the following day, the captain came over the intercom.

"We've got a fix on what we think is your ship. Everybody either find an acceleration couch or get in your beds and secure for maneuvering!"

"Can I stay here?" I asked Beatrice as I was down in Engineering discussing the advantages of different gravity profiles for the different drives. Wilma was off shift, which usually meant she was sleeping.

"Sure, just strap in."

A couple minutes later, everyone reported in as secure, and Emil reported that both she *and* the kitchen were secure. I watched on the bridge repeater that Beatrice had in Engineering as the captain spun us to a new heading, fired up the engines to a full gravity for a minute, reoriented us a second time, ran the drive back up to a full gravity for two more minutes, then flipped us and we decelerated the rest of the way.

"Alright, everyone! We should be there in about six hours. You may go about your business."

I looked at the radar and other detector feeds that Beatrice had up and I really couldn't see anything more than just a big dot. But the course and speed figures looked to be in the neighborhood of what we'd plotted.

Three hours later, I was up on the bridge looking at a long-range enhanced camera view.

"Yup, that's our ship!" I said happily.

"Well, she looks to be in one piece," Captain Hanson said.

"I was allowed to survey the damage before we left. The same shot that killed the fifteen hundred was the one that hulled us and took the air out of the cargo hold. They were either lucky, or really good."

"Doesn't much matter, just as long as it gets the job done, right?"

"I'm just happy my old company passed on salvaging it and let me have it."

"That was a lucky stroke, I'd say."

I laughed. "No, the lucky stroke was finding out that my then-fiancée's family was willing to help us raise the one point five million credits that it's taken us to get to here, and to actually find the ship. Now to get it home and get it earning."

"Not gonna sell it?"

"It's got ten, maybe twelve years left before the SS12G PWRs gotta be replaced. I'm not sure we'd really get all that much for it. But if we turn it into a local trader..." I shrugged. "Who knows? Ten years from now we may have earned enough to put new reactors in it, maybe even have a second ship."

"That's pretty optimistic," Captain Hanson said with a chuckle.

"Well, my personal goal is to get into tuning grav drives for the shipyards and the folks getting rebuilds. This'll just give me a place to put all that money I'm going to make," I replied with a grin.

"If you want to do that, why're you here?"

I shrugged. "Wife's idea mostly, but it's a good one. So why not? I need more hours anyway as a ship's engineer if I want folks to take me seriously. Besides, it's my first ship, I really don't want to just let her die, you know?" I said with a crooked smile. I had a feeling that would connect with the captain, because he'd gone out of his way to get this ship, which I now suspected he'd once served on.

"Now that is about as noble a sentiment as a man can have," he said with a huge grin. "Better start getting your gear ready and suit up. We'll be there soon enough."

"Thanks for getting us here," I said, sticking out my hand. "I'm glad we decided to go with you."

He smiled and shook hands with me. "I'm glad too. We don't have anything signed for another month, and it was getting boring sitting around the house."

I nodded and headed down to my room and got my pressure suit out, then put it on and tested it. Kacey came in while I was finishing up and I unabashedly ogled her while she stripped down and got into hers. We then packed all of our personal belongings into vacuum-proof bags and moved them down to the cargo hatch in the back.

Hank and Chaz were already there, inspecting all of our gear, making sure it was still secure and also making sure they had everything set to unfasten it, get a couple of lines on it, and then winch it over to the *Iowa Hill*, once we'd gotten the main cargo doors open. Both of them were wearing actual spacesuits, not pressure suits with parkas over them like the rest of us were. As deckhands, they were expected to work in vacuum and had the skills to go with it.

I checked to be sure all of our personal gear was hooked to a line, so it wouldn't get lost, then looked around the hold.

"Anybody got anything they need to say?" I asked.

"Nope, I'm good!"

"Let's get this hopping! I want to sleep in my own bed tonight!" Chaz said with a laugh.

"Okay, helmets on, everyone. Hank'll go through first with Chaz behind him, and they'll rig the line. I'll go across next, and the three of us will check everything out. If it looks good, Chaz'll come back and shepherd the rest of you across. Got it?"

Everyone gave me a thumbs-up and I put my helmet up, turned on the radio, and we all checked in with the bridge one at a time.

"We're parked about a hundred feet from your ship, Dave. I've unlocked the airlock—once you give me the green light, I'll start pumping down the cargo hold."

"Understood, Captain. Hank, Chaz, get to it!"

I watched as they cycled through the lock together, then I cycled through behind them. By the time I got out, Hank was standing on the hull of the *Iowa Hill*, and had a line between the two ships. Chaz showed me how to clip on to it, then we both launched over to it. We then cycled through the rear airlock, and once inside I checked my suit's indicators.

"Atmosphere is good, temperature is forty degrees Fahrenheit. I guess Environmental is still working."

"Chaz, why don't you accompany Dave down to Engineering? I'm going to check Environmental out."

"Sure thing!"

✧   ✧   ✧

Ten minutes later, we were down in Engineering with our helmets off, and I was bringing the fusion reactor online. I'd already started the process to bring both of the SS12G PWRs up.

"Dave, how's it going in there?" Captain Hanson called to me over my suit radio.

I pulled my helmet up so I could use the microphone.

"So far, so good. We got breathable air. It's a little cold, but I'm bringing both reactors and the APU up online. Should have full power in a couple of hours. We're going to check the bridge next. Hank's doing an inspection in the back and unless he tells me otherwise, I think we'll be able to open the cargo doors and start shipping our cargo in an hour."

I turned to Chaz. "Go bring the rest of our crew over."

"Let me check in with Hank first."

"Hank's checking our battle damage—if you want to talk to him, I'd suggest touching helmets and *not* using the radio."

"Huh?"

"I'll explain it to you later if he doesn't. Just don't talk about it to anyone, especially not off this ship."

Chaz nodded. "Got it," he said and left me as I went up to the bridge.

Using the codes I'd gotten off Steve Roy after that party, I logged into the main system on the bridge and started changing all the admin passwords. I also locked out all of the old crew, except for Chaz, Hank, and myself. Then I created new accounts for Chris, Kacey, and Emil. I'd share the admin and root passwords with Chris once he was over here, but not before.

I went and checked the freezers in the kitchen next. Everything in the refrigerators had gone bad, so those would have to be emptied out and cleaned. But the stuff in the freezers still looked good.

Then I went out onto the cargo dock to check on Hank. As I'd expected, he was artfully cutting holes in the two catwalks that had been pierced by the "shell" that had hit us.

I got his attention and we touched helmets so we could talk to each other.

"Almost done? I want to open the cargo bay so we can start shipping gear soon."

"Yeah, this is the last of it. I already put a bunch of dents in the ceiling."

"What, no hole?"

"It only made it that far because the catwalk floors are grills instead of solid plate," he said with a chuckle.

"I'll call you when it's safe over the ship's com."

"How's Environmental look?"

"All of the matrices are dead, but we got stuff to restart 'em. Until then the carbon scrubbers will keep us alive."

"Got it. I sent Chaz to get everyone else. They're probably making their way through the airlock by now."

"So, what's our next step?"

"After we get everything moved over, we need to slap a patch on the outside hull, to deal with that hole. I can do a temporary in here while you and Chaz deal with that. I'd like to get an atmosphere back in the hold as soon as possible, so I can change out that drive. That's not something I want to do in a pressure suit if I don't have to."

"Got it," Hank said and, moving away from me, he started packing up the cutting torch, moving to secure it out of sight of the cargo doors as I went back up to the bridge.

Kacey, Chris, and Emil were already up there, helmets off, by the time I made it back.

"We're ready to open the doors, Dave," Hank called over the ship's comm.

"Okay, let me warn Hanson." I pulled my helmet up and commed Captain Hanson.

"We're going to open up the cargo doors. Any side in particular you want to use?"

"Port's good," he replied.

"Got it," I said and went over to the controls and, unlocking the port side, I set them to open.

"Okay, that's done," Kacey said, looking up from the main console she was working at. "Chris, you are now officially logged onboard as the captain of the *Iowa Hill*. I've got your passwords for you. The ship is now officially under your command."

Chris smiled. "Great! Now, Dave, I want the full tour." He then reached over and hit the "all hands" button on the comm unit.

"All hands! Captain Chris Doyle is now in command of the *Iowa Hill*, effective this day, twelfth of August, at thirteen twenty-five, Ceres. Hank, let me know when you're ready to start shipping cargo. You can coordinate that without my help, I'm sure."

"Copy that, Captain!" Hank called back.

"Now, let's inspect my new command. Feel free to join us, girls."

I spent the next four hours giving Chris a much more detailed tour of the ship than I'd expected to. By the time we were finished, Hank and Chaz had shifted all the cargo and were working on the patch on the hull. Kacey was still with us, but Emil was up in the kitchen seeing what she could make out of what was in the freezers for us to eat.

"I still want to run a drive test and a grav panel test before we pull out the bad drive," Chris said as we finished up in Environmental. "I want to be sure we have some level of drive as soon as possible."

I nodded. "I was already planning on doing just that. Let me get the temp patch put in the cargo hold, so we can get atmosphere in there for when Edgar or Stew want to come over and take a look."

Chris gave me a scowl. "Why would they want to do that?"

"Because the official story is that this ship was hit with a shot from a rail gun that took out the grav drive and hulled the ship," Kacey said, "and we have to make sure it looks like that's what happened."

"Wasn't it?"

"That's the official story, so yes."

"What happens if it's not?"

"Don't even think of it," I said with a sigh.

"Okay, but once we're underway, an explanation is due, okay?"

I smiled. "Oh trust me, you're gonna get all the explaining you'll ever want to hear."

Putting my helmet back on, I went out into the cargo hold and started on a temporary patch on the bottom floor. I had to do one on the inside deck, then a second one on the inside portion of the hull. That one would be pretty simple, seeing as Hank and Chaz were now welding the new patch into place. But I had to get down there with the grinding wheel and make sure I removed all telltale traces of the blast, the edges of which were bent out and should be bent *in*.

I started with the floor of the cargo area, that being the easiest to see, and the easiest to deal with as it was bent away from me. But I still had to get some good grind marks around it to make it look like I'd "fixed it" before I went any further.

Then I went to the area between the hulls and dealt with that. That took a bit longer as there was a panel that had taken a direct hit. I unbolted it and moved it out of the way for now. I'd have to get Chaz down here with to help me swap it out later, before we did the drive test.

I was just finishing up the first patch weld when the doors closed and air started pumping into the cargo deck. Once I saw we had atmosphere, I went and checked the safety interlocks on all the doors, the purpose of which was to ensure that the cargo bay door locks couldn't be undone when there was atmosphere inside the bay.

Which made me realize why they'd used a powerful enough device to not only destroy the drive, but to cut through the hull and depressurize the bay. When there was no air in here, you could operate the doors from outside. Assuming that there was no one on the bridge to stop you, of course.

"Cargo bay has atmosphere again and is secure," I called over my suit radio, and then went over to the hatch that led to Engineering to repeat that over the ship's internal comm.

"Hey, Dave, care to show us around the *Iowa Hill*?" Captain Hanson called over my suit radio.

"If it's okay with our captain, sure! Love to show you around. Hey, think you could ask Beatrice or Wilma to come over too?"

"Probably, what's up?"

"Well, these Siz-gees only have ten years or so left, and they've been telling me that I could probably fit an old pair of fusion ones in here to take their place. So I figured I'd let one of 'em look around and tell me whether or not they'll actually fit."

"Ah, got it. Let me raise Chris, and if he's okay with it, we'll be right over."

"Great!"

I hustled my ass down between the hull and deck space and slapped those last two patches on as fast as I could. I only needed one, but the second one would help hide the truth, should anyone ever come down here to inspect.

I was just crawling out of the area when I heard Beatrice calling my name.

"Down here, Bea!" I yelled. "Just finishing up the last patch. Don't want to have to worry about any pinhole leaks!"

I hauled my gear up and left it on the deck for now, and

made my way over to the central catwalk, then climbed up to the mid-deck where she was.

"Come on, let me show you my new domain!" I said with a chuckle and led her off to the engineering deck.

"Wow, been a long time since I've seen one of these!" she said, looking around, once we'd gotten inside.

"I just can't believe I actually *own* it now," I said, shaking my head. "Two years ago I was just some kid who'd just gotten out of engineering school. Now I own a spaceship. That's just weird."

"Have you given any thoughts as to what you're going to do with that old Muller?" she asked, looking over at me.

I shrugged. "I don't know, sell it for scrap?"

She shook her head and smiled at me. "I saw all the *damage* that shell did to your ship. Honestly, why you'd want to haul back something that couldn't be fixed is beyond me. Probably just best if you dumped it out here in the depths of space, right?"

"Umm, I'm missing something here, aren't I?"

"Everything looks like you got hit by a rail gun...well, the decks do, I'm sure the hull does, the catwalks especially..."

It dawned on me and my jaw dropped for a moment. The blast on the top of the grav drive was up, but all the rest of it was *down*. The charge, now that I thought about it, had been placed under one of the inspection plates. If anybody were to see it, they'd know.

"You know what, Bea? You're right. Why would I want to waste energy hauling that hunk of steel around? Probably cost us more shipping it than we'd make scrapping it. Thanks for the tip."

She gave me a nice big friendly smile then. "Just trying to help, David. It's always nice to see a young couple working hard to make a better life for themselves."

"And for our friends, too," I added with a smile. "Can't forget about your friends, right?"

"No," she said with a chuckle, "no, we can't."

Iowa Hill—Deep Space

CHANGING OUT THE WRECKED MULLER DRIVE FOR THE NEW ONE took a little bit longer than I'd expected. About two days longer.

I started off by taking lots of pictures of all the settings, the fittings, even the damn bolts holding it to the keel. Bolts that took me, Hank, and Chaz, along with a lot of swearing and the eventual help of a blue-tip wrench, to get off. This was after half a day of disconnecting every single line attached to it.

Then we hoisted it up a centimeter and spent the next hour making *sure* that everything was disconnected and that it would clear all the lines when we pulled it out. This was more because if we broke any of the lines that connected to it, we didn't have the equipment to repair them.

So a lot of care was necessary.

After that, hoisting it out, setting it by the cargo door for its eventual ejection into space, and putting the replacement on the hoist was pretty trivial.

Lowering the new one into position was not, however.

It turned out that the bottom footing plate on the replacement was a different shape from the plate on the old one. Those plates are cast into the unit's casing and we did not have the ability, or the skill, to swap said casings.

So out came the blue-tip wrench to cut the new one into the shape of the old one. Then Hank, Chaz, and I took turns drilling a dozen four-centimeter-wide holes through a two and a half centimeter thick piece of steel.

Much more swearing ensued, as it was a long, tiring, and difficult job that required the drill bits (we had two) to be constantly resharpened. Also, the amount of oil we used to keep them cutting also made quite a mess, which contributed to even more cursing.

When we finally got the holes all cut, we all decided that a good meal and eight hours of sleep would probably be wise, before attempting to install it a second time.

Next morning at the table in the mess, Chris came in while the rest of us were eating.

"Dave?"

"Yes?"

"Are you aware that we don't have a lifeboat?"

I almost hit my forehead on the table in front of me. The only thing that stopped me was I didn't want a face full of omelet.

"Shit," I swore. "I forgot about that."

"Damn, we *all* did," Hank agreed.

"So, what do we do about it?" Chaz asked.

"Is the *Norse Star* still out there?" I asked.

"Yes, Edgar has agreed to stay a couple of days," Chris told us.

"Okay, my vote is anyone who's not comfortable with this, can fly back with them. I think we're okay, I don't think it's an issue—though I do intend to get a replacement as soon as possible. However, I don't think anyone should take the risk if they're not comfortable with it. We can always take 'em back on board when we get to Ceres."

"What if *I'm* not comfortable with it?" Chris asked.

"Well, I guess I'll ask you to program the route in to Ceres before you left and I'll take my chances," I said with a shrug. "At this point I'm kinda committed and unless I find anything that makes me think we're not safe flying without it, I'm not going to worry about it."

"Why don't we see if we can borrow one from Edgar?" Chaz asked.

"It's going to be months before we get back to Ceres, I don't know if he'd want to be without one for that long."

"I'll talk to him," Hank said. "If we can't borrow one, maybe he'll sell one to us. He's got three and normally, even with passengers, he only needs two."

"But what if we can't get one?" Chaz asked.

"The girls go back on the *Norse Star*," Chris said. "Either or both of you can stay if you want to, your call. But if our engineer is willing to trust his life to the ship, so am I."

"Before anyone says anything," I interrupted, "everyone is now crew and gets paid regardless of if they're going back with us or with Captain Hanson on the *Norse Star*."

"Let's wait and see what happens," Hank said, digging back into his breakfast, "before we make any decisions."

"Good idea," I agreed. "As soon as I'm done here, I'm going back down into the hold and see about getting that drive put back in place. Chaz, you can help while Hank is talking to Edgar. If he gives us a boat, you and Hank can deal with it. Hooking up the lines is pretty much a one-man job anyway."

"Got it," Chaz said, and Hank just nodded.

"Keep me informed," Chris said, and left to go back to the bridge.

It took about an hour to get the drive into place, then another half or so to get it all bolted down. Chaz left at some point, so I guessed that they worked something out with Captain Hanson. I spent the next six hours carefully hooking each of the lines back up to the drive. Thankfully, all the fittings were in standardized locations, so I didn't have to fight with anything there, but each of them took a lot of care and special handling. Then I had to carefully seal each one, and test it. Several of them I had to detach, clean, reattach, and test again, until they worked properly. It was very much a painstakingly slow job, but it had to be done just right, and I was glad I understood it from all of the work I'd done on the panels.

That done, I called for Chaz to come help me if he had some free time and I finally replaced that panel with the big hole in it. Fixing it was going to require some very tricky welding to the case; the rest of it wouldn't be too much trouble. Thankfully, Chaz was a very talented welder, so I left him to it while I went and found Chris.

"What's up, Dave?"

"We can do a drive and panel test whenever you want. Just warn Chaz, he's back in the shop welding something for me."

"Sure thing."

"So, did we get a lifeboat?"

"Yup. Hank's still running checks on it and studying the manual for it. We rented it for six months."

"How much?" I asked with a grimace. Lifeboats weren't cheap.

"Hundred grand."

I nodded. "Guess I need to talk to Kacey."

"She's the one who approved it, so she already knows. Let's do a quick inspection, then we'll run the tests. The sooner we can get underway, the better. We're not making any money sitting out here, right?"

I smiled and gave a nod. "Right."

It was late. All of the tests had been run, and everything had passed. We'd even done a short flight for thirty minutes, flipped the ship, and then decelerated back to our original velocity. The *Norse Star* was now heading off back to Ceres as we'd just radioed our thanks. We were all sitting on the bridge, Kacey and I having called for a meeting.

"Okay, everyone," Kacey said starting off. "As you may have heard either Dave or me saying, we have two options. First is to go back to Ceres, which means we show up there without any cargo, so we don't make any money on this trip."

"Well, we got the ship, isn't that enough?" Emil asked.

"If we were planning on *selling* her, it would be. But we're not. Dave and I have decided to start a cargo hauling company. So it would be a lot better, financially, if we could show back up at Ceres with a cargo."

"But there's a small problem with the cargo we're thinking of hauling," I said.

"And that problem is?" Chris asked.

"I know where the place is that I was held 'prisoner' for six months," I said, making air quotes. "I also know that they're sitting on a lot of processed ore that they'd really like to be able to trade."

"You want to trade with pirates?" Emil asked, giving me a look like I'd lost all sense.

"They're not really pirates," I said with a sigh. "They're refugees.

They're in hiding because they're not strong enough to defend themselves. The only reason they've had to resort to piracy is because they're broke."

"So why aren't they trading, then?"

"Because they can't afford to have the people they're hiding from find out where they are. They can't use their own ships, because someone might recognize them, and sell them out. But I'm not going to rat them out. They were nice to me, they helped me and my crewmate out. They kept their word.

"As far as I'm concerned, they're good people who got a shitty deal and are trying to make the best of it. So we show up, offer to help them out with their trading."

"This way," Kacey said, picking it back up, "not only do we put an end to their piracy in the area, but we make a profit to boot. Win-win. Everybody's happy."

"Okay, but why are you asking us?"

"Because this has to be kept secret," I told her, and looked around the room at everyone else. "Right now, I'm the only one who knows where this place is. I'll share that information with Chris, if he's okay with knowing it, but not with any of the rest of you. You can't share what you don't know, but going even further, I don't want any of you even telling where we got this shipment from. Anyone asks, it was a dark hab, you never set foot off the ship, you never met anyone, I wouldn't let you. That's the line everyone here is going to have, if anybody asks, okay?"

"And if you're uncomfortable with any of this, you have to say something, now," Kacey added. "We'll happily confine you to your cabin once we get there, we'll even put it in the log, so if anyone 'official' looks into it, they'll see you have no idea where we were, or who you were dealing with. Is everyone okay with that?"

Emil looked over at Chris. "Are you okay with this?"

Chris nodded. "Dave, Kacey, and I talked about this before we left. We agreed to do a few things to keep the knowledge just to Dave."

"If I may?" Hank asked.

Chris and I both nodded.

"Okay, on the record, if we all tell everyone what we're told to say, they'll leave you alone, should there ever be a problem. I'd also suggest that you enter into the log that all crew were confined to their cabins from the time we entered the space of where we're going, until we've left it. That'll give us a nice legal backing. These things have happened before, and being totally honest, unless you actively *try* to find out where we're going, you're not going to be able to figure it out.

"Off the record," he said, and looked around the room at everybody. "And I mean this is *off the record*. This isn't something you want to talk about, because you'll get in trouble, but off the record, I'm fairly certain that Ceres's government, Mars's government, probably all of the groups around Jupiter, Saturn, and Neptune, know about these people and what's going on. They're also most likely covertly supporting them, or at least looking the other way. So if they ask, stick to the story. If anybody *else* starts asking, you tell us. If they start pushing, tell the enforcers, maybe even the people in charge."

"Why?" Emil asked.

"'Cause everybody hates the folks that they're running from and are worried that one day there's going to be a war. Having a large population of people from the region who not only fit in, but know how everything works there is the kind of resource you protect, even if you're completely lacking in scruples," Hank said with a shrug. "These folks got a raw deal and are coping best they can. So if we help them, all those folks out there 'looking the other way' just may one day help *you* out when you expect it the least and need it the most."

"Okay, that makes sense, but I think I will ask to stay in my cabin when I'm not working in the mess. Like you said, I can't talk about what I don't know."

"So," Kacey asked. "Nobody has any problems with this?"

I looked around the room, as everyone said they were okay with it. Chris, Kacey, and I had all agreed that we'd tell the lie that only I knew where it was. Though even Chris didn't know that I'd told Kacey. Chris could simply say that I did the navigation myself and didn't share it with anyone. I don't know if people would believe that, but once we got underway, one thing we would be doing is covering all of the windows on the bridge with screens that couldn't be looked through. All of the cameras that looked outside were also being password locked for the duration. Because Eris had a moon, and anyone seeing that would quickly figure out just where we were.

"Well, Dave and I are going to set up the first leg of the course," Chris said. "Once we get there, we'll load in Dave's course and we'll be on our way. So if you'll all clear the bridge, we can get started."

"Oh, and everyone make sure you've got nothing of any value loose down in the cargo hold," I said. "We're going to pump it down and eject that old drive. It's not worth the price of scrap to haul it around and take up cargo space."

"Well, we're on our way now," Kacey said to me, later that night when were snuggling in bed. "We've got our own ship, and we're off to get our first cargo."

"I just hope they don't shoot us." I sighed.

"I wonder if they know we're coming."

"How would they?"

"Well, both you and Hank seem to think that Captain Hanson and his wife were both in the know, on what's going on."

I snorted. "Yeah, looking back on it, it was one hell of a coincidence that they just 'happened' to know we were looking for a ride and that they just 'happened' to have the time off to take us out here. But, I don't know if they realize where we're going next. I mean, I'm not supposed to know where they are."

"Do you think the Ceres government knows where they are?"

I gave my head a slight shake. "Not a clue. Settling on Eris is a pretty ballsy move, so no one expects it, I'm sure."

"What do you think is going to happen when we show up?"

"I think they'll try to play dumb at first. I've given a lot of thought to what I want to say."

"Have you thought about asking them to supply us with an engineer or maybe a couple of mates?"

"Why would they agree to that?"

"Because it lets them keep an eye on us, so they know we're not going to sell them out."

"And why would *we* agree to it?"

Kacey grinned at me. "Because we don't have to pay them."

I laughed. "I'm gonna remember that! But you're right, we could just give them a stipend so they'd have a little money to spend, but that would do a lot for our bottom line."

"We might even be able to get them to give us another lifeboat, so we don't have to buy our own when we return the *Norse Star*'s."

"And what do we offer them for that?"

"Free passage for any refugees?" Kacey said with a shrug and then yawned. "I'm sure they've got contacts and spies all over the solar system at this point. We're just a regular small shipping company; no one's going to connect us to them. I'm sure we'll be able to do them a favor, here and there, to help them out."

"It does bear thinking about," I agreed. "Now, let's go to sleep, my little capitalist. We've got a lot of work to do now that we're underway."

"Yeah, I promised Emil I'd help clean the insides of those refrigerators," Kacey said, and stuck out her tongue. "Bleah, those things are a mess!"

"Yes," I agreed with a chuckle. "Yes, they are."

It was three weeks to get to Eris. In the last seven months, the *Iowa Hill*'s ballistic trajectory had diverged a great deal from where we wanted to go. I was pretty happy with how well the new 1500 was performing and everything else was well under control. The regular maintenance that Dot had always insisted on was paying off now that it was just me doing the work. I did my best to keep up with her old schedule as well, because Eris was starting to pass Pluto's orbit and over time these trips would be to more and more isolated parts of the system.

Not any place where you'd want to have to deal with an emergency of any kind.

When we finally started to draw close to Eris, it was just Chris and me on the bridge. We were keeping the door locked and I had everyone in their pressure suits, just in case there was a misunderstanding.

"Eris Science Station, this is the *Iowa Hill* calling," I broadcast over the radio. I'd done this three times already, each about five minutes apart. I wanted to be sure they knew we were coming and give them lots of warning. I had no idea what kinds of early warning equipment they had, I just didn't want to suddenly show up and surprise them.

Not that we probably weren't already a surprise.

"*Iowa Hill*, this is Eris Science Station. What, may I ask, are you doing out here? We haven't received any notification from our sponsors that they were sending out any kind of shipment."

"Eris Science Station, this is Dave Walker, the owner of the *Iowa Hill*. I was given to understand by Marcus that you might have a cargo you need someone to haul to market for you? Perhaps I could talk to him about it."

There was radio silence for almost five minutes after I said that.

"*Iowa Hill*, what are your intentions?" A different voice came on the radio then.

"To visit some old friends, say hi to my ex, and make money hauling cargo. I'll await your 'customs inspectors' to come up and verify that we're not anything other than what I say we are. Say hi to Pam for me."

"Please enter an equatorial parking orbit. Don't do anything stupid, Dave."

I laughed. "I think this already qualifies," I replied. "We'll be waiting."

Two hours later, we were in orbit and a small, but armed, gunboat was parking itself on our transom, near the rear hatch. I was waiting inside, of course, with Kacey. We'd warned all the crew to stay in their cabins until further notice.

When the hatch cycled, four armed men came in, in suits. I recognized three of them immediately, before they even took off their helmets.

"Miguel! Walt! Greg! Nice to see you all again! This is my wife, Kacey, and yes, we're the new owners of the *Iowa Hill*."

"You got married?" Miguel said, and then smiled. "I think the boss is gonna be happy to hear that!"

"Definitely," Greg said, and actually smiled. "When Pam heard you were up here, I think she got a little worried."

"You can tell her not to worry," Kacey said, "'cause he's mine now and she can't have him back!"

There was a round of chuckles over that.

"This is Kenneth," Miguel introduced the fourth man as the lock cycled and another four men entered the ship. "Now, I have to ask, what in the hell are you doing here? Marcus is pissed and I think people are panicking down below. How did you even find us?"

"Well, first of all, Marcus told me that you guys had all this raw material you needed to trade, but you couldn't trust anybody to trade with. Well, I think I've more than proven you can trust *me*. Seriously, I like you guys—if it wasn't for Kacey here and my brother, who I need to go rescue from Earth, I probably would have stayed.

"As to how I found you? Well, once I decided it might be worth coming back, I recalled what your natural gravity is, the size of just what Mabel wants to build, and a bunch of other clues that I got to see while helping you guys get that factory on line. Wasn't hard after that."

"Huh, I think I need to talk to Marcus," Greg said. "Nobody thought about any of that."

I shrugged. "Like I said back then, I'm not going to sell you out. I don't break my word."

"But what about your crew?"

"Well, I trust my wife, otherwise I wouldn't have married her. Our captain and pilot is a relative and I trust him too. Other than that, *nobody* onboard knows where we are, and we've got the door to the bridge locked, the navigation computer display off, and all the windows covered."

"Plus there's only six of us on board, total," Kacey added. "We picked the crew very carefully for this trip."

"Do you mind if we search your ship?" Miguel asked.

"Nope, go right ahead. When you come to the occupied cabins, I'd like for either Kacey or myself to be there when you search those as well. Those people work for us, so I think we owe it to them to be present."

"We can do that. Let's head up to the bridge first—you four, search the back of the ship, then cover the cargo bay. We'll get the rest."

About an hour after they'd searched the ship rather thoroughly, I was surprised as both Marcus *and* Pam came aboard.

"Marcus! Pam!" I said with a smile, and shook hands with Marcus and gave Pam a hug. "Before you start yelling at me, I'd like to introduce my wife. Kacey, this is Marcus, and this is Pam."

"Nice to make your acquaintance," Kacey said, shaking hands with Marcus and then Pam. "Also," she said, smiling up at Pam and lowering her voice, "thanks for teaching him all those fun tricks!"

I almost laughed as Pam turned the brightest shade of red I think I'd ever seen, and Marcus coughed.

"Now I see why Dave said he couldn't stay," Marcus said, recovering rather deftly.

"He said that?" Kacey asked and turned to smile at me.

"More than once. Now, Dave, why are you *here*? Do you have any idea how dangerous this is? For all of us? You're risking all our lives here!"

"We came here from where the *Iowa Hill* had been abandoned in space, so not like anyone could follow us. And trust me, we checked. Everybody thought we were going to head straight back to Ceres, so no one who might care thought to follow us.

"Besides, you know that they know you're out here, somewhere."

"Oh? And what makes you think that?"

"The bomb that was placed aboard the ship to cause it to stop, of course, even though the government and everyone else swears up and down that the ship was fired on to stop it. There's a bunch of other things as well, and I'll be happy to list them in painstaking detail—if you want." I smiled at him.

Marcus didn't even try to fake it, he just nodded. "Alright, we do have a few allies and the Ceres government is one of them. But even they don't know where we are. And I want to keep it that way, for as long as we can."

"Yes, but you told me yourself you need to trade. Well, I've got a cargo ship, now. True, it's not as large as that monster you've got, but I can show up at Ceres with a cargo and no one's going to ask questions, because the government is going to quickly figure out where I'm getting it from, and I think they'd also rather see you paying your own way instead of relying on their good will and charity."

"But you can't keep coming here!"

"Who says we need to?" Kacey replied. "You've got a big cargo ship. There's no reason why we can't set up places to meet far from here going forward. You can have your frigate playing overwatch, so if anybody tries anything, you can deal with it.

"Look, we're taking just as much of a risk as you are. We're in the red here, financially. We need a nice exclusive trade agreement to put us on a solid fiscal footing. My husband here likes you and wants to help you, that's good enough for me to agree to take the risk. We'll even give you rates just slightly higher than the standard contract, even though—let's be honest—we have you over a barrel because you can't trust anyone else enough to deal with them.

"Further, we'll even *allow* you to put an agent on our ship. We've got openings on our crew and we'd be happy to let you fill them with one or two of *your* people. So you can keep an eye on us."

"Let's continue this conversation on the bridge," I said, and motioned to Pam to join me, while Marcus and Kacey started horse-trading as they followed us along.

"So, how are things with you and Marcus?" I asked Pam in a soft voice. "Happy?"

Pam smiled and nodded. "Yes, actually. When I heard you where here, I got a little nervous, but seeing your wife back there?" Pam laughed. "She's definitely your type of woman! Marcus has eight armed men on the ship, two armed boats sitting outside, and she thinks she's got the advantage here."

"Well, Marcus seems to believe she does too," I said with a chuckle of my own.

"Which is why I can see why you wanted to go back to Ceres. She's definitely the woman for you."

I nodded. "And you weren't. Took me a little while to realize that, even though I was always aiming at getting back to Kacey from day one. So why are you up here, anyway? Other than to say hello, that is."

"I'm going to fly the *Iowa* down to the cargo docks."

"Oh?"

"Marcus was pretty sure you'd give him a good deal, and he was also pretty sure that you'd make a good enough argument that he'd go along in the end. Of course, I don't think he counted on *her*," Pam said with giggle.

"Yeah, that's what I love about her," I agreed, glancing back at Kacey, who was going over the details of the agreement now with Marcus. "She's relentless."

"Anyway, you might want to tell the rest of the crew that we'll be putting in at the loading docks to pick up your cargo, then I'd really appreciate it if you'd head down to Engineering, as much as I might like to catch up with you."

"Oh, I'm sure we'll have a few minutes to talk after we land. If nothing else, we can watch the two of them haggle."

Pam laughed and waved to me as I headed down to Engineering.

Miguel joined me down there as I made the announcement over the ship's comm and we chatted for a while. I'd really only been gone for about four months, but I was still curious about how things were going.

"I hope Marcus is able to work something out with you," he admitted to me at one point. "It would really go a long way toward helping things out if we could start getting regular goods into our shops."

"I'm still impressed that you guys went for Eris. That's going to put you way out in space."

Miguel laughed. "That's the whole idea. We'll be too far away from them for them to come after us, and by the time we're back again?" He shrugged. "None of us think that they're going to survive for four hundred years, much less another fifty. Once we're out of the picture, if they can't focus their hate on us, they either turn it on each other or one of the other planets. Either way, none of us think they're going to survive that."

I shook my head. "That's just so screwed. This is why I stay out of politics."

"Think you'll ever come back? People liked you, you know."

I shrugged. "Hard to say. I married into a pretty big clan, it turns out. Then there's this whole cargo business I suddenly find myself in. I mean, I still want to learn how to tune engines for ships and hope to open a shop doing it someday, but"—I shrugged—"my life has been full of unexpected twists and turns. I still gotta help my brother out; maybe after he's settled I can think about it."

"That's fair," Miguel said, and nodded.

When Pam called down and said we'd landed, I shut down the reactors and brought up the APU as I waited for ground power to be connected. Then I went up to the bridge, where Chris had now joined the others. Kacey had her tablet out and it looked like she and Marcus were hammering out the finer details of our shipping contract.

"They haven't finished yet?" I asked Chris and Pam, who both shook their heads.

"I had to listen to it the whole way down," Pam said with a forlorn sigh, which earned her an apologetic look from Marcus.

"Okay, Kacey, let him come up for air for a minute."

"Yes, dear," Kacey said with a smile. "We're almost done with the shipping details anyway."

"Great. Now, can I let my crew out of their quarters? And what's the deal on liberty?"

"Yes, you can let them out, I'm not going to keep any guards on the ship at this point, as it's more or less pointless. We know what's here and you're now parked inside a hanger, so I don't think any of your crew is going to try and make a daring break for it."

I had to laugh at that.

"As to whether or not they go ashore? I'll leave that up to you. I'll have a couple of my people posted outside, and I'll ask that either you, or one of them, accompany anybody who wants to leave the ship. I don't really anticipate any problems, but I do want to make sure no one tries to figure out just where we are."

I nodded. "Oh, did Miguel tell you how I figured it out?"

"Yes, and I think Mabel is going to be hiding from me all week."

I shrugged. "I couldn't set up the factory without finding out what your gravity was without panels. Now, let me tell the crew what's up and maybe we could all have some dinner, kill a few beers, and relax in a more social setting?"

Marcus smiled. "I'd like that. I'd also like to get to know Kacey here when she's not trying to wring every last concession out of me."

"Hey! I'm just good at business!" Kacey protested.

"I think I can make her tone it down for an hour or two," I said, smiling.

"Great. Pam? Let's go see about getting ready." He turned back to me. "We're at my place, you still remember how to get there?"

I nodded.

"Give us a couple of hours, and we'll see you then?"

"Sounds good!" We all shook hands and Chris escorted them off the ship, while Marcus called the guards and told them they could leave. Meanwhile, I got on the ship's comm and told everyone they could leave their cabins now and go ashore if they wanted to, they just had to take a local guide with them, and please don't try ditching them if you do.

"So, how'd we do on the deal?" I asked Kacey.

"Incredibly well. We get normal haulage plus fifteen percent sales fee on everything we ship, and he showed me the list of what they've got refined! We're going to be coming out of here flying close to max weight."

"What about a lifeboat?"

"I got two. First one they'll put in while they're loading

freight. Second one we'll get when we meet with them for our next load. They're going to provide us with a whole list of stuff they want us to buy and bring back."

"Great, and just where are we going to be meeting them from now on?"

"I got a list of three places. We'll use the first one until it becomes an issue, then move on to the next. They're all empty areas with nothing in them, so navigation will have to be pretty precise."

"And what if all three of those become compromised?"

"We got a couple of backups, as well as a way to get in touch with them in case of emergencies. You know that small ship of theirs that dropped you off?"

I nodded. "What of it?"

"They had to develop a security protocol to keep people from using it to backtrack them, and several have tried. We'll just be using that same basic protocol."

"Good. What about the extra crew?"

"They need to talk about that. They have people who can do the jobs, but the issue will be finding the right people."

"Which means?"

"Among other things, people that they have legal documentation for, to show any inspectors or customs people when we pull into port. I mentioned that we want to make a trip to Earth here in the near future."

"How'd he take that?"

"He said he'd send me a list of things that he'd like us to buy while there. I think he's going to see about putting together a cargo for us as well."

"Really?" I sat back and blinked. "That's unexpected."

"I think they've been mining and processing material for over a decade now, hon. That's a lot of cash they're sitting on, and now they've found a way to use it. So they're not afraid to spend it on high-ticket items."

"This worked out even better than I thought it would!"

Kacey smiled. "I know, right? We could be into the black financially in six months!"

I leaned over and kissed her. "Let's clean up and go to dinner."

"But I'm not dirty!"

"Oh, you will be." I grinned and kissed her again.

TWENTY

Eris

LOADING STARTED THE NEXT MORNING, AND WHEN I WENT DOWN
to the cargo hold to see what was going on, I found both Emil
and Chris going over the manifests and weights of each container,
and making notations on a weight and balance program on their
tablets for the ship as they started carefully arranging the load.

It took me a minute to remember that Emil was a cargo master
and that Chris wasn't deferring to her just to avoid arguments
in the bedroom later tonight.

"Hey! Do you know what's in these containers?" Emil asked,
running over to me.

"Processed metals," I said, and then yawned. Kacey hadn't
let me get a lot of sleep last night, though for some reason she
kept telling me it was my fault.

"We got twenty-six TEUs filled with gold! Completely! Another
twenty full of uranium, and I think sixty full of silver! And rare
earths! We got almost two thousand filled with those!"

I shrugged. "They've been stocking up for a while. We're not
going overweight, are we?"

"I'm giving us a fifteen percent margin—normally I'd go with
seven, but this stuff is all so valuable, I thought we shouldn't
chance it. But the top deck is going to be empty, unless they

253

show up with a cargo that's not much heavier than the shipping container it comes in."

"What I want to know," Chris asked, "is how are we going to sell all of this without causing everyone out there to start spying on us?"

I stretched and yawned again. I'd had this same conversation with Marcus last night. His solution was both simple, and brilliant.

"Simple. We're going to give half the gold to the government, for free, if they'll buy the rest of the gold and all the uranium at market."

"You're going to bribe the Ceres government?" they both said in almost perfect unison.

"Bribe is such a dirty word," I said, grinning back at them. "But basically, yeah. Though the people in charge here like to think of it more as 'paying back the Ceres government for all the free stuff and help they gave us.'"

"*That* they'll love," Chris said.

Emil nodded. "Definitely. Just how much do they think they owe Ceres anyway?"

"Billions. This is only the first installment. Which helps to encourage the government from letting anyone find out just how much our cargo is worth, though I doubt we'll be bringing in any more as hot as this one.

"Anyway, when you're done, Chris. I need you to come with me to do a few interviews."

"Interviews?"

"Yeah, they got a couple of folks here who would like to sail with us, and as Kacey worked a deal on their salary as part of our shipping agreement, I thought it might be a good idea to check 'em out."

"That girl is scary when she sits down to negotiate," Emil said.

"She gets it from her mom," Chris said with a grin. "Maureen Doyle is the head of procurement for Ceres Habitats for a *reason*."

"Really?" I said surprised. "But she seems so sweet!"

"Don't ever get between her and a deal, or you, my friend, will never even know what ran over you. She's very much a 'take no prisoners' negotiator. Once she sees something she wants, she doesn't hesitate, not for an instant."

"Damn, that sounds almost like Kacey and my courtship!" I laughed.

"Send Hank down when you can, he can fill in for me so I can join you. They're going to be loading here all day. Heavy stuff always moves slow."

"Will do!" I said, and waved and went to make my own rounds of Engineering. I'd already hired my assistant, Nicolas, who was one of the engineers Mabel had managing the factory I'd set up. Turned out he held a valid engineer fifth certification. He probably needed to take a refresher course, and then I'd start him working toward his engineer fourth certification, but we'd have plenty of time onboard and I already knew he wasn't a slacker.

But Chris would be working with the two mates that we were hoping to hire more than I would, so they were his call. I'd also told Hank that if he wanted to hire any more deckhands to let me know. We had the space and as they were almost working for free, we now had the budget for it.

Dinner with Marcus and Pam had been a little weird for me, because Pam had pretty much been *mine* for those six months. But Kacey must have realized I was dealing with some conflicting emotions, because I got a lot of attention from her all throughout dinner. Which helped me square my head away, because I really did love Kacey. I was slowly finding out that she was probably as crazy as I was, which was a nice change.

Also, seeing that Marcus and Pam really had connected, unlike Pam and me, and that Pam looked the happiest that I could ever recall seeing, helped a lot. I still felt that she was my responsibility, if only just a little bit. So it gave me a warm feeling to know that she was going to be okay.

I found Hank and told him to head down and relieve Chris, once he was able to, then I sat down with Kacey and we did ship's paperwork until Chris was able to break away.

"How long have they been building this place?" Chris asked me when we finally left the ship to go do our interviews.

I shrugged. "No idea. I know they all fled their homes, like, thirteen or so years ago, then kicked around different parts of the solar system while their enemies started hunting them down, until one of them hit on this place and they all started coming here."

"It's just so impressive how much they've gotten done, and yet no one even knows they're here. That shows a lot of dedication and ingenuity."

"I could say the same about Ceres you know."

"We've been there two hundred years now, Dave. Plus we're not hiding from anybody. I don't know that it compares."

"Well, with our help, maybe in two hundred years this place will be the same."

"In two hundred years the trip here in most cargo ships will take four to six months," Chris pointed out.

"Yeah, but maybe they'll have figured out faster than light drive by then, so it'll be just as close as everything else."

"That or they'll build some faster cargo ships for the long haul," Chris agreed. "So what's the real reason we're getting these people so cheap?"

"Kacey and I thought it would be a nice gesture if we allowed them to put one of their 'agents' onboard the *Iowa Hill*, so they could keep an eye on their investment and also warn them if we sold them out or anything like that."

"Really? You're letting them put agents on our ship?"

I shrugged. "It really does help us with the bottom line and I made it clear that, if we got in trouble, I expected them to help bail us out. I mean, I'm not expecting anything to happen, I don't think anyone's going to link us to these folks in a way that'll cause us harm, but Kacey and me, we're pretty sure that they've got a pretty evolved intelligence network spread out in the solar system.

"Also, we're going to be dealing with a lot of money on these trips and I don't want that flowing through *our* accounts, it'll raise too many suspicions. But they've already got accounts set up to handle everything, and whoever we hire as our new first mate is going to have signing authority with the banks. Hopefully that means no one will connect all that money flowing through their accounts with us.

"And again, our home, Ceres, is backing these people. Or at least the government and the powers that be are. Personally I like the idea of being on those people's good side."

"Why? You're not even from Ceres. Why would it matter to you?"

"Two reasons. First is now that I'm married to Kacey, I'm more than happy to be a part of the Doyle clan. Hell, I even changed my last name to Doyle just to make everyone happy. Second..." I stopped and looked at Chris.

"I'm a gang-banger, as we used to say back home. I grew up in the gangs, I cut my teeth in the gangs, and trust me when I say that I did a lot of really bad shit. So I got a lot to make up for, but still, at my basic *most simplest* self, I need to be a member of a gang. Well, if you need to be a member of a gang, why not pick a nice big one with a solid rep?

"That's what Ceres is to me, Chris. They're my gang. This is like my gang initiation. Eventually they'll figure out where my heart lies and what I'm trying to do, and I'll get an invite to the big table and I'll be read in as a full member."

"Seriously?" he asked, looking at me.

"These people here already made me that offer, Chris. If it wasn't for Kacey and my brother? I probably would have taken it."

"Still, a *gang*? We're talking about a government here with tens of millions of citizens."

I shrugged and started walking again. "It really doesn't seem all that different to me. I mean, my gang back home had so many affiliates that I wouldn't be surprised to find out that we'd numbered in the millions as well."

"That sounds kind of hard to believe for a street gang, Dave."

"There's what, twenty billion people on the Earth? What's so hard to believe that a couple million are all in the same gang?"

Chris seemed to puzzle that one a moment, then shook his head. "I can't fault your argument, even if it seems weird. I can't even get my head around a population that large."

"Yeah, me neither and I lived there," I said with a chuckle. "Well, we're here. Let's go inside and see what the local talent has to offer."

Paul, our new first mate, took us off and flew us out, with Chris keeping a watchful eye on him. They were used to flying that monster cargo ship that they had, so flying something smaller was a little challenging for them, but they had a lot of experience, possibly more than Chris. It was nice to see that Marcus had taken this seriously and sent us somebody good. Especially as they were going to be the ones handling the cash transfers on all of the stuff we were trading for them.

Our new second mate was his wife, Katy, or Kat. Kacey and I were pleased that they were a couple, it'd mean fewer hassles, seeing as most of the crew were now couples. She was also very experienced, though not as much as Chris. That we were getting them for almost nothing, when I thought of what we should have been paying for them, made Kacey incredibly happy.

Hank had hired on two more able-bodied spacers, and boy, were they able-bodied! Both were women, Kei and Yuri, and both were very attractive. As I knew that Hank's tastes didn't run that way, at all, I could only figure that he had some sort of larceny deep in his heart that he would share with me when the time came.

Because, according to Chris, all bosuns had larceny in their hearts and were born crooks and criminals. I didn't think Chris appreciated it either when I told him that idea gave me a warm feeling in my own heart.

The trip back to Ceres was a long one, three weeks. We could have done it in two, but Paul, our new first mate, suggested a dogleg, so no one could look at our incoming vector and figure out just where we'd come from.

We all agreed with him and so we were making quite the detour on our return trip, which worked out well for me because I was teaching Nik, my new assistant, the way we did things here on the *Iowa Hill*—which was, oddly enough, exactly the way Dot had taught me.

I was also making sure that he was doing his refresher materials, because I wanted to be sure he was up to speed. I wanted to get him to third engineer as fast as reasonably possible, and then get him his own grav panel rebuilder certification, so not only would *my* life be easier, but when the time came for him to go back home, they'd have at least one person back there who could check up on things.

"What do we tell everybody about these new people we hired on?" Emil asked when we were only a couple of days out from Ceres. Paul had the watch and Kat was hanging out with him on the bridge; Hank, Chaz, and our two new deckhands were out in the cargo hold doing something, probably target practice. We'd set up a range there and we'd all been getting some practice in during the trip.

"Nothing," I said.

"Nothing?"

"Yup. It's none of their business. They're all licensed and certified and can prove it if they have to, but it's really nobody's business as to who is on our crew, or how they ended up here. We don't pry, we don't ask those questions. If anyone presses, tell them it's none of their business. After all, we're traders and haulers and we don't want anyone figuring out where we go, where we stop, who our customers are, any of that. Because we don't want the competition."

Emil looked at me, then looked at Kacey, who was going over some paperwork that we'd gotten once we'd come close enough to open communications with Ceres.

"What I want to know is," Kacey asked, "are you staying with us, or leaving?" She looked at Emil then and grinned. "I mean, you did get what you were after, right?"

"Ummmm..." Emil blushed a little, and looked over at Chris, who was going over his captain's paperwork.

"She's staying," Chris said without looking up, causing Emil to blush even more. "Though I think there's going to be some sort of long-term agreement here in a few months, am I right, E?"

Emil smiled and nodded and leaned into Chris a little. He put an arm around her and went back to studying the forms he had to file when we docked. "So what are you looking at, Kacey?"

"Outgoing cargo. I have a long list of things that they want and I'm starting to line up purchase orders and all that stuff. 'Course, I can't *buy* any of it until we sell *this* cargo, though I've already told my mom just what we're carrying and asked how much of it Ceres Habs would like to buy, with a special onetime bulk discount offer if she can take at least half of the rare earths and silver off our hands."

"No gold or uranium?"

"I don't want to crash the market. Plus we agreed to offer all that to the government first, or at least allow them to handle the sales so this way we don't have to pay to guard it."

"Don't forget to send an email to your aunt Cheryl, asking her to meet us at the docks when we get in," I said.

"Oh, right! Let me send that now!"

"What do you want to do that for?" Emil asked.

"I need someone to get me in with someone important in the government to deal with all that gold," I said. "I don't think they're going to want to talk to just some random guy off the street."

"Probably not. How long do you think we'll be in port for?"

"At least a week, probably two," Kacey said, sending the

email I'd asked her to and going back to her paperwork. "It's our homeport and selling and securing this cargo isn't going to happen quickly, and then I once I do have enough money, I've got a lot of stuff to buy. We're going to be packed full when we leave, I'm sure."

"Okay, just make sure you ping me when you put the load together, so I can work on the weight and balance."

"Will do."

The landing was pretty anticlimactic, but then no one knew what our cargo was—well, other than my mother-in-law—and we were going to do our best to keep it that way. Once we were docked and on ground power, I secured the two PWRs, shutting them all the way down, then had Nicolas put the APU on standby, just in case.

Then I went and found Hank.

"What's up, Dave?"

"I want you, Chaz, Kei, and Yuri to stay onboard until we get this load dealt with. No one comes on, don't care who they are, without talking to me or Kacey first. Chris has to go deal with captain stuff, so Paul has the watch, but I've already told him to check with you on anything weird, seeing as you and Chaz know this place better than he does."

"Not a problem."

"Thanks, Hank."

"Hey, you're the boss! Gotta keep you happy so I keep getting paid!"

I smiled and waved, went and got Kacey, and we both headed out onto the dock to find Cheryl waiting for us.

"So what's so important that you needed me to meet you here?"

"Oh, I thought maybe we might like to go have lunch with the president," I said with a smile.

"Oh, you did, did you?" Cheryl said with a grin.

"Let's go someplace private, Aunt Cheryl," Kacey said. "You might want to call Uncle Pimm if it'll help us talk to somebody. We've got a...umm, *diplomatic* cargo, I guess you might say."

"I thought you were coming straight back here from picking up the *Iowa*?"

"What? And not make any money?" Kacey looked at her like she'd sprouted a third eye. "What would Grandpa say?"

"That I was the black sheep, just like he always does now that I'm a lawyer and I married a judge," Cheryl said with a laugh. "Come, we can go back to my office and we'll discuss it there. Is everything on the ship alright?"

We both nodded. "Yup, everything was fine. Once our cargo gets off-loaded or sold, we've got a fairly large order to fill, and then some deliveries to make. We miss anything interesting while we were gone?"

I listened while they made idle talk about family comings and goings while I looked around to see if I could figure out just who was paying us too much attention. With all the people on the docks, I honestly couldn't pick anybody out. I guess I would have made a lousy spy.

"So, what's this all about?" Cheryl asked when we got back to her office.

"We've got twenty-six TEUs packed full of gold," Kacey said. "*What?*"

"And half of it goes to the Ceres government," I added.

"Are you..." She looked at each of us. "No, of course you aren't. So you've got something like a couple of hundred million in gold onboard, and you want to give half of it to the government?"

"It isn't ours, Cheryl," I said. "We went back to that place I stayed at, which apparently our government knows about, if not exactly where, and have been sort of 'helping them out.' Well, apparently this is the first of several payments to pay them back for what I guess are some rather large and expensive favors."

"I better call Don; he's got some friends in the president's office, so we should be able to walk right in."

"Good, 'cause we really want to get that stuff off the ship as fast as possible," Kacey said.

"Yeah, I don't blame you. Come, let's walk over to the courthouse. I'd rather not use my phone for this one."

We had to wait about an hour. Which surprised me, because I thought we'd be waiting there a lot longer than that.

When we were finally shown into his office, we were all introduced by the person showing us in, the president nodding to Judge Pimm, who I guess he knew, or at least had heard of.

"Okay, so I hear there's been a lot of strings pulled to get me to talk to you folks, Dan. What's up?"

"David?" Dan said, looking at me.

I looked around the room. "Who doesn't have to be here, other than your security? This is the kind of thing people kill over and I sure don't want that responsibility."

"This isn't about the *Iowa Hill* piracy, is it?" asked a man in a dark suit from where he was standing to the president's right.

I frowned. "No, this is about the thirteen TEUs of gold I'm hauling from the folks who ended up with that gear, who are all mighty grateful for your help, and now that they've hired my wife and me to haul for them, thought they should start paying you back."

I watched as both he and the president exchanged looks, and then the president turned to me.

"You know where they are?"

"And I'm not telling anybody, not even you. I keep my promises. Also"—and I smiled—"I like having the exclusive contract that only me knowing where they are gives me."

"So you're dealing with pirates?" asked a woman who was standing on the other end of the desk from where the first guy who had spoken.

I looked at her. "Please, I'm not stupid and you wouldn't be in here if you were, I'm sure. They're not pirates, and you've all been covering for them for years, if not longer, I'm sure. Yes, I know what happened on the ship was a setup and since taking possession of it, I've made damn sure that evidence is all long gone. But I suspect you know that already?" I said, looking around the room.

"He's got you there, Rachel," the president said with a smile. "So they actually let you take a cargo out of there, and bring it here?"

I shrugged. "I spent six months there, as I'm sure you've all been told by now. They know me and they *trust* me. You all seem to like them enough to be helping them."

"Just how much of a drain on our taxes has supporting them been?" Kacey asked from beside me. "Now they want to start paying their way and paying us back. What's the problem?"

"The problem is," the president said, "none of us expected this. When you didn't show up on time—and yes, you're right, Jack's people in Intelligence have been keeping an eye on you," he said with a nod toward the man in the dark suit. "Anyway, we'd thought you were all dead or something and that there wouldn't be any problems.

"Now you're telling me you've got a ship full of gold?"

"No, we've got a hold full of refined metals. Half of the gold is for Ceres," Kacey said. "The rest of the gold, twenty TEUs of uranium, sixty of silver, two thousand full of rare earths, and another eight hundred of pig iron, that's all for sale. But Ceres government gets first dibs on the rest of the gold, and the uranium."

"Why do we get first dibs?" Rachel asked.

"Because I want it off our ship as fast as possible and I don't want anyone to even know we were carrying it," I told them. "If you don't buy it, we'd rather you handled the sales for it—again, so no one knows where it came from. We've got account numbers from them for you to put the funds in, but the sooner we get the rest sold and clear the ship, the sooner we can buy the cargo they asked us to, and start earning our pay."

"And I think it's only fair to let you know that Ceres Habitats has already bought all the iron and half of the rare earths and silver, and put options on the remaining stock," Kacey said, looking up from her tablet that I guess had just alerted her to a message from her mom.

"The government owns a couple of docks over there," Jack said. "We could move all the gold and uranium off there, and no one would know about it."

I watched as the president considered it a moment, then turned to Rachel.

"What'll this do to our budget?"

"That'll depend on if they'll let us make payments on the remaining gold and uranium they want us to buy, because we really can't afford to let that out all at once or it'll put a severe dent in the market."

"We were told to give you at least a year," Kacey said. "But no more than two."

Rachel smiled. "In that case, I think we need to make the deal. Our budget is still hurting after we paid off the insurance on that last claim that we so *foolishly*," she said, chuckling, "agreed to cover. Though I think we're going to have to have a private meeting with the finance group to let at least some of them know what happened."

"I think we should wait a few months, just to keep anyone from associating the *Iowa Hill* or its crew with this unexpected windfall," the president said, looking rather thoughtful.

"I have a question," Jack said looking at me.

"Shoot."

"Why are you doing this?"

"What?"

"Why are *you* doing this? You took a fairly large risk, you're still taking a large risk—we could have just confiscated your ship and taken everything onboard. You're not from here, you've only just recently come here, and well, to be honest, the reputation of people from Earth isn't really all that great out here."

"Ah, fair question," I said with a nod. "Well, honestly there's four reasons. The first is that after living with those folks for six months, I realized that they weren't bad people—trust me, I know all about bad people. That they could use some help, and I figured, why not? Second is the money. We'd just started a new business"—I gave Kacey a hug as I still had my arm around her—"and I figured a solid contract like that would definitely get our balance sheet out of the red."

"They could have just killed you."

I laughed and shook my head. "No, once they knew it was me, I knew they'd want to ask me, personally, just what the hell I was doing there. Third was, I'm going to file for citizenship here in about a year, after one last trip to Earth. I'd already figured out what was going on between Ceres and them, and I thought if I showed all of you just how helpful I could be and that I'm on the side of Ceres, that you'd be happy to have me."

"But you told us you wouldn't tell us where they were," Rachel pointed out.

"If I don't keep my word, why would you even want me here?" I asked her.

"Good point."

"What's your fourth reason?" the president asked.

"Oh, I'm going to bring my brother here, maybe our parents and sister too. I want to be sure you don't let Earth extradite him."

"Why would they want to do that?"

"Because he's a genius and he wants to live someplace where he can make a difference, not just make rich people richer."

"Well, if he's anything like you," the president said with a smile, "I'd say he's more than welcome here. Jack, Rachel, work out the details, I've got a meeting to go to."

We ended up back at the ship not long after that, and had Chris come back to move it from the current dock into the private yard for Ceres Habitats, who immediately unloaded all of what they'd bought, then a "special crew" came over to unload the gold and uranium for the government.

That done, we flew back to the public docks and made arrangements to put the remaining cargo units into secure storage, though Kacey sold the rest of the silver and almost half of the rare earths that we had left. The stuff that was left was all cerium and europium, which were probably the cheapest of them right now and consequently sold the slowest.

Then we gave everyone two weeks of shore leave, because it would take at least that long to assemble the cargo.

"We're going to need to actually rent an office now," Kacey told me as we lay in her bed, in her parents' home.

"And we're going to need someone to sell off that remaining cargo while we're gone," I agreed.

"And maybe buy our own home?"

"What, is your mom pushing you out?"

"Nooo, actually I think she and Dad both like our staying here."

"So do I," I said, and rolled over to give her a kiss. "What's wrong with staying here?"

"Have you looked at our bank account? We could easily afford our own place!"

"And just how much time would we be spending in it? Maybe when I get around to opening my own shop, we could live in the back," I said, grinning at her.

"We are not living in the back of your shop," she grumbled.

"I need another year or two aboard ship as an engineer so I'll have the hours to take the test for my second engineer rating when I hit my five-year mark."

"I thought you were going for the tuner's cert."

"I want both. I may even see about going for chief eventually, though I'm not really in a rush for that one."

"So why do you need the second?"

"Because as second I can work as chief engineer on almost any boat out there without worrying about legalities. I suspect when we buy our next ship, I'll have to make a few trips on it until we've got a crew for it."

"Thinking ahead, are we?"

"I've been told that you probably won't stop until you've got a fleet of a hundred ships," I said with a smile.

"Only a hundred? I should feel insulted!" she replied, smiling back at me.

"Well, you're the one in charge of long-term planning. Right now I'm just focused on my next goal. After that, I guess you get to tell me what to do."

"Oh, I like the sound of *that*!" She laughed. "So, just what *is* the next goal? Your brother?"

I nodded. "Yeah, I promised him I'd get him out of there. I think he wanted to go see the stars more than I did. For me, it was just an escape out of a world and a life I hated. For him, I think it's a whole lot more than that. Ben's always been the one with the big dreams."

"And what about the rest of the family?"

"I don't know. Our sister, Dianne, is definitely smart, though I don't know if she's as smart as he is. I guess I'll leave that decision up to my parents when the time comes. But once that's done? I don't think I'll ever go back there. I like the idea of having my own shop, my own wife, and"—I kissed her again—"my *own* family. If you want to run a cargo company, I'm fine with that and I'll do whatever you need to make it happen."

"There are a lot of men out there who wouldn't be happy with their wives having a bigger job than they do."

"Oh? Well, we'll just have to see who makes more money," I said with a chuckle. "But I really don't know the cargo business like you do. I know engines, reactors, ships—those are the things I went to school for. They're the things I enjoy working with. And I know how to deal with people, because I wasn't given much of a choice. But I'll admit, the idea of owning a big corporation of our own is tempting."

"This whole thing has happened kind of fast. I had no idea they'd load us down with such a rich cargo, and on our first trip, too!"

"No one knew we were coming; it made the most sense, really. From this point on, I suspect our cargoes are going to be a lot less valuable."

"Oh, I know. I don't think they'll even load us down with gold again until our trips have become routine. I just wonder how many people are going to spy on us to try and find out where Marcus and the rest of them are."

"As long as nobody figures out who we're hauling for, I don't think there'll be any of those. More likely just folks trying to find out who we're trading with, so they can try and butt in on our contracts."

"Don't you think someone from the government might try following along? To find out?"

"Nah. They're a lot better at this kind of thing than I am. I mean, it's possible they don't know where we went. But think about it. They helped set up the theft of all that gear we were hauling. I don't see them doing that if they didn't know where it was going. They're just playing dumb."

"Like you are," Kacey giggled.

"I'm not so sure I'm playing," I teased her back. "So, when do you think we'll start loading?"

"The twenty-third. We should have it all loaded by the twenty-fifth and be ready to go."

"So a week from now."

She nodded and I snuggled her up close. It would be a ten-day trip to where we were meeting their cargo ship, the *Astro Gerlitz*. The *Astro Gerlitz* was a Radon-class cargo ship and they were the second biggest haulers out there. With a gross capacity of twenty thousand TEUs, they could carry four times the cargo of the Argon class. So they'd be able to take all of our cargo and then provide us with the cargo we were going to take to Earth.

It would take us about four or five days to transfer cargo, then we'd be off to Earth which was currently about nine days from there. We'd be landing at Holloman again, and it'd probably be two days to unload and reload, maybe three. In that time I had to get Ben onboard without anybody knowing about it, then get out of there and far enough away that they couldn't stop us.

I really had no idea how to do any of that—well, not yet at least. In the morning I'd drop Ben an email and maybe ask if he'd be able to get away from his studies to visit with me and the folks when I went to see our parents the next time I made it back to Earth? That was the signal we'd agreed on, to let him know I was going to be there within a month or two.

After we left Earth, we'd be heading back to the *Astro Gerlitz* with the cargo we were to pick up there. Then another cargo swap and back here to Ceres. So maybe two months after we left we'd be back here. Any money my brother might have would probably be seized by then. So he'd be broke with whatever he was able to bring along.

Not all that different from how I started out.

Sighing, I closed my eyes and tried to sleep. I could tell that Kacey had already drifted off from her breathing. Maybe after this was over I could finally start training for that next cert.

TWENTY-ONE

Above the Ecliptic

WE RAN A STRAIGHT OUTBOUND COURSE FOR THREE DAYS, THEN executed a sharp turn up out of the plane of the ecliptic. There were two purposes; one was, of course, to make it harder for anyone trying to get a read on where we were going. The other was to make it easier to tell if anyone was following us. Gravity drives are pretty easy to track, if you're close and if you have the equipment. Anybody who wasn't flying a military ship probably wouldn't be able to follow us, not at least without being close enough that we could see them.

So we cut drive for eight hours just to see what showed up.

Thankfully, nothing did. I know that Jack's people did a lot to keep us from being associated with the "Let-Be's" as Hank called them. Or with the expensive shipment that we'd brought in.

None of the governments helping Marcus and his people wanted it known that they were helping them, and so Ceres would hopefully provide us cover, but I had no idea how good they were, or how long it would last. I also hoped there wasn't a downside to their wanting to keep things quiet that would mean them looking the other way if anything bad happened to us.

Still, the money was good and eventually enough people would have been encouraged to look the other way, so that no one would bother us. It wasn't like we were trading illegal arms or contraband—though there was a fair deal of high-end machinist equipment and tech gear that was not at all easy to build if you didn't have a dedicated factory.

I was working on the engineering deck when we finally got there and got the all clear. A day later, the *Astro Gerlitz* showed up and we moved so close that the cargo decks were almost touching.

Paul gave me and Kacey a tour of the ship, seeing as he used to be the first mate on her before he was asked to sail with us. I have to admit it was an impressive sight.

"How'd you come by this ship?" Kacey asked as we were finishing up the tour of the engine room, which had six very large fusion reactors.

"We took it with us when we left Venus," he said with a shrug. "We had about eight of these when we first left. Two major shipping companies were among the refugees. We probably had a couple hundred Argon- and Krypton-class cargo haulers as well as a pretty large fleet of Neons and other private ships."

"Oh? Where are they?"

"Well, five of the sister ships to the *Gerlitz* were destroyed by the navy, as well as dozens of the smaller cargo ships. Fortunately, some of them had already made it to a hab someplace and off-loaded most of their passengers, but we lost a lot of people that way."

"Oh," Kacey said a little embarrassed. "I'm sorry, I didn't know."

"It was a long time ago, back in the first years of our flight from home. I was only a kid then, I really didn't understand any of what was going on. To be honest?" He turned and looked at the two of us. "I *still* don't understand it. Yeah, we disagreed with them. We still disagree with them. Rather than fight over it, we left. Yet they still spend billions every year trying to hunt us down."

"Remind me never to visit Venus," she said with a sigh.

"After this trip to Earth, I don't think I'm ever going to go inside of Mars's orbit again," I said with a smile, and gave her a hug. "They're not as bad as Venus, but I'd still rather not have much to do with the Earth government either."

When we got back to the ship, I was surprised to find a man waiting for me. I recognized him from that one time I'd been in

Marcus's office, back when they'd gotten rid of Kiesler. He hadn't said anything back then, however.

"Hi, Dave, I don't know if you remember me, but I'm Jarvis Armstrong. We met briefly a few months back."

I shook hands with him. "I remember you. This is my wife, Kacey. What brings you here?"

"Well, I need to go with you to pick up the cargo you're getting on Earth."

"Hon," I said turning to Kacey, "could you check with Emil to see if we have enough food?" I looked back at him. "There is just the one of you, I hope?"

He nodded. "If it's a problem, I'm sure we can have some more sent over."

"That's why I want to check now."

"Be right back," Kacey said, and went off to find Emil.

I looked at Paul. "Paul, I think you have a pressing meeting on the bridge."

"I do?" he said, then saw the look I was giving him. "Oh! Right! I do!"

Jarvis watched him quickly walk away and snickered.

"Oh, don't think it's funny yet. I want to know why you're here, and trust me when I say that if I think you're lying to me, it won't go well."

"We're buying targeting gear and early warning sensors for our defenses. It's all legal enough, we've got the proper papers and all the rest of that," he told me. "But we had to float a few hefty bribes to get those clearances and I want to make sure that we got what we ordered before I turn over any money. Also, this is secret. Very secret. With all the money you brought in on that first trip, we decided to put in some defenses."

"Okay, I'll buy that. Though if you get us shot down, you folks are on the hook for a new ship, got it?"

Jarvis smiled at me. "If you're still willing to keep trading with us after getting 'shot down,' we'd be fools not to give you one, now wouldn't we?"

"Not as big a fool as me, I'm sure," I said, smiling back at him. "Now, let's make sure we really do have enough food before they finish loading and button up. We don't want to buy supplies on Earth; the cost will kill our profits."

❖   ❖   ❖

"So what's the story on Jarvis?" Kacey asked me later that night in our quarters. I'd taken the chief engineer's room, after clearing out all of Dot's stuff and leaving it for her to pick up the next time she hit Ceres. It was actually just as big as the captain's quarters, but then engineers designed the ship in the first place, and apparently we look after our own.

"Some of the stuff we're getting is sensitive and expensive. He wants to make sure we don't get ripped off."

"And handle any last-minute bribes, I'm sure."

"Probably. I just need to make sure that none of the people he's doing business with are around when my brother gets here. I don't want anyone seeing him board the ship. They may figure out eventually that he left with us, but I'd prefer for us to be way far away from here before they come to that conclusion."

"Doesn't he have a different last name than you?"

"Yeah, but it still shows up that we have the same parents, if anyone takes any time to do a real search."

"What about your parents?"

"What about them?"

"Do you think they'll come?"

I shrugged and shook my head. "No idea."

"Well, what happens if they do?"

"They'll probably get fined, but beyond that?" I shrugged again. "I don't think anything will happen. If they were to go back, *then* they might get in trouble, I'm sure there's some law against emigrating without a license or some such."

"Do you think they'll get in trouble for Ben's leaving if they stay?"

I shook my head, "I don't have a clue. Maybe if Ben was working on some sort of supersecret program they would. But back when we started planning this, I told him not to get hooked into anything where they'd want to kill him so he couldn't tell anybody their secrets. He was smart enough to see the logic."

"So just why is it so hard to sneak off of Earth? Do they have enforcers everywhere?"

"Worse, they have cameras everywhere. Cameras and people who are too stupid to mind their own business," I said with a frown. "There are always people willing to rat other people out, and they don't even do it for money! Just for a pat on the head and to be told publicly that they're a 'good person.' It's part of why the gangs are so popular with teens. It's the only way you can lash out and go against the grain. People are terrified of the gangs, so at least you get left alone.

"Well, most of the time at least. Every once in a while the government goes on an 'anti-crime' crusade and they crack down for a few months, maybe even a year or two. They rarely take in any of the big criminals, of course, but they do make a few examples out of some of the gangs and their members. But six months later, it's always back to business as usual.

"Ben once said that it's a safety valve to siphon off all the malcontents. Most kids realize it's a dead-end street and go back to a normal life having learned their lesson. The rest either get killed, kill themselves, go to jail, or end up in one of the organized crime syndicates."

"Was that where you were headed? For the syndicates?"

"I don't know," I said, shaking my head. "I really don't. I had status because they couldn't put me in jail."

"They couldn't? Why not?"

"Because my mother was an elie and that made me immune to the law, as long as I wasn't harming other elies. I was so mad at her back then, for having abandoned me, that I grabbed onto that one thing she left me, that power, and I used it. I was fixing to take over the gang and make myself into a very nasty young man, when something changed."

"Oh? Ben?"

"No, my grandfather, my bio-mom's father, sent a couple of pros to take me down and administer a beating. They didn't break anything, but I was in bed for a week and did it ever hurt. And when they were done, they told me that my grandfather was 'very unhappy with how I was living my life' and that 'I was bringing shame to the family.'

"And finally that the next beating I 'wouldn't be waking up from.' And then they knocked me out."

"Wow, that sounds pretty harsh."

"They were right. He was right. Ben told me I should get into engineering. Get a job on a ship and get the hell off of Earth and start over someplace else. So I did."

"So is that why you're helping him? Because he helped you?"

"Some. But you have to understand, helping Ben was my job. My dad sat me down when he and Mom got married and told me straight out, that Ben was my brother now, and as the older brother I had a responsibility to him. That you always take care of family—first, last, and always. And with the way Mom had left us, that made an impression on me. I hated her for it, and there was no way I'd do anything like that to my own brother. So taking care of Ben became a big part of my life. Man, he was such a clueless kid. He was so smart, but in other ways, just so stupid."

"How can you be smart and stupid at the same time?" Kacey asked with a laugh.

"He thought knowing the answers would protect him from bullies and people who didn't like a kid telling them things like they were an adult. It took me a while to get him to understand what he eventually told me were *social dynamics*. Once he figured out the basics with my teaching him, he started reading books on it and studying it. Pretty soon he really didn't need me anymore, but I was always there, just in case."

"You really love your brother, don't you?"

"Yeah, I guess I do. Dad was so proud of me for watching out for him. Mom was so happy that I'd taken him under my wing, just like if he'd been born my brother. It made us a family again. It was the second best thing I ever did in my life."

"Oh? What was the first?"

"Marrying you," I said, and smiled at her.

Flying to Earth is easy, until you get to the last ten thousand kilometers or so. I'd remembered Dot's warning about the age of the ship and passed it on to Chris that once we got into Earth's gravity, as the chief engineer and ship owner I didn't want him pulling a tenth of a gee acceleration, that it would be best to keep us at a constant velocity and keep that velocity low.

He grumbled a little but didn't argue. Falling out of the sky would ruin everybody's day and a bent spaceship would mean that we wouldn't be flying out. So I fired up the APU to give us all the power we had onboard and kept a close eye on the Siz-gees to make sure they didn't have any hiccups on the way down. Both Paul and Kat joined him on the bridge. Neither of them had been to Earth before either, and with all the traffic around and controllers you had to deal with on the radio, the extra hands definitely helped. I think only Mars had airspace as crowded as Earth's.

It took us three hours, from the time we entered an orbit at a couple hundred kilometers altitude until we landed.

And the very first thing we did when we landed was pay a landing fee. Then a parking fee, estimated on how long we thought we'd be staying, and a takeoff fee for when we'd leave.

I could have waited on that, but I decided to get it out of the way in advance.

I kept the APU running, because I didn't want to pay for ground power, or deal with all the hookups and other stuff. I sent my parents an email as soon as we grounded that I was on Earth for a few days while the ship I was working on shifted cargo, and when could I come for dinner, and would they invite Ben, please?

I got a response from Mom before I'd even finished powering down the reactors.

Can you come tomorrow night?

I thought about our schedule. Our official one, as well as our unofficial one.

Sure, ask Ben if he can get away for a few days. We're flying out Tuesday night and will stay till Wednesday night.

Fifteen minutes later I got an *Okay.*

"Hey, Dave, the crew wants to know if they can have liberty?" Chris asked over the comm.

"Let's have everyone meet up in the mess. Don't pop any of the hatches yet, I want to go over a few things first; after that, sure."

"Understood!"

A few minutes later, as I was securing a few last items, Chris called for an all-hands meeting in the mess. So I went up the back ladder to join them, taking my time so I'd be last.

"Okay, has anyone besides Hank and Chaz been here before?" I asked, looking around the mess.

Nobody raised a hand or said anything.

"Alright. Guns are illegal. Put them in your cabin and *keep* them there. Do *not* bring them onto the cargo decks for any reason after the doors have opened, and if there's a gun range set up in the hold, tear it down as soon as I'm done here."

"Why's that?" Kei asked.

"Guns are illegal here for damn near everyone. The penalties are pretty stiff too—as in you won't be around when we take off or be seen again for years.

"And here's another thing to remember. Once the cargo bay doors are open, the cargo bay is subject to Earth law. *But* not the rest of the ship, as long as you don't let any Earth officials into those spaces. So I want all of the hatches leading off the cargo bay sealed. No one is to be allowed into any other part of the ship under any circumstances, no matter what they say.

"Sometime before we unload, a customs guy is going to show up to 'inspect' the cargo. He's not allowed into any other part of the ship. Whatever he says, the answer is no. If he's got to pee, he can pee out the hatch. If he has a heart attack, push him out the cargo door to the ground below.

"Next thing to remember is that this place can be pretty screwy. Don't take a lot of money with you; stay out of fights, there are cameras damn near everywhere. Prices are a lot more than you remember them, and we're in a very hot and dry place right now. So don't stand out in the sun, or you'll pass out.

"Also I would suggest sleeping on the ship, and I would definitely stay away from the hookers here as well as any black market folks. It's not that they're any more deadly than anywhere else, it's just that they're a lot more crooked and the cops are on their side. Because the cops know them, and are probably getting kickbacks under the table.

"So take Hank or Chaz with you, if you go out. They've been here before."

"What about you, Dave?" Chris asked.

"I'll be here tonight, but tomorrow I'm taking Kacey to go meet my folks and we'll be gone until the next day.

"Any questions?"

Nobody had any.

"Great. Chris, let me know when Customs shows up. You and Emil will probably need to be with me for that as well. Normally the captain signs off, but if there are any issues, as the heads of the company that owns the ship, Kacey or I can handle it too, I'm sure."

Everyone ended up going into town that night, though Kacey and I elected to stay and keep an eye on the ship. I was surprised that even Jarvis went with them, but then again, most people never get the chance to visit Earth, so I'm sure he didn't want to pass it up.

Sure enough, the customs inspector showed up while they were gone. I think he was hoping to stir up enough trouble to get a bribe or something. I popped the port side cargo bay doors and made him use the ladder on top of the truck he came to the ship on. When he tried one of the tricks that Steve Roy had told us about, back when he was the captain of the ship, I refused.

He tried to push me on it, but after I told the inspector that I was from Boca Chica and my dad was a union man, he backed off quickly as I was obviously not one of those "system rubes" he was used to fleecing.

Two hours later, he was done and I ended up supervising the unloading until the rest of the crew returned. I picked the least drunk of them to keep an eye on things while I went and got some sleep.

The next two days were going to be eventful, I was sure.

TWENTY-TWO

Earth—Texas District

WE TOOK ONE OF THE SHUTTLE FLIGHTS THAT CONNECTED THE Holloman Spaceport with the Boca Chica Spaceport. Kacey was sitting in the window seat, gawking out the window with a death grip on my left arm.

"I just can't get over it! All that open space! And there isn't anything to keep the air in!"

"Actually, it's called gravity, Kace," I teased her again for probably the tenth time. The wide-open spaces were a bit hard on people who'd never really been out in them without a pressure suit of some kind. Hank was used to it from growing up on Mars, where you really only needed a face mask these days, and could actually survive without one if you needed to. Chaz, of course, had been here before.

But Kei and Yuri were definitely getting a little "heady" over it, which had been pretty funny to see, and Jarvis, Paul, and Kat were all rather nervous and uncomfortable whenever they stepped outside in the daylight. At night it wasn't so bad, because it wasn't all that obvious that you were out in the open without a dome of some kind above your head.

Chris and Emil were doing about the same as Kacey, as there were all those large open spaces on Ceres. But I thought even they were getting a little giddy over it at times.

"How far is your parents' house from the spaceport?"

"Thirty minutes by tube. The quad they live in is within walking distance of the station."

"Where's the college you went to?"

"It's on the west side of the spaceport."

"That's convenient."

"It makes it easier for them to get the students stuff to work on. Also more than a few of the instructors work at the different shops around the spaceport."

I pointed out a few of the landmarks that I was familiar with during the short flight.

It was late when we got in; I'd timed it to coincide with my dad getting off work, so we could go back together. I wasn't surprised to find him waiting for us when we came out of security.

"Dave!" he called out and I all but dragged Kacey over to him, hugging him when I got there.

"Dad! Great to see you again!" I said, and then let him go. "This is Kacey, my wife!"

"Welcome to the family!" he said and hugged her too. Then he held her at arm's length and looked at her. "You're even cuter than the pictures he sent!" he said with a chuckle. "Come on, let's go home so Jenny can start bugging you about grandchildren," he said with a wink as he let her go.

"It's so nice to finally meet you, Mr. Walker," Kacey said, getting her wits back. Dad was like that—charismatic and outgoing and at times a bit overwhelming. I often suspected that was how he'd ended up with Eileen, my bio-mom. Of course I never really saw that side of him until he'd taken up with Jenny. On reflection, that probably had a lot to do with why I loved her too.

"Please, call me Kurt. Or better yet, Dad," he said, grinning as we started to make our way to the tube station.

"When's Ben getting here?" I asked.

"Tomorrow. He had a few papers to submit or something, I guess. But he wanted to be able to stay a few nights, so he could stay for dinner and spend some time with all of us."

"How's Dianne doing?"

"Great! She's about to make the jump into high school, two years early. So, not as smart as Ben, but still way smarter than you, Dave," Dad joked, and I had to laugh as well. We spent the first half of the trip back to the quad hearing all about how she was doing both in and out of school.

Next he talked about how Ben was doing up at MIT and how he was struggling with the decision to either stay and teach, or go into corporate research. Neither Ben nor I had told our parents that Ben was leaving Earth with me. What you didn't know, you couldn't accidentally give away, after all.

When we got off at the housing district and started to walk to the quad where my parents lived, I was struck by how run-down and dirty it was. I wondered if it had always been like that and I just hadn't noticed. Or were things getting worse around here?

There were the usual kids hanging out in and about the place, most of them Howlers, and when I flashed one of the older ones the old gang sign, I got a double take and then a smile and a wave after he recognized me.

Just because I'd stopped running with them, it didn't mean I'd stopped being friends. It was a lot safer to walk the streets at night when they all knew and remembered you. It also didn't hurt that my reputation had been a pretty nasty one. There are times when being feared is just as good as being respected. Perhaps even better.

"Old friends?" Kacey asked in a whisper.

"More or less. It's the gang I used to run with. This is all their territory."

"It helps," Dad said in a soft voice as well. "They all remember Dave, and Ben still builds those maskers and a few other toys for them. So they keep an eye on your mom and Dianne when I'm at work."

"What about the enforcers?" Kacey asked.

"The cops?" He sniffed contemptuously. "They come around here less and less every year. There are places with 'more problems' that need their attention. I think the Dolers are starting to act up again. Probably be another purge in a few years if they start rioting again."

"Wow, Dad, I had no idea it was getting that bad."

"You picked a good time to leave—in the last year things have really started to slide around here. I'd like to move too, take your mother someplace nicer. But I don't know if we can afford it. Maybe after Dianne goes to college and we can fit into a smaller place."

"Maybe you should come live with us on Ceres," Kacey said with a smile. I'd warned her that they didn't know the real reason for this trip, but I'd also told her that after seeing Ceres, I wanted to see if we could talk them into leaving with us.

"There's no way we could afford a trip like that!" he protested. "Besides, what would I do?"

"Oh, you could come back with us," Kacey said. "I'm sure the owners of the shipping company wouldn't mind."

Dad laughed. "Sure they wouldn't, and what would I do for work?"

"Same thing you do here, Dad," I told him. "Techs like you are in demand pretty much everywhere. As for hitching a ride, the ship's gotta move anyway and what's a few more passengers? We got the space and I can pay for the extra food you'd eat out of my pocket. Ceres is nice, Dad. A lot nicer than *this*," I said, and gestured at the surrounding area as we walked into the building and headed for the elevators.

"What about your sister?"

"I think she'd have a lot more opportunities there than here. There's a lot going on out there, Dad. Mom probably would like it more as well. They don't have doles, proles, any of that. You either pull your weight, or you don't."

"Your mother's a housewife, Dave."

"The shipping company we work for is looking to hire a receptionist for their new office on Ceres," Kacey said with a smile, and I could see she was shifting into "negotiation" mode. "I'm sure they'd be more than happy to hire her."

"Really?"

"Of course! Low-skilled jobs are actually harder to staff because everyone's always going for the higher-paid skilled jobs. Plus the company is family orientated. A lot of places on Ceres are."

I watched as Dad "hmmmed" a bit, obviously thinking about it. Which again made me wonder just how bad *had* things been getting in the two years I'd been gone. Dad had always been proud of living here; getting into this quad back before I'd been born hadn't been easy. All of the families living here were skilled technicians. Or at least they had been back then. I wondered just who was living here now.

I had a few worried thoughts about just what the future held for my old quad.

"Dave!" Mom yelled as she ran over. She hugged and kissed me, followed by a second "David!" from my younger sister, who came over and hugged me as well, driving all those thoughts from my head.

After they'd mobbed me a few minutes, I introduced Kacey, who was then equally mobbed as well. Mom was still as lovely and outgoing as ever.

"You must be tired after all that traveling," she said. "I could make dinner at home, if you'd rather not go out tonight?"

Kacey lit up, smiling. "That would be great, Mrs. Walker. I'm still getting used to all this open space!"

"Please, call me Jenny."

"Can I help?"

"Of course you can!" she said, and I watched as the two of them headed off to the small kitchen. As always, the apartment was as neat as a pin, Mom really did take care of the place, as well as Dianne and my dad. It was a two bedroom, one bath, with a small kitchen and a family room, which also served as the dining room.

Looking at it now, it was kind of odd. Here on Earth there was so much open space, still, even now with whatever the population was up to. But everyone lived in such small apartments; this place was around six hundred square feet. On Ceres, where everything was dug out of the planet, the apartments were huge. They even called them "houses" most of the time because they were so big. The Doyles lived in a three-thousand-square-foot home and Kacey was already looking at getting one made for us just as big.

I shook my head, trying to reconcile all of that.

"So what's it like living in space?" Dianne asked, coming over to sit with me.

"Being on board a ship is different, it's a lot like living here, only you're not able to leave the apartment for weeks at a time," I said, then shrugged. "But there's always work to be done, so you don't notice. But the habs? They're huge. Same for the orbitals. They're like gigantic and never-ending indoor malls!"

She asked a lot more questions and, after changing out of his work clothes, Dad came back and joined in. I could hear Kacey and Mom talking in the kitchen, though I didn't know what about. If I had to guess, she was telling her all about how great life was on Ceres. She could be relentless once she started in on the hard sell.

When dinner was served the conversation died off, but then afterward we all settled down in the living area and just talked about everything and anything. Kacey floated the idea past all of them about coming to Ceres, and I could see that both Dianne *and* Mom looked interested.

"Tell you what," I said with a thoughtful look. "How about you all come on out to look at the ship we came here in tomorrow, after dinner? Ben's already dropped a few hints that he wouldn't mind a tour."

"Do you think that'd be okay?" Mom asked. "Wouldn't your boss, the captain, mind?"

Kacey coughed and blushed a little, and I smiled.

"Truth is, Mom, Dad, Kacey and I *own* the ship we came in. The captain works for us. We're the bosses."

"*What?*" Dad said, looking shocked. "How did you buy a spaceship?"

"Remember the ship that got taken out by pirates?" I asked and they all nodded.

"We went back and salvaged it," Kacey said, jumping in. "Dave here got all the orbital data before he had to leave with the pirates, who didn't care, because they didn't want the ship, just the cargo."

"And by the time I got back," I continued, "the company I'd been working for had already collected the insurance on her and didn't care either. So we went out, repaired all the damage, and claimed her."

"That couldn't have been cheap!" Dad said, probably running the numbers in his head.

"No, it wasn't," Kacey said. "But we got a bunch of investors and took out a business loan. We've managed to secure an exclusive deal with a good customer, and we're doing quite well for being such a new company."

"Which is part of why Ben wants to see it," I told them. "I think he wants to see if he can figure out how to help me make even more money."

"If anyone can, it'd be him," Dad agreed.

"I know, I'd be stupid to turn him down. So, everyone feel up to a trip tomorrow?"

"What about school?" Dianne asked.

"We'll go after dinner, like I said. This way you won't have to miss class."

"Awww," she sighed. "Can't we go earlier? It's not like I'll really miss anything!"

"Now, don't start taking after your brother and start ditching school," Dad warned.

"Yeah, but he's got a *spaceship*!" Dianne said with a grin.

"That may be, but if Ben had gone with him, they'd probably have a dozen of them by now."

"Listen to Dad," I said with a smile. "I just got lucky."

"Okay..." she said with a frown.

"Great! It's settled," Kacey said with a clap of her hands. "After dinner tomorrow we'll all head out and we'll give you a tour!"

I looked around the room and smiled. Even if they decided not to leave with me, the trip would be fun and maybe give them something to consider for the future. If they changed their minds I could always see about making another trip out here to get them. It would also help us separate Ben from any prying eyes, and make it easier for him to split off from the group and stay aboard ship until we left.

When we came out of my sister's room in the morning—she'd been relegated to the couch for the night—I was surprised to see Ben sleeping on the floor.

"Ben! When did you get here?"

"Late last night," he said, yawning. "I thought it'd be easier to come then, rather than wait until this morning."

I pulled my brother up and gave him a hug, then dragged him over to Kacey, who was staring at him.

"I thought he was supposed to be in a wheelchair?" she asked, looking over at the very expensive chair parked in a corner of the apartment.

"Welll, maybe we lied just a little," Ben said, smiling.

"Lied? How do you lie about something like ALS?"

"Eh, hacking the lab that the doctor sends the tests to so you can manipulate the results helps. Also, there's a few drugs you can take before any examinations to help them see what you want them to see," Ben said with a shrug, and then gave her a hug. "The hard part is explaining why my muscles aren't wasting away, but I told them I'm using a couple of TENS units to try and keep from 'looking like a freak.'"

"Oh. What's a 'tens unit'?"

"Transcutaneous Electrical Nerve Stimulation. It stimulates the muscles with an electrical current. It's not a lot of fun; I've actually tried the ones I bought. A lot of paralyzed folks use them while they're waiting for corrective surgery."

She nodded, then smiled. "Well, it's nice to finally meet you. So you're the brains of the family?"

Ben laughed. "That's what they say, but after meeting you I'm starting to think that maybe it's been Dave all along!"

"No problems in getting away?" I asked as Kacey blushed.

Ben shook his head and yawned again. "I haven't taken any time off in over six months, and they all heard the story about how my 'poor beleaguered brother' was taken hostage by pirates and only barely managed to escape. So they weren't surprised when I told them I wanted to go see him."

He smiled evilly at me then. "So, what did you do to the pirates? Something epic, I'm sure!"

"Truth is, he made them his friends," Kacey said with a snicker, "and they're all but paying us now to help them."

"Really?" Ben said, looking surprised.

"Oh, they're not really pirates," I said. "And they're actually pretty nice people. Sit down, I'll tell you all about it."

"I'm going to make some coffee," Kacey said.

"Mom already beat you to it," Ben said. "So what's this I hear about you owning a spaceship?"

"Sit, please, and I'll tell you *all about it*," I said, and, sitting down on the couch, I did just that. Truth is, I wanted to brag, and I felt that, for once, I had something to brag about: a hot wife who loved me, a spaceship that I'd salvaged, and my own trading company.

I didn't hesitate to mention that the hot wife had a lot to do with the rest of the stuff.

"Wow, nice to see how well you've been doing now that you're out from under my shadow!" Ben teased.

Kacey came out and handed us each a cup of coffee and a bowl of cereal.

"Where's Mom and Dad?" I asked, looking around the room. Dianne was at school and Dad had said that he was taking the day off.

"Shopping. She wanted something a little better to go see your ship in than what she currently has. She didn't want to make you look bad."

I snorted. "Like she could do that."

Ben chuckled. "You know how she is. She's always afraid she's holding us back."

"Why would she think that?" Kacey asked.

"Because mom's a doler."

"Huh?"

"She grew up on the dole, she's bottom rung. Technically, because my original father died, I guess I could be called that too, because when he died she got tossed out on the street with me. That's what they said we were."

"So your original father wasn't a . . . doler?"

"No, he was a prole, just like our dad here. Mom always wanted to do better for any kids she had, and if you think she looks good now, back when she was young, she was hot. So she found a good, steady man, threw herself at him, and did everything she could to make him happy, which included giving him a son and staying home to take care of him.

"From what she told me once, life was good, until he was killed in an accident at his job. His family wanted nothing to do with her, and, well, she *wasn't* a prole, so she got tossed out of their home. Dad found us, out on the street. Mom was begging for food and he needed someone to watch Dave while he was at work, so the deal was, she would come here and be his full-time babysitter and cook, and he'd take care of the both of us."

"Nice to see it worked out."

"Dad's a good man. He treated me and Mom okay, and when he married her, well . . ." Ben shrugged. "Mom worships him. He still spoils her."

"Take notes, dear," I said, grinning at Kacey.

She stuck her tongue out at me. "Start spoiling me, and I'll think about it!"

"I would, but how do I top a spaceship?" I said, giving Ben a panicked look.

"I may be smart, but I'm not *that* smart!" Ben said, and laughed.

"So where do we do the switch?" I asked him, nodding at the wheelchair.

"Well, if we do it here, no one will know I went out to your ship. I have a fake ID that'll get me past security onto the shuttle flight. But it's only a ten-hour tube ride back to Boston, and not much farther to my apartment, so they'll figure out something happened to me as soon as someone decides to drop by and say hello."

"They're supposed to finish loading us up tonight after the sun sets. So we'll probably be out of here about three or four in the morning," I said. "Couldn't we just leave the chair here?"

Ben shook his head. "They're tracking it—for my safety, of course. So if it sits in any one place too long, they get an alert. I had to tell them I was parking it and going to bed when I got here."

"Why are they tracking you so closely?" Kacey asked.

"Because I wrote a paper on quantum mechanics that's now being hailed as the breakthrough they've been looking for, for the last two hundred years."

"What breakthrough is that?"

"Faster than light travel," we said together and then yelled "Jinx!" at each other.

"When did that happen?"

"When I was in high school trying to get into MIT, before I knew any better," Ben admitted with an embarrassed look. "When I saw how everyone was reacting to it, I started to look around, beyond the local school, and the gangs, all that stuff. I soon discovered that I'd probably never get the credit, if I did discover it. I wouldn't get a dime, out of all the billions it would make. *That* money would go to someone 'better' than me. But worst of all, I'd never be allowed to travel anywhere on it. Hell, they'd probably chain me to the lab I worked in out of fear someone might try to kidnap me and steal the secret."

"So we came up with this plan," I told her. "I was already planning on engineering school to get away from here."

"So for years now, I've been stalling them. Going down dead end after dead end. Making mistakes that it takes them years to figure out. But sooner or later I'm worried they're going to discover I'm holding back."

"So we made up the whole ALS thing, so they'd think he was tied to a wheelchair and not be able to easily run away."

"Where'd that idea come from?" she asked.

"A really old movie about some stage magicians who live this whole fake lifestyle so no one could figure out their tricks. It's so simple, it's brilliant," I said with a grin.

"Dave's not as stupid as he likes people to believe," Ben added with a grin of his own.

"So what are you going to do, just send the chair back by itself? Won't anyone notice?"

"Actually, we were going to find a bum, drug him, stick him in the chair, and send him home," Ben said.

"What? You can't be serious!"

"Sure, why not? Stick a couple hundred credits in his pocket and he won't care."

"Well, I have a better idea."

"Oh, and what would that be?"

"Pay one of the gang members downstairs to ride it back. Then at least you can even tell them when to go."

"Huh, that *is* a good idea. Especially as I just gave them a half dozen maskers when I got here last night."

"Did I mention how I married the smartest woman I could find?" I said, grinning.

"I thought you said 'hottest,'" Kacey frowned.

"Brains are sexy," Ben teased.

"Very sexy," I agreed.

"Well...You may have a point." She grinned.

"So after dinner we can all fly out to Holloman so I can show Mom, Dad, and Dianne the ship, and we can get you situated onboard."

"And as my chair hasn't gone there, they'll 'know' that I didn't go."

"What will you tell them if they ask why we didn't take him along?" Kacey asked me.

"That he was tired and wanted to take a nap before heading home, and wasn't all that interested in seeing an ancient cargo ship."

"I'll ping them before we leave," Ben said, "and let them know I'm taking a nap before I travel back. This way they won't start asking any questions."

"Have you talked to Mom and Dad at all about going with us?" I asked Ben.

He shook his head. "No, I still haven't told them I'm going

and I was afraid if I suggested to them that they should leave, they'd figure it out. Have you?"

I nodded. "Last night I dangled the hook."

"I talked with your mother while she was cooking," Kacey said. "She was definitely interested. I think she's figured out that you're going, Ben."

Ben nodded. "I've been coaching Dianne to hold back just enough so she doesn't get the genius tag. She's been studying a lot of cultural anthropology, as well as history lately, and she *really* doesn't want to be here for the next round of riots. She thinks the proles are going to take it in the short hairs again."

"Things do seem to look a lot more run-down than when I left. Have they been moving any doles into the quad?"

"No, but a lot of the folks here have started retiring, and are living on their pensions. I guess all of the retirement communities are full up or something."

"Which means that as far as the government's concerned, they might as well be doles," I said with a sigh.

Ben nodded. "And if a few places like this get burned down, they won't really be losing that much productivity, but they can claim that they've punished the evil proles once again to make the doles happy."

"They'd do that?" Kacey said, looking shocked.

"They've done worse," Ben told her. "They'll probably schedule the 'riots' to start just before rush hour, so the workers who are returning home won't get caught up in the mess, just the folks who aren't working."

The look on Kacey's face said it all.

"Now you know why I wanted to leave," I told her.

"Okay, I think it's time I switched to hard-sell mode with your parents," she said with a serious look on her face.

"Hard-sell mode?" Ben asked, looking at me.

"Her mother is one of the most ruthless negotiators on Ceres and apparently"—I smiled—"the fruit didn't fall all that far from the tree."

Ben's phone buzzed then and, pulling it out, he looked at it, then frowned.

"Yes, Mom?" he asked, answering it. "No, she's not. No, I don't know. I'll have Dave go talk to the Howlers. Don't worry, Mom, we'll take care of it. Yes. Bye."

"What's wrong?"

"Dianne's not at school."

"What?"

"She never showed. I think we should go downstairs and talk to Blu."

"Blu? What happened to Merks?"

"Blu told me last night that he got taken out a few months ago. Someone from the Crawlers, I guess."

"What the hell are the Crawlers doing 'round here?"

"The Howlers here are starting to shrink, Dave. With the number of retirees growing, that means no new families moving in and that means fewer kids, less new blood."

I nodded and stood up. "Kacey, wait here for our parents. Come on, Ben. Let's see if Blu knows anything."

"What are you going to do?" she asked worriedly.

"Whatever I have to." I sighed with a sinking feeling. "Whatever I have to."

Ben followed me out of the apartment, locking the door behind us, and down to the elevator.

"You up for this?" I asked him.

"That depends. I'm not as strong as I used to be, because I do have to spend a lot of time in that damn chair each day at school, so they don't figure out I'm faking it."

"Does Blu know about your whole ALS scam?"

"Yeah, I think all the Howlers know. They all think it's funny that I'm pulling one over on our elie bosses."

"And did you bring any maskers?"

"Actually, I brought two!" Ben said with a grin as the doors to the elevator opened. He passed me one as we went inside. I checked to be sure it was on, then pressed the button for the basement. The Howlers had a "clubhouse" down there, and the folks in building maintenance knew better than to say anything about it.

Blu looked up from the table he was sitting at the moment we stepped inside.

"I didn't have anything to do with it," he said immediately, holding up his hands.

"You know why we're here, then," I said, making it a statement.

"Donde did it, he only just called me. He's got your sister down at his clubhouse. He says he wants to *talk* to you."

I frowned; Donde was the man in charge of the Howlers at one of the other quads.

"So you're just gonna let another quad leader walk all over you?"

"He just moved up a few months ago; he runs *all* the quads in the city now."

"What happened to Kauf?"

"Kauf moved up to regional. Look, all I know is he wants to talk to you. Says he has a job for you or something. I even told him you left the gang six years ago. But the little shit wouldn't listen."

I shook my head. "Where is he?"

"He took over Kauf's digs."

"I need a ride. You got any drivers left?"

Blu frowned. "'Course I do! What, you think I can't do the job?"

"No, it's just that I've been gone for a couple of years now. If they put a *puta* like Donde in, who knows what else changed?"

"Tal! Get your ass out here! Goose needs a ride!" Blu said, turning and yelling into the back room. A moment later a teenager dressed in a well-tailored outfit walked in.

"Hey Professor," he said to Ben, then he looked over at Blu. "Who the hell is 'Goose'?"

"It's short for 'Mongoose,'" I said, and frowned at him.

He blinked. "Wait, that's you? I thought you were a myth or sumpthin'!"

"Yeah, well, he isn't. Don't piss him off and do as he says," Blu said. "Now, he needs a ride over to Donde's. So go!"

"Yeah, yeah, I'm going, I'm going."

We followed him out of the clubhouse over to a fairly nondescript electric sedan, and got in.

"So what's 'Tal' short for?" I asked as he pulled out of the garage.

"Tailor, 'cause I make clothes. And before you ask, they don't call me 'Tail,' 'cause I'll glue or sew one to the ass of anybody who does the first chance I get. And I get a lot of chances."

I snickered at that. "Good one."

"So, did you really kill all the people they claim you did?"

I shook my head. "I don't even want to know what they're saying about me now."

"Why'd you stop?"

"Because I was given a very good incentive."

"And that was?"

"You know, you ask way too many questions, Tal," Ben said, speaking up. "In some circles, that's not very healthy."

I saw Tal glance up in the mirror and look at me. I wasn't very happy right now, and I'm sure it showed.

"Yeah, right, I'll shut up now."

The rest of the ride was in silence.

"Wait here, don't go anywhere," I told him when he pulled into the garage of what was now Donde's place.

"You sure?"

"Very sure."

Walking over to the entrance, I saw there just happened to be two guys sitting out front and having a smoke. Cigarettes were supposed to be illegal, but people still smoked. I didn't think the cops even bothered enforcing the law because a lot of them smoked too.

"What do you want?"

"Donde called, said he wanted to talk. Now, how about you go inside and tell him I'm here. Or would you rather I tell him I left a couple of dead bodies out front?" I said with a frown. If they were still telling stories about me, I figured I might as well make the most out of it.

"And just who would *you* happen to be?" he said, standing up and giving me his "tough" look.

"Mongoose—you may have heard of me?" I said, staring right through him. I don't know why that look always bothered people, but I was just glad that it did. I wasn't looking forward to playing the "cold, hard killer" routine again. I'd had enough of that back with Marcus's people. But the gangs have their own subculture, their own ways, and a lot of it required a certain amount of posturing. I just hoped I could still pull it off. This wasn't a couple of losers in a hab, or some cut-rate killer. These were all experienced bangers.

My reputation must have preceded me, because he backed down and was almost polite after that.

"Go on in, he's expecting you."

"Come on, Prof," I said and went inside, with Ben following me. The first thing I saw was Donde sitting behind an actual desk. Kauf *never* had a desk, just a beat-up old card table. I guess that wasn't "upscale" enough for Donde. He wasn't armed, that I could tell. I'm sure he had a knife or a pick someplace on him, but I doubted he had a gun of any kind. The penalties for those were so stiff that, assuming you could even find one, everyone avoided them in the gangs.

The second thing I noticed was Dianne, who was sitting in a chair looking very scared. Her eyes were wide as she looked at me.

There were three other people in the room, not a one of whom looked over sixteen. I didn't recognize any of them, of course; they were probably Donde's crew from his quad. One was sitting by Dianne; the other two were standing behind Donde.

Donde was possibly the only person in the room older than me. The quad leaders were typically in their midtwenties, and moved up to regional when they hit thirty—assuming, of course, they both stayed out of jail, and lived that long. He had the same short black hair that Ben had, but a more muscular build. He actually looked more like Ben's brother than I did.

"Well, if it isn't the Mongoose himself!" Donde said with a smile.

"You know, Don, if you'd wanted to talk to me, you just could have called."

"Oh, but I wanted to be sure I had your full and *undivided* attention."

"Point made. Prof, take her home."

"Oh no, I got something I need for you to do first."

I walked up to the desk and, putting my hands on it, where they were clearly visible, I leaned over and said in a low voice, "Don, are you telling me you *don't* control the quad my parents and my sister lives in? That you *can't* grab her whenever you want?"

He flushed a bit at that.

"Take your sister and go, Prof."

"Thank you," I said and, straightening back up, I turned and nodded toward the door. Dianne looked torn for a moment, but she was smart enough to see I wanted her out of there, and she let Ben lead her out of the room.

"Before you think of taking us all on, my men here are armed with Tasers, so don't go getting any ideas."

I snorted. "I'm not armed. Airport security kinda frowns on that sort of thing, so I left my pick back on the ship."

"Ah, so you've stayed in practice, I see!" Donde said with a predatory smile.

"What do you want from me, Don? I walked away from the head picker role quite a few years ago. Hell, I believe you were actually here, in this room, when Kauf wished me luck and I gave him my old pick."

"Yeah, well, Kauf ain't here and I got a problem."

"So? I don't care about your problems, Don."

"Well, you'd better—like you said, I can get to your sister whenever I want to. Or your mother."

I frowned at that; threats against family were never a good thing.

"Fine, what's the problem?"

"Crow, over at the Creepers. I want him dead."

"You want me to kill the Creepers' head boss for the *city*?" I said looking at him in disbelief. "Are you trying to start a major gang war?"

"He's the one who killed your old boss, Merks! I can't let that go without retaliating! I'd look weak if I did that! Then they'd be coming after me next!"

"What about your own men?" I asked, nodding at the others.

"Crow's people know what they all look like, plus, let's be honest here, Goose. None of my guys have the ability to carry off something like this!"

"So you thought you'd endear yourself to me by kidnapping my sister?"

"No, I thought I'd make it clear to you that you're going to do this, or I'm going to give your sister to my boys to play with. And then once they're done with her, I'll slit her throat and part her out on the black market!"

I was amazed that I didn't jump over the desk and throttle him, Tasers or no. If I'd had my pick, yeah, he'd already be dead. But I didn't, and I also wasn't looking to die today.

Or any other day, truth be told. The very last thing I wanted was to get involved in a gang war. Sure, when I was fourteen it would have been a hell of a rush. But not anymore. I was a grown man with a wife. I wondered if I could just go home, pack 'em all up, and get to our ship before anybody noticed.

"Besides, what are *you* worried about? You'll be on that ship you're working and be out of here before the police even find out! What's the name of that wreck? *Iowa Hill* or something?"

"Or something," I said as *that* idea went right out the window. "Just how am I supposed to hit this guy? He's gotta have bodyguards, just like you do!"

"That part's easy," Donde said with a smile.

"Oh, is it now?"

"Crow eats lunch at one of six restaurants. We just find out which one he's going to, my boys subdue the waitstaff, and you go in dressed as a waiter."

"Are you serious?" I said, giving him a look like he was mental.

"Goose, you're what, twenty-three now? Most of my guys are under sixteen! Same for Crow! He won't look twice at you, trust me."

I frowned, but he had a point.

"Okay, so I kill him, then what? You're not gonna leave me there with my dick in my hand, are you?"

"You run out the back and leave with my boys. They'll bring you back here. Once I'm satisfied Crow's dead, you can go home."

"Once you're satisfied?"

"Yeah, bring me back a trophy, something I can hang on the wall."

I just shook my head. "Do you have a pick for me at least?"

Donde smiled. "As a matter of fact, I do."

"Let's just get one thing straight: I'm doing this for Merks, not you, got it? 'Cause yeah, he was *my* boss and shit like that needs to be punished."

Donde smiled even wider as I said that. I didn't mean any of it, of course; I was lying through my teeth. But I knew it was the kind of thing he expected to hear.

"Great! Now we just need to wait to find out which restaurant he's going to."

"I also need a weapon," I told him.

"One of my boys will give you one when you get there."

I nodded and sat down. So much for any ideas that started with my killing him.

An hour or so later I was sitting in the passenger's seat as we drove to a Pho Noodle house. We pulled up to the rear of it and the two guys in the back of the car piled out. There was another car here already. I guessed Donde wasn't taken any chances.

"Here," the driver said, and passed me a pick. Looking at it,

I had to shake my head. It was the same pick I'd given Kauf over six years ago.

"Hello, old friend," I said. I spun it in my hand, then; the balance was just as I remembered it.

"Time to go to work, I guess," I said, and, getting out of the car, I slipped it into my pocket and went inside. The entire waitstaff, which was all of two people, were bound, gagged, blindfolded, stripped to their underwear, and lying on the floor. What I guessed was the cook was with them. The guy working the cook's job now looked more like some bum off the street who'd been paid a couple hundred creds and had no idea what he was getting himself into.

I put on one of the "uniforms," which was mainly just a fancy shirt, and peeked out of the back room. I didn't even have a chance to figure out where he was, or what I was going to do, as the kid behind me unceremoniously shoved me through the door.

At least I didn't stumble or drawn any attention to myself.

I spotted Crow almost immediately as I grabbed the busboy cart and started bussing the tables. There were several that needed it, thankfully. There were about a dozen people in here eating, a mixed crowd—late teens, early twenties, if I had to guess. I really had no idea what I was going to do. I really didn't want to kill Crow, but I didn't want to have my sister raped and murdered either.

I'd just come around the last table between me and Crow when I saw what looked like a four-year-old girl sitting at the table with him.

"I am just so screwed." I sighed and shook my head. There was no way I was killing somebody in front of their four-year-old daughter.

"You can say that again, Dave," Crow said looking over at me.

I noticed then out of the corner of my eye that at least two of the twenty-ish looking guys had guns, actual pistols, and were pointing them at me.

"I'm surprised you still remember me," I said with a shrug.

"I'm surprised that you didn't go for it when you had the chance. Though honestly, I had no idea Merks meant that much to you."

"I'm not here for Merks."

"Then why are you here?"

"Because Donde has assured me, after kidnapping my sister this morning, that if I *don't* kill you, she's going to be raped and murdered by him and his boys."

Crow looked over at me and frowned.

"So why'd you stop?"

"Do you have any idea what it takes to kill a man in cold blood in front of his daughter?"

Crow shook his head. "Not really."

"Yeah, well, neither do I. I'm not even sure I could have done it back when I was actually *in* the gang."

"Why does Donde want me dead? Other than the obvious reasons."

"Because you killed Merks. Because he's afraid of looking weak."

Crow snorted. "Actually, Donde killed Merks. Kauf wanted Merks to take over after he left, so Donde decided to get rid of the competition. He just told everyone that I did it."

"And I'm just supposed to believe that?"

"I'm sure he's going to tell everyone that he had no idea you were going to kill me, that you just went and did it on your own to avenge Merks's death."

Shaking my head, I dragged a chair over and sat down.

"The guys in the back who brought me here left already, didn't they?"

"As soon as they shoved you through the door, they ran out the back."

"And I take it that Donde knows you have armed bodyguards, which is why he's afraid to take you on himself?"

"Correct again. Now, if you wouldn't mind surrendering your weapon? I'd feel a lot better about things if you did, Dave."

I laughed. "*Damn!* Don't tell me you're starting to believe all those stories too!"

"You forget, I saw some of those 'stories.'"

I slowly took out my pick, then I rolled it across the floor to him.

"You did? Huh, I hadn't known."

"So what happened to you? You were really climbing up to the top in the Howlers, and then one day...gone. I found out that you'd quit, finished school, and left town not long after that."

"Someone told me that I was wasting my life, and I believed them."

"Your brother, that genius kid?"

I shook my head and laughed again. "No, this was a much more painful and professionally administered suggestion. But"—I shrugged—"they were right."

"They were?"

"You're alive, aren't you? Sure, your men would have gotten me, but I really didn't want to kill you. Hell, I'm not sure I want to kill Donde, and if anybody deserves it right now, it's him."

"For setting you up?"

"For promising to rape and murder my sister. You don't think you can take care of him before that for me, do you?" I asked him as the reality of my situation started to sink in. I was surprised at how calm I was. I'd always thought I'd go out raging.

"What, not going to do that yourself?"

I looked at the two guys still pointing guns at me. "Unless those guys are really terrible shots, I don't think I'm going to be dealing with anybody."

Crow bent over and retrieved my pick from the floor, where it had stopped rolling.

"So is this it?"

"Yup. I gave it to Kauf when I quit. I guess Donde got his hands on it. They gave it back to me just before I got shoved through the doors."

Crow nodded slowly and looked at it.

"What is that, Daddy?" his daughter asked.

"Pain. Pain and suffering. A lot of suffering," he said, looking it over.

"Is it evil?"

"No, baby doll, it's not evil. Men are evil. This is just a tool."

"Is he evil?" she asked and nodded toward me.

"No, he's just another tool. Ain't that right, Dave?"

I laughed. "Mongoose was a tool. Dave just wants people to stop messing with his family. I'm sure you can understand that."

Crow laughed, surprising me. "You know, I find myself with a bit of a dilemma, Dave."

"Enlighten me, Crow."

"If I kill you, I know that there's a chance, a good chance, that your elie mom and her family will come down hard on me, if for no other reason than to make an example out of me. Wouldn't surprise me one bit if Donde was counting on that if you failed today."

"Makes sense," I agreed, curious as to where this was going. That probably was the reason I wasn't already dead.

"How much longer are you planning on being in town?"

I looked at the clock on the wall and did some quick mental math. "Thirteen hours. That's when the ship I'm an engineer on is due to lift."

Crow looked impressed. "You're an engineer on a spaceship?"

I nodded. "I'm only here to visit family. I'm not the person everyone seems to think I am anymore."

"Interesting. The other part of my dilemma is, if I let you go, people might start thinking I'm weak."

"But I didn't try to kill you," I pointed out.

"And they're going to believe that?"

I shrugged. "You've got a lot of witnesses. You've also got my pick, which I gave you."

"True, and without his teeth, the mongoose really isn't all that much to fear now, is he?"

"Not anymore."

"If you're still in town come tomorrow morning, I'll have to kill you, you understand that, right?"

I nodded, surprised at what I was hearing.

"Take this." He grabbed the necklace that he was wearing, yanked it off, and tossed it to me. I caught it and looked at it: a silver chain with a pendant hanging off it. A pendant in the shape of a scarecrow.

"Huh, always wondered why they called you Crow."

"Well, now you know. You can give that to Donde. Goodbye, Dave. You can consider us even."

"Goodbye, Crow," I said and went out the way I'd come in, shucking the "uniform" shirt on the way and grabbing my own.

I got about a block before my legs gave out as all the adrenaline just quit at once and I ended up sitting on the ground.

I thought about what his last words were, and tried to remember just *why* he said we were even. But for the life of me I had no idea, and I wasn't about to go back and ask him.

It took about five minutes for my legs to stop shaking before I could stand up again. The first thing I did was send Kacey a message telling her I was alright and I'd be home soon. The second was to call a taxi. There was no way I was going to walk to Donde's headquarters.

The driver wouldn't get within half a block of the place, so I paid him and walked the rest of the way. When I got there, the two toughs by the door looked surprised but didn't say a word as I walked by them and went inside. The look on Donde's face was priceless. I just threw the necklace at him, turned and walked back the way I'd come.

I had to walk two blocks before I could get another taxi to come and pick me up. But fifteen minutes later I was back at my parent's apartment.

Kacey all but tackled me as I came in through the door. Dianne, whose eyes were red from crying, got there next.

I kissed Kacey and held the two of them for a moment.

"What did they want you to do?" Ben asked first.

"Donde wanted me to kill somebody."

I heard my mom gasp at that.

"Who?"

"The head of the Crawlers, guy named Crow."

"What'd you do?" Kacey demanded.

"Got very lucky. Right now, Donde thinks he's dead."

"He's not?"

"Nope."

"So what's going to happen when Donde finds out you didn't kill Crow?" Ben asked.

I shook my head. "I don't know. For all I know, Donde's first inkling that Crow isn't dead is going to be when Crow kills him."

Ben stood up then and sighed. "Mom, Dad"—he looked over at our sister, who was still holding onto me—"Dianne. I think you need to pack."

"Why, Ben?" Mom asked.

"Because I'm leaving with Dave and I think you all should too. Dianne's never going to have the kind of life here that she'd want, and they're not going to be all that happy when they find out I emigrated. And even if this Crow guy manages to kill Donde, I don't think you're ever going to be able to trust Dave's old gang to keep you safe again.

"But it goes beyond all of that! Look around outside, the government has already written off this quad. The doles are starting to act up again. Who do you think they're going to attack when the next set of riots hit? Look, Dave's made a name for himself already; if nothing else, *he* and Kacey can probably give you all good jobs.

"They've got a great school system on Ceres that Dianne will love. I know because I checked when Dave told me he was settling there. I'll probably end up teaching in it as well. Dave broke the ice. We need to leave, while we still can."

"Why are you running away, Ben?" Dad asked. "MIT offered you a teaching position; the corporations are lining up to hire you. Why would you want to throw that all away?"

"Because if I ever publish the research that's in my head, they'll throw me in a cage 'for my own protection' and you'll never see me again."

"Is it that dangerous?"

"No, it's worth that much money, Dad. And you all know the *last* thing the elies want is for proles to have money."

"Or power," Dad agreed with a sigh. "Still, it's a big change, you're asking a lot of us. All of your sister's friends are here, everyone I've ever known is here. I don't know if I can."

"I want to go, Dad," Dianne said, looking at him. "Ben's right, without the protection of the local gang, it's not safe anymore—if it was ever really safe to start with," she said with a sniff. "I can make new friends, and I don't want to end up like Ben is, worried that someone will find out that I'm smarter than everybody else and suddenly I'm nothing more than a slave to some corporation."

"Jenny?"

"If Ben and Dave both say we should go, we should go, Kurt. I remember what it was like the last time my world fell apart, and if I lost you, it would kill me. Plus it would be nice to have something to do now that Dianne's growing up and will be starting college in a couple of years."

"Do you think we should go?" Dad asked, looking at me.

I nodded. "Yeah, I do."

"Pack a small bag," Ben said. "Take only what you really can't live without. We're just going on a day trip. We don't want anybody to think you're not coming back."

My father looked around the room a moment before he finally nodded. "Jenny, Dianne, go pack."

As soon as Dianne let go of me I went over to the couch to sit down.

"How bad was it?" Ben asked after Dianne and our mother and father had left the room.

"Bad. I thought I was dead. I'm still not sure why Crow let me live, but it seems like a combination of he's afraid of what Eileen might do and he seems to think he owes me for something."

"He owes you?"

"I guess." I shrugged. "Maybe it'll come to me. But he recognized me the moment I set foot in the room. I'd have sworn I'd never seen him before, but he sure remembered me," I said as I got out my tablet and reserved six tickets on the shuttle to Holloman. "Now, how about we change the subject?"

"Sure. What kind of cargo are you taking on that loads only at night?" Ben asked as the three of us sat there waiting for the others.

"The kind that you pay large bribes for, I guess. Some sort of high-tech early warning system. One of the few things that Earth is still the best at making these days."

"You do know that most of those come with interceptor missiles, don't you?"

I sighed. "Well, I do *now*. All the more reason to lift ship and get out of here tonight."

"He's always been like this," Ben said to Kacey, sotto voice. "He just can't help himself. If there's trouble, he's just got to be in the middle of it."

Kacey laughed. "I think you're right."

I just grumbled. After the day I'd been having, all I wanted to do was crawl into my bunk and pull the covers over my head. Too bad it was never that easy.

"What about that?" Kacey asked, pointing to the wheelchair.

"Oh, right!" Ben said. "Dave, could you come with me downstairs? I need to talk to Blu again."

Sighing, I got up. "Hopefully this will be a lot easier than our last conversation."

Ben got in the chair and we took it out to the elevator and down to the basement again.

"What are you doing back here?" Blu asked when we came into the clubhouse.

"I took care of what Donde asked me to do, but now my brother here needs a favor."

Blu nodded, a little cautiously. "What?"

"I need to disappear for a while," Ben said. "So I was hoping you could get somebody to help me out?"

"What do you need?"

"I need someone to take this wheelchair back to Boston. I got the tickets and everything."

"Sure, I can get someone to do that. Hundred credits."

"I'll give you two and a half, but they can't leave until the eleven o'clock train tonight. That's the one I got tickets for."

"What do you want them to do when they get there?"

"The chair's programmed to go to my apartment, the door's keyed to it. So tell 'em to help themselves to whatever they want and then split."

Blu smiled then. "Whatever they want?"

"Yeah, knock yourself out."

"Oh, I got *just* the guy for this."

"Great!" Ben got out of the chair, counted out the money, then took a moment to show him how it all worked.

"That was easy," Ben said.

"For a change," I agreed.

"Well, let me call my minders so I can tell them I'll going to be spending the afternoon with family, and taking a nap before I catch the last train out to Boston, and to leave me alone until I see them all at school in the morning."

"Think they will?"

"I'll tell 'em that I'm turning off my tablet," Ben said with a laugh.

He made the phone call while we were in the elevator. I guess someone wanted to know if he'd tell them about what happened to me, and he agreed that he would, but for now, he just wanted to have some time with his family.

Then he hung up and turned off his tablet.

"How'd it go?" Kacey asked.

"Easy peasy," Ben said with a smile. "Mom! Dad! Dianne! You guys ready?"

"I'd say so," our mother said as she and Dad came out of their bedroom, each carrying a small overnight bag.

"I'm ready too!" Dianne said, coming out with her schoolbag.

"Is that thing full of books?" I asked.

"Data cube and my tablet. Oh, and a change of clothes," she said with a grin.

"Ah, that's my sister," Ben said, grinning. "Books first, clothing second!"

"I take it there's a story there?" Kacey asked.

"It only happened the once!" Ben said with a wink.

"And it was more than enough, trust me," I said with a heavy sigh.

I watched as Mom and Dad paused for a moment and took a look around the room, then Mom went and got the picture of all of us that was hanging just above the flatscreen.

"Can't forget this!" she said with a smile and added it to her bag.

We all followed her out after that.

Dad closed the door behind us, locked it, and then led the way as we went down and caught the tube to the spaceport. Boca Chica was busy, as always, but things moved fast, because the police didn't care much for loitering. A lot of the elies moved through here, so trouble wasn't tolerated.

"Why do we have to go through security, anyway?" Kacey asked as we went through the scanners looking for explosives and other contraband. "I meant to ask on the way out."

"Nobody knows," I said with a shrug.

"I used to think they did it just to mess with us," Ben said. "But nowadays I think it's just government momentum. If they stopped doing it, thousands of government employees would be out of a job and hundreds of millions of dollars wouldn't get spent, and then who knows? They might even have to lower taxes!"

Kacey looked a little shocked as everyone within earshot either laughed or muttered some kind of agreement.

I noticed they didn't even look twice at Ben's ID, though they *did* look twice at Kacey's, until I told them she was my wife, we both worked on a ship docked in Holloman, and I had taken her to visit family. Mine still showed me as a resident of the Texas District; I'd decided that I'd change that part after we'd gotten Ben. I'd only filed for the change to my last name just before we'd left on this trip. I'd update all my licenses and documents when we got back, and who knew? Maybe a lot of folks would lose track of me after that.

Security at Holloman was as screwed up as ever once we got out of the air terminal portion and headed over to the spaceport. Not that I was complaining. We breezed through the corridors and out on to the tarmac and over to the ship.

If you can call walking a couple kilometers "breezing." At least the sun wasn't overhead anymore, so it wasn't unbearably hot.

"Wow! A spaceship!" Dianne yelled when we finally walked up to it, proving that she wasn't yet as jaded as I might have feared. I could see the port side cargo doors were still open, but the bottom two cargo decks looked to be halfway packed and loading was well underway with dozens of containers parked by the ship waiting to be loaded.

"We better check with Emil and Chris to make sure it's all being packed right," I said to Kacey as we made our way over to the stairs, which were still down.

"Oh, I'm sure they know what they're doing, but I'll look it over if it makes you feel any better," she said with a smile.

"I'm just worried about Jarvis's cargo," I admitted to her in a soft voice. "I think we've had enough things go wrong today."

Kacey just nodded and I gestured for the others to go up the stairs, then followed them up into the center of the hold.

"Well, Mom, Dad, Dianne, Ben, welcome aboard the *Iowa Hill*. She's old, she's tired, but she's ours and she still flies great."

"Wow, this is really amazing!" Mom said.

"What are you running on the bridge?" Dad asked unsurprisingly.

"The third-generation Honeywell Stratus guidance, comms, and nav package."

"Why so old?"

I waved a hand at the ship around us. "Old ship, old systems. Trust me; it does the job for us more than well enough."

"Now, come on upstairs and we'll introduce you to the rest of the crew," Kacey said. "Then we'll figure out who's staying where. Not that there's any shortage of space on this thing."

I followed them up the steep stairs to the top deck, where Chris, coming off the bridge, found me.

"We just got a call from the Port Ops. Seems there's some paperwork that you need to sign?"

"Huh?" I said.

"Apparently the last time the *Iowa Hill* put in here, the paperwork for the nav systems upgrades didn't get signed off and now that you're one of the new owners, they want you to initial it before the union throws a fit," Chris said with a shrug.

I sighed. "Fine, I'll go deal. Has Jarvis said if his people were still on schedule for their delivery?"

"So far."

"I want to get off as soon as reasonable after they're done."

"Is that your family?"

I nodded. "Yeah, and they're about to become refugees, something I'm sure a lot of our crew is familiar with." I turned to Kacey. "I'll go deal with this, get everyone settled and give Ben one of my shipsuits, but don't put him on the roster just in case anyone comes looking. Log my parents and my sister as VIP passengers deadheading to Ceres—unless someone has a better idea."

"I'm on it, hon," she said and gave me a kiss.

I ran down to my quarters, got into my shipsuit, then went back out and down to the tarmac and started heading toward Port Operations, which was at the base of the ground control tower. It was barely past noon and I was definitely getting hungry. The next twelve hours would be a little worrisome. I'd planned for a four a.m. lift and Blu had promised us that he wouldn't put his guy on the train back to Boston until eleven like Ben had asked. So hopefully they wouldn't know about Ben being gone until after we'd passed the Moon's orbit and were well out of Earth's sphere of influence. But I could see there was still a lot of cargo to load and Jarvis's "special cargo" wasn't here yet, and I knew that loading that would take hours and it was already past seven.

"Dave Walker?" someone said as I walked in through the door.

"Yes?" I said, looking up. There was a guy in a suit who I recognized.

"Sorry, no beatings today," he said and, pulling out a shocker, he lit me up until I passed out.

TWENTY-THREE

Morgan Family Estate, Colorado District

I WOKE UP AND MY HEAD HURT. I FELT A BRIEF STING IN MY arm and then things started to feel better.

"Give that a moment to take effect; you've had quite a shock."

"Don't quit your day job," I groaned and then opened my eyes. It was the guy who'd shocked me, of course. Last time I'd seen him, he'd administered an epic beating with the help of two others, and then passed my grandfather's message on to me.

I looked around. I was sitting in a chair, in a *very* expensive-looking room.

"What time is it?" I asked, looking for a clock. I could feel that my hands were cuffed behind my back. "And where am I, why am I here—you know, the usual questions."

He smiled. "It's after five p.m., local. You're in Colorado, at the Morgan family estate. Your grandfather apparently wants a word or two with you."

"You could have just *asked*, you know," I grumbled.

"You've killed three assassins that I know of, plus the last time we met, you weren't very happy when I was done with you."

I sighed and looked at him. "As much as I want to hate you and my grandfather for that little 'meeting,' I can't."

"Really?" he said, looking just a little surprised.

"He was right, and the only way I would have gotten the message back then was to have it beaten into my head. It changed my life. For the better, I might add."

"But you still had this on you," he said and held out my pick. I'd forgotten I had that in the pocket of my shipsuit! Talk about stupid! And on Earth no less.

"Yeah, well, Eileen's husband wanted me dead, so what was I supposed to do?" I said, looking around the room again to hide my embarrassment as things started to come into better focus.

"You mean your mother."

I snapped my head around and stared him in the eye, "Don't start. Or I will hit you."

He gave a small nod, acknowledging my point.

"Now, can we get these cuffs off and can I get some water? I'm dying of thirst over here."

"Will you promise to behave?"

"I promise not to hurt or kill Grandfather or Eileen."

"What about her husband?"

"Jefferson?" I laughed. "If he so much as takes a swing at me, he's going to the hospital. But I promise I won't attack him first."

"Fair enough. One last thing."

"What?"

"Do you promise not to kill me?"

I laughed. "As long as you're not trying to kill me, sure."

"Good enough."

He came over and helped me up out of the chair, undid the cuffs, then led me over to the small table in the room that had a pitcher of water sitting on it with several glasses. He poured out two, picked up one, tipped it to me in a toast, and took a drink.

So I picked up the other one and drained it.

"Feel any better?" he asked me.

"Mostly. Can I have my pick back?"

"Not until we're done here."

I just nodded and set the glass down.

"Come with me," he said. Taking my elbow, he carefully led me out of the room and into a hallway that probably cost more than the *Iowa Hill* had cost to build when it was new. I actually recognized some of the artwork hanging on the walls and, while I couldn't name any of it, I doubted they were reprints. Elie ego wouldn't allow for something like that.

He then opened a door and led me into a room with a lot of very comfortable chairs around a small table, though at the far end of the table, instead of a chair, was an imposing desk with an old white-haired man sitting behind it.

Sitting beside each other in two chairs on the left side of the room were a woman and a man. Both were richly dressed and attractive looking. The woman might have been my mother, but my memory of her was so dim I really couldn't tell. Dad had burned or deleted every single picture of her that he'd had.

"David!" the woman said, jumping to her feet.

"And you would be?" I asked, looking at her.

"I'm your mother!"

"No, my mother is currently sitting in a cabin on my space-ship back in New Mexico. *You* lost the right to call me that when you dumped me and ran home to Daddy, leaving me to grow up in poverty." I looked up at the old man behind the desk. "No offense, sir."

"How can you say that? Your father wouldn't let me take you with me! He threw me out!"

I rolled my eyes. "Save it for the press, Eileen. You want me to believe that Kurt, my father, stopped you from calling me? Sending me letters? Contacting me in *any* way? You've got more money than *God*, Eileen. If you wanted to talk to me, there is nothing he could have done to stop it.

"But you didn't. Fine, you left him, all but destroyed him. But you're both adults, not my business. However, you dumped me like a bad habit and never once, not *once* in the last eighteen years, tried to reach out to me! Yeah, thanks for having me, but that's about as far as it goes. You lost your rights to being my mom when you walked out the door."

"See? I told you he'd be an ungrateful whelp! Those proles don't know how—"

"Shut it, Jefferson," I growled, looking down at him. "Sending all those people to kill me does not endear you to me in any way."

"You mind your manners, boy!" he yelled, jumping to his feet.

"Or what? You'll hire another lame-ass assassin? Seriously? I *am* curious; did Eileen know you were trying to kill her son? Did she even *care*?"

"That was uncalled for, David," the man behind the desk said.

"That may be," I admitted to him. "Grandfather, I presume?"

He nodded.

"That may be, but it's a question I would love to know the answer to, as much as I probably shouldn't. *You* at least made the effort to teach me a lesson. A lesson I realized I sorely needed to be taught and took it to heart."

"And what lesson was that?" Jefferson asked, looking back and forth between us.

"That *family* matters and you don't go dragging their name through the mud," I told him. "That there was at least *one* person in this family who thought I could be more, who wanted me to make something of myself."

I looked back up at my grandfather. "Again, thank you for that, for all that I was pissing blood for a week."

I was surprised to see him smile.

"You're welcome."

I turned and dropped into one of the chairs. I noticed the man who had brought me into the room was no longer there.

"I must say, son, I'm impressed. You've got your own ship, a cargo company, and a growing bank account. Plus you survived Jefferson's attempts. Attempts which neither I *nor* your mother, Eileen, knew about."

I gave a small sigh of relief. "Thank you for telling me that."

"There were several reasons why I wanted you here today, before you left. The first is that Jefferson there is going to apologize for trying to have you killed and is going to swear to never do it again..."

"I will do no—"

"Jefferson, if you do not, I will not ask David to refrain from hiring his own assassins."

"Like he could afford such a thing!"

I watched as my grandfather pinched the bridge of his nose between his thumb and forefinger. He closed his eyes and sighed heavily.

"Jefferson, you know that nice Mr. Smith who came in here yesterday and paid us one hundred million credits, *cash*?"

I noticed the very slight involuntary shiver that Jefferson gave. Obviously Mr. Smith had made *quite* the impression on him.

"Yes, what about him?"

"They're going to be loading that missile targeting system we sold them onto *David's* ship tonight. Now just what do you think Mr. Smith is going to do to you if he finds out you had his friend here killed? Or, for that matter, if he discovers that *you're* the one who has been *trying* to have him killed?"

I was surprised at just how white Jefferson turned.

"Now, apologize and promise not to ever try again!"

Jefferson got up out of his seat and turned to me. I could see he was actually scared. I guessed that "Mr. Smith" was a very intimidating man.

"David, I apologize for all of my past actions. I swear to you that I will never try and have you killed again. Please forgive me."

"I don't know if I'll forgive you, but I promise not to kill you. Grandfather is right—I do have access to some very good assassins, and not just the ones this Mr. Smith knows."

"You may leave now, Jefferson," Grandfather said, in a tone that brooked no argument.

Jefferson nodded and left the room quickly.

"Now, Eileen, you had something you wanted to say to your son?"

"She's not my—"

"David," Grandfather growled at me. "Mind your manners."

I shut up.

Eileen sighed and turned to face me from her seat. "When I got the message of your capture and probable death when the pirates took your ship, I suddenly realized what I had done. Yes, I was a vain and selfish young woman and I ran away from my responsibilities and tried to pretend that none of it had ever happened. I'm sorry, David. I'm sorry for what I did to Kurt, and most of all, I'm sorry for what I did to you.

"You can hate me all you want, but I owed it to you, to admit that, yes, what you said before about me was right."

"I don't hate you," I said with a soft voice. "I gave up on that a long, long time ago. But I am upset with you. So let's just leave it at that."

"Can you ever forgive me?" she asked, and I could see that she was actually crying. I didn't think it was an act. I noticed the look my grandfather was giving me. I didn't know how he felt about me, but it was pretty obvious he cared about his daughter, for all that he'd put her up to this.

"Maybe? One day? I don't know, I really don't. This isn't something you can just say you're sorry for and expect it to all just go away. It's been years, *years*... Yeah, maybe one day I can forgive you, but you're going to have to work at it, Eileen, if you ever want to hear me call you 'Mom' and mean it."

I noticed my grandfather nodding his approval while my bio-mother, the woman who gave birth to me, nodded with tears in her eyes.

"I promise to try," she said and then, getting up, she hurried out of the room.

I sighed and shook my head. "Why am I here, Grandfather? I think the beating was a lot easier to take."

He snorted and then smiled at me. "Oh, those things were important. Jeffery needed his leash jerked. Sometimes he thinks he's allowed to make the decisions around here. And my daughter, your *mother*, needed to find some closure and perhaps start on making amends. She really did cry when she thought you were dead, and she suddenly realized just what a bad thing she'd done. Honestly, she should have just brought Kurt home with her. Lord knows he's a better man than that Jefferson is. At least their children turned out okay."

"So why didn't you do anything?"

"I'm not omniscient, son. I had no idea you even existed until you got in trouble that first time with the police. Until then you were totally off my radar. Then it took months to puzzle it all out and find out that it wasn't a mistake in the system. I have to admit; I'm pretty damned chuffed to see that you turned out okay. When I sent Havier there to give you a little tune-up, I was worried that I might have to come back and follow through on that threat. I'm just surprised you actually understood the message."

I shrugged. "You could have had me killed. By that point in my life I'd killed quite a few people myself, Grandfather, and I knew that you'd shown restraint. Which meant you actually *cared* enough to go right up to that line, but not cross it. You did that for some bastard brat you didn't know, never met, and up until that moment had never cared about. Oh no, I got that message loud and clear. Loud and clear."

"Which brings me to my next point: how would you feel about changing your last name to Morgan?"

That floored me! I stopped, leaned back in my chair, and blinked. "What? You want me in the family? Me? With *my* history?"

"Sure, why not? It would definitely let the other families out there know that this one still has a lot of spine left in it."

I snorted at that. "Yeah, only the elies would think of someone like me in those terms. But I don't think I could see myself living in a house like this, or even on Earth anymore."

"So stay on Ceres. This family has a lot of resources, son. A mover and a shaker like you? You could take us places. Think of what you could build with access to the assets that we've got. Hell, you're already one of us! You ended up with Smith's people and had them eating out of your hand by the time you left! They let you come and go as you please! They even trust you to haul a billion credits of their gold around without anything more than your word!

"I mean, damn, son. I should send my other grandkids out to work for you so they'll learn how business *really* gets done!"

I gave a small laugh and shook my head, "Grandfather, I don't know. It's one hell of an offer, but the truth is I already changed my name to Doyle when I married my wife."

"Yes, I saw that. Might I inquire as to why?"

"The Doyle clan is both large and important on Ceres. It's the same reason I agreed to put their name on the company: I wanted the folks who run things back there to know that I was serious about 'joining their gang,' you might say."

"I could see where that would be important. Still, the Morgan name carries a lot of weight, son, a lot of weight."

"Not on Ceres, Grandfather. Besides, if you were to make me a member of this family, I can guarantee you we'd be having some *very* loud arguments over how you do business!"

"Oh, what I wouldn't give to have someone with enough balls to do that!" He laughed. "Look, David. Think about it. Just promise me that if I do send one of your half brothers or cousins out there, you won't kill them out of hand."

I nodded slowly and paused a moment to think about what he was saying. Sure, it was a great offer, but where were the downsides? A hook is still a hook, no matter how great the bait. Respecting family was one thing, but trust was the important issue here, and I definitely had trust issues with both elies and with my bio-mother's family.

"Something on your mind, son?"

I nodded again and looked him in the eye.

"You know why the people you just sold all of that stuff to trust me?"

"Not really, son, though I do admit I'm curious."

"It's because they know I have their back, just as I know they have mine. They trust me, because I've proved to them that I'll do what I have to, to protect them, and they've proven to me as well that they'll keep their word and watch out for me.

"Even the government on Ceres, for as much as you can trust any government, has made it clear that as long as I play the game their way, they'll do what they can for me. They can see I'm committed, that I'm trustworthy, and they understand. Changing my name was part of showing that commitment, not just to them but to the community at large."

"Ah, so what you're saying is you don't want to change your name."

"No, what I'm saying is I don't know that I can *trust* you, Grandfather, that I can trust any of the Morgan family. How do I know that you have my back? That you're going to take care of me and mine?

"Yeah, it was nice what you did here today, but none of that was anything I wasn't already dealing with. If anything, it was more you dealing with family issues, just like when I got that little tune-up. I have to warn you, Grandfather, while I do respect you, and you are family, I'm still not sure that I like you, or that I can *trust* you. So for all that your offer is tempting, until I know I can trust you to do whatever you have to, to protect me like Mr. Smith's people will, I don't know that I can agree."

He frowned a moment, thinking about what I said.

"I could say the same about you, son. It's not like you'll be here on Earth where I can keep an eye on you."

"True, but with the friends I have, if I break trust with one, then the others will all start thinking about breaking their trust with me. I'm still the one taking the greater risk."

He considered that and nodded. "I have to concede your point there. When all you have is your reputation, you have to guard it carefully. Will you at least give me the opportunity to win your trust? Not just shut me out cold?"

I almost told him no, but I realized that wouldn't be fair. He'd never done anything to me that I could honestly fault him for.

Still, it wasn't easy to say it.

"I will, I promise."

He surprised me then by getting up and walking around his desk and sticking out his hand. Standing up, I shook hands with him and he looked me in the eye. "I'm going to make it clear to everyone that you're my grandson, that you've been accepted into the family, that regardless of your last name, you're still a member in good standing of the Morgan family. If I have to start somewhere, then I guess I might as well start there."

"Thank you," I said, feeling rather shocked. By elie standards I was well beyond a black sheep, I was more like a leper.

"Havier is waiting outside to take you back to your ship."

All I could do was nod mutely.

"Give my regards to your lovely wife, and your mother, as well as my apologies to your father. Oh"—he paused a moment—"do you *really* know a good assassin? Because I can't believe you meant your old gang friends back in Boca Chica."

"Yeah, I do. And I already had to warn them off of killing one idiot, though honestly? I really didn't want to kill Jefferson. Just *why* was he trying to get rid of me, anyway?" I asked as I regained my wits. Today had definitely been a day of unexpected surprises.

"Because you had a police record with a very long list of victims, and he was worried that if it got tied to him in the last election, it would ruin his chances."

"Oh? So what happened?"

"I had it deleted. You were a minor, they're not supposed to keep those kinds of things," he said with a wink.

I just sighed. "Goodbye, Grandfather."

"Good luck, Grandson."

I stepped out of the room and sure enough, Havier was there.

"Didn't kill anyone, I see."

"No, no, I didn't. I need to get back to my ship."

"Come, I'll take you there."

I pinged Kacey on my tablet to let her know I was on my way back, that *yet again* something unexpected had come up, and I'd let her know about it once I was back onboard.

It was about eight when we landed at the spaceport.

"Don't forget your pick," Havier said as I got out of the car, offering it to me.

I took it from him and looked at it a moment, and thought about what I'd told my grandfather. Then I handed it back to him.

"Give that to my grandfather when you get back."

"You sure? I hear it's pretty wild out there."

"Yeah, I'm sure."

Closing the door, I turned and walked across the tarmac to the ship. The sun was setting and there was a large line of haulers with containers waiting to be loaded. I could see Jarvis was inspecting one of them. When he finished they closed and locked the doors and he put a seal on it, wrote down the numbers, and went to the next one as Emil looked at her chart and told the loaders where to put it in the hold.

He looked up and saw me, and waved me over.

"Hi, Jarvis, what's up?"

"Where were you?"

"Family business," I said with a shrug.

"Family business? I thought your family was all onboard the *Iowa*?"

"It's complicated. Oh, just how scary is Mr. Smith?"

"Mister . . . who the hell are you talking about?"

"The guy who gave my grandfather a hundred million for this stuff."

"Your *grandfather*?" he said, giving me a sidelong look of disbelief.

"Like I said, complicated."

I watched as he considered that a moment, then shrugged. "He was a leading actor on the stage back before we all had to leave Venus. He can act about as scary as you'd want him to be. But truth is"—Jarvis grinned—"he's harmless."

I shook my head and chuckled. "Figures. So how goes the inspection?"

"Good. With any luck we'll have it all loaded before midnight."

"Guess I better start prepping the ship to lift," I said with a smile, and went over and took the stairs up to the cargo deck. As soon as I slipped in through the hatch to the engineering deck, Kacey ran over and gave me a hug.

"What happened?"

"Just a sec. Nik!" I called into Engineering.

"What's up, Dave?" he said, popping out from behind one of the Siz-gees. He must have been sitting at the main control panel.

"Start waking up the reactors. Take it slow, but I want them online by eleven."

"I'm on it!" he said and disappeared.

I smiled at Kacey. "I had a very interesting meeting with my grandfather."

"Isn't he the one who had you beat up?" she asked, giving me a concerned look.

"Yeah, but like I've told you, I had it coming. Long and short of it, my bio-mom's husband has apologized and promised to stop bothering me. My bio-mom apologized for abandoning me as a child, and I think she might actually mean it." I shrugged. "I guess we'll see.

"Oh, and my grandfather wants me to join the family business."

"And what, stay here on Earth?" she said, making a sour face.

"No, from Ceres."

"Really? Sounds like they must be desperate."

I had to laugh when she said that.

"You know? I hadn't looked at it like that. Then again, I get the impression he thinks I'm going somewhere and that I'm a solid investment. Hmm, where have I heard *that* line before?" I asked, rubbing my chin and looking thoughtful until Kacey poked me in the ribs.

"Oof!" I said and then laughed again.

"So what did you tell him?"

"That I'd think about it. So I'll think about it. I don't think there's a due date on it. Now let's go upstairs and I'll give my parents the edited version, and maybe see if Emil left anything in the fridge for me to eat."

I passed a much less detailed account of what had been going on to my parents, only telling them that Jefferson had been causing problems, my grandfather had found out, made him apologize, and put an end to it.

"Was that it?" Dad asked.

"Well, he did apologize to me for everything that happened and asked me to convey his apologies to you as well." I grinned at Dad. "Honestly, I think he's a little unhappy with his daughter for having dumped you. He doesn't seem to like his new son-in-law very much."

I watched as he shook his head. "Probably for the best. I

wouldn't have known how to act around those kinds of people and"—he looked up at Jenny and lit up with a smile—"I wouldn't have met Jenny. Yeah, don't get me wrong, Eileen was nice and she did give me you, but I wouldn't get rid of Jenny for all the money in the world."

It was fun to see Mom lean into him and pretty much melt after he said that. I also got the feeling he was right. Eileen didn't strike me as the kind of person who could devote themselves to someone else, while Jenny had done just that, devoting her life to her family.

"So what happens next?" Dianne asked.

"What happens next is once they finish loading, we deliver our cargo and then head home."

"How long will that be?"

"About a month."

"That long? I thought these ships were fast?"

"Ten days to our delivery, a week to unload and reload, then about ten more to get home." I shrugged. "Ask Chris or Paul or Kat to teach you about navigating and all that if you want to know the details."

She nodded. "I think I will."

"Anything else?" I asked, looking around.

"When would be a good time to let my manager know that I'm not coming back?" Dad asked.

"Probably when we get to Ceres," I said with a smile. "After we pass the orbit of the Moon, sending messages gets pretty tough."

"Anything else?"

Everyone shook their heads.

"Great! I'll be down in Engineering, getting the ship ready to launch."

Ben came down with me and watched as Nik and I got everything ready. He had a few questions about what *really* went on at my grandfather's place, and was happy to hear that Eileen's husband had been forced to swear off any more attempts on me.

TWENTY-FOUR

Holloman Spaceport

SOMETIME AFTER TEN O'CLOCK I WENT OUTSIDE TO CHECK ON how the loading was progressing.

"How many containers do we have left?" I asked Jarvis as I walked up to him. He was putting a seal on another container.

"I've got about sixteen left of the special ones that I need to inspect. I think there's about a hundred left to be stored. Emil would know."

"Still think you'll be done by midnight?"

Jarvis winced. "It takes about ten minutes to inspect and seal each of these."

"So, by one, then?"

"As long as there aren't any issues, yes, by one. Sorry, Dave."

"Don't worry about it. As long as we're out of here by three, I don't think anybody's going to complain. I'll let Chris know; maybe he can get our departure moved up."

"What's the rush? We'll make the four a.m. deadline easy."

"With the day I've been having, the sooner we're gone, the better."

"I thought people from rich families didn't have bad days," he joked.

"The black sheep do," I said, looking around and pulling out my tablet to ping Emil. "And I think I'm one of the blackest sheep out there."

"I'll keep that in mind," Jarvis replied, heading off to the next container in line.

I checked my tablet to make sure I was on the ship's network, then pinged Emil for an estimate of how long it would take to load the remaining containers, and could she provide that estimate to Chris, so maybe we could get out of here ahead of schedule?

"Well, if it isn't my old pal!"

I sighed and turned, lowering the tablet.

"Donde, what the hell are you doing here?" I asked, looking him over. He was dressed like one of the usual cargo handlers who moved the containers for loading. I noticed the other cargo handlers were all avoiding him, because he looked union and they weren't.

"Well, I could say I was here to ask you why the hell Crow isn't dead, but it seems I've got even bigger problems!" he growled in a soft voice, looking around to make sure no one was close enough to eavesdrop on us. "What happened there, anyway?"

"He knew I was coming and of course your 'men' abandoned me the second I stepped inside. Oh, and his men all had guns, and guess what? They really were men, not a bunch of juiced-up fourteen-year-olds. So, why are you here, or do I just kill you and hope no one notices?"

I was bluffing, of course; about the only weapon I had now was harsh language.

"Kauf believes that I had Merks killed, that Crow wasn't the one who did it, and now *he's* after me as well! Yeah, I could hold off Crow, if it was just him, but my guys all abandoned me the minute Kauf told them I was *out*."

"Yup, sure sounds like you got problems, but that still doesn't explain why you're here and why we're having this conversation."

"I need to *leave*, man. Like *off the planet*, leave! And you, Goose, are going to make that happen!"

I frowned at him.

"And just why would I do that? You set me up to get killed, Donde! I don't owe you shit."

"Oh, then maybe I'll just go over to the tower and inform them that you're smuggling your brother off planet? Blu told me what you paid him to do. I'm not stupid, Goose!"

Actually, I thought he was pretty stupid to have gotten himself in this mess. But I didn't tell him that.

"Oh? So what do you want me to do? Go tell the captain that I need to smuggle a gang-banger off planet? One with a price on his head and a record a mile long?" I looked at him like he was mental. The bit about Ben was worrying me, though. Then again, if he was on the run from that many people, how long before somebody from one of the gangs caught up with him?

The last thing I needed right now was to draw any attention to the ship with the cargo we were carrying, as well as with Ben being onboard.

"I have a better idea," I said and put my hand in my pocket. "How about I just kill you instead?"

"I wouldn't do that, Goose," he warned.

"Oh? And why not?"

"Because I'm wearing enough explosives to kill me, you, and make a nice dent in that beat-up old hull you call a ship."

That stopped me!

"You're wearing a suicider?"

He nodded.

"Where the hell did you get that from? That's a doler trick!"

"Desperate times, Goose, desperate times! You're right about Crow's people having guns; they shot my best man while I was getting away. At least this way, if they get me, then I'm gonna take 'em with me! Now, are you gonna get me onboard your ship? Or are me and you gonna be decorating the outside?"

I looked at him as he opened his jacket, and sure enough, the bastard was wearing one of those vests. Dolers used them because they bought into the whole "martyr myth." At least the younger and dumber ones did. Part of why doler riots were always such a mess, as well as why the police used heavy weapons when dealing with them.

My tablet pinged then and I looked at it. It was Emil. She confirmed that she'd have it all buttoned up by one. She had to go slow because some of Jarvis's containers had to go along the centerline.

That gave me an idea.

"Look," I said to Donde, looking him in the eyes. "If I go to the captain and try and smuggle another guy onboard, he'll throw *all* of us off. I don't have enough bribe money, and ship's security *does* have guns and they'd be more than happy to shoot you if you try to board without the captain's permission. We got a big money cargo and the captain's really worried about hijackers."

"Goose!" he growled, putting a hand in his pocket.

"Wait!" I said and waved the tablet. "What if I stuck you in one of the TEUs?"

"What's a TEU?"

"These are," I said, patting the sides of one of the containers.

"You want to lock me in one of *those*?"

"I'll find one with food in it and hopefully some water too, so you don't starve. It's only ten days to our next stop, I can smuggle you out then!"

"Right, and leave me in there to die? I'm not buying it, Goose!"

"Donde, you're wearing a suicider! You set that off inside the cargo container and it'll be, like, ten times worse! You just might destroy the ship! I'll check on you every couple of days! It's not like I have a choice, right?" I said, putting a little desperation in my voice as I tried to sell him on it. I figured once we got into space, I could always just jettison the TEU he was in. Yeah, Jarvis or Marcus might be pissed at me, but I was beyond caring right now. There was just too much at stake here.

He frowned and thought about that.

"Don, what have you got to lose? If you stay here, you die. You weren't expecting to travel first class, right?"

"There better be enough food!" he grumbled.

"Hold on, let me see what we've got in cargo."

I started typing on my tablet.

Emil, I need a cargo container with food and drinks in it. Cheapest one we got.

What for?

Don't ask! Just find me one! I need it ASAP. Is there one still on the ground, or can you move one out for me?

I'd have to move one out. It'll take me a few minutes. I gotta move two others out of the way.

Do it.

You sure?

DO IT NOW! I typed back.

No need to yell! It'll be the third one I set down.

I sighed and looked up at Donde with a smile as I cleared the tablet. "You *owe* me. I just had to bribe the loadmaster a couple *K*. They're gonna off-load a couple of containers to 'fix' a balance issue. The third one they set down I'll put you in. But we gotta be quick, because I have no idea how long it'll be before they reload it."

"Won't they know what you're doing?"

I snorted. "They probably think I'm trying to smuggle a whore onboard without the captain finding out."

"People do that?"

"The male-to-female ratio ain't the greatest at some of the places we go. A good whore can make serious bank. So yeah, it happens," I said, spinning him a story that I knew he'd believe.

Donde nodded with a thoughtful look. "Huh. Maybe after the heat dies down and I come back here, we can do some business. I know some hot working girls."

"Whatever. Come on, let's find a safe place to wait and start counting containers."

I led him 'round to one of the landing gear legs, which on a ship like the *Iowa Hill* were pretty massive. The next ten minutes were spent in relative quiet as I waited for containers to come off. When the third one hit the ground I immediately jogged over to it, with Donde hot on my heels.

I looked at the seal on it; everything was sealed, of course. Getting by the seal wasn't hard, it was just a piece of wire looped through the holes where a padlock would normally go, then crimped with a special wafer. The problem was that the device that crimped the wafer had a very distinct design, which was different for every company, along with a date, time, and random number that was recorded on the shipping manifest. Which made forging them almost impossible.

I pulled out one of my engineering tools and cut the wire on the backside, away from the wafer, pulled it off, and, undogging the door, I pulled it open.

"I don't have a flashlight!" Donde said.

"Use your phone."

"It's off!"

"Once I close this door, you're not going to be getting a signal, so don't worry about it. Set a timer so you don't lose track of time. I'll be back to check on you in twenty-four hours, got it?"

"Yeah, yeah. I got it. Thanks, Goose."

"Oh, one other thing. It's Dave. Nobody here knows about

Goose. You go calling that out, and they'll think you're just a random stowaway."

"Fine, fine," Donde said and I pushed him inside. The container was pretty full, but everything inside was palletized for shipping and there were two "aisles" that ran from front to back for customs inspectors.

I slammed the doors behind him, locked them, then ran the wires back through. I'd come back with some epoxy and "fix" it later, not that I expected anyone to be inspecting us, we were outbound, after all. Pulling out my tablet I messaged Emil again.

I need this put on the very outside of the stack, right next to the cargo door.

What? Do you have any idea how much trouble that will cause?

I'll give you a thousand credit bonus if you just do it and don't ask any more questions.

Two.

Have you been taking lessons from my wife? Fine.

I got back a smiley face and, shaking my head, I went up the ladder and back into the ship in search of some epoxy. I now had a ticking time bomb inside my ship, but if worse came to worst, I could just jettison this one out into space and be done with it. I actually wasn't too worried about Donde popping the bomb off now. TSU containers were actually built to withstand all sorts of nastiness after a few accidents and intentional bombings over a hundred years ago. Yeah, it'd do some damage, maybe even rip open a hole in the container.

But that was a whole lot better than my being turned into a bloody paste on the outside hull of the ship, or having a bomb go off in one of the living areas.

I shook my head as I looked at my watch; it was after eleven. Five more hours and we'd be gone. Twelve more and we'd be well on our way. Too bad I couldn't just go crawl into bed and wait for it all to be over.

I went and found Ben, who was still in Engineering, and pulled him aside so we could talk without being overheard.

"We've got another problem," I told him.

"What now?"

"Donde showed up. Seems Crow *and* Kauf both want him dead. So I stuck him in one of the containers."

"Alive or dead?"

"Alive. He's wearing one of those doler bomb vests."

"Who else have you told?"

"Nobody. Once we get out of here, I'm thinking we can just jettison it."

"Maybe you could drill a hole and gas him? Then pull him out while he's unconscious?"

"Gas him with what? This is a cargo ship, Ben."

"Oh, I'm sure I could whip something up."

I pondered that. The problem with the suicider vests was they had heart monitors in them. If the wearer died, they went off.

"That might work," I said thoughtfully.

"You could just give him an air bottle full of the stuff when you check on him."

I shook my head. "I'm not opening those doors back up. Last thing I need is for him to come running out to hijack the ship."

"Yeah, he's asshole enough to do it too. Let me go through the ship's tools and supplies. I'll see what I can make based on what you've got."

"Sure. It's going to be a while before we can do anything anyway."

"You know, I have to ask: are all your days always this interesting?" Ben asked and then laughed at me as I swore.

"And to think, I gave up an aspiring career as a cold-blooded killer for all of this!" I grumbled as I threw my hands up in the air and left him laughing even harder as I went to check on Nik and the reactors.

We actually got off the ground a half hour past one o'clock. The shipment had come with its own cargo loaders and they must have been getting paid extra as they all busted ass to get done as quickly as they could. Surprisingly, the union guys at the spaceport didn't say a word or get in the way, or even get anywhere near the ship during loading.

Which made me wonder just how many people were looking the other way tonight. My grandfather had clearly stated that this was a weapons system, and I suddenly wondered just how many missiles were in those TEUs that had been loaded.

And if any of their warheads were nuclear.

Chris took it up and out slowly. He was just starting to increase the throttle as we cleared regular traffic a few hours later when suddenly he started to cut it back. He commed me from the bridge immediately.

"Dave! We've got an Earth Guard Navy ship coming up behind us fast, advising us to cut thrust and prepare for boarding!"

"What?"

"They want to inspect us."

"Find out what for!" I then hit the all hands. "Ben, Jarvis, get down to Engineering!"

Ben was in almost immediately.

"What's happening?" Ben asked.

"We're about to get searched. There's only two things they can be after, and one of them is you."

Jarvis slid to a stop in the hatchway.

"They can't be here about the weapons," he said.

"Oh? And how do you know that?"

"Because your grandfather's son-in-law is a senator and he personally approved this shipment. If they open up any of those special containers I sealed they'll spend the rest of their careers cleaning toilets with their tongues!" he said with a frown.

"Great," I said, shaking my head. "We need to hide Ben, and we need to put him someplace they won't look."

I thought a moment, mind racing, and then thought about the *other* problem I had hiding aboard ship.

"Can we have Ben hide in one of your containers? If they know about them, then they won't search them, right? The only problem is how do we fake the seal?"

"I've still got the seal device in my cabin. Remember, I had to inspect them and re-seal each one personally."

"Great! Get it and meet us up on the top cargo deck."

I hit the comm to Chris. "Stall as much as you can!"

I then ran to my cabin, grabbed my pressure suit, tossed Ben the helmet and the backpack, and ran up to the cargo deck with him hot on my heels.

When we got there, Jarvis called out and waved us over to a unit that he'd opened.

"Do you know how to wear one of these?" I asked Ben.

"I've read the instructions, but that's about it," he said.

"Well, that should be fine. Work your way to the back, get into it, the air turns on when you seal the helmet. Turn your tablet off and don't make a sound."

"Got it," he said as I thrust the suit into his hands, then watched as Jarvis hauled the door far enough open for Ben to get in.

Sure enough, it was full of missiles.

"Go down to the other end, there's enough space to hide in front of them," he said.

Just then I heard the clang of magnet grapples on the back of the ship.

"Go!" I said and I helped Jarvis seal the doorway. Then watched as he put a new seal on it that matched the one he'd removed, right down to the time, date, and random number.

"They're entering the airlock," came over the all hands comm. "Everyone report to the mess!"

I followed Jarvis out of the hold, hitting the switch to kill the lights in the cargo bay.

When we got to the mess, everyone was there, except for Chris, who was still on the bridge.

"Now what?" Emil asked.

"We wait, and no one volunteers anything," Paul said. "We have no idea why they're here, and we have no idea what's in the cargo."

"What Paul said," I said, looking around the room. "No matter what happens, nobody says anything."

Everyone nodded and we all just sat there.

Two minutes later, a large party of men wearing Earth Guard Marine space suits stopped outside the mess, though one was in an Earth Guard Navy suit. He was wearing senior grade lieutenant's bars, so I figured he was the one in charge. The marines were all carrying sidearms, and a few had some hand held scanners. They all had radios.

"Is this the entire crew?" the navy officer asked. His nametag identified him as Lieutenant Stewart.

"The captain is still on the bridge, as per regs," I said.

"Who are you?"

"Dave Doyle, Chief Engineer."

He frowned and looked at me. "Aren't you a little young to be a chief engineer?"

"My certs are on the wall down in Engineering and I can show you my guild ID if you need to see it. I'm a certified third engineer, which is enough to be chief here." I then added, "Sir."

He turned to the marine lieutenant, who he obviously ranked. "Lieutenant, secure the crew. You two"—he pointed to a pair of marines—"come with me to the bridge."

"Okay," said the marine lieutenant, "if anybody has any weapons on them, now would be a good time to tell us. We're not after any of you, but we are going to search the ship. We will be searching you for weapons. Nothing else. Now, any weapons?"

Yuri and Kei both were armed, surprisingly, Kei with a rather large pistol and Yuri with a knife as long as her forearm. After they'd set those aside, they had us each come up one at a time, and they checked us over with a wand. The only things that turned up on anybody was the mechanical pencil, grease marker, and folding tool in my pockets and the pens in Jarvis's.

"Okay, I have a manifest here from Lieutenant Stewart," he said, looking at his tablet. "Please sound off when I call your name."

He went down the list then. When he got to my parents and Dianne he looked at them. "What are you all doing here? I don't see you on the crew list."

"Lieutenant, if I may?" I asked.

"I take it you can shed some light on this?"

"My last name used to be Walker; I changed it when I married my wife and joined the Doyle clan on Ceres."

He gave me a funny look then. "Does that mean they're related to you?"

"Yes, that's my father, mother, and younger sister. They're coming with us to Ceres to meet my in-laws."

"Oh, are they now?" he asked, giving me a suspicious look.

"As I already mentioned, my wife's name is Doyle—you know, the same as in Doyle Shipping, the company that *owns* the *Iowa Hill*."

"And that would be me, sir," Kacey said with a wave of her hand.

The lieutenant sighed and then came to the bottom of his list. "Which one of you is Jarvis?"

Jarvis raised his hand.

"And just why are *you* here? You're not an in-law too, are you?"

"No, I'm the buyer's rep for some of the cargo that was purchased on Earth."

"And which cargo is that?"

"The white TEUs with the StayCo markings on them."

"I see. And just what's inside those containers?"

"I'm not at liberty to say."

"Oh? Then perhaps you wouldn't mind if we *inspected* them?"

"You might want to talk to your superiors about that," Jarvis said with a faint smile on his face.

"And why would I want to do that?"

About that time the navy lieutenant came back, minus the two men who had gone with him.

"Why would you want to do what, Lieutenant?"

"Jarvis here is the buyer's rep for the cargo in the StayCo cans and he won't tell me what that cargo is."

"We're not here to inspect cargo, Lieutenant Jones. Now take your team and start the search."

"But, sir!"

"Our orders were quite clear, Lieutenant. Opening any of the sealed containers on the cargo deck without proof that our man is inside will be a career-ending move. After a very long stretch sweeping floors and cleaning toilets on Darkside Station. Understood?"

"Yes sir!" the marine lieutenant said and saluted.

"Now, take the first team and start on the bottom deck. Sergeant Hobbs, take the second team to the back of the ship and start on the bottom as well. Once that's done, search the cargo decks with both teams from top to bottom."

"Yes, sir," the sergeant said and saluted.

Lieutenant Stewart sighed and shook his head. After they'd left he pulled out a picture of Ben in his wheelchair.

"Have any of you seen this man?"

Everyone shook their head no.

"This boat ain't exactly wheelchair friendly, Lieutenant," Hank spoke up.

"How long is this going to take?" Kacey asked.

"Why?"

"Because if we're going to miss our shipping deadline, I want to send a message out before we get too far away from the Moon to have it relayed back to my parents," she said with a shrug. "I'm in charge of scheduling. I've never been on a ship that got searched before."

"They'll be done with the crew spaces and the engineering spaces in short order. Not a lot of places for a man in a wheelchair to hide onboard one of these old General Ships Argon Sixes. The cargo deck, however . . . that could take a couple of hours."

"Sir, I demand to be on the cargo deck when they are searching, to ensure that none of my containers are opened," Jarvis said from where he was sitting.

"Oh, I'm sure they'll be okay."

"I must insist, Lieutenant. If not, well, I'm sure it will be mentioned in my report to *my* superiors."

I watched the pained expression that passed over Lieutenant Stewart's face and wondered what he would do.

The lieutenant triggered his mic and spoke into it. "Lieutenant Jones, when you're ready to start searching the cargo hold, please detail one of your men to come to the mess. The buyer's representative is going to watch to make sure that none of his containers are disturbed."

"Thank you, Lieutenant," Jarvis said with a relieved sigh.

"Understand that if any of those containers have had their seal broken, that will be grounds to look inside," Lieutenant Stewart warned.

"If any of their seals have been broken, I will most certainly want to inspect them, Lieutenant. I do not need some sort of criminal destroying sensitive gear!"

Over the next ten minutes, Lieutenant Stewart had several short conversations over his radio, though I couldn't hear what he was hearing, as he had an earpiece. From the responses he was giving, it sounded like each of the floors was being cleared and nothing had been found.

When one of the Earth Guard enlisted men showed up and escorted Jarvis out of the mess, it was obvious that they were now searching the cargo hold and Lieutenant Stewart must have gotten a call from one of *his* superiors, because there were a lot of "yes, ma'am," "no, ma'am," and "I understand, ma'am" replies from him into his microphone. But the most telling one was when he said, "I've told them not to open up any of the StayCo containers without first getting clearance from you, ma'am!"

"If we're going to be here a while, is it okay if I make everyone some food?" Emil asked when he was finished.

"Sure, knock yourself out," Lieutenant Stewart said with a wave of his hand. "Hopefully we'll be out of your hair in an hour or two."

Over the next hour I could tell the lieutenant was getting more and more annoyed. It sounded like his bosses were checking in with him every ten minutes to know if he was done yet.

Then he got a call from what I guess was someone on the search team, as his whole demeanor changed and he immediately called his superior.

"Captain, they found a container with a broken seal. No, ma'am, it's not one of the StayCo containers. They're looking through the manifest right now. Yes, ma'am."

A few conversations later and I heard him reporting to his boss again. By now Jarvis had been escorted back to the mess and was looking concerned. I knew which container it was and I was starting to be worried as well.

"Ma'am, the container is marked as foodstuffs. Yes, ma'am, my thoughts exactly. I'll direct Lieutenant Jones to inspect it, ma'am."

A minute later Lieutenant Stewart's face blanched. "What? A bomb? Corporal Vanek! Order the captain to fire-evac the cargo hold! Immediately!"

A moment later the fire alarm sounded, followed immediately by the sounds of something like gunfire, but which I knew where eight explosive bolts.

"What's happening?" Emil asked, looking at me.

"They're blowing the bolts in the safety interlocks on the cargo doors; it's in case of a fire on the cargo decks. The doors will be pushed open by the air pressure on the cargo deck and all of the air will evacuate in seconds."

"Why?"

A soft *thud* vibrated through the deck plates.

"Because bombs do less damage in a vacuum," Lieutenant Stewart said. "I think we may have found our missing person."

Mom gasped and Dad suddenly looked concerned.

"Do you know something, Mrs. Walker?" Lieutenant Stewart asked, looking at her.

I swore to myself. The last thing I needed was for my mom to be questioned. While she didn't know about Donde or where Ben was, she knew more than enough that she might say something to arouse suspicions. The didn't want to see her in trouble—or worse yet, arrested and hauled off for "further questioning." Then there were the ship's internal chat logs—if they searched those, they'd see I was the one who'd called for that container.

Like it or not, this one was on me, and I had to do something to protect my mom.

"Lieutenant," I said standing up. "He showed up outside while we were loading. He was high on drugs, quite irrational, and was wearing what he claimed was an explosive vest. He threatened to kill me if I didn't take him with us."

"Oh? Is that so?" he said, frowning at me.

"Sir, could we please have this conversation somewhere else?" I said and gave a slight nod to my mother, who was starting to quietly cry.

He looked at her, then back at me. "Sergeant Hobbs, keep an eye on everybody. Mr. Doyle, let's go to the bridge. You can lead."

Sighing, I left the room and walked down the hall to the bridge and starting thinking about just what I was facing. I knew that getting an ID off of someone who used one of those vests was difficult. Someone who'd just undergone explosive decompression would undoubtedly make it even more difficult. Not impossible, just difficult. What I needed was to get them off the ship, and to get the ship back on its way. Both Ben and Marcus were counting on me to do that and right now all I had going for me was the ability to think under pressure and a general suspicion that there were a lot of powerful people who didn't want this ship delayed and were making life uncomfortable for the lieutenant and his superiors.

When we got to the bridge, Chris looked at me and I noticed the warning lights for the cargo deck were all flashing. Hopefully we'd only lost the atmosphere.

"So, Mr. Doyle, it seems you have a story to tell?" Lieutenant Stewart said.

I nodded. "First off, did any of your people get hurt?"

"Thankfully, no. When they opened the doors to that container, they saw a man matching the description of who we were looking for. They saw the vest immediately and he started screaming your name, and how he was going to get even with you for betraying him and kill everyone onboard."

I sighed again. "I'd honestly hoped that whatever it was he was on would have been out of his system when I came to check on him. That he'd be more reasonable."

"Oh? Is that so? Well, perhaps you'd like to tell me why you didn't warn me about a man with a suicide vest who was obviously irrational?" he said rather angrily.

"And have you go in there with guns blazing? I grew up on Earth, Lieutenant, I know all about how the marines just love to shoot people! I'd been hoping that he'd be passed out and unconscious from lack of air and you'd be able to go in there and just take him wherever he needed to go—and yeah, *of course* I didn't want to admit to any part in this. It's not like I did it willingly."

"Why don't you tell us what happened from the start?" Chris asked. Lieutenant Stewart shot him a look, but didn't say anything.

"I went outside to check on how the loading was going. The reactors were still being brought up and I wanted to get an idea of when I'd need to start warming up the gravity drive." I looked over at Lieutenant Stewart. "On a ship this old, thermal shocks cause problems, so we like to bring things up slow to cut down on maintenance.

"Anyway, he shows up, dressed as one of the cargo movers. Starts accosting me, yelling at me. Says I'm taking everything he loved away from him, stuff like that."

"Why would he say that?" Lieutenant Stewart asked.

"I've made no secret of wanting to find my dad a better job—it's part of why I want him to come out and see what Ceres is like, because I want him to emigrate, which would mean my stepmom and sister going as well." I shook my head. "I don't know, he was going on about how he wouldn't be able to see her if she left and all that kinda thing and then he started going on about how they wanted him to do things that he couldn't and they were gonna find out he was a fraud and wasn't going to solve this big problem everyone wanted him to solve." I shrugged and looked back at Lieutenant Stewart. "I know he was a little strange at times, but I figured that was because his real father had died when he was a little kid and all that."

"Why do you think he was on drugs?"

"Because of the way he was acting, erratic and all jerky like. Plus he was sweating and yelling, waving his arms, it wasn't like him at all! And then he showed me that vest and told me it was a bomb and if I didn't get him on the ship, he'd blow us both up!"

"So why'd you put him in a container?" Chris asked.

"What choice did I have? I didn't want a crazy guy with a bomb running around inside the ship. I also didn't want to get blown up myself. I mean, I *hoped* the vest was fake, but with him you never knew. Besides, the containers are all bomb resistant, so if he did set it off, it wouldn't destroy the ship!"

I looked at Lieutenant Stewart. "I mean, what would *you* have done? He's always been like a brother to me and you saw how upset my mom was getting. I was hoping he'd calm down and

then I could go to the captain here and tell him what I'd done!"
I shook my head and sighed again. "Why are you even looking
for him? Did he kill somebody?"

Lieutenant Stewart did a double take. "Huh? No! Don't you
know?"

"Know what?"

"They passed a brain-drain law about fifty years ago. Geniuses
like your brother aren't allowed to leave the planet. Not without
permission, that is. When you put your brother onboard that
container, you committed a felony."

"I was trying to save a life! Mine too!" I complained.

"Yes, well, that's for a judge to decide, not me. I'm afraid
we're going to have to take you back with us."

"*What?*" both Chris and I exclaimed at the same time. I'd
been afraid this might happen, but better me going through this
than my mom. I could just imagine the scene between Dad and
Dianne and the Marines if they tried to take her off the ship.
That wouldn't end well at all.

"We're also going to have to have you take the ship back,
Captain Doyle, so we can do forensic testing on the body."

"I think you'd better call Jarvis to the bridge," I said.

"Jarvis? Why him?"

"Because I'm sure he'll want to let *his* superiors know just
what you're going to do."

Lieutenant Stewart frowned a moment, then keyed his radio.

"Captain, we have a possible problem." He paused a moment.
"I think the company representative for those StayCo containers
is going to throw a literal shit-fit when I tell him we're taking
this ship back for examination."

I could see him wince almost immediately after that. I could
only assume she wasn't pleased with that information.

"Why not just take the container he killed himself in?" I
suggested, because there was no way Ben would be able to avoid
being caught if they took the whole ship back.

"Yes, why don't you?" Chris agreed. "The cargo bay's already
evacuated and the doors are open."

"Captain, could we just take the TEU container? The remains
are still inside it."

There was a brief pause and then Lieutenant Stewart sighed,
looking relieved. "I'll have my men start moving the container out

immediately. Also, I have a prisoner, the deceased's stepbrother, who has admitted to helping him onto the ship, though he claims it was under duress."

Chris gave me a look then, and I could just imagine what was going through his mind. He was about to lose his only "real" engineer. Nik wasn't bad, but he really wasn't rated for the job yet. But right now, what choice did he have?

"He had a bomb, Chris, with a suicide switch! What was I supposed to do?"

"Suicide switch?"

Lieutenant Stewart looked up. "They make those vests so that if the wearer dies, the bomb goes off. It's more likely that the vacuum killed him and set off the bomb than he set it off himself."

"So then why'd you tell me to blow open the doors?" Chris said, looking at him like he's lost all sense.

"Because doctrine says that you kill anyone with a vest, immediately. If he'd been wearing a space suit, we would have shot him as soon as the air was gone. We only had you open the doors to minimize our own casualties. Which it did, thankfully.

"Now, if you don't mind, I'll gather up my marines and then we'll be on our way."

Twenty minutes later, I was sitting in some sort of navy boarding boat and we were making our way to the navy corvette that was stationed "above" the *Iowa Hill* by a thousand meters.

I waited as I sat in my seat and tried to figure out what my next possible move was. Eventually they'd find out that what they thought was Ben, *wasn't*. I knew they had handheld fingerprint scanners, but I had no idea what shape the corpse was in, as I hadn't seen it. If they had any medical personnel aboard they *could* check his dental records, as the head usually didn't get too messed up when the vest went off.

I just really had no idea. In any case, wherever they took me, I was sure I'd be languishing in a jail long enough for them to figure out I'd misled them. Then the real fun would begin. But with any luck the *Iowa Hill* would be long gone by then.

"Turn around, please," said a young female petty officer, holding what looked like a fingerprint scanner as I stepped out of the boat onto the deck.

I nodded and did as I was told, holding my arms out a bit

and spreading my fingers. It might have been years since I'd been through this routine, but I still knew what to do.

"Thank you," she said after she'd scanned each of my fingers. "You can turn back now."

I turned back and noticed she was doing something with the unit.

"Something wrong?"

"It's not giving me the correct results. It says your name is Dave Walker."

"I only changed it last month."

"That shouldn't matter."

"On Ceres."

She looked up at me and sighed. "Oh." Then went back to the display. "The rest of your records are...missing. Must be the name change."

"I didn't have this problem on Earth."

"The navy's database is separate from Earth's. I'll have to put in an update request," she said with a frown and then looked up at the lieutenant. "I'm done, sir. You can take him to the brig."

"Come on," Lieutenant Stewart said and, taking hold of my upper arm, he led me out of the small bay. The brig was just past the exit, and it was small. Really small. Less than three feet on a side small.

I looked at him as he pushed me inside.

"How long am I going to be in here?"

"Until we finish our patrol."

"And that is?"

"Twelve hours, give or take."

"Can you at least take the cuffs off? It's not like I'm going anywhere."

"Face the back wall."

I did and he removed the cuffs, then stepped back as the door slid closed. It had a glass port in it, but that was about it.

It took me a while to figure out the one small set of controls, as I'd never seen anything like this before. There was a very small toilet that doubled as a seat and I found that if I slouched a little while sitting on it my knees hit the opposite wall, keeping me in place.

Ten minutes after figuring that out I fell asleep, the narrow walls keeping me from falling over. It wasn't comfortable, but as the adrenaline drained and the fatigue hit, it was good enough.

TWENTY-FIVE

Jail Time

I WOKE AS I HIT THE FLOOR. APPARENTLY SOMEBODY HAD A LOW sense of humor as they hadn't thought to wake me before opening the door.

"Oh, sorry!" said Sergeant Hobbs, who'd opened the door. The expression on his face made it quite clear that he wasn't.

"We there yet?" I groaned as I slowly got to my feet. My body was stiff and sore from the way I'd been sleeping.

"Captain wants a word with you."

"Oh? She does?"

"Seems they finally got an ID on that guy who killed himself."

"You mean the guy you spaced," I corrected. That earned me a smack to the back of my head.

"Don't be an asshole. You're already in a lot of trouble."

"Any more and they'll make me a marine, right?" I grumbled back at him and got smacked in the back of the head a second time.

"Sorry," I mumbled. "I haven't had my coffee yet."

"Just turn and face the wall," he said, helping me along with a none too gentle shove. At least I managed to turn my face to the side so I didn't get my nose broken as he pulled my hands behind my back and put the handcuffs back on.

The bridge wasn't that far a walk—this ship was just a corvette, which made it pretty small inside after you added the boat bay and all the weapons.

When I stepped inside, the captain turned her seat to look at me. "Mr. Walker."

"Doyle," I corrected. "I changed it when I got married."

She rolled her eyes. "Fine, Doyle. Just *where* is your brother?"

"My brother?"

I got smacked on the back of the head by Sergeant Hobbs again.

"Is he allowed to do that?" I said, glancing back at him.

"I didn't see anything," the captain said with a frown. "Now, answer the question."

I glanced back at Sergeant Hobbs again. "I'm assuming that you mean my *step*brother? Benjamin?"

"Yes, Benjamin. Where is he?"

"Dammed if I know," I said with a shrug, and immediately got smacked in the back of the head again.

"Dammit! Try MIT! That's where he's going to school!"

"According to the police, they arrested a young gang member who was using your brother's wheelchair when he failed a spot ID check."

"What? When did that happen?"

"About three a.m., Eastern. We were alerted and sent after the *Iowa Hill* to retrieve him."

"Why would you think he was on the *Iowa Hill*?"

"Because when authorities questioned the young man, he said you were smuggling your brother off planet. So of course they assumed he was on board your ship."

"But he wasn't, you searched it," I said, looking at her with a frown.

"We know that the man who died wasn't Benjamin."

"Huh? Why'd you think that?"

"Our medical technicians ran a dental records check on the head, that's why!" she said, giving me an angry look.

"No, I meant why did you think it was Ben?"

"Because you told us that it was him!"

"No, I didn't! That was Donde, one of my brothers from back when I was in the Howlers, my old juvie gang!" I replied, lying through my teeth.

"We have everything you said on vid," she said with a predatory smile. "I'm sure you didn't know that!"

Actually I'd noticed the small pip camera on the uniforms. They were the same as the ones the cops had always worn and I was quite familiar with those from my childhood.

"No, but I never claimed it was my stepbrother either."

"Oh? Then why did you tell us he was upset about you taking away his mother?"

I sighed and rolled my head around like I was talking to an idiot. I would have face-palmed for the added effect if my hands weren't cuffed behind my back.

"Don was dating my *sister*! My father forced her to come with us because he didn't approve! That was why I figured he'd calm down! Because he was on the ship with her! Ben's got ALS, how the hell would he have gotten there on foot?"

That earned me an even harder smack, but the look on the captain's face was the same look I'd seen on the faces of people playing cards when they rudely discovered that they'd lost the hand.

"Take him back to the brig! The police can deal with him!"

The trip back was a lot more painful than the trip out had been.

"Hey, don't take it out on me! The guy had a bomb!" I grumbled at Sergeant Hobbs as he threw me back in the cell.

"Yeah, tell it to the judge!"

It wasn't until after the door had closed that I realized the bastard hadn't taken off the handcuffs. Swearing, I spent the next several minutes fumbling with the controls until I got the seat back out and sat back down to try and get some more sleep.

The next time the door opened, I was already awake as I'd felt the slight jolt as the ship landed. The two men waiting for me had MP bands on their arms and one of them turned to Lieutenant Stewart, who was also there.

"Why is he still handcuffed?"

"I have no idea."

"I was fighting with the other prisoners," I said with a yawn. "Could someone please help me stand?"

One of the MPs helped me get out, then they stood me up, faced me at the wall, and changed handcuffs.

They then each grabbed an arm and escorted me off the ship. It was at that point I realized we were in a gigantic hanger with rock walls.

"Where the hell are we?"

"The Moon," one of them said as they led me over to two other men who weren't wearing any uniforms. But the haircuts and the cheap suits made it clear. So did the badges hanging out of their suit jacket pockets.

Once again they changed my handcuffs, but this time I appreciated it. Police handcuffs were actually much more comfortable by comparison, as they were required to be "humane" by the government after one too many doler riots.

"Come with us, Walker," one of them said.

"It's Doyle now," I told him. "Not Walker."

"That's not what the navy guys told us," the other one said.

"Yeah, seems that they don't update their files all that much. You might want to fingerprint me."

"Don't worry; we'll take care of that at the station. So what did you do that they sent the navy after you?"

"Apparently I failed to kidnap my stepbrother," I said with a shrug. "Guess not finding him on my ship pissed them off."

"Says here you killed somebody."

I snorted. "Typical, the marines space a guy, blow him up, and then I'm the one responsible."

"That's not what they said."

"Please, do a net search. They're marines. You know damn well one of them is gonna upload the video under some 'see idiot kill himself' tag as soon as he gets shore leave."

They both laughed at that one.

"Well, whatever you did, our captain told us you sure pissed off the navy gal running that ship!"

We bantered a bit more on the way to their station, though I was careful about what I said. Mostly I was just trying to avoid the "asshole" treatment. I'd learned—the hard way, of course—that if you were nice to the cops, they were usually nice to you. Or at least pleasant.

We got to the station, they took my prints, and then immediately moved me into interrogation.

"Okay, now you can tell us your side of the story," one of them said.

"I want a lawyer," I said, looking at each of them in turn.

"You sure? You could cut a deal, right here and now. You get a lawyer and all of that goes out the window."

"Look, I appreciate how nice you've been. But I'm done talking.

Save yourselves the time and go get some coffee or lunch. I want a lawyer."

"You've been through this before, haven't you?"

"I want a lawyer."

"Yup, he's been through this before," the other one said, and a minute later they locked me in a cell with a couple of other guys and I went back to cooling my heels.

The only thing that was different this time was the guys I was in the cell with weren't playing any "dominance" games. Then again, I wasn't a tough-shot kid being shoved into a holding cell with a bunch of other juvies who all had something to prove.

They served us lunch, which was nice because I was starving. Sometime after that they pulled us all out to go before the judge for a bail hearing. Which was when I met the public defender assigned to me.

"You're being charged with violating the Exporting of Persons Against the Will of the State Act, as well as being an accessory to manslaughter."

I looked at the guy sitting at the table I was standing at. He hadn't even looked up.

"Look at me," I said.

"Why?" he asked, looking up. "This is just a bail hearing. The judge is going to deny it and someone else will be assigned to handle your case. There's two felonies here."

"I want you to make a motion to have the first charge dropped."

"Oh? On what grounds?"

"Lack of evidence. The navy searched the entire ship I was on and found no evidence that the person they were looking for was on it."

"They are saying you admitted to him being there."

"Well, they're lying. Go through the recorded interviews. I never once mentioned the guy they were looking for, I only mentioned my dead friend who those idiot marines killed."

"The judge will still deny it."

"Make the motion anyway. Now, has anybody here run my background?"

"Not really, why?"

"Because I want to hire a better lawyer, that's why," I said with a sigh. "Are things on the Moon always this screwed up?"

"What, are you some kind of 'elite' back on Earth? I'm afraid you're not going to find that to be much help up here."

"Just make the motion, run my background, and let the best lawyer you know, who you want to owe you a favor, that you've got a guy with money looking to hire him. The only reason they even arrested me was because they were pissed that they fucked up and wasted the wrong guy."

"What about the other charge?"

"I'm innocent, obviously. Now, can we go see the judge?"

"What's the rush?"

"I want to get out of here and go home to my wife, that's what." I sighed. This wasn't looking good. I'd been hoping that once they figured out who I was, I'd get some sort of priority and the old "elie treatment" that I'd used to. Either what he just told me was true or somebody wanted me kept here and was using their influence to do just that.

"It doesn't say here that you're married," he said, glancing his tablet.

"Does it at least say that my name isn't Walker anymore?"

"Umm, no. When did you change it?"

"Let's just go and see the judge."

He at least did what I asked him to, and sure enough the judge denied both his motion and bail. An hour later I was in a real jail. I'd never been to jail before, and while I'd heard stories, I still had no idea what to expect.

When they turned us out into the general population, it wasn't as bad as I'd feared. Yeah, there were more than a few bad characters watching as they sent us in, but I'd grown up around bad characters—hell, I'd been one myself! So they didn't worry me, much. Also, several of the people in the group I was sent in with looked a lot easier to prey on than I was.

So I just separated myself from the crowd and left them to fend for themselves. I didn't know if there were any gangs on the Moon, and I sure as hell didn't know if there were any Howlers up here. I looked around and flashed the Howler gang sign at a couple of folks. There was safety in numbers, and having a friend or two here wouldn't hurt.

The third guy I flashed flashed it back at me, so I went over to join him and the three he was hanging out with.

"Howlers?" he asked.

"Yeah, on Earth. Texas District."

"Man, you are a long way. How'd you end up here?"

"Was working on a ship and one of my old crew from back home was pulling too much heat. Well, they found him onboard, smoked him, and now I'm being blamed for everything since the original sin."

They all laughed at that, and we all shook hands and made introductions. His name was Ghost, because he liked ghost peppers; the others were Cam, Buc, and Vod. They were all locals, so thankfully none of them had ever heard of me, though I knew once they put the word out—and they would, of course—word would get back soon enough.

"How bad is it in here?"

"First time?" Ghost asked.

"Prison? Yeah. When I ran on the streets I was underage, so we only got stuck in juvie."

"Well, we're not the biggest group in here, but that's not a problem. A few of the guards used to be bangers like the rest of us, so as long as we act nice and get along, they do us favors. Easy on them, easy on us."

"What about the guys who aren't bangers?"

He frowned. "Sometimes they'll ask us to teach one of 'em a lesson. But mainly they pick on the new meat." He motioned back toward the others I'd shown up with, and sure enough, they were "fitting in," and for some of them that was already looking like it was going to be an unpleasant process.

It hit me then, I was in trouble. *Serious* trouble. I was in jail on two felony charges, both of which were trumped up beyond belief and apparently *no one* knew I was here. What made it even worse was unlike the previous times I'd been in trouble, *now* I had something to lose. I had a *lot* to lose! My wife, my job, the company I'd just started building, all of my plans, everything!

Sure, I *was* guilty of the smuggling charge, but they had no evidence of that, and until Ben showed up on Ceres, no one even knew where he was. Hopefully he wouldn't be seen coming off the *Iowa Hill*, because if I was still in here, that would definitely be the final nail in my coffin.

Then, of course, there were the charges surrounding Donde's

death. Yeah, I was happy he was dead, and not just because of what he'd done to me. If they'd gotten him alive, he would have told them about Ben. Which would have put me in jail anyway, and possibly gotten the ship impounded and a few others thrown in here too!

If only that idiot hadn't come looking for my help! If only.

I sighed and shook my head. If only, if only.

"Something wrong?"

"I need a lawyer, a *good* lawyer," I told Ghost as all of the possible consequences started to sink in.

"Good lawyers ain't cheap, bro."

"I can afford it."

"So why don't you have one?"

I shook my head. "I don't know anybody here. Hell, I don't think anyone even *knows* I'm here. I asked my public defender to get me one, but somehow I don't think he cares."

"Yeah, they're all like that. I can let the gang mouthpiece know you're looking."

I nodded. "Sure, why not."

"So you're on the ships now? How'd that happen?"

"Went to school to learn ship's engineering. Took a while, but it was worth it," I replied, welcoming the change in topic.

"What's it like out there?"

"Different. Everywhere you go, the rules change. Still, it's way better than Earth, because they don't have any elies or doles. It's just proles everywhere."

"Think they'd take a guy like me?"

"If you got the skills someone needs, yeah. There's always places that need people who know how to keep the faith and can be dangerous when the time comes. Why? Looking to leave?"

He nodded. "I've got six months left here. After that?" He shook his head. "I'm gettin' too old for this. But it's all I know."

"Yeah, I hear you on that. Just don't sign up as a worker on any of the company mines without checking them out first. Some of those places are worse than jail."

Two days later, I found myself unexpectedly being dragged off to court. Not long after that I was sitting in a conference room with a lawyer I'd never met before and two other people who, again, I had no idea who the hell they were.

"Dave, I'm your court appointed attorney, Jill Small. These two gentlemen represent the government. They'd like to make a deal."

"Why haven't I been allowed to retain my own lawyer?" I asked her, ignoring the other two for a moment.

"Because you're indigent with no funds, of course."

"Indigent? I own a fucking shipping company on Ceres!" I said, giving her a look. "Hell, I'm related to the Morgans of Earth and they've got more money than the government!"

I turned and looked at the two guys sitting on the other side of the table. "As for you two, you can both just fuck right off. I haven't broken any laws, so I'm not making any deals."

"They're here about your brother," Jill said in what I guess was a "soothing" voice. "If you tell them where he is, they're willing to make a deal."

"Dave, just tell us what we want to know, and all of this will go away," one of them said.

"The only thing that's going away is you two," I said, looking at them. Then I turned back to Jill. "If you *truly* represent me, we should be having this discussion, in *private*. Not with other people in the room."

"I'm sorry, but I can't do that, Mr. Walker," she replied.

I leaned over suddenly and put my lips by her ear, moving my hands up to block the view of any cameras that might be in the room.

"If you possess an ounce of self-preservation, you'll get me a *real* lawyer before my family finds out what's going on."

I sat back up then as the doors to the room opened and several guards swarmed in. Jill looked white as a sheet.

"Are you okay, ma'am?"

"Yes, I'm fine."

"What did he say to you?"

"He . . . he propositioned me!" she said, and turned and glared at me. "I can't represent this man. Get yourselves another lawyer!" And with that she grabbed her stuff and left the room.

"Well, we tried the nice way. Why don't you guys see if you can soften him up for us?" said the guy who had spoken before.

Thankfully, these guys were amateurs and I passed out early on in the "softening" process.

✧   ✧   ✧

I woke up as they dragged me back into the prison and literally tossed me into the main room as I passed out again. When I woke up the next time, I was on my cot, and Buc was keeping an eye on me.

"Damn, Goose, what happened?"

"I wouldn't give them what they wanted."

"Yeah, I can see that. What do they want?"

"Something that I don't have, obviously." I sighed and tried not to move. They may not have been pros, but it still hurt like hell. "Care to help me up? I think I need to use the bathroom."

Come the next morning, I got dragged out again, and this time they didn't even ask about Ben. They just went right to the beating.

After that one, I woke up in a hospital with my arm in a cast and a couple of IVs stuck in the other one. From the colors of the bruises on my body, I'd been here at least a day, maybe two.

"Ah, you're awake."

I looked up. There was a man in a suit there. A very expensive suit.

"And you are?" I whispered.

"Your lawyer."

"Sure you are."

"Marcus sent me."

"About time," I said, and passed out again.

The next time I woke up, I felt a lot better. The nurse came in, gave me a quick checkup, raised the head of the bed a bit, and brought me something to eat.

"How are you feeling, Mr. Doyle?"

"Finally! Somebody got my name right. I'm feeling okay, I guess."

"The man who was here before, your lawyer, he asked me to call him when you were ready to see him?"

"That would be nice," I said with a smile. "How long have I been here?"

"Three days. The internal bleeding was pretty bad. That must have been a really bad accident you were in."

"Accident?"

"Yes, the two government agents who brought you in said you fell down a shaft when an elevator door opened too early and you stepped in without looking."

"Why didn't they just say I got hit by a reckless driver?"

"We don't have cars here," she said with a wink.

I just sighed and lay back in the bed. She came back with something for me to drink and the man in the suit returned sometime after that.

"What's going on?" I asked him.

"Well, the judge released you to this hospital, seeing as you weren't able to go anywhere. But once you're released, you'll have to go back to prison."

"Ah, I see. So back to the beatings, I presume?"

"No, there won't be any more beatings. Several of those officers have suffered unfortunate incidents and will be recovering for a few days."

"How sad. Is it safe to talk here?"

"Not really."

"You know that they didn't find my stepbrother onboard, right?"

"Yes. And apparently the government knows that as well. It's getting them to admit it. They claim that because *you* believed he was onboard, that gives them the power to charge you."

"But I didn't."

"Yes, but the navy is claiming you did."

I sighed. "Let me guess, they 'lost' the recordings of my interview?"

"Bingo."

"Why do they keep calling me by my old name? Doesn't anyone update their files here?"

"Every time your file updates, someone deletes the updates. For the most part, you don't really exist here."

"What? How can that be done?"

"The Clark and the McVay families consider MIT to be their personal domains. They're rather pissed that some pissant black sheep from the Morgan family managed to do an end run around them and smuggle out their prize possession. They had plans for your brother, it seems."

"So they're behind this?"

"Yes, though it's only a matter of time until your presence here is discovered. Hence the beatings. They're getting desperate."

"Well, I have no idea where he is. And I obviously never said he was onboard or even claimed the dead guy was him."

"Yes, I know, and I can prove it too."

"You can?"

"The captain of the *Iowa Hill* saved the cockpit recorder after you were escorted off the ship. So I have a copy of your interview with that navy lieutenant. I submitted it to the judge yesterday with a motion to dismiss the charges against you."

"Will he?"

"That depends."

"On what?"

"On just how much outrage your grandfather can summon up when Mr. Smith informs him of just what happened to his favorite grandson." He smiled then. "I'm sure it will be epic."

"One can only hope. Oh, and you are?"

"Craig Kinyon."

"How'd you find me, by the way?"

"Once we learned you'd been arrested, we just found out where the navy ship you'd been on had put in. Then a few discreet enquiries and we discovered who your last public defender was."

"And here I'd been hoping she'd found you somehow."

"No, she's on an extended leave of absence. Apparently something you said to her caused her to decide to change the focus of her legal career."

"Ah."

"Did you really proposition her?"

I laughed at that. "I told her she needed to find me a real lawyer or when my family found out, it wouldn't go well."

He nodded. "Yes, I suppose things won't be going well for a number of people after this. I've given your judge clear legal grounds for dismissal of all counts without looking like he's being forced."

"Like that matters," I grumbled.

"To his ego it does," Craig said with a smile. "Now, get some rest, they'll be moving you back to the prison in a few hours."

"Shouldn't I be going to a prison hospital?"

Craig shook his head. "Trust me, the gen-pop is a lot safer for you right now, especially as I hear you have friends there?"

I nodded and gave a weak smile. "Say what you will about us gang-bangers, but when push comes to shove, we stick together."

Going back to prison wasn't as bad as I thought it would be. Ghost and the others helped me out, and I made sure to get all of their real names. I was going to pay them back, especially when I heard that when I'd been dumped unconscious on the floor they'd had to administer a few beatings to people who'd tried to mess with me while I was out.

The next morning, I was hauled off to court, and when I got there, Craig had someone give me a wheelchair, which I gratefully collapsed into. I still hurt everywhere and could barely stand.

They shepherded us into a waiting room, and shortly after that we got called into the courtroom.

"That was fast," I remarked.

"The people on the Moon might like to think that they're beyond the games played down on Earth, but the truth is, elie money has just as much power up here as it does down there," Craig said as his assistant wheeled me into the courtroom.

"All rise!"

We stood up and the judge same in, then we all sat down again.

I didn't pay much attention to the different introductions, though it was nice to hear that they got my name right. I did listen, however, as the prosecutor read the list of charges along with all of the associated issues and other crimes that I had supposedly committed.

Craig immediately moved for a dismissal as soon at the prosecutor had finished.

"On what grounds?" the judge asked.

"On the grounds that the defendant, my client, has no knowledge of Benjamin Strossner's whereabouts, either on that day or even now, eight days later. That the navy captain's testimony, as well as that of the navy lieutenant's, as to what my client, Mr. Doyle, said was misleading."

"Objection!" the prosecutor called out.

"Your Honor, at this time, I would like to submit item one of my intended filing against the government, *Doyle versus the State*, into evidence. It has significant bearing on the case currently before you."

"Which evidence is this?" the prosecutor demanded.

"The recording of Mr. Doyle's interview with Lieutenant Stewart."

"The navy said that that recording was inadvertently destroyed!"

"Yes, well, the ship's cockpit recorder also recorded the interview, and I've submitted one of the copies."

I saw the prosecutor wince.

"*Doyle versus the State*, item one is admitted. I assume that monitor over there is so we may view it?" the judge asked.

"Yes, Your Honor."

Craig's assistant then loaded the recording into the monitor and ran it.

It was interesting to watch myself talking to the lieutenant. I could see that Chris was noticeably upset by some of my admissions, but then paled when I mentioned the bomb and my fear of letting Donde onboard with it. Though at that time I never once mentioned anyone by name.

"Your Honor! The defendant clearly referred to the deceased as his brother!" the prosecutor said.

"True, he did. What is your response to that, Mr. Craig?"

"Your Honor, while growing up, my client had ties to one of the street gangs that is also present here on the Moon. He grew up with the deceased and apparently they were quite close. I've also been led to believe that 'Donde,' as Mr. Severson was known, was dating my client's sister, something which her father did not approve of. He became frantic when he heard she was leaving, hence the confrontation."

"That still doesn't explain his calling him his brother."

"Your Honor, I would like to introduce *Doyle versus the State*, item number two, into evidence."

"What's that?"

"Recordings from the prison general area. It turns out that there are several members of my client's former gang there, and he immediately joined with them in search of protection."

The judge nodded. "I'll allow it."

I sat up a little and watched it. I should have known things in prison would be recorded, but it hadn't occurred to me. The scenes were mainly shots of us calling each other "bro" or "brother," which *was* fairly common in the gangs. For some of us, it was the only family we had.

"Mr. Doyle," the judge said, looking at me. "Why didn't you mention your friend—'Donde,' I believe—by name during the interview?"

"You don't have to answer that," Craig told me.

"It's okay," I said and then turned to the judge. "Honestly? I never realized it," I lied. "I was pretty shocked and upset with

what had happened. I didn't expect the marines to just kill him
out of hand. I'd hoped he'd be passed out when they found him,
and at the very least they'd try to talk him down first. Honestly,
I had no idea that they'd kill him."

I also didn't mention how happy I was that they had, however.

"I did mention him by name in the second interview onboard
the corvette that brought me here. Before they started asking me
where my brother was."

"I see. Do you know if that interview was taped?"

I shrugged. "It was on the bridge with the captain, so I'd
guess so."

The judge turned to the prosecutor. "Do you have a copy of
that interview?"

"No, Your Honor, they told me that it was also inadvertently
deleted."

"In that case I have no other choice than to dismiss the
charges against Mr. Doyle here involving the Exporting of Persons Against the Will of the State Act due to lack of evidence."

"Thank you, Your Honor!" Craig said. "Now, about the rest
of the charges?"

The judge opened his mouth to say something, but was rudely
interrupted by Eileen's husband, as he barged into the room.

"What is this I hear about you holding my stepson on these
ridiculous charges?" he yelled, storming up to the judge.

"Who do you think you are, barging in here! Bailiffs!"

"I'm Senator Harold Jefferson! *Earthgov* Senator Jefferson! And
I demand these charges against my stepson be dropped immediately! How *dare* anyone bring such scurrilous charges against a
member of the *Morgan* household, as well as my beloved stepson!"

I watched, amazed, as everyone in the courtroom just froze.
Even the judge was looking like he'd just been hit with a shock rod.

The judge turned to me and asked in a very soft voice, "Mr.
Doyle, is this your stepfather?"

I struggled a little as I quickly stood up. "Yes, Your Honor,
Senator Jefferson is my stepfather." I smiled for the benefit of the
onlookers and nodded to him. "Hi, Dad. I'm sorry I didn't call
you, but I didn't want to drag you into this."

"Think nothing of it, David! If I'd known sooner, I would
have come here immediately!"

I smiled again. I couldn't believe this was the same man I'd seen my grandfather berate into submission last week. Now I could see why he was a senator—he sure could act and, out here in public, in front of everyone, he was fearless.

"You could have warned us, Mr. Doyle," the Judge said.

"I tried to tell the public defender, but she wouldn't listen to me."

"I see."

"Well, what are you waiting for?" Jefferson demanded.

"Senator Jefferson, the more serious charge has already been dismissed due to lack of evidence. As for the other charges, I'm assessing a fine of ten thousand dollars to cover the equipment that the navy had destroyed, and all other fines or penalties are waived! Court's adjourned!"

With that, he smacked the gavel on his desk and all but fled from the room.

The bailiff didn't even get to tell everyone to stand. In fact, they fled almost as fast as the judge had, but by then I noticed the four bodyguards who had followed Jefferson into the courtroom. All of them were obviously professionals, and I suspect none of them had left their guns outside the courtroom.

"How are you doing, Dave?" Jefferson asked, coming over to me.

I smiled at him again, and this time it wasn't just for show. "Better, a lot better. Thanks for doing this; it really means a lot to me."

He looked surprised. "Honestly?"

I gave a small nod. "Yeah it does. Trust me, the next time I talk to Grandfather I'm going to make sure he knows it too. You didn't have to do this, yet you did."

"If I hadn't," he said in a voice so soft I almost couldn't hear it, "he would have been very upset with me. He all but ordered me to do it."

"That may be, but you really gave it your all and went over the top. I think the judge even shit himself!"

Jefferson smiled at that, so I stuck out my hand and he smiled even wider as he shook it.

"You know, I think I understand what that old bastard sees in you. You really were handling this, weren't you?"

"Yes and no. It's been hinted that the Clark and the McVay families were behind this and I don't have the ability to deal with something like that. At least not on my own. Now that they know you and grandfather are involved, hopefully they'll stay away."

"While I hate to break up this family reunion," Craig said. "I believe there are better places for us to talk?"

Jefferson nodded. "Yes, and I know of a good one. Oh, and Mister...?"

"Kinyon, Craig Kinyon, I'm your son's lawyer."

"Ah yes. Please send his bill to me, and don't be afraid to pad it, heavily. I'm sure you took a risk here today, and that deserves to be rewarded."

"Why, thank you, I will," Craig said with a smile, which made me wonder suddenly if he had been planning to charge me when this was all over. Then again, suits like the ones he wore don't come cheap.

We followed Jefferson out of the courtroom; surprisingly, he had a transport. Most people on the Moon used mass transit. But then again, an Earthgov senator probably had more power than the old heads of state. They *made* the laws, they didn't follow them.

And my grandfather had one completely in his pocket.

That was something to remember.

"So who was that guy who died onboard the ship?" Jefferson asked me after his men had told him that it was safe to talk.

"A convenient tool who got what was coming to him," I said with a frown. "He really did threaten me, and I'd already made plans to fix his ass, but what those marines did made it so much better. I'm a bit annoyed at those navy officers, though, for not turning over that evidence."

Jefferson lowered his voice again. "Your brother is okay, right? Or do you need me to help you with him?"

I blinked. That was probably the last thing I expected to hear.

"He's fine. Or at least he should be. I guess my next step is to see if I can get a ride on the next cargo ship to Ceres."

"I'm sure we can find you something better than a freighter. Is there anything else you need? I'll stick around until tomorrow at the very least, to drive the point home to the local politicians and police that they're to keep their hands off you."

I smiled again, "Thanks, Jefferson. And actually, there *is* a little something you might be able to help me with."

✧   ✧   ✧

A week later, I was on a nice passenger ship that was also rather fast. It would get to Ceres in four days, which was pretty quick. I'd gotten my four friends from prison paroled as a thank-you for their help. I'd also gotten each of them into a tech school or college so they'd be able to get real jobs and get off the Moon, like Ghost wanted.

They were all getting a bit too old for gang life—Ghost was already eighteen, and if you didn't want to move up into a real "organization," well, there wasn't much of a future beyond menial work.

I also had a fair bit of time to reflect on how I'd been living my life over the last few years. While it wasn't as bad as my childhood years, I realized that I'd fallen back into those patterns more than was probably good for me. I'd rationalized it then as not having any choice. But now? Now I had a family, I had connections, and a business that was thriving.

I also had a grandfather who was rather hot for me to join the "family business," and that didn't just mean money—it meant responsibilities. I was sure there would be times ahead where I'd have to resort to crude methods and foul language; I had a bit of a reputation now, after all. But if I wanted to be taken seriously, I'd have to put that stuff behind me.

And I very much wanted to be taken seriously.

TWENTY-SIX

Ceres

WE GOT TO CERES BEFORE THE *IOWA HILL* MADE IT INTO PORT, which showed up several days later than our original plan. I met them at the docks and was almost knocked off my feet by Kacey, who literally threw herself at me. Mom wasn't much better, and thankfully Ben had figured out that being seen publicly coming off our ship probably wasn't a good idea.

We all went back onboard then, so I could fill them in on everything that happened, well away from any prying eyes or ears.

The first thing I did was take care of business with Chris and Kacey.

"I'm a bit pissed that you didn't tell me about that guy in the hold," Chris said.

"He didn't even tell *me* about it," Kacey replied.

"He didn't?"

"I only told Ben. I didn't want to involve anyone else before I had to."

"So why tell *him*?"

"Because he's better at planning that I am?" I said with a shrug. "But he was going to see if he could make some sort of knockout gas from what we had onboard, so we could pacify Donde, and then toss his ass overboard."

"You were going to kill him?"

"He kidnapped our sister and threatened to rape and murder her if I didn't kill somebody for him. Hell yeah, I was going to kill him. I just can't believe he was fool enough to show up," I said, frowning.

"Well, at least you don't ever have to go to Earth again," Kacey said, patting my arm.

"Hell, I don't think I want to get any closer to the sun than Mars," I replied with a shake of my head. "On the other hand, both Marcus's people and my grandfather did help, once they knew what was going on that is."

I turned to Chris. "Thanks for sending them that recording."

Chris chuckled. "I did it to let them know what happened. I didn't think they'd believe anything I told them, so I just let them see it for themselves."

"How did you get the ship going again? When I left, all the interlocks were broken."

"Hank and Chaz strung a bunch of cables and chains and winched the doors shut. When we got to our rendezvous, Marcus's people used the machine shop onboard the *Astro Gerlitz* to fabricate replacement parts, and helped fix everything. We do have six panels that now need to be repaired, however. Nik didn't think it would be wise for him to fix them without you there to approve them, and I agreed."

I nodded. "What's in the hold now?"

"No gold, but a lot of high-value ores and rare earths," Kacey told me.

"No gold?"

"Apparently they packed almost all of what they had left into the shipment we took to Earth to pay for that massive anti-ship missile system. Just about the entire shipment that we brought back, even those containers that hadn't been done by dint of bribes and convincing a great many people to look the other way, were all for setting up the system."

"You should have heard them, they *cheered* us when we docked with them," Chris said, looking a little embarrassed. "I had no idea they were *that* desperate."

"Well, after so many years of living in fear, I guess they figured that now that they had the money along with the ability to spend it, that they might as well do something about protecting themselves," I told him. "Hank once told me that they used to be a fairly pacifistic group back on Venus before the purges started."

"And now they're anything but," he said with a nod.

"Can you blame them?" Kacey asked.

"Not at all. Just kinda sucks that they had to learn the hard way. They really are nice people."

"Well, not to change the subject, but how much of the cargo did your mother buy this time?" I asked Kacey.

"All of it."

"*What?*" I said looking at her in shock. "*All* of it?"

"I gave her another discount. Not as much as last time, but they've been using the last batch to corner the market to help cover the funding for a major expansion. If we sold this ourselves, we might soften the prices. So it was in their best interest to buy it all up. Especially when I promised them it would be five months before making another dump like this one."

"Oh? So what happens the next time we run out to trade with our friends?"

"I already lined up a buyer on one of Neptune's moons," she said with a sweet smile. "As well as one with Mars. We'll be doing a triangle route on the next few trips."

I shook my head and laughed. "We're really going to be in the money here, aren't we?"

She nodded. "They pushed so much gold through on that last trip that we really made a killing off the percentage I negotiated. I almost feel guilty!" she said with a giggle.

"But not guilty enough to give any of it back, I'm sure."

"Nope. But, if this keeps up, in a couple of years we might want to start looking at some of the older ships like this one, that have timed out on their fission reactors, and see about putting in rebuilt fusion reactors."

"I guess that's one of those things we're going to have to talk with our investors about. We've got a couple of weeks before we have to leave to meet the *Astro Gerlitz* for another cargo. I guess we'll give everyone leave after we move the ship for unloading. I can grab Chris or Paul to come with me and move it back to the public docks once they've finished. Yuri and Kei can stay onboard during the unloading and make sure nobody goes anywhere they're not supposed to.

"Chris, tell Nik not to shut the engines down. After I finish talking with Kace here, I'll do an inspection to make sure there aren't any problems. Then we can move the ship over to Ceres Habitats' private docks."

"Sure, what about leave?"

"Anyone we don't need for the move can go. Except for Ben, we'll smuggle him off after the move."

"On it!" he said and left the room.

"What about your family?" Kacey asked.

"Huh?"

"We need to find your parents a place to live with Dianne. *Then* we need to get our own office going now that we have someone to mind it. Any idea what Ben is going to do?"

"He's thinking about working at the local university, but I'm sure he'll get so many offers he'll be able to take his pick."

"Maybe *we* should hire him," Kacey said, looking thoughtful.

"If Ben is going to pursue his theory on FTL drive, it's going to cost more than just the price of a spaceship or two, Kace, and then there's always the chance he might be wrong and there's never any payback."

"You talked to him about it?"

I nodded. "Yeah, I did. He said it would be a year before he was ready to start. He had a lot of stuff he wanted to finally put down on paper and then go over and double check before he even considered making an attempt at it." I paused a moment. "There's something else I wanted to discuss."

"What?" she asked, eyes narrowing.

"I'm starting to wonder now if the whole reason my grandfather wanted to talk went beyond just burying the hatchet, as they like to say. I'm starting to wonder if he *knew* I was going to smuggle Ben off the planet. I mean, why else offer me access to the entire Morgan empire?"

"And what triggered this?"

I pulled out my tablet and queued up my email, opening up the one that I'd gotten a few days ago while I was waiting for Kacey and the *Iowa Hill* to arrive.

"'David,'" I read. "'I want to congratulate you on your little escapade leaving Earth. I must say that using the cover of Mr. Smith's shipment was really brilliant. The amount of pressure brought to bear on that Earth Guard ship's commander was truly a sight to behold, and as you no doubt had planned. While I do apologize for what you had to go through after your arrest, I must also applaud your brilliance in setting up the diversion in the cargo bay.

"'Clearly you had contingencies in place for whatever happened during the trip.'"

I looked up at her a moment. "Here's the good part."

Continuing on I read, "'In regard to my proposal back at the estate, I'm starting to see the wisdom of your response. I'd like to propose a partnership, with three equal splits: myself, you, and your brother. Anyone I show the prospectus to, should we need help or extra funding, will see your heritage and immediately assume that I have things well under control, and that the Morgans are the ones actually managing this effort, and will therefore rest easy and not seek to interfere.

"'You and I know the truth, however. All I ask is that you don't make that truth obvious to the public or the other families.'"

I looked up again and couldn't recall ever seeing her eyes quite that wide before.

"He knew."

I nodded. "I think so. Or at the very least, suspected. He probably sees all of this as a plan hatched by my brother and me to get him away from Earth so we can develop his FTL drive and keep the profits."

Kacey nodded slowly. "It makes a certain amount of sense, especially with how much risk you've taken, and how ruthlessly you appear to have pursued every opportunity that came your way. You already told me just how impressed he was by your making Marcus and his people your friends and gaining their absolute trust. And then on top of all that, you turn down joining a family that's worth probably a trillion dollars, and then...*this*?" Kacey laughed. "Oh, he wants in so bad I can taste it from here."

"So you think we should do it?"

"Yes, I think we should do it. And not just because of the money. If Ben's idea works out, think of just how many people are going to want to get their hands on it. On *him*. But if the Morgans already control it..." She gave me a wicked smile. "They'll know we can *defend* it. Plus Earthgov won't panic, because they have ties to the Morgan family that they'll be looking to exploit in their favor!

"Think about it: If a lone inventor changes the world, everybody panics. But if one of the big families who run everything does? Nobody gives it a second thought!"

"I guess now I know why he runs the family."

"I think you just became his favorite grandson!"

I sighed. "You know what's going to make this difficult?"

"I don't know, what?"

"That everyone thinks I'm some sort of genius like Ben. I just got lucky, that's all."

"I don't know... There's a lot to be said for making your own luck. You just took advantage of things no one else would have considered."

"Still..."

Kacey put her finger on my mouth. "Hush, just go with it. You, me, and Ben can discuss it after dinner tonight."

I nodded.

"And here I thought the hard part was over."

"Oh trust me, the fun is only beginning," she said with a grin.